KT-370-364

Ken McCoy was born in wartime Leeds and has lived in Yorkshire all his life. For twenty-five years he ran his own building and civil engineering company. During this time he also worked as a freelance artist, greeting card designer and after-dinner entertainer. He has appeared on television, radio and as a comedian on the Leeds City Varieties' *Good Old Days*.

Writing is now Ken's first love – not counting of course his wife Valerie, to whom he has been married since 1973. He has five children and twelve grandchildren.

www.kenmccoy.co.uk

Change for a Farthing

Ken McCoy

piatkus

PIATKUS

First published in Great Britain in 2005 by Piatkus Books
This paperback edition published in 2011 by Piatkus

A CIP catalogue record for this book
is available from the British Library.

ISBN 978-0-7499-5668-4

Typeset by Palimpsest Book Production Limited
Falkirk, Stirlingshire
Printed and bound in Great Britain by CPI Group (UK),
Croydon, CR0 4YY

Piatkus
An imprint of
Little, Brown Book Group
100 Victoria Embankment
London EC4Y 0DY

An Hachette UK Company
www.hachette.co.uk

www.piatkus.co.uk

To my daughter, Angela

Part One

Part One

Chapter One

31 October 1880, Bradford, Yorkshire

'I wouldn't mind you pressing up against me as hard as you're pressed up against that loom! What d'you say, Beth?'

Godfrey's remark drew no reaction from her, but it spurred one of the older weavers into sniggering, 'Watch it, Mr Godfrey, I can see yer shuttle's on the move.'

The cackling woman was in no danger of being the object of Godfrey's banter – he only picked on the young girls. 'Doesn't take much when you've a shuttle as lively as mine. Liveliest shuttle in Bradford – what about it, Beth? Like to give me shuttle a try?'

Many of the women laughed but Beth kept her head down and carried on with her work. He was the son of the mill owner; she was seventeen and one of Samuel Farthing's youngest and best weavers. It was rewarding and companiable work if you could stand on your feet for hours on end. She wore a long and voluminous mill skirt that washed as white as snow, and a small leather apron about two feet square, worn where her belly pressed against the loom. The only thing she hated about the job was Godfrey Farthing and his crude talk, delivered at the top of his voice above the chatter of the machines.

'I'm told you wear nothing but bare skin under that skirt. Is that right, Beth darling?'

Most of the girls laughed off his crude remarks, but when he directed them at Beth there was something more sinister and lewd about them that made her feel decidedly uncomfortable. One of the coarser girls shouted out, 'She's still got her cherry has our Beth, and she's not likely ter give it up too easy – unlike some I could mention.'

'Unlike you, yer mean,' someone else shouted.

Beth got on with her work and didn't join in the banter, totally ignoring Godfrey, which annoyed him no end. He walked to within a couple of feet of her and, without looking at her, hissed in a low voice, 'Ignore me at your peril, Beth Wainwright. As from next week I'm manager of this floor. You'll see the good sense in being nice to me then.'

'I'm paid to do a good job, nothing more,' she retorted, with her eyes fixed intently on her loom. 'There's other jobs for me in this town if you're not satisfied with my work.'

'Not if I put the word around that you're a thief and a common whore!'

Beth froze, shocked at such awful lies. 'You wouldn't,' she protested. 'I'd tell your fathe—'

'My father takes notice of me, not of the likes of you!' he roared, loud enough to attract the attention of the nearby girls, who hadn't heard his original threat. 'I'll soon be master in this mill and I'll do as I damn well please!'

4

Beth was one of prettier mill girls and many a lad in the town had set his cap at her – but she didn't want to wed the first young man who took a liking to her. Godfrey was twenty-two years old and fancied himself as a good-looking young buck. Beth considered him to be a charmless braggart who, without his father's money, would struggle to hold down a job as lowly as a piecener (joining up broken threads for the weavers) much less a mill manager.

Once a week she stayed behind to clean her loom with brushes and emery paper. A good and fastidious weaver was always given the most valuable pieces and Beth had ambitions way beyond working at a loom for the rest of her life. If she hadn't stayed back that night her life might have taken a very different course.

The other girls had all left and Beth was working quietly; happy with the calm of the room after the incessant noise of the day when all conversations were done by either shouting or lip-reading, and Beth had become adept at both. Her hands worked automatically leaving her mind to attend to the other problems in her life. If she did leave here she'd have to be certain of getting a job with at least the same pay; she couldn't manage on a penny a week less. So God help her if Godfrey went round telling his lies. Maybe she ought to humour him without actually succumbing to his unwanted advances.

After her father died in a quarry accident, Beth had begun work at Samuel Farthing's Mill, at the age of ten, as a half-timer – dividing her day between school and work.

Over the past few weeks her mam had been stricken with the consumption and Beth's life was full – a mill girl during the day and a nurse at night. Mrs Wharmby, an elderly neighbour came round during the day to tend to her mother's needs. Beth gave her five shillings a week which didn't leave much to live on after the rent had been paid.

She put aside her emery paper when she saw Godfrey come in through the door at the far end and scan the vast weaving room with his glinting, piggy eyes.

'Oh no!' she murmured to herself. 'What the devil does he want? As if I didn't know.'

Before his searching gaze fell on her she had ducked behind her loom. He was a determined man who thought he was entitled to have his way with any mill girl he chose. Well, he could damn well think again as far as she was concerned. Samuel Farthing was the man she worked for, not his loud-mouthed son who wasn't fit to lace his father's boots, much less run his mill for him.

'Are you there, Beth Wainwright?'

His voice boomed around the empty room. Beth didn't answer. She was a good hundred feet away from him but she could swear he'd be able to hear her breathing. She heard his heavy footsteps clumping around. If he walked down the room and saw her she'd simply tell him the truth, that she knew what he was after and she wasn't interested. Even if he gave her a florin, which was twice the sum some of the other girls reckoned they'd been paid for their 'services to Godfrey'. The footsteps stopped. When she looked up again he was nowhere to be seen so she continued with her work.

'So, value your job, do you?' He was standing behind her in his stockinged feet with his boots in his hand and an inane grin on his face.

Beth tried to contain her shock at his sudden and unwelcome appearance. 'Yes, thank you,' she said, coolly.

'Well, thanks might not be enough, now I'm to be made manager. I might want more than thanks.' He sounded as if he'd been drinking.

She turned to face him and asked, 'What do you mean?'

The fact that there was no one else in the vast, machine-filled room now disturbed her. His face was flushed and his smile humourless. He dropped his boots to the floor.

'I mean I've had my way with all the good lookers except you and I think it's about time I put that right.'

'I don't think so. Can I get on with my work, please?'

'Well, I damn well *do* think so!' he snarled. 'You either lose your bloody virtue or you lose your job. What's it to be?'

'Neither,' she said, keeping as cool as she could. 'Maybe we should ask your father?'

His arm swept round in a wide arc, knocking her down. She struck her head on the edge of the loom – by the time she reached the floor she was unconscious, with her skirt in disarray around her knees. It was all too tempting for Godfrey.

For a disoriented moment, just before her vision returned, she thought her insides were exploding. As the grey mist cleared, she saw him on top of her, his sweating face contorted with lust, grunting and thrusting at her like a rutting hound. She screamed but he clamped his hand over her mouth and held her down until his lechery was fully sated.

Breathing heavily, he put on his boots, got to his feet and fastened his trousers. Then, taking a handful of change from his pocket, he selected a shilling and threw it at her. 'Here, never let it be said that Godfrey Farthing never pays full value for services rendered. This makes you no better then the rest of the whores in this place.'

By Christmas Beth knew she was definitely pregnant and she daren't tell anyone. Had she known she'd fall pregnant perhaps she would have reported Godfrey to the police, but he'd already told her what his story would be if she was so stupid. It was she who had made the first move, that's what he'd tell them. Why should an eligible young man like him have to force himself on a lowly mill lass? He could have any girl he wanted by snapping his fingers.

Beth didn't trouble her mother with her news, for it seemed she hadn't long for this world and there was nothing to be gained by sending her off with an extra worry on her mind; she was worried enough about leaving Beth. Her mother made this plain on Christmas morning as she was struggling to open the gift Beth had bought her – a silk head square.

'It's beautiful present, Beth love. Not that I'll have much chance ter wear it, but it's the thought that counts.' She looked at her daughter with weary eyes. 'I'm troubled, lass. I worry so much about leaving yer on yer own.'

'There's no need, Mam. I'm a young woman now with a good wage. I can cope. There's many a young man giving me the glad eye. Anyway, there's lots of life left in you yet.'

Her mother went into a fit of coughing that had Beth worried. She had no way of knowing if this was the end. But her mother's breathing eased after a sip or two of water and a tablespoon of Dr Kilmer's Indian Cure Consumption Oil which Beth had bought in good faith from a travelling healer who had sold his wares

8

from a wagon outside Brown and Muffs on Market Street.

'Ee, Elisabeth lass,' she whispered. 'I doubt I'll see the New Year in – and I'd like ter see yer settled afore I pop off. It's a mother's duty ter see her daughter settled.'

'I'm all right, Mam, honest.'

Her mother became agitated as if she'd suddenly remembered what had been troubling her. 'But yer not all right, are yer? I've seen it these past few weeks. If I didn't know better I'd have said yer with child.' Her eyes searched Beth's and she got her answer in her daughter's hesitancy. 'I bloody knew it! Some man's left yer with child. Was it that young bastard Godfrey Farthing? It was, wasn't it? By God I'll curse him with me dying breath.'

Her mother's quick progression from suspicion to conviction left Beth speechless. How on earth could she work all this out just by looking at her face?

'I've had me suspicions,' explained her mother, reading Beth's thoughts. 'Yer've had some nasty words ter say recently about Godfrey Farthing. And I remember them nights yer spent cryin' in yer room. Just because I'm poorly dunt mean I'm daft.'

Beth fell on her mother in floods of tears. 'Oh, Mam, what am I to do?'

Her mother stroked her head, like she had when Beth was a young child and Beth took great comfort from it. 'I'll tell yer what yer'll do. Yer'll tell young Alfred from me I said he's ter marry yer.'

Beth straightened up and looked at her mother in amazement. 'Alfred? You mean Alfred Crabtree?'

'Aye, him. I happen ter know he's not courting anyone.'

'Really? And how would you know that?'

Her mother summoned up the energy to tap the side of her nose. 'That's fer me ter know and fer you ter find out. I'll tell yer one thing, when he looks at you he's got eyes like a soft puppy. He'll look after yer proper will Alfred. He's got a nice head of hair and he's a very amiable lad. Yer father was amiable. Them's very good qualities in a man – plenty of hair and amiability. That and putting bread on the table. Promise me yer'll tell him what I said.' She patted Beth's stomach. 'And as for how that got in there – well, I reckon I'm not up ter knowin'. Just you make sure that arrogant young brat gets his come-uppance one day. There'll be no rush.'

Beth's thoughts had turned to Alfred Crabtree. She liked him quite a lot – but she couldn't say she loved him. Was her mother right about how Alfred felt about her? And would he still feel the same when he found out she was pregnant? Her mother interrupted her thoughts with what turned out to be her last words.

'Promise me yer'll tell young Alfred what I said.'

'I promise, Mam.'

Her mother gave a satisfied nod then closed her eyes and drifted off to sleep. She died in that same sleep an hour later.

The funeral was held mid-week because it was cheaper and was well attended despite the absence of many of her mother's friends due to them being at work. Funerals were only accepted as an excuse for time off if it was an immediate family member.

Although Beth was now five shillings a week better off – with not having to pay for her mother's care – she'd be paying that weekly sum to Harold Pratts, the under-taker, for the next nine months. The day after the funeral she went in to see Samuel Farthing. He rose, briefly, from his chair then motioned her to sit down opposite.

'I'm sorry to hear about your mother. She was a fine woman and a good worker.' He took out his wallet and counted out five one-pound notes which he pushed across his desk towards her. 'I know funerals cost money. This might help.'

It was more money than Beth had had at one time in her life. She looked at it but made no move to pick it up. 'That's very generous of you, sir, but you might change your mind after what I've got to say.'

'Oh, and what might that be?'

'I've come to tell you that I'm leaving.'

He left a long silence before saying, 'Well, I'll be sorry to lose you, but you must still take the money.'

'You haven't asked me why.'

It was as if Samuel didn't want to know why. He took his time lighting a large cigar then said, 'All right – why are you leaving?'

'It's because of your son.'

He didn't seem surprised. 'What about my son?'

'He – he's made my life most unpleasant ever since you made him manager. I'm going to work for Brammah's.'

'My loss is their gain,' said Samuel. Then, rather than give her an argument, he explained his position – even though he didn't have to, not to such a lowly member of his workforce. But somehow he felt obliged. 'I'm getting on in years,' he said. 'And I intend handing over the reins very soon. He'll learn, will Godfrey. Not all at once, but he'll learn. Man management takes time, you see. Woman management takes even longer.' He smiled at his own joke and Beth gave him one of hers because she thought

11

he deserved it. 'I spent twenty-one years learning how to manage my wife, then she died . . . and Godfrey's all I've got to show for it.'

Beth flashed him a look of sympathy that didn't say whether she was sad about his wife or about him only having a waster like Godfrey to show for twenty-one years of marriage.

'I just want to say that all the time I've worked for you you've been fair with me, Mr Farthing, and that goes for my mother as well – God rest her soul. She always said you were the best boss in Bradford.'

'I thank you for that, Beth, and I thank your mother as well – God rest her soul, indeed. Now take this money and I wish you well.'

Beth took the notes and got to her feet. 'Thank you very much, sir. This will be a great help to me.' It crossed her mind what he would say if he knew she was carrying his grandchild in her belly, but to tell him would cause too much trouble. She turned as she reached the door and asked, 'I don't suppose you know if Alfred Crabtree's in today, do you?'

'Alfred? Yes, saw him not half an hour ago. I believe he's been working in the cutting room these past few days. They're short-handed up there this week; turn his hand to anything, that lad. I do hope you're not thinking of taking him with you to Brammah's. Put a few years on his back and he's overlooker material, is Alfred.'

'I just wanted to talk to him, if that's all right.'

Samuel took a gold half-hunter from his waistcoat pocket and scrutinised it. 'I imagine he'll be due a break any time now.'

Beth found Alfred up on one of the loading bays eating cheese and lettuce sandwiches from his snap tin. He wore

12

a cap tilted over one ear, a dark-blue workcoat that had seen much better days and brown fustian trousers patched at both knees and held up by braces. On his feet were a pair of substantial clogs that looked to have transported him many a mile. The light that her mother had seen in his eyes switched on the minute he saw Beth. She saw it and felt guilty for what she was about to do to him; she was about to take selfish advantage of his infatuation for her.

'Hey up, Beth. What're you doin' up here?'

'I came to find you.'

'Me?' He pointed at himself and raised his eyebrows in surprise.

'Yes.' She gave him a look of appraisal. He was quite tall and not at all bad looking, and he had lovely thick black hair that didn't looked as if it might drop out by the time he was forty. A mother had to think about such things on behalf of any future sons.

'Look, I'm sorry I didn't come to yer mam's funeral,' he said. 'Did yer get me flowers? I had the shop send 'em special.'

'They were lovely, thanks.'

'I thought a lot about yer mam. She took me under her wing when I first came ter work here. Taught me a lot when she'd no need.'

'She thought a lot about you as well.'

'Yer makin' me feel guilty now. I should have made time ter go ter the funeral. It's just that we're pulled out in here.'

'I was wondering if you might want to come round for a bit of tea after work,' Beth said. 'I've got something to ask you.'

'What sort o' somethin'?'

13

'Something I can't talk about here.'

'Well, I must say it's all a mystery ter me is this,' he said, rubbing his chin. 'The problem is, me mam'll have me tea ready and she gets proper narked if I don't turn up on time. She'll be double narked if I say I don't want none because I've been invited elsewhere.'

Beth wasn't prepared for this reaction. She had her pride and she wasn't going down on hands and knees to him.

'Well, I wouldn't want to upset your mam,' she said, huffily, turning to go. 'It was just something my late mother wanted me to ask you. Anyway – I'll see you when I see you.'

'No, no – hang on!' He took her by her arm, then let go lest she thought he was being too forward. 'I'd never be so ungracious as to turn down a request from a proper lady such as yer mam. If yer just want ter talk ter me, couldn't I come round after tea?'

'That would be fine. Shall we say half past seven?'

'On the dot. Best bib and tucker. At your service. I must say, it's set me thinkin' has this. Sounds very important ter me.'

'It is important, Alfred.'

He arrived at seven twenty-five with his face scrubbed, hair neatly combed and dressed in a dark-blue worsted suit, a collar and tie he was obviously unused to wearing, and well-polished black boots.

'You look very nice,' she said, allowing him past her, into the living room. She noticed his cheeks bore the marks of a couple of recent shaving accidents and had been liberally dabbed with cologne. So he was here to impress – which was good.

14

'Thank you,' he said. 'I er – you look very nice as well.'

'Thank you, won't you sit down.'

'Thank you.'

They sat on opposite sides of the dining table but there was an awkwardness about the situation which Beth was struggling to deal with. She'd been trying to work out the best way to broach the subject without immediately scaring him off. How do you tell a young man with whom you only have a casual acquaintance that you'd like him to marry you because you're pregnant by another man and need him to make an honest woman of you? It was a puzzle she hadn't quite come to grips with. Alfred smiled at her, displaying two rows of white, even teeth. This was good. Thick hair and good teeth. He was a strong looking young man as well. Between them they should produce fine sons. Pity about the first offspring; she'd just have to take pot luck with that one. But would she love it as much as the others? Her mind was adrift as he mentioned, politely, 'You said your mam wanted you to ask me something?'

'What? Oh, that's right. It was the very last thing she said on this earth and I promised I'd do it.'

'Then you must.'

'I know – but before I do I need to explain something. Because if I don't you'll run a mile.'

'I don't think there's much you can say to me that will make me run a mile from you, Beth Wainwright,' he said. 'I might run a mile in your direction but not away from yer.'

Her mother had been right about him. 'That's a very nice thing to say,' she said, genuinely. 'Because I've always thought a lot about you, Alfred.' She placed her

15

elbows on the table and laced her fingers together, forming a bridge upon which she rested her chin. Her eyes held his in her gaze as she told him her story. 'I was assaulted by a man a couple of months ag–'

'What! A man assaulted you? The dirty coward. What man? Did you tell the police?'

'No, I should have done but I left it too late – and even if I had I'm not sure he'd have got what he deserved. You see he–' Beth paused because she'd never used this word before '–he raped me.' She said it quietly as though she couldn't bear to hear the word herself, then she dropped her gaze from his. Alfred leaned across the table and lifted her chin up with a finger that was quivering with rage.

'By God, you give me his name and I'll deal with him meself! I'll make sure he gets what he deserves.' He took her hand in his and she felt the strength of it. It was a strength she desperately needed.

It was at this point that Beth decided not to reveal Godfrey's identity. Such knowledge would have Alfred doing something he might get into a lot of trouble for, and what she needed right now was a husband, not revenge.

'Alfred, I want you to promise you'll never ask me his name,' she said, earnestly. 'Promise?'

'But–!'

'Promise? Alfred, this conversation ends here if you can't make that promise.'

Such a promise went against everything he felt at that moment but the pleading look in her eyes was too much for him.

'I promise,' he said, 'but he deserves to hang for what he did.'

'I know. But what's done's done and can't be undone. If I'd gone to the police it would have been my word against his, and I'm afraid his word probably carries more weight than mine. He'd have blackened my name and called me a low and common woman. I didn't want that, Alfred.' She paused again, then said, quietly, 'I didn't want that, any more than I want his baby.'

Alfred released his grip on her hand for a second and her heart sank. This was all too much for him.

'He's made you pregnant?'

'Yes.'

'Does anyone know about this?'

'No, not even him. My mother guessed before she died.'

He took her hand again. She felt something else in his grip this time, something more than just the strength of a friend. He was reading her face just like her mother had, trying to work out why she had asked him here – him and no one else. What was the question her mother wanted her to ask him? It seemed fairly obvious, but it must be a difficult question for her to ask. She needed the help to start here and now.

'Yer could really do with a husband at a time like this,' he said. 'A man who'd do anything for yer.'

'Someone like that would come in handy,' she admitted. 'But I'm a ruined woman. Who would want to marry a ruined woman? Who would to take on another man's child as his own?'

He cleared his throat, nervously. 'I don't know if it's any help,' he said. 'But I've held you in high regard for quite some time now. And I'd marry yer like a shot – but I don't s'ppose yer'd want someone like me.'

He had relieved her of the humiliation of having to ask

17

him herself. This alone told her he was the right man. Maybe a better man might never have come along.

'Is this a proposal, Alfred Crabtree?'

'By God, if yer think it might be worth my while it most certainly is.' He got down on one knee and took her hand. 'Beth, I haven't got much to offer, just more love than yer'll ever be able ter cope with.'

She stayed his next words with her free hand over his mouth. 'Alfred, before you say anything else I want you to know I like you very much but I don't think I truly love you. It won't stop me being a good and faithful wife to you but I think you should know the truth. If I wasn't in such trouble I wouldn't be looking round for a husband just yet.'

'In that case maybe yon rapist's done me a favour,' he said. 'But it's a favour I'll kill him for if ever I find out his name.'

'That's why you never will.'

'Beth, I've got enough love inside me for the both of us – all three of us. Will yer marry me?'

'Yes, Alfred, I'd be honoured.'

Chapter Two

October 1881

Beth was surprisingly pleased with her lot. She and Alfred were living in the same rented cottage in Cinder Yard where she had lived with her parents. Baby Amelia had arrived in July of that year, six months after the hurriedly arranged wedding at Saint Barnabas's Church. No one but them knew that Alfred wasn't the father and he couldn't have loved the baby more had she been his own.

'Happen we should start thinking about a brother or a sister for her,' he suggested one evening as Beth was bathing Amelia.

'Alfred, I'm eighteen years old. There's plenty of time for more children. I'd like to enjoy what's left of my youth while I can. It's all right for you, you're an old man of twenty-one.'

Alfred hobbled round the room like an old man, holding his hip and stroking an imaginary beard. 'Ee, when I were a lad any man worth his salt'd give his wife a round dozen kids afore she were thirty.'

Beth laughed at his antics. 'Two more and no more,' she said. 'And none until I'm twenty-one and past enjoying myself. Until then we do it when it's safe. I want no surprises, thank you very much.'

He put his arms around her and hugged her to him. 'You're the boss, Beth love.'

'Watch it, Alfred! You'll have Amelia out of the bath.'

'Oh heck, sorry love.'

She wrapped the baby in a large towel and laid her in her crib, then she turned to face her husband. 'Alfred, you've nothing to say sorry for. You've made a happy woman of me. I thank you for that.'

'Yer'll always be happy while ever I'm around,' he said. 'That's a promise.'

It was a promise that would expire the next day.

During that year Samuel had gradually handed over the reins to his son who had brought in two managers, one to manage the office side of things and one to run the mill. This left Godfrey to concentrate on drumming up business – a job he appeared to be cut out for.

Before his retirement his father had made known his displeasure at having to lose one of his most promising workers due to his son's heavy-handed management style. This left Godfrey with a grudge against Beth's new husband.

He had been wining and dining a client for several hours that day before he decided to go on a tour of the mill. Alfred was working on the third floor gantry, loading bales of cloth, when Godfrey strode past.

'How's married life, Alfie boy?' he called out.

'It's fine, thank you, Mr Farthing. How's married life treating you?'

Godfrey had been married six months to the daughter of a local businessman. He walked up behind Alfred as he lowered a bale down to a haulier's horse-drawn wagon.

'Married life's fine enough when the woman knows her place – which is either on her knees or on her back. Surprised at you getting married right out of the blue like that. Never seen you with a woman before. Always had my suspicions about you. Maybe that's why you married a pregnant woman, eh? To stop people talking about you being a bum boy.'

Alfred reddened. 'I think you've got the wrong idea about me,' he said, gruffly.

'Wrong idea my arse,' chortled Godfrey. 'I rode your wife like a donkey once. Did she ever tell you that? I fettled her good and proper. Gave her a right good seeing to. In fact I did you a favour – fathered your bastard child for you, saved you the trouble. I reckon you prefer to stick your key in the back door.'

Alfred had his back to Godfrey. He stiffened and spun round with fists clenched. 'You,' he hissed. 'You're the dirty bastard who raped my Beth!'

Godfrey laughed out loud at Alfred's anger. 'Rape?' he sneered. 'You can't rape a mill lass any more than you can steal rain from the sky. They're there for the taking. It's all right, I'll not lay claim to your wife's bastard. I've a wife of my own now.'

Alfred aimed a heavy blow at Godfrey's mouth, knocking him to the floor, where he lay, spitting out blood and teeth but still smiling with drunken glee. 'I don't suppose I need tell you that you're fired,' he said, getting to his feet. Alfred hit him again, several blows to his body. He was weeping with rage, further exacerbated

21

by Godfrey's drunken taunts, even though he was doubled up from Alfred's assault.

Godfrey spat out a mouthful of blood. 'She loved every minute of it,' he sniggered. 'Wanted me to pay her for her services like the whore she is. I gave her a shilling – which was more than she was worth.'

'Liar!' screamed Alfred. 'You raped her. She told me she was raped.'

'Well, she's liar. Why would I need to rape a mill girl? There's not a woman in here that I couldn't have for a handful of change and your wife's no different. Face up to it, man, you're a bum boy who's married a whore and you're looking after a whore's bastard.'

Alfred squeezed his eyes together and pressed his hands to his ears to block out the sight and sound of this foul man, screaming at him. 'I'll kill you for this, you bastard.'

The sudden hissing of a steam engine in the yard below distracted him for the split second it took for Godfrey to put his head down and run at him, butting Alfred in the stomach like a charging goat. He staggered backwards until he felt nothing under one of his feet. He tried to regain his footing, windmilling his arms as a grinning Godfrey watched him topple backwards, out of sight.

Thirty feet below, the haulier, who hadn't heard the fight because of the noise of a steam wagon going past him, looked up in surprise as Alfred's falling body hit the horse with a force enough to break both the animal's neck and Alfred's back. He landed on the ground head first and lay there in a widening pool of blood with the horse collapsed between the wagon's shafts, whinnying in agony. The stunned haulier looked from horse to Alfred then up at the empty gantry before running for help. But Alfred was beyond help.

Godfrey heard the thud as Alfred landed but he didn't bother to reveal his face to any curious eyes below. Instead he checked all around him to see if anyone had seen what had happened, but he saw no one. If Alfred didn't survive his fall it would be a careless accident. If he did it would be his word against Godfrey's.

The news of Alfred's death saddened Beth immensely but it broke neither her heart not her spirit. It was like hearing of the death of a dear friend, and she felt guilty at not being completely heartbroken. He was a good man who deserved to have a heartbroken wife. At the back of her mind it was as if he'd served his purpose in legitimising her baby and had now left her free to marry whomsoever she chose. But time would prove that Alfred was a hard act to follow – her greatest concern was lack of money. Neighbours advised her to apply to Farthing's mill for compensation but she knew that Godfrey wouldn't be overly keen to part with his money. She could swallow her pride and apply for parish relief, queuing once a week for seven measly shillings – barely enough for the rent – then joining another queue for second-hand clothes. The wages Alfred was due from the mill wouldn't even pay for his own funeral; She'd only just finished paying for her mother's funeral; now she'd have to start all over again.

Harold Pratts, the undertaker, had told her to pay in her own good time – he wouldn't chase her for the money. His kindness brought tears to her eyes and relief that the world wasn't made up of people like Godfrey Farthing whom she vowed to deal with one day, as per her promise to her mother.

A knock on the door three days after the funeral came

as a greater relief. It was Samuel Farthing. He wore a long, dark coat and a top hat which he removed when she opened the door.

'Mr Farthing.'

'Good day to you, Mrs Crabtree. I hope I haven't come at a bad time. Sorry, that was a silly thing to say. Of course it's a bad time for you.'

'Won't you come inside, Mr Farthing? Your driver as well, rather than him stand out in the rain.'

Samuel called out to his carriage driver who was tethering the horse to the hitching rail at the end of Cinder Yard.

'The kind lady has invited you in, Josiah.'

'Very good, Mr Farthing.'

Samuel and Josiah followed Beth into the living room where Samuel looked around, approvingly, at the cleanliness and good taste of the furnishings. 'You're obviously a woman with great pride in her ways,' he said.

Josiah, stood by the door, suitably sub-servient, with his cap in his hands, but with a look in his eyes that told Beth it was only an act. He was a frail-looking man in his thirties and there had always been rumours flying around the mill that he was Samuel's illegitimate son, but there were rumours in every mill so Beth had always paid it no heed. If it were true she could see no family resemblance. She turned her attention to Samuel.

'If you've come to give me my old job back the answer's no.' she said quickly.

'I've not come to take advantage of the situation,' he replied. 'You know me better than that.'

Amelia, who had been sleeping in her cot, awoke with a sudden cry. 'Excuse me, Mr Farthing,' Beth said, going to pick her daughter up.

24

Samuel's eyes twinkled with pleasure. 'She's a grand-looking girl.'

Beth smiled back as she held Amelia in her arms and she could have sworn there was more than just a friendly interest in Samuel's eyes. Just for a second she thought of telling him he had a granddaughter, but that would have bespoiled her dear husband's memory. 'Alfred doted on her,' she said, instead.

'I'm sure he was a wonderful father. The funeral was well attended, I noticed.'

'Yes, thank you for coming.'

'It was the least I could do, in fact that's my purpose in being here. I came to discuss compensation with you. The accident occurred on my premises and I accept some of the responsibility.'

Only some? thought Beth. *Ah well, some's better than nothing.* All thoughts of revealing Amelia's parentage went from her mind. 'That's very good of you, Mr Farthing.'

He took out his wallet and laid ten one-pound notes on the table. Beth looked at the money and was about to ask him if he thought that's all Alfred's life was worth.

'This is to cover the funeral,' he said. 'And I'll give you a promisory note to pay you half of Alfred's wages every week for the next five years, including any pay rises he would have been entitled to. That should keep you off parish relief until you get back on your feet.'

It was more than she could ever have expected. There was also seamstress work she could do from home. She'd be able to manage. 'It's more than generous, Mr Farthing,' she said.

'It's only right and proper. We Farthings look after our own.' He looked at Amelia when he said it and held out

25

his forefinger for her to grip. 'My, my – she's got a good strong grip on things, has the girl. That's what you need in this life, Beth – a good strong grip on things.' He paced up and down the room before adding. 'There's a job waiting for you back at the mill if you so choose.'

'Thank you, Mr Farthing, but I think it's best I don't come back.'

'You know Godfrey's married now,' he said. 'Calmed him down I expect.'

I doubt that, Beth thought. 'Yes, I had heard. But I still don't want to work for him. I'd work for you at the drop of a hat but not for him.'

'Beth, I've been working since I was ten – rarely taken a holiday. I'm sixty-one years old and I reckon I've got ten good years in me and, if I'm lucky, ten declining years after that. I intend enjoying those years.'

'I hope you do, Mr Farthing. There's no one entitled to a happy retirement more than you, but I'll not work for your son.'

'I understand,' he said, then turned to go. 'You can pick up your money once a week. It'll be there for you, every Friday for the next five years.'

June 1882

Beth was sitting out in what bit of sunshine Cinder Yard afforded. A chimney sweep was working at one of the houses opposite and he'd asked her to give him a shout when the brush emerged from the chimney pot.

'It's out, mister,' she shouted.

The chimney sweep raised and lowered the brush in acknowledgement of her shout then he brought it back down again. In half an hour he'd be gone and she'd be able to put her washing on the line strung across the yard. No one hung out washing when a sweep was at work.

Mrs Tattersall from Number 3 came out and called across to Beth. 'D'yer know if they're still tarrin' up Lupset Lane? Our Benny's got whoopin' cough.'

'They were this mornin'. Is he bad?'

'Bad enough. Poor little beggar dint get a wink o' sleep last night. I'd take him ter t' doctor but I haven't paid me panel money since my Walter popped his clogs.'

'I'm sure the doctor won't worry under the circumstances.'

Mrs Tattersall gave this some thought then shook her head. 'It's not life and death or nowt. I'll take him and stand him by t' tar wagon. A few lungfuls o' them fumes is as good as owt t' doctor could do for him.'

Beth thought about Amelia and vowed to keep paying the doctor his fourpence a week panel money – if only for the baby's sake.

With the warm weather came the bedbugs, which Beth had already dealt with. From where she sat she could smell the delousing going on at Number 13. Sulphur candles would have been lit in all the offending rooms, which would then have been sealed with brown sticky paper. The fumigation would take twelve hours, leaving in its wake the smell of bad eggs. Earlier that day the school nit nurse had visited two houses in the yard checking the kids for nits, ringworm and impetigo. Within a couple of days Beth knew that some of the kids from these houses would be going round with shaved heads, dabbed with gentian violet – and there would be little embarrassment. It was the price they had to pay for living in such a poor and dirty part of town.

A young, elegant woman strode through the archway

27

and paused to scrutinise the numbers painted on the house walls. Her head turned round in a half circle, following a small boy who was running round the yard with a hoop and stick. Her eyes settled on Beth and she smiled, uncertainly.

'Mrs Crabtree?'

'Yes.'

'My name's Lydia Farthing – Mrs Godfrey Farthing if I'm to be correct.'

'If you're Mrs Godfrey Farthing then you have my sympathy,' said Beth.

'Oh dear, I thought I might. That's why I came to see you.'

'To see me? What business might the wife of Godfrey Farthing have with me? There's no love lost between me and that ma—' She stopped when she saw that Lydia Farthing's lip was quivering. 'I'm sorry, Mrs Farthing,' she said. 'That was very rude of me.'

Lydia pressed her lips together. Her face was pale and she looked ill. 'Look,' Beth said. 'I think you'd better come inside. She got to her feet and took Lydia by the elbow, guiding her across the threshold into the cool room where eleven-months-old Amelia lay sleeping in her cot.

Lydia went over and looked down at her. 'Oh my, she's quite beautiful,' she said. Then she looked up at Beth and asked, with a note of accusation in her voice. 'Is it true?'

'Is what true?' Beth asked, guardedly.

'Is it true that my husband is her father?'

Beth was stunned by such an impertinent question from right of the blue. Since Alfred had asked her to marry him the question of Amelia's real father had never been raised. Alfred had assumed the role of father-to-be that day and had never wavered from it. She knew it was likely that Godfrey would correctly guess that her child was his, but it was a thought she hid away in a deep recess of her mind. But it seemed to Beth that this woman had the right to know the truth about her vile husband. She thought for a long time before replying, 'It's true that your husband raped me and made me pregnant. But I'll thank you to keep this between the two of us. I don't want my daughter to grow up knowing she's the daughter of a rapist.'

'Raped? He didn't say anything about rape to me.'

'Well, he's hardly going to admit it? What exactly did he say to you, Mrs Farthing?'

Lydia sat down in a chair and breathed a long sigh. 'Please call me Lydia,' she said. 'Might I call you Beth?'

'Of course.'

'Oh Beth, it's such a mess! I only married him to please my family.' Then, in belated answer to Beth's question she said, 'He was drunk – and he gets horribly vexatious when he's in drink. He got into bed and demanded his rights, which I refused due to his drunken state. He punched me and told me I wasn't his first by a long way, in fact he had a daughter from one of his – his conquests.'

'Conquests? I doubt if he used that word,' Beth commented, bitterly. 'Are you sure he didn't say whores? Some of them probably were. For your information I wasn't. I was a virgin until he raped me.'

'Oh dear, how terrible for you.' There was genuine pity in the woman's eyes as she continued, 'He began ranting at me, so I ran from the room. He followed me and – and he told me it was you who had had his bas– baby.'

'His bastard. He refers to my daughter as his bastard.'

'Actually, he probably didn't mean to mention you. I

29

think he was too drunk to know what he was saying. I suspect he doesn't remember even telling me.' Her hands trembled and drew Beth's attention to a diamond engagement ring, as big as a lark's egg. She was screwing it around her finger, half taking it off then pushing it back down. 'For two pins I'd take this damn ring off and throw it away.' Lydia was sobbing now.

'Well, it looks as though it's worth a nice few shillings,' said Beth. 'Why don't you sell it? Use the money to run away from him. You've obviously made a mistake marrying the brute. Why don't you leave him while you're still young?'

Lydia let out another deep sigh and shook her head, hopelessly. 'Would it were that simple.' She looked up at Beth with watery, hazel eyes and said, 'I'm pregnant.'

'Oh,' said Beth.

There was a long pause as Lydia looked around the room. At the wedding photograph of Beth and Alfred on the mantelpiece, and then down to the sleeping Amelia.

'But not to Godfrey,' she said, eventually.

'What?'

'I'm pregnant, but not by my husband.'

'You have a lover?'

'Well, I don't actually love him, nor does he love me – at least I don't think he does. He's a kind and decent man who happened to be around to comfort me when I was lonely and at a low ebb.'

'They can be very good at comforting lonely women, can men.' Beth failed to hide her cynicism.

'Please don't condemn me.'

Beth took her hand. 'I'm sorry. I didn't mean to condemn. In fact, anyone who's married to Farthing is entitled to the comfort of a decent man.' She sat down in the other chair, at a loss what to advise in such a complicated situation.

'Why did you come here?' she asked, at length.

Lydia got to her feet and walked around the limited confines of the room. 'You don't have any cigarettes, do you?' she asked.

'Sorry – I don't smoke cigarettes.'

'It's wonderfully therapeutic, tobacco. Helps me think. I didn't start until after I married Godfrey. Had I started before I would probably have thought better of marrying him.'

'Is this . . . sorry, what's your lover's name?'

'I'd rather not say. You wouldn't know him, anyway.'

'Is he married?'

Lydia shook her head. 'No.'

'Well, why not leave Farthing and run off with him? He sounds like a much better prospect. I wouldn't need to give it a second thought if it were me.'

Lydia stopped walking and looked down at Beth from the edge of her eyes. 'I threatened to leave him once and do you know what he said?' She answered her own question as Beth knew she would. 'He said he'd deal with me like he dealt with Alfred Crabtree. That scared me.'

Beth felt herself going cold. 'No, he can't have – surely.'

'I'm not saying he had anything to do with your husband's death,' said Lydia. 'You know what an empty braggart he is at times. I'm just repeating what he said – but if you ask me, a man who's capable of rape is capable of anything.'

'I couldn't stand it if I thought he'd murdered dear Alfred.' Beth said to herself, then she looked up at Lydia. 'You must leave him before the baby is born. Leave him

31

right now. Stay here tonight then tomorrow go to your decent man.'

'Oh, Beth, I wish leaving Godfrey were that simple. I can't, don't you see. I can't even tell him he's the father of my child. He's not exactly a man of substance, and Godfrey's in a position to destroy him if ever he found out. I can't inflict that on him. Not only that, but my own family would turn on me.'

'Your own family,' said Beth, 'why would they turn on you?'

'Because to them I'm just a pawn to be pushed around and used to their best advantage. They're quite big in the wool trade and I'm a weak woman, which is why I allowed myself to be pushed into marriage with Godfrey. My family told me it would be good for their business and I hadn't the guts to argue. So, you see,' Lydia said, dismally, 'I'm trapped.' She sat back down in the chair. 'The reason I came to see you is because I need to talk to someone. I need a shoulder to cry on. A confidante who won't tell on me.'

'But you don't even know me.'

'I don't trust anyone I know, but I know I can trust you because we both have secrets we don't want betrayed. I need a confidante who's outside my circle of acquaintances.' She gave Beth a bleak smile. 'Actually, I know *of* you. I've heard Samuel speak of you in the most glowing terms.'

'He was always good to me,' Beth said.

'It sometimes seemed as if there was another connection – does he know about your daughter being his granddaughter?'

'I don't think so,' Beth said, with an uncertain shake of her head. 'But he was very generous to me when

Alfred died. You won't tell him, will you?'

'No more than you'll tell anyone about me. Tonight I'll tell Godfrey I'm pregnant and my child will grow up with him as the father. I wouldn't wish such a fate to befall your lovely daughter.'

Beth smiled. Somehow she was glad this woman had come in to her life. Each could share the other's burden. Lydia got to her feet again and walked over to the cot. 'Amelia,' she said. 'Such a beautiful name for a beautiful child.'

'Have *you* thought of any names?' Beth enquired.

Lydia nodded. 'Only if it's a boy. If it's a boy I'm going to call him Henry.'

'Would you like a cup of tea?'

'I'd love one, thanks.'

The two of them chatted all afternoon. Amelia woke up and sat on Lydia's knee quite cheerfully, bringing a rare smile to the desolate woman's face. At five o'clock Lydia left to go home. Beth never saw her again.

A few weeks later she received a letter from Lydia telling her that she wouldn't be seeing her again because Godfrey had found out about the first visit and had maltreated her. It was dated August 1882 and as a postscript she added:

I realise you may not want to hear this but Godfrey told me once again that he had killed Alfred. Apparently they had a fight and Godfrey pushed him off a gantry. I am quite sure he killed your husband; this is why I fear him so. Please tell no one that Godfrey is not my baby's father. If he ever found out I dread to think what he'd do to me and the child. He would try and force the name of the father from me and I'm such a weak person I might reveal it. He's capable of the most awful frightfulness. I would therefore be obliged if you would destroy this letter.

November 1884

Henry's eyes flickered as Lydia's tears dropped on to his sleeping face. Her own eyes were wild and unbalanced. The youthful glow had gone from her face despite her being only twenty-four years old. Eight-month-old James was sleeping in a cot next to Henry's bed.

She had provided Godfrey with the heir and the spare, as he called his sons, and he had little more use for her. Samuel had championed her during the early days of their marriage, but in the last two years he'd scarcely been at home, seriously devoting his remaining years to travel and pleasure, leaving Godfrey in charge of everything.

Surprisingly, the mill was flourishing under Godfrey's system of delegation, hiring three men to do the work his father had done on his own, which left him free to drum up business and cream the odd bonus off the top. His treatment of Lydia bordered on sadistic. Word had got back to him that she'd been seen leaving Beth Crabtree's cottage, and his punishment had left Lydia confined to her room for a week until her bruises subsided. It was only when she screamed that she was pregnant and that he was killing his own child that his brutal assault on her stopped. Her complaints to her own family fell on deaf ears. Since the marriage they had struck up a fruitful business arrangement with Godfrey Farthing and they didn't want a whining woman who couldn't cope with a few slaps to upset the applecart.

'Goodbye my darlings. Your father's kinder to you than he is to me, so I expect you'll be all right. I know your grandpa won't let any harm come to you as long as he's alive. I pray to God that he lives long enough to see you both through to adulthood.'

Early the next morning she was found by a gamekeeper on the rocks at the bottom of Eaglescliff Crag. She had apparently died instantly. Godfrey put it down to chronic melancholia which he had done his best to alleviate. She had left a damning suicide note in the nursery which Godfrey found and tore up without a word to anyone.

All in all she had served her purpose and the outcome had been most satisfactory. Saved him the trouble of doing it himself.

Later that day the father of Lydia's child found a note she had sent him. It said she felt it only right for him to know that her eldest boy was, in fact, his son. It also swore him to secrecy and obliged him to burn the note immediately. It confirmed his suspicions but he knew there was nothing he could ever do. Her death had shaken him, and robbed him of his dream of one day running away with her. He had loved Lydia Farthing and had hoped that one day she might return his love; but it was a love now destined to be forever unrequited. He lit a match and watched through tearful eyes as the note burnt to a curled up crisp and dropped to the floor.

26 August 1900

'I could have come to you, Mr Farthing,' said John Sykes. 'It would have been no trouble.'

'It was better I come to your offices,' said Samuel. 'I

don't want to arouse the sort of suspicion that will have me end my days arguing with my son.'

Sykes was a partner in Sykes, Sykes and Broom. He nodded, then looked at the door. 'What about–?'

'Josiah? Trust him with my life. He's been with me since he was a lad – over thirty years now. He won't tell anyone I've been here, not if I tell him not to. On top of which I've chosen to see a junior partner so that if anyone *has* seen me come here then I can say it's on a minor matter which is my business and my business only.'

The solicitor sat back in his chair and smiled. 'To use an expression I read in a Wild West magazine, you seem to have covered your tracks well, Mr Farthing.'

Samuel gave a deep, rumbling cough and banged at his chest with a frail fist as though trying to encourage his heart along. 'I wish I knew how to cover the angle that says I haven't long for this world.'

'I'm sure you've got many good years in you yet.'

Samuel opened his mouth to give the young man an argument but decided against it. He had little time to waste on irrelevances. 'I want to change my will,' he said. 'I assume you're qualified to do that?'

'Yes I am.'

'Will anyone else need to know?'

'The junior clerk, Robert Burns can act as witness. You can be assured of his discretion.'

'Good. And I don't want to leave any loopholes. I want it to be as watertight as a duck's arse. My son has been robbing my company blind for years and I want to rob him of his inheritance and pass it on to my grandsons – and what's more I want to tell him in my will just why I've done it.'

*

Samuel clung to life for just over a year when, with only Josiah at his bedside, he opened his eyes for the last time.

'Ah, Josiah. I'm glad you're here to see me off. You've been a good and faithful servant.'

Josiah also knew the rumours regarding his parentage, but he was *fairly* certain they weren't true. He'd been brought up in an orphanage, the abandoned son of a woman of ill-repute and an unknown father. He'd harboured dreams of the rumours being true and wondered if Samuel's deathbed might be a good time to settle the doubt.

'Thank you, Mr Farthing. I've always looked upon you as the father I never knew.' He searched the old man's eyes for the truth but saw only a twinkle.

'Sadly that rumour isn't true, Josiah,' whispered Samuel. 'Had it been true you'd have been inheriting much of my fortune about now. But I've left you well catered for. My grandsons should be pleased as well . . . mind you, Godfrey's got a bit of a shock coming to him.'

With that he closed his eyes as if giving death permission to take him. He was eighty-one-years-old and met his end with a most inappropriate grin on his face.

Part Two

Chapter Three

RMS *Lusitania*. Friday, 7 May 1915, 1.30 p.m.

The waiter gave the girl a discreet wink because he knew it would earn him a smile, and of course she didn't disappoint him. Then she rolled her deep-blue eyes and inclined her head in the direction of her parents who were busy arguing. Again. They'd scarcely argued at all before the letter arrived from England. *That damn letter,* as her mother frequently referred to it.

The letter had contained two sadnesses. First, the news that Uncle James had been killed in France, and second that Grandfather Farthing wanted her daddy to go to France to fight in the war that had killed his younger brother. This made no sense at all to Amy but she was only ten so what did she know?

Their voices were low and modulated and didn't rise above the polite hubbub of the lunchtime diners around them, most of whom would be dead within the hour. There was a gentle clink of silver cutlery and an aura of understated wealth in the room, apart from a well-preserved dowager at the next table who wore a tiara and pearls to lunch.

Only their mannerisms betrayed the animosity between the pair. An elegant, jabbing finger; arms folding in frustration; a shake of one head, a toss of the other; a cigarette stubbed out just a little too vigorously.

'Henry, if you must go and fight in that damn stupid war I don't see what's wrong with us staying at my mum's house.'

'It's . . .' He tried to think of a description that wouldn't insult her mother. Amelia leaped upon his hesitation like a cat on a mouse.

'Go on. It's what – not good enough?'

'It's very small,' he murmured, inadequately.

'It's a home, which is more than can be said for that soulless mausoleum your father rattles around in.'

'Hey! That was *my* home once.'

'It was where you lived,' Amelia countered. 'There's a difference.'

Henry needed to change the subject. 'It's *not* a stupid war,' he said, firmly. 'It's an honourable war. If the blasted Americans had any sense of honour they'd be helping us out – and as you well know my father has very kindly agreed to put you up.'

'Put us up, or put up with us?'

'Amelia!'

'Oh, come on, Henry – in all the time I've been with you your father hasn't given me so much as a smile. It's as if he thinks I'm carrying the plague or something. And why he got us tickets on this floating target beats me – or is he trying to get rid of us in style?'

Amelia Farthing, daughter of Beth Crabtree, was a real head-turner. There was a luminescence about her that drew the eye. Ten years of living in New York and, before that, all her life in Yorkshire, gave her no right to her cut-glass English accent. Raised in poverty, Amelia was an ambitious woman who had bettered herself to a degree where she had been considered a great catch for all the eligible young Yorkshiremen who had set their caps at her. Henry's father, Godfrey Farthing, had told him she was a bloody gold-digger but, had money and status been her prime motive in life, she could have done even better than Henry. In turning down the young and persistent heir to the earldom of Kirkby, Amelia had missed out on one day becoming a countess and the mistress of a size-able estate in North Yorkshire. But money, position and title cut no ice with Amelia Crabtree; she knew what she wanted and what she wanted was Henry Farthing, with all his irritating ways. Apart from a long nose and unruly hair Henry was not unpleasant to look at. He was kind, amusing, very clever and had effortlessly eased his way into Amelia's much sought after affections. It made no difference to her that Henry's father was one of the wealthiest mill owners in Bradford; in fact, as things turned out, it was more of a hindrance. Beth Crabtree's strangely triumphant satisfaction at this match was almost as mysterious as Godfrey's resentment of his vivacious daughter-in-law.

'Darling, we've been through all that. It's one of the fastest ships in the world. It'll easily outrun a submarine.' Henry's accent came courtesy of the public school to which his father had sent him. It had opened many doors for them in impressionable New York society.

Amelia wasn't impressed. 'That's just it, we shouldn't have to be outrunning submarines. We should have trav-elled on an American ship. There are posters all over

New York harbour warning about making this crossing on board a British vessel!' She waved a contemptuous arm at their lavish surroundings. 'Heaven knows what we need all this for. Complete waste of money. I'd have been just as happy travelling steerage and spending the difference on something useful. Heaven knows we could have done with it. Twelve years of marriage and nothing to show for it but a rented apartment and a few sticks of furniture.'

'I provided for you as well as I could, Amelia. We had an expensive lifestyle, that's all.'

'We lived way beyond our means, just like we are now. The people in Britain are living hand to mouth and we're wallowing in luxury. It's obscene.'

Her voice carried to the next table, earning her a disapproving glare from the bejewelled dowager who ignited a luxurious cigar and aimed the smoke in Amelia's direction. The woman obviously considered it her station in life to wallow in obscene luxury.

'It's father's way,' Henry said. 'I look upon it as an olive branch.'

'Olive branch?' snorted Amelia, wafting away the drifting cigar smoke with an irritated hand. 'He wants his only surviving son to go off and play soldier-boy just to satisfy some warped family honour and you call this an olive branch? There wasn't much family honour around when he cut you out of his will – as if it might make me change my mind about you. From what I hear about your grandfather I bet he'd have made provision for you in his will had he known how disgracefully your father was going to behave. And refusing to come to our wedding was just petty. I bet if your mother had been alive she'd have made him come. '

'I'll thank you not to bring my mother into this.'

The anger dropped from her eyes for a second, but her tone remained unpenitent. 'I'm sorry,' she said. 'It's just that my mother knew her and said she was a good woman.'

Henry nodded. 'I wish *I'd* known her.'

'I know,' said Amelia. 'I wish I'd known my father, but there you are. The thing is we have each other now – and Amy. And I'm frightened to death that I might lose you.' She placed her hand on his, and said, as persuasively as she could, 'Henry, we love you. You're our whole world. Without you we have nothing. For one last time, don't leave us just to try and please your father. We need you more than he does.'

He placed his other hand on hers and steeled himself to resist those normally irresistible eyes.

'Darling,' he said, slowly and deliberately, 'I'm not joining up to please my father. I'm not a fool, I know what he's like. I'm joining up so that I can live with myself, and I'll be back before–'

'Live with yourself!'

Amelia's combustible temper popped like the cork from one of the lively champagne bottles that had been in such abundance the night before. 'What about living with us? In fact never mind me, what about Amy?'

Amy nearly said, 'Hey, leave me out of this,' but she was interested in what her mother had to say.

'What about interrupting Amy's schooling, leaving all her friends behind, her violin lessons?'

'Darling, she can make new friends, go to an English school, take violin lessons there if she wants to go on with it.'

'Oh, for God's sake Henry!'

The girl had had enough. She pushed her chair back

45

and wandered over to the waiter, standing by a wall like a corpulent, black and white statue. He pretended not to see her and gazed at a point well above her head. She stood in front of him with arms akimbo, silently willing him to give in and look down before she spoke to him. O'Keefe's mouth twitched and his eyes narrowed with determination not to be beaten by this young bewitcher. His eyes swivelled left at the emptying tables which would be soon cleared by waitresses, then to the right where the exchanges between Amy's mother and father were hotting up. What on earth people like that could find to argue about was beyond him. They appeared to have everything, including the most charming child he'd ever had the good fortune to meet. The charming child gave in first.

'I know you know I'm here, so please don't pretend you don't.'

O'Keefe looked upwards. He cupped a white gloved hand to his ear and asked in a tremulous voice, 'Did someone speak?'

'I'm down here,' giggled Amy.

His eyes travelled fearfully downwards and he gave a heart-clutching start at her unexpected presence. 'Heaven help me, madam. I didn't see you there.'

'You couldn't rustle me up a chicken sandwich, could you, O'Keefe? Mom and Dad are having one of their family meetings.'

The waiter gave a grin. Even after six days of serving at her table her accent still surprised him. It should be English, like her parents, but Amy Farthing, to all intents and purposes, was a New Yorker, having lived there all her life. He glanced across at her parents once again. They were unaware that their daughter had left their table. Amy had dark, curly hair and an interesting, rather than pretty, face – one of those ugly duckling faces that could one day blossom into spectacular beauty or go the other way. At her age it was hard to tell. She had inquisitive eyes and a singular smile that could light up any room, even the spectacular first-class dining saloon of the Royal Mail Steamer *Lusitania*, one of the two largest ships in the world and former holder of both Blue Ribands for eastbound and westbound crossings of the Atlantic.

'I'll see what I can arrange, madam.'

'Why don't you call me Amy?'

He looked around in an exaggerated fashion and said furtively, from the side of his mouth, like a spy passing on a top secret to an enemy agent, 'I'd love ter call ye Amy, madam, but I'm not allowed ter be on first-name terms with the passengers. Ye wouldn't want me walkin' the plank now, would ye?'

She giggled again. 'Don't be silly, this isn't a pirate ship.'

O'Keefe warmed to his theme. 'Ye'll change yer tune when yer see me bein' keel-hauled and swingin' from the yardarm.'

'Fair enough. I'll let you call me madam.'

'Ah, ye just saved me life. Fer that I'll whistle up the finest sandwich this side of the Spanish Main. Would madam like a nice apple to go with it?'

He had an amiable face. His hair had once been ginger but was now grey going on white. His nose had the texture of orange peel, only much redder, and there was a cheery, dancing light in his blue eyes. O'Keefe was fifty-two years old and he came from County Cork which, at that very moment, was just 10 miles off the port beam.

'That would be just great, thanks. I'll be at the top of the stairs.'

Amy went up to the balcony, from where she could observe the animated conversation of her parents who were now drawing disapproving glances from other diners. Her mother usually won these exchanges but it seemed she was on a loser this time because Dad could be real stubborn when he set his mind to it. He had a way of setting his jaw and narrowing his eyes and his words came out quietly and firmly. When it got to this Mom usually let him have his own way. Which was a shame because, for once, Amy was with her mom, although it would never do to take sides. She would never take sides against her dad.

From her elevated vantage point Amy looked around the huge and lavish room. Decorated in the style of Louis XVIth it occupied two decks and was capped with a beautiful plaster dome. Their first-class passage had apparently been paid for by her paternal grandfather. Amy knew something bad had once gone on between her parents and Grandpa Farthing that had prompted their move to America before she was born, but she didn't know what it was. All she knew was that her dad was viewing this as a chance to make up and mend.

She had never met Uncle James who had been killed by *the damned Hun*. Apparently her grandfather had said in his letter that he would sign up himself if his other son hadn't got the courage to go and fight for king and country and avenge his brother. By the sound of it, her mother didn't have much time for Grandpa Farthing, whom Amy had also never met. Amelia had poured scorn on her father-in-law's empty words. 'Your father wouldn't have the guts to join the Salvation Army, never mind the proper army.'

This had made Amy smile for a second until she saw the hurt look in her dad's eyes. She concealed the smile behind her hand until it went away of its own accord.

To Amy it didn't matter who they stayed with, she most definitely wouldn't like it – she had made up her mind about that. Hedley Cooper, one of the boys at her school, recently over from England, had told her that Yorkshire was cold and the kids all had snotty noses and no shoes and something called rickets that made you bow-legged. Amy looked down at her legs and bowed them out, then she turned and looked at her reflection in a glass door. It made her smile.

Captain William Turner allowed himself a rare smile as he strode across to the port side of the bridge and looked over the calm sea at the southern Irish coastline about 14 miles away. The Old Head of Kinsale was slumped on the horizon like a pale green puppy, sleeping in the afternoon sun. At the end of it was the lighthouse with its black and white horizontal bands. The captain had passed it so many times it seemed like an old friend welcoming him home. He'd had a nervous few hours, but his last Admiralty signal had read: *'SUBMARINE FIVE MILES SOUTH OF CAPE CLEAR, PROCEEDING WEST WHEN SIGHTED AT 10 AM.'*

This meant the danger was many miles behind him and heading in the opposite direction. Up until then the signals had been troubling him sufficiently for him to have the lifeboats swung out on to their davits and to turn the ship 20 degrees to port so sharply that it had caused many passengers to momentarily lose their balance.

Then, as he looked at the distant lighthouse, another message from Vice Admiral Coke in high grade naval code ordered him into Queenstown immediately – standard procedure in situations of grave peril. Captain Turner, who had planned reaching Liverpool exactly in time to catch the high tide, cursed under his breath in an undiluted Liverpool accent. He lacked the social sophistication that shipping lines preferred in their top captains, but he made up for it in seamanship. The social side of the *Lusitania*'s captaincy was taken care of by another captain with supposedly superior breeding. William Turner turned to the newest officer on the bridge, Junior Third Officer Albert Bestic, whom he called Bisset because Bestic was difficult to pronounce in scouse.

'Mr Bisset. Do you know how to take a four-point bearing?'

'I do sir.'

'Then kindly take one off that lighthouse, will you?' With that the captain left the bridge and went into the chartroom.

Kapitan-leutnant Walther Schwieger was up on the conning tower of the German submarine U20 with the lookouts. In an earlier voyage he had narrowly missed a hospital ship with a torpedo, which meant he wasn't above destroying a British passenger liner.

At around noon they had sighted an old war cruiser, the *Juno*. It escaped because it was zig-zagging and difficult to fire at. Captain Turner of the *Lusitania* did not do this because he considered it a waste of time and fuel, a decision that would come back to haunt him.

At 1.20 Schwieger saw smoke off the starboard bow

and focussed his binoculars on it. All he could see above the horizon were four funnels. It was big, and at least 12 miles away. He gave the order to submerge and alter course to intercept. As the ship and the submarine converged, Schwieger studied the vessel through the U20's attack periscope. He called to the pilot, 'Four funnels. Upwards of 30,000 tons, making about 20 knots.'

Lanz, the pilot, checked in his copies of *Jane's Fighting Ships* and Brassey's naval annual.

'It is either the *Lusitania* or the *Mauritania*. Both are listed as cruisers and used for trooping.'

'Which makes it a legitimate target.'

'Yes, Herr Kapitan-leutnant,' confirmed Lanz.

To their delight the liner began to turn to starboard, presenting the submarine with an unmissable target.

Amy took her sandwich and apple out on the boat deck where lots of people were at the rails watching Ireland pass them by. The sea was calm and an inviting blue, contrasting with the patched green landscape and faraway, hazy hills. The afternoon sun winked brightly from windows in the distant town of Kinsale, tucked deep within its harbour. In between she could see the flapping, white sails of fishing boats tacking to a fro in pursuit of an elusive breeze. Squawking seagulls dived and wheeled and flew alongside, hoping for titbits. Amy threw the remains of her sandwich and laughed as one bird swooped and caught it well before it reached the water. The very thought that there was any danger lurking near at hand was unthinkable. She leaned on the rail and munched away at the apple, wondering what lay ahead of her. Strange country, new people, new family, and all because her dad wanted to go to war and maybe get killed. It troubled her deeply that she might lose her dad. Hedley Cooper said millions of men had been killed already because the Germans had the biggest guns in the world. When she put this to her father he had dismissed it as foolish talk and said he was only going over there for a few months to help finish them off.

'Tis a beautiful country, right enough,' said a voice, from over her shoulder. O'Keefe was carrying a tray of drinks, presumably destined for someone out on deck. 'I was born just a few miles over there and I'll be goin' back when this journey's over. There's a whisper that we're callin' into Queenstown. If we are I'll be after signin' off there – if they'll let me. Save me comin' back from Liverpool. Might have a word with old Bowler Bill.'

'Who's Bowler Bill?'

'He's the Lucy's captain – but ye'd never know him. Doesn't like all the fancy socialisin' with the passengers, doesn't old Bowler. He has another feller ter do all that fer him. I take him his meals up on the bridge. He's a good old scouser. Let me off at Queenstown if I ask him, no problem.'

'Do you have a family, O'Keefe?' Amy asked.

'I have three grown-up boys. They all went to America.' He jabbed a thumb towards aft and America. Amy looked, then returned her eyes to O'Keefe as he went on: 'My wife was never the greatest traveller or we might have gone with them. She once went off ter Killarney for the day an' got homesick.' He smiled to himself at the memory. 'Ah, me darlin' Maggie wouldn't leave Ireland for all the money in the world – and neither will I after I get back.'

'I expect she misses you when you're away.'

'Well, I expect I miss her a lot more than she misses

me – she died ye see. I went off to America to be with me boys, but I belong over here.'

Amy allowed a respectful silence to pass before she said, 'I'm very sorry to hear about your wife.'

He looked down at her and saw the deep sincerity in her eyes. 'By God, so ye are. I never seen so much truth in such a small package.' Then he smiled and shaded his eyes at the distant green hills. 'I wonder if she's out there, dreamin' of me right now. That's what she called death, ye know – the big dream. She had her own way o' thinkin', did my Maggie.'

Amy leaned on the rail and stared out to sea, meditatively. The passing breeze plucked at her curls which she pushed back over her forehead. 'O'Keefe – do you think I'll miss my home? I'm going to live with my grandparents in England.'

He smiled. 'Ye home is where ye mammy an' daddy are. I expect ye'll come to no harm at all.'

'My dad's going off to war.'

The smile dropped from his weathered face. 'Ah, so that's the craic, is it? King an' country an' all that. They like their wars do the English. He'll be an officer will he, givin' out all the orders?'

'No idea,' said Amy, still staring into the distance. 'He's never been in the army before. He's an architect.'

'Jeez, that's a good number is that architect stuff. I wouldn't be goin' off ter no war if I was an architect.'

'Mom doesn't want him to go either, neither do I. Do you know what the war is all about?'

'Well, as far as I can figure it out, Amy, it's like a barroom brawl. A couple of fellers start fightin' and before ye know it the whole pub's at it.'

'You called me Amy.'

'Now don't ye go tellin' my superintendent that. I'll be walkin' the plank before we get ter Queenstown.'

'O'Keefe, you are funny.'

A loud, American voice from further up the deck called out, 'Waiter – are you going to be all day bringing those drinks? We could die of thirst waiting for you. God only knows where Cunard get their staff from nowadays.'

An equally loud, woman's voice said, 'I suppose all the good men are away fighting.'

'I don't see too many Americans away fightin',' muttered O'Keefe, under his breath, before giving Amy an expressive wink that said, in a voice meant for her ears only, 'Someone has to humour these people.' Then he called out in a thicker than necessary Cork brogue, 'Comin', sor.'

As Amy watched him go she overheard people expressing their relief at having made a safe crossing. The man with the loud voice was saying, 'Honey, we were safe from the minute we left New York harbour.' Amy remembered him making an almighty fuss at there having been no lifeboat drill. 'The Germans will know this ship's carrying Americans,' he went on. 'Never in a million years would they dare attack Uncle Sam.'

The torpedo struck the other side of the ship with a sound, which the captain later recalled was 'like a heavy door being slammed shut'.

Almost immediately there was another explosion that sent a column of water high in the air. Amy was flung back across the deck into the wall of the dining room where she banged her head and passed out. Just 30 feet away, her parents' argument was instantly forgotten, replaced by two more immediate concerns. What the hell was happening and, more importantly, where was Amy?

All the chairs were sliding across the polished wooden floor to the starboard side. People were involuntarily following the chairs, sliding across the floor like ice skaters, and the Farthings could do little else but go with them. 'Amy!' screamed Henry as he and Amelia got caught up in an inescapable crush, but his daughter couldn't hear him.

Up on Amy's side of the ship many of the port lifeboats were filling up with panicking passengers, but lowering them over the side would be impossible because of the ship's list to starboard. Third officer Bestic was trying to explain this to the people in lifeboat 2 when he heard the sound of a hammer striking the link pin that would release the snubbing chain holding the lifeboat to the deck.

'No!' he shouted, but before the word had left his lips the chain was freed and the lifeboat, laden with over fifty passengers, swung inboard like a gigantic pendulum and crushed those standing on the deck against the super-structure. The screams of agony and terror stirred Amy into consciousness. Blood was running down the deck past her legs. Beyond the rail there was only blue sky and to her right loomed the lifeboat that had just killed half a dozen people, maimed even more and was about to wreak further carnage. She crawled sideways and into the dining-room balcony just as her parents were leaving by the starboard door on the lower level. The lifeboat dropped from its davits and crashed to the deck where Amy had been only moments before, then it slid for'ard, leaving behind a grisly, screaming collection of dead and injured passengers and taking with it more of the same, including the loud American and his party, before it jammed under the bridge with a morbid finality.

Officer Bestic was running to lifeboat 4 to stop the same thing happening when someone knocked out the linkpin. He jumped out of the way just as this boat followed the same path as lifeboat 2, killing more passengers.

Driven by panic the passengers swarmed into lifeboats 6, 8, 10 and 12. One after another these boats all careered down the deck and smashed into lifeboats 2 and 4. Amy was in the dining room hanging on to a balcony rail and screaming for her mother and father. The sea was pouring through the lower level doors and smashed windows, and rising quickly. Tables and chairs were now floating around and banging into each other as the water sloshed around in great, untidy waves.

The dowager in the tiara, her face covered in blood, was thrown through the door and straight down the stairs into the water where she thrashed around helplessly for a while before fighting her way, with the last of her strength, back to the stairs only to be washed down again by the heaving water. Frozen with horror, Amy watched the beaten woman drown. A hand closed around the girl's arm and pulled her against the wall of an annexe. She looked up and was grateful to see O'Keefe.

'Here, put this on.' He helped her on with a lifejacket then donned one himself. 'Come with me.'

'What happened?'

'I think we been hit by a torpedo.'

'I want my mom and dad.'

'Amy, I don't know where they are. Maybe they're in one of the boats.'

'They wouldn't go without me.'

'Right oh, we'll go and find them. Just stick close by me.'

The ship was now sinking fast and the water was surging in through the balcony level starboard side doors as the list grew ever worse. The shouts and screams of panic and terror were deafening. O'Keefe put a strong arm around her as the sea surged up to her waist and lapped backwards, taking the two of them with it, straight through the door, out on to the starboard boat deck, across the rail and into the cold Atlantic.

The four great funnels loomed ominously above them, bowing to the sea as if in noble acceptance of defeat. People were jumping into the water from the stern of the ship which was high out of the water with its four great propellers still turning, slowly and uselessly, like an unpopular fairground ride. Some of the jumpers hit the boats, with sickening thuds; others hit the water, not all of them surfacing. There were screams of anguish and terror all around. Parents frantically looking for missing children, wives for husbands, children for parents.

'Can ye swim?' O'Keefe asked. 'We need to get clear of the ship.'

Shock had taken away Amy's power of speech but she answered by striking out in as good a breast stroke as her lifejacket would allow. O'Keefe struggled to keep up with her.

Many people in the water couldn't swim. Amy saw the arms of a drowning woman reaching upwards; expensively jewelled hands clawing for help that wasn't there. But the wealth on her fingers couldn't save her as she disappeared beneath the unkind waves. The girl paused, momentarily, wondering if she should do something. Perhaps tell someone.

'Keep going,' O'Keefe urged her. 'We don't want to be near when she goes down.'

Amy swam on as fast as she could until she was a good hundred yards away from the doomed liner. Then she turned and began to tread water as O'Keefe caught her up.

Eighteen minutes after the torpedo first struck, the great ocean liner slid, helplessly, beneath the waves, leaving in its wake a great, boiling froth of bubbles and a sense of shock among the survivors that the gigantic and world-famous *Lusitania* could be despatched to the bottom of the sea with such contemptuous ease.

All Amy was interested in was the whereabouts of her parents. There were bobbing heads and lifeboats all around, some overturned; the handful which had been successfully launched were overloaded to the point of sinking, with desperate people still trying to climb on and being repulsed by those already on board, who gave apologetic cries. 'Sorry, we can't take you. There are too many on already.' She knew her parents must be on one of these, hidden from her view. The possibility of them not being alive wasn't something she even considered. Her parents were the best, most capable people in the world. If anyone could manage to get on a lifeboat it was them. No way could Amy survive and her parents not. That was just too silly to contemplate.

'Mom, Dad. It's Amy. Where are you?'

She shouted until she was hoarse, with O'Keefe helping. The people in the boats were numb with shock. Blood-drained faces looked at the screaming girl without seeing her. Water was being baled out of a grossly over-laden boat which desperately needed to shed some of its cargo. A semi-conscious man either fell or was pushed overboard. His awakening cry of panic was choked off as he splashed into the sea, head first. He wasn't wearing a lifejacket and presumably couldn't swim because he sank, boots last, with no reaction from those he had left behind.

'Is my mom and dad on there? My name's Amy Farthing.'

Her name was passed around the boat with diminishing interest. An old man in an incongruous top hat said a guilty, 'Sorry, my dear.'

'Take the girl,' shouted O'Keefe. 'Ye must have room for at least one.'

No one said she couldn't, but no one made a move to help, and without help she couldn't climb on board. They knew that even her weight would sink them all. The old man in the hat seemed to give some thought to the notion that he could let her take his place – at the cost of his life. But he realised he wasn't that brave and turned his head away in shame.

'Bastards!' shouted O'Keefe. Then to Amy he apologised for his language. 'Sorry, about that. We'll be picked up soon.'

In the distance they could see the sails of fishing boats. There was something cheerful about them that didn't seem right, but it gave Amy hope. What she didn't realise was that the boats were over 10 miles away and in such a light, unhelpful wind it would take hours of tacking for them to reach the scene of the disaster.

Their kapok-filled lifejackets were cumbersome and not entirely reliable. But Amy was a lightweight, high in the water and bobbing up and down like a fisherman's float, while heavier people, such as O'Keefe, were having problems.

She was unwittingly wearing him out as he swam loyally by her side to visit each lifeboat and check on all the bobbing heads and enquire about her mother and father. After two hours the cold was getting to him and his head slumped occasionally forward into the sea. Animation had gone from many of those in the water. The swell of the heartless Atlantic provided their only movement; some face down, some face up, it didn't matter to them. They were dead. The hysteria and general shouting had lessened considerably due to cold, exhaustion, and there being progressively fewer people to shout. Amy looked across at the sails, tacking to and fro in the distance like pieces of paper fluttering in the breeze.

'Why don't they come and get us?' she asked O'Keefe. But, even if he knew, he was too tired to reply. 'O'Keefe, keep your head up,' she shouted.

He lifted his head and tried to smile, then rolled on to his side with his head under the surface. His submerged breath came out in bubbles. Amy swam over to him and turned him on his back. His lungs were choked with sea water and he coughed violently, then rolled over again.

She screamed at him, 'O'Keefe!' Then she grabbed his hair and pulled his head clear of the water. The coughing had stopped, but so had his breathing. Panicking now, she kicked out at him and caught him in the groin. The force of her kick was lessened by the water but it was enough to cause his eyes to slam open and for him to splutter out a mouthful of water and take a rasping gasp of air as Amy shouted encouragement.

'Keep kicking your legs!'

O'Keefe was choking, but he did as he was told for a

few seconds, before his energy drained away and he slumped forward again. She pushed his chin clear of the water and knew she wouldn't be able to keep this up for much longer.

'Help me!' she shouted to anyone who might care. 'Help, help – O'Keefe's drowning!'

A nearby voice said, 'O'Keefe? We can't have that.' Captain Turner swam over to them. He had been swept off the bridge just before the ship went down. Taking hold of one of O'Keefe's arms, he placed it across his shoulder. Without being told, Amy did the same with his other arm. Between them they just managed to keep the now unconscious waiter's head clear of the water.

'Do you know O'Keefe?' enquired Amy, totally unaware of who had come to her aid.

'I do. He brings me my meals when I dine on the bridge.' Turner had a strong Liverpool accent.

'Does this mean you're the captain?'

'I am – or was.'

'So you're Bowler Bill?'

The captain managed a glimmer of a smile; she could extract a smile under the most trying of circumstances. 'You're supposed to call me Captain Turner.'

'Oh, sorry.'

'You're doing well,' he said. 'Better swimmer than most.'

'We live near a swimming pool . . . Captain Turner.' Amy kicked harder than ever now to support her extra burden. 'I go there all the time.'

'Good girl. If we can hold out for another half hour we should get picked up. We got a message out before she went down. Do you think you can manage it?'

'I'll do my best.'

'I never doubted that.'

'You haven't seen my mom and dad have you?'

'I expect they're safe enough. No doubt as worried about you as you are about them.'

Such a reassurance coming from no less a person than the captain gave her hope and cheered her up somewhat. 'If I could find them I could stop them worrying,' she said. 'I expect they've got enough to worry about without me adding to their troub— Oh no!'

A dead woman floated past on her back, clutching an equally dead infant to her breast. Amy and the captain watched them drift away on the slight swell. Despite the horrors of that afternoon they were both moved to tears. Tears that were washed away by the sea.

A chorus of discordant shouts from the boats took their attention. People were waving and screaming. From where Amy was she couldn't see anything.

'I think help is at hand,' said Captain Turner; then to himself he added, 'God help those who have perished and I hope I didn't do anything to contribute to all this.'

But there were those who would say he had.

It was another hour before Amy, O'Keefe and Captain Turner were picked up by the steamer *Bluebell* and taken to Queenstown. After they had been hauled on board the captain said a polite 'Goodbye and good luck' to his two recent companions and was taken away by the *Bluebell*'s captain. Along with other rescued passengers, Amy and O'Keefe stood on deck in the cheerful sunshine, shivering and soaked in their bare feet, having discarded their footwear in the sea. Blankets were produced and Amy slipped, discreetly, out of her clothes and hung them out to dry on a rail. O'Keefe had been helped into a lifeboat where he lay, drinking hot tea and thawing out in the warmth of a sun that had never seemed so life giving and wondering how he could ever repay Amy for saving him.

After two hours they docked in Queenstown and an eerily silent river of survivors was ushered off the boat and along the quayside to the Cunard wharf, where a first-aid post had been set up. Bodies were being delivered to a different part of the wharf and placed in coffins. Some people sobbed, most seemed totally at a loss what to do or say or even think. Amy and O'Keefe were taken to a makeshift desk where a man took their names and added it to a list of survivors he was compiling.

'Please, are my mom and dad on your list?'

'What are they called?' asked the man, kindly.

'Mr and Mrs Farthing – Henry and Amelia.'

The man ran a pencil down his list and slowly shook his head. 'Not so far, but they're bringing people in all the time.' He glanced, pointedly, at the line of coffins which were all open for ease of identification. Amy and a now revitalised O'Keefe followed the eyes and knew what had to be done.

'I'm sure yer mammy and daddy are all right,' O'Keefe assured her. 'I'll just take a look to see if there's anyone here I know. You go inside and get yourself a cup of tea. I'll be wid yer in a few minutes.'

'O'Keefe, you need to rest,' protested Amy.

'I've got a whole lifetime to do me resting,' he said. 'Thanks ter you.' Then, to the man at the desk he said, 'She saved me life did this young lady and she could do with a pair of shoes – so could I for that matter.'

The man glanced down at Amy's bare feet as O'Keefe turned towards the line of coffins and took a deep breath.

'You'll tell me if you – if you see them,' Amy said, hesitantly.

'The minute I see yer mammy and daddy come strollin' up the road I'll be in to tell yer like a shot.'

'Thanks, O'Keefe.'

She watched him go, then turned as the man said, 'Right, young lady, you'd better tell me who you are, who you belong to and the address to where you're headed.'

'My name is Amy Farthing. I'm the daughter of Henry and Amelia Farthing. I don't have an address other than it's my grandpa's house in a town in England called Bradford.'

'Were there just the three of you on board? I mean, were any other relatives travelling with you – brothers or sisters?'

'No. I don't have any brothers or sisters.'

'I imagine your grandfather will get in touch with Cunard when he finds out what has happened,' said the man. 'In the meantime we'll fix you up with shoes and find you a nice billet in the town.'

'I just want my mom and dad.'

'Survivors are being brought in all the time. I'm sure your parents will be among them.'

'What makes you so sure?' Amy asked, innocently.

The man stared at her and wished her parents could come walking around the corner – but the odds were heavily stacked against it. He lowered his eyes and muttered, hopelessly, 'You mustn't give up hope.'

It was dark when O'Keefe returned. He was shivering once again, as if the hypothermia hadn't left his body yet. Amy looked at him, hopefully. He arranged his face into a smile and said, 'They're not back yet.' He could have added that all the survivors seemed to have been brought in, but he couldn't bring himself to be the bearer of such bad news. Not just yet.

Out of the 1,959 passengers who had set off from New York six days earlier only 761 survived. Amy, O'Keefe and Captain Turner were among the lucky ones.

Chapter Four

Saturday, 8 May 1915, Bradford, Yorkshire

A wide yawn allowed Godfrey Farthing's heavy face a moment's respite from its customary scowl. He eased himself from his bed, glanced at his image in a cheval mirror and picked up a comb from the dressing table to part his thinning hair down the centre. Then he tweaked his thick, black moustache and stood back to admire what he considered to be a handsome face; it was an opinion few shared with him. He strode to the window and opened the heavy, brocade curtains to illuminate the dark room with grey, morning light. Then he yawned once again, scratched his fat belly and pulled a bell rope to summon his manservant who would bring him his morning tea and take his order for breakfast. He took in the view as he made his first decision of the day – what to have for breakfast. It would be bacon that morning; six rashers, along with two eggs, mushrooms and tomatoes.

In the distance, beyond a regiment of smoking chimneys, were the raw green hills that would grow bleaker as they rose up to become the Pennines, the backbone of England. The backbone of the Farthing fortune was standing in the valley below him. Farthing's Mill, built in millstone grit – grimy grey from its own chimney and all the others. Four storeys high with rows of windows as dark and hostile as the gunports of a man o' war. Beyond those windows over three-hundred people toiled away to make him a rich man. He looked at his pocket watch, 7.10.

The boiler firer, who lived in the mill yard to be at hand for early morning stoking, would be taking a well-earned break as the steam from the boilers was fed through to the three massive engines which drove the looms. Work started at 6 a.m. At five minutes past the gates would be slammed in the faces of any latecomers, who would be left standing outside until after breakfast time, thus losing part of their wages.

Right now the looms were producing the drab, khaki material that would be made into army uniforms by a Leeds tailoring firm. The outbreak of war had had no adverse effect on his business, quite the opposite in fact. Like his father before him, Godfrey Farthing was a shrewd businessman and had secured the army contract the day after the Archduke Ferdinand had been shot dead in Sarajevo.

He had been expecting his son and family the previous night and was more irritated than concerned at their non-arrival. If it was as he suspected, that Henry's unnatural wife had persuaded him to spend the night in her mother's hovel, there'd be hell to pay. Josiah's knock seemed more tentative than usual.

'Come,' boomed Godfrey, decorously fastening his dressing gown across his great stomach.

His manservant shuffled in, stooped, skeletal and ancient, with the tray rattling nervously. Godfrey turned around. Josiah was watery-eyed and as pale as a ghost.

'What's the matter, man?' snapped Godfrey. 'Been at the drink last night? If you've been at my cognac I'll dock it from your wages.'

'No, Mr Farthing, nothing like that.'

'Then, what is it, man?'

'I think you'd better read this, Mr Farthing.'

He handed Godfrey a copy of the *Yorkshire Post* and stood back, nervously, as his boss's eyes scanned the front page headlines.

LUSITANIA SUNK OFF IRELAND BY GERMAN SUBMARINE. MORE THAN 1000 FEARED DEAD INCLUDING ALFRED VANDERBILT. CAPTAIN TURNER SAVED.

'Damn!'

Godfrey sank on to the bed and held his head, dramatically, in his hands. 'I wasn't expecting it to happen like this. How the hell can a submarine sink a floating city like the *Lusitania*?'

The newspaper had dropped to the floor. Josiah picked it up. 'It says there are hundreds of survivors, Mr Farthing – perhaps Mr Henry and his family are among them.'

Godfrey, stared at him for several seconds before saying, 'What?'

'Survivors – there are many survivors, sir. You mustn't give up hope, Mr Farthing.'

'Let me have a look.'

He snatched the paper from his manservant's hands. The report was extensive and covered the whole of the front page. His eyes raced up and down the columns searching for some mention of his son but all it told him was that the survivors had been taken to a place called Queenstown in Southern Ireland and would be brought to Liverpool at the earliest opportunity. Still in his dressing gown he strode out of the room, almost ran down the stairs to the telephone and bawled into the candlestick mouthpiece, 'This is Godfrey Farthing of Farthing's Mill. I want to be connected to the Cunard offices in Liverpool.'

'Do you know the number, sir?'

'Damn you, woman! Of course I don't know the number! What the hell do they pay *you* for?'

'Cunard – could you spell that, sir?'

'Oh, for God's sake, woman! C . . . U . . . N . . . A . . . R . . . D. They've got ships, bloody big ones! My son was on one until it damn well sank. I need to know if he's still alive if that's not too much to ask!'

'I see, sir. Just one moment, sir.'

The unhurried clock on Godfrey's wall ticked away two minutes before the operator came back on the line. 'I'm afraid the Cunard telephone lines are tied up, with many people waiting to be put through. Would you like me to try again later, Mr Far–'

He slammed the earpiece down on its bracket. 'Josiah, pack me a bag and bring the car round to the front, we're going to Liverpool.'

'But Mr Farthing we don't know–'

'What we don't know we'll find out, Josiah.'

'Very good, Mr Farthing.'

As hovels went, Beth Crabtree's was pristine clean, well kept and neatly furnished, as were most of the houses in Cinder Yard – apart from number eight where Gertrude Earnshawe lived. Amelia had been happy living there and

69

might have been even happier with a brother or sister to keep her company. But fate had put paid to that. Amelia was just three months old when her father, Alfred, had been working a ginny wheel up on the third-floor loading bay of Farthing's mill, hauling up bales of wool from a haulier's cart when he mysteriously fell off the gantry's cantilevered floor. He hit the carthorse first, breaking the beast's neck before breaking his own on the cobbled yard. At least that was the story her mother had told her and Amelia had no cause to believe differently.

Shortly afterwards Samuel Farthing had handed over the running of the mill to his son, who had different ideas from his father. For a start, old Samuel would never have approved of cashing in on the war quite so readily, nor would he have approved of sending his only surviving grandson to the front to follow in the unfortunate foot-steps of his other grandson, now dead. Godfrey himself had always managed to avoid volunteering for any form of armed conflict.

When Amelia Crabtree became engaged to Henry, Godfrey became outraged and threatened to cut Henry out of his will if he went through with this unnatural union. He told his son that she could only be marrying him for his money and that her bitch of a mother was probably behind it all. In truth, Beth was quite shocked at the way Henry and her daughter had been drawn together, but she accepted it as the mischievous hand of fate. She would have had her daughter fall in love with anyone other than a Farthing, but when she met Henry she realised he was as different from Godfrey as chalk was from cheese – which of course he would be. Beth derived a certain perverse satisfaction from her daughter marrying Henry against his father's express wishes. All through the courtship she expected Godfrey to blurt out the truth in order to avoid his son becoming involved in what he thought to be an incestuous marriage. Right up to the wedding itself she enjoyed the agony he must have been going through and wondered if he might try and halt the wedding with his shocking revelation – as any decent father would. If he had she would have denied his being Amelia's father and insisted that the wedding go ahead. It wasn't strictly true but it would have sorely damaged Godfrey and ensured the wedding took place. She had harboured her hatred of him for thirty years, so anything she could do to hurt him was fair game to Beth. But, as Beth truly suspected, Godfrey valued his reputation too much to admit being Amelia's father and the wedding went ahead.

At this point Beth could, and probably should have told the couple about their true parentage but then she thought, *What does it matter? They're happy and Godfrey's mortified. Best of both worlds really.*

When Beth read of the sinking of the *Lusitania* she knew who would be to blame if her daughter, granddaughter and son-in-law were among the dead. With the newspaper still clutched in her hand and a shawl wrapped around her head and shoulders she made her way up to Godfrey Farthing's grand house on Heaton Hill. She had left work the instant the paper had been shown to her by Dan Cullen in the time office at Brammah's Mill.

Godfrey's Daimler was coming down the drive towards her as she went in through the gate. She held up a hand and the car drew to a halt.

'What the devil do you want, woman?'

Beth couldn't see him but she could hear his obnoxious voice coming from the back seat. She walked alongside the car and stared at Godfrey in severe silence. The only sounds came from the soft purr of the engine and her clogs clicking against the stone paving beneath her feet. Eventually he lowered his eyes beneath the force of her gaze.

'Well?' he asked, roughly. 'Have you come to mourn this unnatural family of yours? You should have stopped that marriage, you vindictive old cow.'

'You know very well why I'm here, you poisonous devil. I know you killed my husband. If I find you've been responsible for the deaths of any more of my family I swear I'll swing for you, Godfrey Farthing!'

'What the hell are you taking about, you stupid woman. Drive on Josiah.'

Beth took a quick step back to where Josiah's ears were pricking with prurient interest in this conversation. He didn't much like his employer, but at his age the job was all he could get. For the life of him Josiah couldn't understand what had happened with the old man's will. Samuel had promised him he'd be well catered for. In the event he'd been left nothing, nor had Godfrey's sons.

Beth reached inside the car and, with her left hand, she grabbed Josiah by the scruff of his scrawny neck. In her right hand was the starting handle which she had by now taken from the running-board tool box and was holding against his face, threateningly.

'Switch the engine off or I'll switch you off!'

Old Josiah needed no second bidding. Beth returned her attention to Godfrey and thrust the handle under his nose, forcing him to recoil within the confines of his car.

'By God, you callous bastard. I'd do it here and now

if I thought there was no hope of my family being still alive. I'd ram this down your throat and pull your innards out, so help me I would!'

'What the hell has this got to do with me?' protested Godfrey. 'It's the damned Germans who sank the ship, not me.'

Beth shook her head at his stupidity. 'It was your idea they should travel on the *Lusitania* and not on an American ship. I got a letter from Amelia not three days ago telling me how worried she was at having to travel on what she called a floating target. She didn't want to come at all, and wouldn't had it not been for you insisting that her husband goes off to war to be killed. If they are dead I reckon you'll be really satisfied at having killed three of my family and not just the one.'

'I'm not listening to this. Josiah, get this thing started.'

'I can't without the handle, sir,' said Josiah, who was beginning to enjoy himself.

'Give him the bloody starting handle, you ridiculous woman, or I'll have the law on you.'

Beth gave him a stare that sent a chill through his body. Her voice was colder than the sea that had become the *Lusitania's* grave. 'If anything's happened to my family you won't have to call the law, Godfrey Farthing. I'll give myself up the minute I do you in and I'll have a smile on my face when they hang me, because I'll know I'm coming to torment you in hell!'

With that she hurled the starting handle over the garden wall into deep bushes on the other side.

O'Keefe managed a few hours restless sleep before returning to the dock to await incoming vessels, each tragic cargo offloaded with reverential silence. It was late

73

Saturday afternoon when the *Flying Fish*, an old side-wheel paddle steamer, came chugging in. It had made seemingly endless trips to and from the disaster area, bringing back the living and the dead; but on the last few trips the cargo had consisted of entirely the latter. Its skipper, Captain Brierley, stood at the top of the gang-plank as the corpses were brought off and taken to the waiting coffins. After the unloading had finished, O'Keefe walked up the gangplank and spoke to the weary skipper.

'Excuse me, sir, but I'm looking for a man and wife. Nice looking couple in their early thirties. She had blonde hair, he was dark.'

'Are you a relative?'

'No sir. I'm enquiring on behalf of their daughter who's most concerned.'

'We did pick up a youngish couple on this trip, could be them. They were lashed together by the man's belt and braces. She was wearing a lifejacket, he wasn't. My guess is that he drowned and dragged her down with him. She probably wouldn't have had the strength to untie herself. They were both floating no more than six inches underwater, but it might as well have been six fathoms.' The captain pointed to where the off-loaded bodies were being placed into coffins. 'They'll be over there, but if it is them I must warn you that I've only got your word that they were ever good looking. They've been in the water a good twenty-four hours.'

'Thank you, sir. I see what yer mean, sir.'

Amy had been placed with a local family who took it in turns to sit with her as she sat by the window overlooking the lane along which her parents would come. O'Keefe would be with them of course, leading the way with his red nose. As the hours dragged on a sepulchral gloom descended over the whole town, added to by each arriving boatload of corpses. Amy's spirits sank with each tick of the noisy clock on the fireplace wall. There had been no good news, no word of any more survivors being brought in all that day. Only bodies. Deep down she knew the worst and no one in the family was prepared to offer any false hope which they knew would be shattered before long. It was the saddest time in Queenstown's history.

She sat up as she saw O'Keefe coming around the corner. Her eyes were glued to the road behind him to see if her mother and father were following, but the road was as empty as her heart. Slowly and resignedly Amy got up from her seat and went out to meet him. She was standing at the gate by the time he arrived and she looked up at him, guardedly, from beneath a furrowed brow, expecting the worst and not knowing how she'd take it. He shook his head. The expression on his face told her his bad news with greater eloquence than any words he knew. They looked at each other in silence and O'Keefe said, eventually, 'Amy, I'm so sorry.'

'Did – did you actually see them?' she asked, trying to battle against the tears.

'Yes, me darlin' girl. They were brought here together. I guess they were together when they . . .' His voice tailed off, not wishing to commit himself to the actual word.

'Drowned?' Amy's voice was little more than a whisper. The tears brimming up in her eyes overbalanced and tumbled down her cheeks.

O'Keefe nodded; he had never felt as sad since his darling Maggie had died. He went down on one knee, took her in his arms and allowed her to sob her grief on

75

to his shoulder. The watching family stood with hands clasped, the mother reciting a silent rosary.

'I want to see them,' Amy said, in a voice O'Keefe could scarcely hear.

'I don't thin—'

'I want to see them.' There was desperation in her voice now. 'It might not be them.'

O'Keefe drew away from her and held her at arm's length, studying her pale, damp face. 'Do ye trust me, Amy?'

She nodded, hesitantly, and he spoke in a slow, soft voice, 'Then will ye believe me when I say it's definitely yer mammy and daddy?'

Another reluctant nod.

'And do ye believe me when I say this isn't how ye'd like to remember them?'

Her moist, red-rimmed blue eyes stared deep into his and she brought her hand up to her mouth. 'Why?' she asked.

He took her by her slender shoulders. 'Well, I have an image of my Maggie's last day on this Earth that I'd rather not have in me mind. And I'm sure yer mammy an' daddy would prefer ye to remember them as the happy, beautiful people they were.'

'Do they look horrible?'

'Well, I have to say they're not at their best and I'm sure yer mammy hated people seeing her when she was not at her best.'

'Mom was always at her best,' said Amy. 'Always. She was the most beautiful lady in the whole world.'

'Now, I'd have to agree with yer there. A real beautiful lady. Put all them big-time actresses to shame would yer mammy. And that's how ye should remember her.'

'And my dad was the nicest man in the whole world.'

'Nice? I'll say he was nice. He was a high-class feller was yer daddy. High class but not so high that he ever looked down on anyone. That's real class. He was a good man with the joke as well. I'm sure he'd like ye to remember him with a smile on his face.' O'Keefe took a handkerchief from his pocket and wiped away her tears. 'So, am I right or am I wrong? Isn't that the way ye'd like to remember them? Remember people at their best is what Napoleon O'Keefe always says.'

'OK,' she said tremulously, 'I guess you're right.' Then she added, 'I didn't know your name was Napoleon, it's a swell name.'

'Ah, well now, when yer a waiter the people yer serving don't like to think ye might have as many names as them.' He took her hand in his. 'As a matter of fact I have three Christian names and I'm not partial to any of them. Napoleon Francis Bertram O'Keefe, at your service, madam.'

'And are you?' she asked.

'Am I what?'

'At my service? I'm not sure what I'd do without you right now.'

'Amy, me darlin', there's a ship leaving for Liverpool on the Monday morning tide. I'll come with ye until yer properly sorted with yer grandad.'

'Thank you. Will Mom and Dad be coming?'

'Yes, me darlin', they'll be comin' as well.'

'Can I call you Napoleon?'

'I prefer O'Keefe. Me dear mother favoured Mr Bonaparte due to his active dislike of the English. As a child she suffered the potato famine, lost a sister and a brother due to the starvation.'

'Potato famine?' said Amy, vaguely. 'I think they told us about that in school.'

'Well, with it bein' an American school I imagine they did. I don't suppose the English schools will cover it, though.'

'Why was it the English's fault?' She asked the question without any curiosity, just something to say.

'I don't think they bent over backwards ter help. But if it was anyone's fault it was the Irish, fer relyin' too much on the ole spud. It's the only country in the world where failure of the spud crop would leave everyone starvin' ter death.'

He looked down at Amy but she wasn't really interested in the Irish Potato Famine.

She had troubles of her own.

Beth Crabtree had a friend who worked on the Post Office telephone exchange in Cartwright Road. With a little more patience than Godfrey had shown she got through to the Cunard offices and learned that the survivors would be brought to Liverpool on the following Monday. The lists were far from complete yet but they could confirm that an Amy Farthing had been rescued alive. There was no mention of Amelia or Henry.

It was noon on Monday, 10 May when Amy and O'Keefe disembarked from the cruiser *Minerva* and stepped on to the pier in Liverpool dock.

There was a crush of people waiting behind a metal barrier, guarded by police as the group of survivors were led to the offices to be *processed* – whatever that meant. In Amy's case it meant uniting her with one of two relatives.

Beth, who had come by train to Liverpool that morning, and Godfrey, had already been shown the list of survivors, which included Amy but not her parents. Beth had already prepared herself for the worst, but Godfrey had all but taken a shipping clerk by the throat.

'Is this the complete list?'

'Yes, sir.'

'Then how the hell can the daughter be alive and not her parents, man?'

'I don't know, sir,' replied the clerk, as coolly as he could, with a nod at a policeman who was standing by the door.

Beth followed the man's glance and placed a restraining arm on Godfrey as the policeman took a step towards them. 'Don't be a damned fool all your life, Farthing. It's hardly this man's fault. Our children are dead but we must thank God our granddaughter is still alive.'

Godfrey whirled around to face her. There was more anger than grief in his eyes. '*Our* granddaughter?' he roared. 'She's no granddaughter of mine and if you think I'll be handing out money just because she's carrying the Farthing name you've got another think coming.'

'Is that what your son would have wanted?' asked Beth, heatedly. 'For you to disown your granddaughter when she needs you most? What kind of monster are you, Farthing?'

There were other people in the office who turned to look at Godfrey for his answer. A thought came into his head that would disentangle him from this predicament without loss of face.

'Who says she's my granddaughter?'

'What?' exclaimed Beth.

He stepped close to Beth and said, in a low, sneering

voice. 'You know as well as I do that this girl isn't my natural granddaughter.'

'You vile-minded reptile,' screamed Beth, hurling herself at him. She had to be restrained by the policeman.

'Excuse me, sir,' said a small voice. 'I'm Amy Farthing.'

Amy was standing in the doorway, holding O'Keefe's hand. The big Irishman was glaring with disgust at Godfrey, his free fist opening and closing. Beth rushed towards her granddaughter and tried to take her in her arms but Amy pushed her away and enquired, 'What's happening?'

Beth looked over her shoulder at Godfrey, then back at Amy, who addressed herself to Godfrey.

'Sir, are you saying my father isn't my father?' enquired Amy. 'How can that be?'

'He's an evil old liar,' said Beth, looking at Godfrey with contempt. Amy's eyes were wide with innocent confusion. Godfrey looked away from her.

'I asked you a question, sir,' said Amy, gravely.

'And she asked very politely,' said O'Keefe with distaste in his voice. 'So she deserves a polite answer.'

Godfrey looked about him at all the accusing faces. 'What the hell do you want from me?' he muttered. 'I've just lost my son.' From his waistcoat pocket he took a handful of coins, from which he selected the smallest. He walked up to Amy and said, 'Hold out your hand, girl.' Amy frowned but did as she was told. He pressed the coin into her palm, wrapped her fingers around it and snapped, 'This is as near as you'll get to the Farthing fortune.'

Amy opened her fingers and looked down at the small, copper coloured coin. On it was a wren, surmounted by a date, 1912, and underneath was the word, *Farthing*. She stared at it, then showed it to O'Keefe. 'Look, it's got my name on it. Isn't it pretty?'

O'Keefe nodded. 'It's not the prettiest farthing I've ever seen, but it's pretty enough.'

Amy looked up at her grandfather and said, 'Thank you, sir.'

Godfrey stood there, awkwardly, not knowing what to make of Amy's reaction to his insulting gift. Beth placed herself in front of him. Her voice was low and belligerent and only meant for his ears. 'As you didn't come to their wedding, Farthing, I don't suppose you'll be bothering with the funeral. I doubt if my daughter would have welcomed you, and Henry wouldn't have gone against her wishes.'

'You know full well why I didn't come to the wedding.'

'I know full well you're a foul old lizard and the sooner you crawl back under your rock the better. I'll organise a decent funeral for both of them. I can't stop you coming but I wish you wouldn't.'

Godfrey made a grunting noise and walked out of the door to his waiting car.

'I guess it was nice of him to give me this,' Amy said. She looked up at Beth and gave a sudden smile that stole her grandmother's heart in an instant. Then the smile was gone and the deep sadness, that had darkened her face since the tragedy, returned. 'I expect he's sad because my dad died,' she concluded. 'After all, he didn't know me any more than I knew him.'

Beth reached out a tentative hand for her granddaughter to take. 'I'm your grandmother,' she said. 'And I can't tell you how delighted I am to meet you.'

'I kinda figured you to be my grandma,' said Amy.

'Mom and Dad both said you're a very good person. Is it all right if I come and live with you?'

'Yes, Amy,' said Beth, hugging her granddaughter to her. 'That would be fine.' She looked up at O'Keefe.

'Do you mind if I ask who you are, sir?'

'I'm O'Keefe, the delivery man, madam. Making sure I deliver this young lady into safe hands.'

Beth looked down at her hands, calloused by years of hard work. 'Well,' she said, 'they're not rich hands, and they're not very pretty hands, but you have my word that they're safe hands.' Then she looked up at him. 'Tell me, O'Keefe, how do you come to be with my granddaughter?'

'We saved each other's lives,' explained Amy, placing the coin carefully into the pocket of her dress. 'First he saved mine, then I saved his.'

Beneath her solemn features was a matter-of-fact modesty and charm that continued to disarm everyone in the office. Amy looked up at O'Keefe and asked, 'Would you come and stay with us for a while until I know I like it?'

'What are yer goin' ter do if yer don't like it?' he replied.

'Then I'd have to stay with you in Ireland.'

'Ah, fancy me not thinkin' o' that,' said O'Keefe, snapping his fingers. 'And why would I want a heap of trouble like you messin' up my life?'

'I guess it's because you love me,' said Amy. Her sad eyes looked deep into his, effortlessly destroying any defences he might have.

He shook his head. 'Even if yer right,' he said, 'and I'm not sayin' ye are, I doubt yer grandma will be able ter put me up.'

'I can only offer you a small attic, Mr O'Keefe, but you're most welcome to stay as long as you like.'

'You're supposed to call him O'Keefe, not Mr O'Keefe,' corrected Amy. 'It's like a Christian name, only it's not.'

'I'd be pleased ter accept yer kind invitation fer a while,' said O'Keefe to Beth. 'Then it's back to Ireland.'

Chapter Five

Beth smiled at herself in the dressing-table mirror as she listened to O'Keefe singing upstairs. He had a strong, melodious voice that cheered the place up. It was good to have a man in the house again. Come October it would be thirty-four years since Alfred died. Since then there had been just one mild flirtation with a local man who, when push came to shove, didn't like the idea of a ready-made family.

Although Beth hadn't married Alfred for love, what she missed was his kindness – a quality she hadn't come across in any man since; maybe she'd set her sights too high. Widowed at the age of eighteen, with a child, very little money and very fussy about men. It was the latter that had kept her alone since Alfred's death.

The face staring back at her was coming up to fifty-two years old. Once it had been considered attractive; it must have been or where else did Amelia get her good looks? Certainly not from her father.

All her good years had slipped by. In her darker moments she thought they had been stolen from her by Godfrey Farthing. The revenge she had sworn that day in his driveway had been cooled by the arrival in her life of Amy, who had been quite morose for the first few weeks but who was now coming out of her shell.

A New York accent was a much admired novelty in Amy's new neighbourhood, especially by her school pal Billy Eccles so, when she greeted him one day with the old Yorkshire salutation, 'Sithee, Billy lad,' it just didn't sound right. He took her to task on it.

'If I had an American accent like yours I'd guard it with me life.' he said. 'I wouldn't try an' swap it fer a Bradford accent, any road up.'

'OK,' she grinned, embarrassed at her feeble attempt. 'I'll guard my accent with my life, then,' she added, although she had decided to drop 'mom' from her vocabulary and replace it with 'mum', to avoid odd looks. Mom had always called her own mother Mum so it somehow seemed the right thing to do. It might be a while before she progressed to the Yorkshire 'mam'.

'It's my birthday tomorrow. I'll be eleven. If I'd still been in New York with Mum and Dad I'd have had a great party with all my friends and a whole heap of presents.'

'I got a new pair o' socks, an orange and a bag o' spice for my eleventh birthday,' Billy said. 'I were due a new pair o' socks any road, so it were just an orange and a bag o' spice really.'

'What's spice?'

'Sweets,' he explained.

'You mean candy?'

Billy gave a broad grin. 'I reckon there's a few Yorkshire words yer might need ter learn if yer want ter be understood.'

The two of them were on their way home from school. He was a sharp-faced, skinny boy with unruly, mousy hair protruding from beneath a checked cap that was too small for him. His grin was frequent and easy and accompanied by a pair of cheeky brown eyes. His legs were quite noticeably bowed and a playground fight had cost him one of his top teeth. He was a lad who would be unwise to rely solely on his looks to capture the girl of his dreams.

He wore a ragged shirt tucked into patched trousers which ended at scarred knees and gave way to poorly darned socks. On his feet he wore steel-segged boots that clattered noisily on the cobbled paving. By comparison Amy was smartly dressed in a tartan smock, knee-length woollen stockings and black leather shoes. Beth had made sacrifices to ensure her granddaughter was well turned out.

'I bet yer miss livin' in America,' Billy remarked. 'Land of milk and honey, that's what me dad calls it. Did yer see any cowboys an' Indians?'

Amy giggled. 'No, silly, not in New York. There may be some cowboys out west but I don't think there's many Indians.'

'What happened ter them?'

'The American soldiers ran them off their land.'

'Hard flippin' luck fer the Indians,' said Billy. 'I make no wonder they went round shootin' soldiers with their bows an' arrows. I'd have done the same.'

There was a lull in the conversation before Amy said, 'I miss my parents. They'd have had me playing my violin.'

'What?'

'At my birthday party.'

'Oh, right. I've never had a birthday party.'

'I was always asked to play my violin. I was pretty good too.'

'I prefer the trumpet meself.'

'You play the trumpet?'

'I didn't say I played it. I just prefer it. If I were gonna play owt I'd play a trumpet in a brass band. Trouble is they cost money do trumpets. Money we haven't got.'

'So do violins. Mine's at the bottom of the sea, I guess. I can't ask Grandma to buy me another, it's too much to ask. Any way, I'm not sure she knows I play.'

'Why don't her tell then?'

'I guess I don't want her to feel guilty if she can't afford to buy me one.'

'She either can or she can't,' said Billy. 'Yer'll never know if yer don't ask. What d'yer think of school?'

'It's OK, I guess. You're a bit behind where we were back in my old school. We'd started doing French and algebra.'

'Everybody says yer clever. Yer should have taken your scholarship to go to grammar school,' Billy said. 'You'd have passed, no problem. I might have passed meself if I'd spent more time at school than knockin' off.' He grinned then added, 'No I wouldn't – me dad reckons I'm as thick as two short planks. Any road, I'll be twelve in November, I might get a job as a half-timer at Farthing's.'

Amy pulled a face at the mention of the name Farthing, but said nothing.

'Isn't owd Godfrey Farthing your grandad?' enquired Billy.

'He was, but he's not any more.'

'How come?'

'He doesn't want to be my grandpa.'

'But he's a millionaire. I thought he'd be buyin' yer a pony or summat fer yer birthday.'

'Maybe he blames me for my parents dying. Old people have funny ways of thinking. He doesn't like me, so I don't like him.'

Billy shrugged and kicked at a stone. 'If I had a granddad who were a millionaire I think I'd make an effort ter like him. Me granddad Eccles hasn't got a penny ter scratch his arse, but I still like him.'

'But you'd like him a whole lot more if he was a millionaire, is that it?'

'Prob'ly.'

'What if he hated you?'

Billy kicked at another stone and sent it over a wall into a yard where it clanged against something metallic. He grinned as it drew a shout of anger from a woman hanging out her washing. 'Do that again an' yer'll be laughin' on t' other side of yer face yer barmy little beggar!'

'Me dad says he's just got one of them omnibus things.'

'Who has?' enquired Amy, confused by the seeming change of subject.

'Who d'yer think? That bloke who's not yer granddad. Me dad says this bloke owed him some money so owd Farthing took his omnibus instead. Me dad says he's a thief.'

'My grandpa?'

'I thought yer said he weren't yer granddad.'

'Maybe he is, maybe he's not. He's sure an old skin-flint though.' She looked up at the grey sky. 'Does the sun ever come out in this country? It's the middle of July and it feels like winter.'

Billy gave her a broad smile; the type that made her smile back. 'Not in Bradford,' he said. 'Me dad says sunshine makes yer bone idle. There's no slackers in Bradford, that's what me dad says. Hey, we break up next week; d'yer fancy doin' owt?'

'Such as?'

'There's a stream down in Granny Beck Woods. We could dam it up and go swimmin'. Me and Nipper Boothroyd did it last year. We tied a rope to a tree branch and swung out over t' stream. Mostly we fell in. It's a good laugh. Can yer swim?'

'Some – sounds like fun. I hope you're kidding about the weather.'

'It'll warm up a bit,' Billy promised. 'Have yer gorra cozzie?'

'What's a cozzie?'

'Swimmin' costume.'

'What, you don't go skinny dipping?' Amy said it with tongue in cheek, to see if she could shock him.

'What's skinny dippin'?'

'Swimming with no clothes on.'

He reddened and Amy took his arm. 'I was kidding,' she said.

'I should flippin' think you were.'

'Would it be so bad?' she asked, intrigued by the way she'd made him blush.

'Yer what? Swimmin' knacker-bare with a lass? Dunt bear thinkin' about if me dad found out. Tan me arse from here to Heckmondwike. I wouldn't sit down for a month.' He gave Amy a light smack on her bottom then ran away. 'Might be a bit of a laugh, though,' he called back over his shoulder.

Amy ran after him, and as she ran she envisaged the

skinny, short-trousered boy with no clothes on. It made her smile and like him even more. It also made her curious.

August brought with it a spell of good weather and Amy went down to Granny Beck Woods with Billy – with her grandmother's words ringing in her ears:

'Don't get up to anything daft, and don't be fooled by that smile of his. He can be a right scallywag can Billy Eccles – he doesn't get that from his dad. Too straight laced for his own good is Ernest.'

'Billy's always talking about his dad. He seems to think he's OK.'

'Hey, I never said he weren't OK. He's a bit strict with young Billy, though – not that it does much good.' Beth paused and said, 'You know his mam died, don't you?'

'No, he never talks about her.'

'Well, she died just after Billy were born – pneumonia.'

'I see. So, Billy never knew her?'

'No, he didn't, poor little beggar. His dad went to seed a bit after that, didn't look after Billy properly; that's why his legs are like they are – rickets, poor little beggar. Couldn't stop a pig in a passage, couldn't young Billy. Takes after his mother in many ways, though. Smashin' lass. She were your mam's best pal. They got married within a couple of months of each other. I think she missed our Amelia so much she just wanted someone to keep her company. I can't think of any other reason a lass like her would marry Ernest Eccles.' Beth laughed and shook her head. 'God, he could bore the balls off a buffalo.' She clapped a hand to her mouth. 'Oh – wash my mouth out with soap! That's what comes with working

in the mill too long. Don't you ever let me hear you say
that, do you hear me?'

'What, bore the balls off a buffalo?'

'Amy!'

It took the two of them a whole afternoon to dam up the
stream with rocks, twigs and mud. Billy, having done it
the year before, was something of an expert. Exhausted
they sat on a large, weathered rock, to watch the pool
they'd created fill up with sparkling water until it was
just about deep enough to swim in. Amy nudged him and
said, 'You first.'

'What? I haven't got me cozzie.'

'There's no one looking.'

'There's you,' he pointed out.

'I won't tell anyone.'

'It's not . . .' He stopped and grinned. 'I will, if you
will.'

'What – you think I daren't?' There was a mutual
curiosity driving them to meet the other's challenge. 'You
first,' she said.

Billy nodded and gave a nervous grin, then he took off
his boots and socks. Amy followed suit. Then Billy took
off his shirt, turned his back to her and walked down to
the pool. In a quick movement he took off his trousers,
threw them behind him and splashed into the water,
where he sat down and shivered as the cold hit him. The
sight of his naked bottom amused Amy. She was laughing
as he shivered, scared to stand up and reveal himself.

'Hey! What's so flippin' funny?' he said.

'Your bare ass.'

'At least I did it, which is more than you dare do.'

'Who says I daren't?'

'I do.'

'You turn around and I will.'

Billy sat with his back to her as she undressed and stepped warily into the water, tensing herself against the cold.

'Don't you dare turn around,' she warned him. 'Not until I sit down.'

'I'm not gonna turn around.'

Amy sat down until the water was just below her shoulders, then she splashed some over his head. Billy turned, with a broad grin on his face, and splashed her back. This went on for a while with both of them laughing and splashing whilst retaining their modesty beneath the water. Then Amy said, 'What do we do now?'

'Get out and get dressed I reckon, before we catch us death o' cold.'

'OK.'

'Do you want me to go first?' he asked.

'Can if you want. I don't mind.'

'Or we could do it together. It means we'd see each other.'

There was a long silence as Amy weighed up the pros and cons of this. 'Okey dokey,' she said, at length. 'I'll count to three then we both stand up and get out.'

'Fair enough.'

Amy counted very slowly to three. With their eyes fixed on each other's faces they both stood up, climbed out of the stream and stood in a patch of warm, afternoon sunlight. The only sounds came from the summer birds twittering in the trees, and the miniature waterfall they'd created. It was a brief, innocent moment that they would remember forever. Both pairs of eyes ventured down to see the parts of the other they hadn't seen before.

Neither of them felt qualified to comment on what they saw.

'I don't know about you, but I've goosebumps,' Amy said, after a while, wrapping her arms around her shivering body.

Billy picked up his shirt and handed it to her. 'Yer can get dried on that, if yer like.'

'That's very gallant of you. What will you wear?'

He blushed with pleasure at being called gallant, then said, 'I'll hang it up ter dry fer a bit, then I'll put it on.'

'Thanks.'

Billy turned his back to her, allowing her privacy while she dried and dressed herself before handing him back the damp shirt. He gave himself rub down, hung it on a tree branch, and pulled on the rest of his clothes. A pair of prying eyes looked on from behind a bush, disappointed that the show had finished.

'Better not tell anyone about this,' Amy decided. She looked at Billy. 'Promise?'

'Promise,' he confirmed. It wasn't a difficult promise to make. No way would he ever tell anyone about this, especially his pals – he'd never hear the end of it.

'Do you promise as well?'

'Most definitely,' said Amy. She started giggling, for no reason she could think of. What they'd just done was so outrageous that it amused her. Then Billy, on exactly the same wavelength as her, started giggling too. Their giggles turned to laughter as they got up and chased each other around the trees in an energetic game of tig.

They sat back down on the rock and stared at the pool, their thoughts drifting back to the forbidden sights they'd just seen. Then Billy gave her a demonstration of how he could whistle through the gap in his teeth. Satisfied that she was suitably impressed with this talent he fired a stream of spit, through the same gap, a good 10 feet, into the stream. Amy had a go herself but could barely manage to stop it going down the front of her dress.

'It takes practice,' he said, sagely. 'I'll teach you if you like, but first I'll have to knock your tooth out.'

'Oh yeah, you and who's army,' laughed Amy, putting up her fists and having a mock boxing match with him, which Billy eventually lost by throwing his hands to his face in pretend pain and falling, pole axed, to the ground.

The next time Billy went to the pool there wouldn't be quite so much to laugh about.

Nipper Boothroyd was so named because his elder brother had already inherited the nickname 'Young Napper' from his late father, killed in the last week of the Boer War, six months before Walter – Nipper – was born. He and Billy were playing on the swing above the pool, both of them wet through, having fallen in the water more often than not.

'I thought it were a couple o' monkeys and I were nearly right,' shouted a voice. 'Except monkeys are brainier than you two.'

'Clear off Heptonstall!' retorted Billy.

Hubert Heptonstall was a tall, angular youth, with volcanic acne, near-set eyes and a reputation for picking on smaller kids, mainly because boys his own age didn't want anything to do with him. He approached Billy with a sneer on his mean face. Hubert was fifteen years old and a little doffer at Farthing's Mill.

'Shouldn't you be at work, playin' with yer bobbins?' asked Billy, who wasn't particularly scared of him. 'Or haven't yer learned how ter do that yet?'

'Get lost!'

'From what I hear yer spend enough time playin' wi' yer own bobbin that yer should be expert at it by now.'

'I'll rattle yer bloody ear'ole if yer give me any cheek!' snarled Hubert.

'Oh aye, you and who's army?'

'All right, Billy?' called out Nipper, who was just about to launch himself out on the rope swing.

'Course I am, Nipper – I'm not scared of a big daft lass like Hubert.'

'Well you'd know all about lasses, wouldn't yer?' sneered Hubert. 'I saw yer – yer bandy legged little bugger, muckin' about wi' that Yankee lass.'

Billy coloured and had no answer.

'Wait till I tell my gaffer you an' his granddaughter were muckin' about knacker bare. I saw your bobbin, so did she. It were bobbin all right – bobbin' up an' down like a worm between two wishbones.'

All Billy could think of was to deny it. 'Yer a lyin' sod, Heptonstall! Is that what yer do, go round spying on people? Why don't yer just sod off an' squeeze yer spots?'

Hubert took a pace forward and thumped Billy in the chest, knocking him to the ground. 'Nah then, what've yer got ter say for yerself, yer mucky little bugger?'

Billy lay there, out of breath, as Hubert stood over him, then he kicked at the bigger boy's shin with the segged heel of his boot. Hubert screamed in pain and hopped around, clutching his leg as Billy got to his feet with clenched fists and punched his adversary on the end of the nose.

Nipper launched himself into mid-air in the vain hope that this might be his time to actually complete the arc and land on firm ground – thus coming dramatically to his friend's rescue. The rope snapped as he was on the final, upward, curve causing him to fall backwards into the water. Billy heard the splash but he was too busy fighting to take any notice. He was pressing home the advantage he now had over Hubert, who was cowering beneath a rain of blows as he clutched his injured shin.

'All right, all right,' he screamed. 'I think yer've broke me leg.'

Billy stepped back and glanced at the stream, wondering where Nipper was. Rings of water were still widening where his friend had gone in.

'Nipper?'

The only sounds came from the chirping of a few watching birds, and Hubert, who was sitting on the ground, moaning.

'Nipper?' shouted Billy once more. He waded into the stream to where Nipper was lying under the water, looking upwards with a drifting cloud of dark blood obscuring his face. Billy leaned down and pulled his friend's head out of the water but it slumped to one side. Forgetting the fight he shouted back for Hubert to help him, but the older boy remained where he was, watching the proceedings with a sullen interest, but no sympathy.

Billy dragged Nipper on to the bank, completely at a loss what to do. There wasn't an ounce of life in his pal. He turned him on his front with his head to one side and pushed at his back, trying to force out the water. But Nipper hadn't drowned, he'd hit his head on a rock under the water.

'Yer bloody mad, you are,' Hubert sneered, getting to his feet and limping painfully away.

'Hubert, will yer go get someone?' pleaded Billy. 'I think he's dead.'

'If he is, it's your fault!'

'It's not my fault,' cried Billy, tears streaming down his face. 'How can it be my fault?'

'It's your fault and I'll tell everyone.'

Billy, his face candle pale, was sitting with his father down at Heaton Royd police station when Sergeant Dicks came over to them. It was a sombre corridor and a smell of vomit emanated from a nearby cell housing a midday drunk. The policeman displayed no apparent compassion for Billy, who had just lost his pal in harrowing circumstances.

'My inspector would like a word with you,' he said, then added, ominously, 'There's been a development.'

The father and son followed the policeman into a small, windowless room, furnished with just a table, four chairs, a patch of worn lino that didn't reach any of the walls and a coloured picture of King George V hanging above an empty fireplace. Sitting on one of the chairs was a uniformed inspector with a bald head and an unnaturally back moustache. A former army major, now in his early sixties, he was too old to fight the Hun and were it peacetime he would probably be too old for the police. But this was wartime when women and old men did young men's jobs.

He looked, sternly, at Billy as the ashen-faced boy sat down opposite him. Then he addressed himself to Ernest Eccles, as if it were beneath his dignity to speak to someone as lowly as Billy. 'We seem to have conflicting stories, Mr Eccles. Your son tells us it was an accident, but a witness says your son was to blame.'

'Well, I can't see how that can be true,' said Mr Eccles.

'Our Billy and young Nipper Boothroyd were best pals.'
He looked down at his shocked son. 'What have you got
to say for yourself, our Billy?'

'It wasn't my fault.' Billy's voice was barely audible.

'Speak up, boy,' said the policeman, sternly.

'He said it wasn't his fault,' said Ernest.

'I didn't see it happen,' muttered Billy. 'I were scrappin'
with Hubert Heptonstall.'

'Ee, Billy. How many times have I told you about
fighting?' said his father. 'No good ever comes of fighting.
Now look what's happened.'

'It's not the first time we've had to have words with
your son, Mr Eccles,' the inspector went on. 'According
to our files he's been spoken to on several occasions by
my officers – once for breaking a window at this very
police station. On top of which he ran away rather than
face the consequences – definitely not cricket, Mr Eccles,
not cricket at all.'

'I never did it on purpose,' protested Billy. 'We were
kickin' a ball about on us way home from school. It were
an accident.'

'He's nobbut a scamp, Inspector,' said his father.
'There's no harm in the lad.'

The inspector gave his moustache another tweak then
remarked, sourly, 'Hubert Heptonstall says your son deliberately knocked the deceased boy off a swing of some
description, causing the boy's death.'

'I didn't knock him off,' said Billy, stoutly. 'Hubert's
telling lies.' Then he thought of something else Hubert
might have told them, and decided to get his two penn'orth
in first. 'He said he saw me and Amy Farthing playing
without any clothes on – he were lyin' about that as well.
That's why we were fighting.'

'Yes, well, that indeed is another accusation the witness made,' concurred the policeman, looking at his file. 'And you're telling me this didn't happen?'

'That's right. I mean I were playing with her, but all we did was build a dam in the beck and go paddling.'

'So neither of you took your clothes off?'

'No mister – well, we took us boots and socks off, but that were all.' Billy looked down at his hands in case the policeman saw the lie in his eyes.

'I hope you're telling me the truth,' the inspector said, brusquely, 'because if we find you're telling lies we may have to think about a charge of indecent exposure in a public place.'

Billy's father looked shocked, but sprang to his son's defence. 'Good heaven's, Inspector, surely you can't just take one lad's word against another.'

'No sir, we can't. That's why I'm sending my sergeant round to the girl's house to find out the truth. Find out which one of these boys is the most believable.'

Billy gulped as he realised his fate was in Amy's hands. It was to be hoped she'd lie as well, or he was in it up to his neck. Then he remembered the promise they'd made to each other and he felt more confident.

Amy's immediate reaction at the sergeant's question was one of annoyance at Billy for breaking his promise not to tell. Why on earth had he told them? It was this last thought that stopped her blurting out the truth. It wasn't a bit like Billy to have told the police something like that, especially after having promised not to. He hadn't told them, somebody had seen them – that was it.

'I'm sure I don't know what you're talking about,' she said. 'Did Billy Eccles tell you this?'

She noticed that Sergeant Dicks held his helmet under his arm the same way that Anne Boleyn's ghost held her head in a picture she'd seen in a book. The policeman lowered his gaze from the challenge in her eyes. Noisily, he cleared the embarrassment from his throat and wished the inspector had come to ask the question himself. 'So you're saying it didn't happen?'

'Billy and me were playing in the stream, that's all that happened,' Amy told him. 'Anyone who says different is a fat liar.'

'For heaven's sake, what on earth do you take her for, sergeant?' chided Beth. 'Taking her clothes off in front of a boy. You should be ashamed of yourself for asking such a question.'

'I'm only doing my job, Mrs Crabtree,' he muttered uncomfortably. 'A young boy's dead and we've got to get to the bottom of things.'

'Well you seem to be going about it in a funny way, if you ask me,' Beth retorted.

'Is Billy all right?' Amy asked, concerned. 'Nipper was one of his best buddies. I don't think it's right to keep him at the police station.'

'We've got loose ends to tie up,' said Sergeant Dicks, disappointed that Amy hadn't confirmed Hubert's allegation. Maybe the youth *had* been lying after all. If he'd lie about that he'd lie about anything, even seeing Billy push his pal into the water. Then an idea struck him. It was a bit unconventional, definitely not cricket, as the inspector might put it, but it might get to the truth.

Billy sat nervously opposite as Sergeant Dicks riffled, studiously, through his notebook. Next to Billy was his father and next to the sergeant sat the inspector who was in on the ruse and didn't approve. If it didn't work it was the sergeant's head on the block, if it did work the inspector would take the credit. That's the way things were in the force.

'Well, I've been to see young Amy Farthing,' the sergeant said, as if reading from his notes, 'and she admitted it.' He looked up at Billy and noted, with some satisfaction, the sudden guilt written all over the boy's face. Had he been wrong it would have been a look of protest.

What upset Billy the most was that Amy had told on him. He thought she had more about her than that. 'It was only a bit of daftness,' he muttered.

'Billy!' admonished his shocked father. 'So you did take your clothes off.'

'We didn't do nowt rude,' said Billy, red faced with embarrassment. 'We just took us clothes off an' put 'em back on again. It were a bit of a laugh, that's all.'

'Do you know what this proves to me,' said the inspector to Billy, who couldn't help but notice that some of the blacking on the policeman's moustache had rubbed off on his nose. 'It proves to me that you're an untruthful boy. It proves to me that Hubert Heptonstall's word is more reliable than yours.'

Mr Eccles glanced down at his son with deep disappointment in his eyes and Billy knew he wouldn't be getting much support from that quarter.

The inspector got to his feet and spoke to Billy's father. 'I'm bailing your son to appear at juvenile court,' he announced, 'probably some time next week. Please ensure he turns up, Mr Eccles.'

'Oh, you can be sure of that, Inspector.'

*

The next day Amy had tried to contact Billy to offer her support and good wishes but Mr Eccles said he wasn't allowed out before the court date and in any case his son didn't want to see her and hadn't she done enough damage? Billy had done wrong and would have to take his punishment like a man. The only person in the world who believed he didn't do it was Amy and she wanted him to know she hadn't told on him. As she walked away from his house an upstairs window scraped open. Amy looked up at Billy's forlorn face.

'Yer broke yer promise,' he said, just loud enough for her to hear. Then he closed the window and vanished from view.

Amy shouted up to him. 'Billy, Billy.'

Mr Eccles came to the door and asked her to go away. The following week Billy was sent to a reform school for two years for his part in the death of Walter (Nipper) Boothroyd.

Chapter Six

August 1917

Cinder Yard was a motley collection of thirteen early
Victorian brick houses, three lavatory blocks and a bin
yard. They were built in an eccentric rectangle around a
stone-flagged enclosure, approached through a high
archway and lit by a single gas lamp, more often off than
on. Surrounding the yard, on three sides, was a cemetery,
a clog and boot factory, the Cobbler's Arms and an iron-
monger's shop. Four of the houses faced south and, in
the absence of gardens, they had window-boxes that took
advantage of the erratic Bradford summers; the rest of
the houses didn't enjoy enough sunshine for a window-
box to flourish. Some of them had tubs with small shrubs
and another had a 3-foot high statue of a heron with a
fish in its beak, guarding its front door. Each stone step
was scoured, with a donkey-stoned line drawn around
each angle. Each window had spotless curtains and woe
betide the reputation of any household that fell down on
the job. Number Eight had long been a let-down, but
Gertrude Earnshawe didn't care. In any case she didn't

live there, now that her son Sefton was back from the war. According to the newspapers he was fortunate to be alive, having been reprieved from a death sentence for 'Cowardice in the face of the enemy'. His mother had left him to face his ignominy on his own and had gone to live with a tally man in Shipley.

Amy had never seen Sefton. He had been home a month and, as far as she could tell, had never gone out of the house. She was playing hop-scotch in the yard with Euphemia (Effie) Slack when a column of belligerent youths marched, in an unco-ordinated military fashion, up to Sefton's door. Their leader, a boy in an ancient bowler hat that was too big for him, took out a white feather, pinned it on the door, then banged on it.

'Come out, Earnshawe, yer bloody coward!'

Amy saw a bedroom curtain twitch and a brief glimpse of a pale, shadowy face. Effie nudged her and said, in a low voice, 'He's in – don't sayt nowt to 'em.'

'I wasn't going to.'

'Sefton used to be a nice lad,' Effie went on. 'Me dad says there's more to it than's in the papers. I've heard Sefton's gone daft in the 'ead.'

'He's not in,' lied Amy to the youths. 'He went out about an hour ago.'

The youths turned to face the two girls. 'Who d'yer think you're talkin' to?' said one of them.

'Not much,' said Amy.

'Why aren't you lot in the Army?' Effie asked, provocatively. She was fifteen. 'I thought the White Feather Brigade only handed 'em out to men who weren't in khaki – Sefton's been in khaki. I don't see any khaki on you lot, do you, Amy?' Amy shook her head, the boys were stuck for an answer. Effie continued with her taunting, 'Happen yer

104

should be handing 'em out to yerselves instead of to lads who are brave enough to sign up.' She reached out and tipped the leader's bowler over his eyes. 'Yer know what they say – if yer can't fight, get a big hat.'

The boy blushed and straightened his hat. 'Yer can tell him we'll come back – and when we do . . .' He bunched his fist and pulled a fierce face.

'I don't think a bunch of daft boys will worry him,' said Amy, contemptuously. 'He's had to face real men.'

'If yer want ter fight yer should join up,' Effie sneered. She pointed to a poster stuck on the archway wall:

> YOUR KING AND COUNTRY
> NEED YOU
> A CALL TO ARMS

Despite conscription for single men being introduced eighteen months previously there was still a shortage of married volunteers whose wives had all heard of the horrific carnage in France.

'We're too young else we'd be off like a shot,' protested one of the youths. 'We're only fifteen.'

'Sefton was only fifteen when he joined,' said Effie. 'All yer've got ter do is lie about yer age. Me dad says they're so desperate they'll take anybody – even you pimply lot.'

The youths had no answer to this. They retraced their steps with a boot-stamping, arm-swinging march. One of them was skipping to try and get in step, his segged boots sparking on the stone flags. After they had gone the curtain twitched again and Amy smiled up at the window.

'Don't,' said Effie, looking the other way. 'Yer'll only encourage him.'

'I thought your dad said he was OK.'

'He also told me not ter talk to him, else I'd be tarred wi' the same brush. Me dad reckons Gertrude Earnshawe's a right floosie.'

Amy walked across to Sefton's door and gave a polite knock. Effie stood, undecided for a few seconds, then walked away. Amy knocked again and a voice from within said, 'What d'yer want?'

'I was being neighbourly,' called out Amy. 'I came to say hello.'

'Oh.'

'Aren't you going to open the door?'

'It's a trick.'

'It's not a trick. Those idiots have gone away.'

A bolt was slowly drawn, the door opened a fraction and a frightened voice said, 'Me mam allus says I haven't ter let anyone in.'

'I thought your mum had left.'

'She has and she hasn't.'

It was Amy's turn to say, 'Oh.'

'She says I've brought shame on her so she's gone ter live with me Uncle George, but she still brings me food twice a week.'

'My, that's good of her.'

He missed Amy's sarcasm. 'It is, int it? I didn't even know I had an Uncle George – never seen him or nowt. Me mam says I won't be seein' him neither, cos he dunt like cowards.'

'Can I come in and talk to you?'

There was a long pause. 'Why?' he asked, eventually.

'Because we're neighbours – and neighbours should help each other.'

'Yer don't sound like a neighbour. Yer sound foreign ter me.'

'I used to live in America.'

'America?' He was impressed. 'Whereabouts in America?'

'New York.'

It was as if she'd found the right password. The door opened and she saw Sefton Earnshawe for the first time. If her arithmetic was correct he should be eighteen, but he looked thirty at least. His eyeballs trembled in their sockets, never focussed, never still. But there was an engaging symmetry about his face which might even have been considered handsome except for an inner ugliness that the features could not mask. His limp brown hair was flecked with grey and his skin was pallid and lifeless.

'By the way, they didn't shoot me because I wasn't eighteen!' He blurted this out before she had even set foot inside his door. 'They thought I were eighteen, then an officer ran up an' told 'em not to shoot because I was only sixteen – so they didn't shoot me. Yer've got ter be eighteen before they can shoot yer. Good job really.'

'Wow!' said Amy. 'You mean you actually faced a firing squad when you were sixteen?'

Sefton nodded vigorously, then he gave a smile that betrayed a mouthful of rotting teeth.

'Why didn't you tell them you were only sixteen?'

'I thought I might get into trouble fer tellin' lies about me age.'

Amy stared at him, incredulously. 'Trouble? How much more trouble could you get into?'

'I didn't think,' he said. 'Me mam allus says that's the trouble wi' me – I don't think. They locked me up in jail instead. Then they let me go after a bit because I'd gone daft in me 'ead – that's what me mam says. She reckons

I should've been sent to a loony bin. Do you think I'm daft?'

Amy stepped inside and looked around. 'Strikes me you're ill, Sefton. My name's Amy by the way. Amy Farthing.'

'Amy,' he said, as if her surname was too much for him to manage. 'Do yer think I'm daft?'

'No,' she said, decisively. 'I think you're very brave going off to war like that – very brave indeed.'

The living room was sparsely furnished and covered with what seemed like years of dust. To one side was a scullery with a Belfast sink, a gas ring and a tin bath full of water.

'I'm going ter have a bath,' he said, almost boastfully. 'Me mam allus says I've got ter keep meself clean an' tidy, so I'm goin' ter get a bath.'

Amy stepped into the scullery and dipped her hand in the bath water. 'It's cold,' she observed.

'Me mam allus says it's best cold. Kill the germs. Germs don't like cold. That's what me mam says.'

'Your mum sure has a lot to say – mind if I sit down?' Without waiting for an answer Amy banged a cloud of dust from a worn, easy chair, then decided further banging was futile and sat in it anyway.

'I could make yer a cup o' tea if yer like,' Sefton offered.

'That's very kind of you, Sefton.'

He went into the scullery, lit a gas ring then filled a huge kettle from the tap. 'I'll use the rest ter warm me bath water up,' he called out.

'Very wise.'

Sefton came through and sat on the only other chair in the room, a rickety dining chair. Amy looked at him with a million questions in her head. He was five years older than her, looked twenty years older and behaved five years younger.

'I got very frightened,' he said, without any prompting. It was as though no one had ever wanted to listen to his story and he wanted to get it out before she lost interest. 'We were at a place called the Western Front. I think it's in France or somewhere.'

'Was it very bad?' she asked, somewhat inadequately.

His face brightened. 'Christmas were good.'

'Christmas?'

'Christmas Eve. It'd been snowin' – only it stopped and then all the guns an' stuff stopped.'

'Why?'

Sefton seemed surprised she had to ask. 'Out of respect for baby Jesus Christ. The Huns stopped as well. That's what they call Germans – Huns. It were very quiet.'

The memory of the quiet softened his face. 'I remember lookin' out over the top of the trench and everythin' were white an' glowin' as though – as though the snow had lit itself up.'

'Snow does that,' Amy agreed.

'Then we could hear singin'. Fellers singin' Christmas carols only it were miles away at first. Then someone not far off started. It wasn't one of our lads because he were singin' in German. It were a song I used ter sing in t' choir but I only knew it in English, so after he finished I started singin' it as well.'

'What song was it?' Amy asked, curiously.

'A lullabye. Do you know what a lullabye is? It's a song yer sing ter babies ter make 'em go ter sleep. I wonder if me mam ever sang me lullabies? I bet she did.' He got to his feet and began to sing with perfect pitch:

109

'Sleep my child and peace attend thee,
All through the night.
Guardian angels God will send thee,
All through the night.
Soft and drowsy hours are creeping,
Hill and vale in slumber sleeping,
I my loving vigil keeping,
All through the night.'

His voice was out of keeping with the rest of him. It was a trained voice; strong and sweet and deep with emotion. His eyes became still and clouded and Amy could see that he was back in the trenches. He was enjoying a brief time of peace with his comrades; some of whom would later point their guns at his heart and cock their rifles, only to be stopped from killing him by an officer who had actually lied and placed his own job and freedom at risk to save Sefton's life.

As he sang Amy looked beyond him to where her grandmother was standing in the doorway. Beth put a finger to her lips to indicate that Amy should ignore her arrival and let Sefton finish, such was the sweetness of his voice. All four watching eyes were brimming with tears as he came to the end. He smiled and sat down again.

'Me sergeant said, "Well done Private Earnshawe. That's showed 'em what a proper English voice sounds like. Our man sang the bollocks off their man, didn't he, lads?" And everyone said I had.'

'I bet you did,' said Beth.

'I've gorra right voice on me, haven't I?' He said it without conceit, then added an odd non-sequitur that seemed to please him, 'I can play cribbage as well.'

110

'You always did have a right voice on you, Sefton,' said Beth.

He turned around and his face registered no surprise that Beth had been listening. 'I have, haven't I, Mrs Crabtree? That's what everyone says. He's gorra right voice on him has Sefton Earnshawe.' Then his face fell. 'I'm a coward as well, though. That's what everyone says. Sefton Earnshawe's a coward.'

'We don't think you're a coward, Sefton,' Amy assured him, 'Do we, Grandma?'

'We most certainly do not. We think you're a young lad who got badly done to by a load of daft men.'

'His head came off,' remembered Sefton, distantly. 'Bounced like a football right in front o' me.' His restless eyes turned first to Amy, then to Beth, as if pleading for her forgiveness. 'He were me mucker were Jim and his head came off. I were cryin' when they found me and I'd lost me rifle. They said I were runnin' away. It were all the noise.' He clasped his hands to his ears as though the thunderous sounds of battle were still howling all around him.

'I think I'd have run away,' said Beth.

'Ah, but yer not allowed,' Sefton told her, earnestly. 'Yer not allowed, Mrs Crabtree. If yer run away they shoot yer. It's in the rules.'

'It's a damn pity everyone on both sides doesn't run away,' commented Beth, heatedly. 'There's men out there being killed by the thousand and no one really knows why. If women had the vote I doubt we'd have been in such a rush to go to war.'

'Women,' said Sefton, as if the word had triggered a thought. 'I've never had a woman.' He looked from Beth to Amy.

111

'Well, you're not having either of us.' Beth said it with a half smile.

Sefton suddenly roared with laughter, as if she'd cracked a really funny joke. He went through to the scullery where the kettle was steaming. 'Hey, that's a good un is that, Mrs Crabtree,' he called out. 'As if I'd want either of you.'

Amy and her grandmother looked at each other, not knowing whether to be relieved or insulted. Sefton poked his head back into the room and asked, guilelessly:

'Do yer want a cup o' tea, Mrs Crabtree. I make a very nice cup o' tea. People allus say that about me. Sefton makes a very nice cup o' tea. Yer can put yer own milk and sugar in. I allus let people put their own milk and sugar in. I wouldn't mind a girlfriend though. I've never kissed a girl.'

'Your time will come, Sefton,' called out Beth. 'Good-looking lad like you.'

Sefton roared with laughter again. 'People used ter say that about me. Good-lookin' lad, that Sefton. That's what they used ter say. Never had a girlfriend, though.'

An hour later Amy was helping Beth get the tea ready. O'Keefe would be home soon from his job at the munitions factory. Many times he'd suggested going back to Ireland, but each time Amy had protested that she wasn't ready to be left alone with Beth just yet. Beth would argue that for O'Keefe to leave her to look after Amy on her own was just too much to ask. O'Keefe wasn't keen on leaving anyway, so he stayed on.

'It's a sin and a shame,' Beth said, slicing angrily through a loaf of bread. 'He used to be such a bright lad. If anyone's to blame fer what happened to him it's his mother.' She waved the carving knife in between slices. 'That woman

112

drove his dad away with her loose ways. I think young Sefton grew up just waiting for the day he was old enough to run away from her. Now this has happened to him. All this bombing and shelling's addled his brain. Any mother worth tuppence would look after him. If I had my way I'd stick *her* in front of a damn firing squad. I don't think anyone'd be in too much of a rush to save *her* life.' She looked up at Amy and smiled. 'Listen to me going on. You'd think he was my lad. I best improve my temper in time for his lordship coming home.'

'Lord O'Keefe,' laughed Amy. 'I think I'll start calling him that.'

'He's a good man,' remarked Beth, looking down again.

'And your generation,' added Amy, pointedly. She was at the match-making age.

'Looking forward to the trip on Saturday?' asked Beth, changing the subject. 'Should be a good day out. There's a spare seat, so why don't you ask young Billy along? I'm told he's home again. Been home a fortnight. I'm surprised you haven't been round.'

'I thought he might come round here. I don't think I'm Billy's favourite person.'

'If I know young Billy he'll be as fretful to come round to see you as you are to go see him.'

'Do you think so?'

'I know so. To be honest I think he'll be more worried about making his peace with Nipper's family. Billy won't know what to do. His dad's a right useless lump. He'll be no help to the lad.'

'Maybe I should help.'

'Maybe you should, love.'

*

'Is your mother in?'

Napper Boothroyd knew who Amy was. With her good looks and American accent, who didn't? For the life of him he couldn't figure out what she wanted his mother for. 'Er . . . yeah. Do yer want me ter get her?'

'Yes please.'

Mrs Boothroyd came to the door, wiping her hands on her pinny. She gave Amy a cautious smile, not saying anything, just curious to know why she was at the door.

'Hello Mrs Boothroyd, my name is Amy Farthing.'

'I know who you are, love.'

'I've come about Billy Eccles.'

'Have you now?'

'He blames me for him getting locked up and I think you blame him for what happened to Nipper.'

'I think yer'd best come in, lass.'

Amy followed the mother and son into the house that was furnished as cleanly and sparsely as every other house in the district. Nipper's face smiled out from half a dozen photographs around the room. On the mantelpiece was a class photograph, with Nipper and Billy sitting side by side on the front row, arms folded, faces uncharacteristically serious – as per the photographer's instructions.

Mrs Boothroyd had heard what had gone on between her and Billy just before her son had died. Chinese whispers around the neighbourhood had exaggerated a bit of harmless curiosity into something far more sinful. Amy waited to be invited before sitting down. Mrs Boothroyd sat opposite and Napper hovered, uncertainly. He was a couple of years older than Amy but still found her most impressive.

'For a start,' Amy began. 'A lot of this stuff that went around about Billy and me being sinful is about as true as Hubert Heptonstall's story about Billy pushing Nipper into the stream. Billy and me were just having fun. Just like Billy and Nipper.'

Napper tried to speak, 'I allus said, didn't I Mam–'

Mrs Boothroyd stayed her son with a wave of her hand. 'When you lose a son, Amy, you think the worst in everyone. I don't know this Hubert lad so I had ter believe what I heard in court. It hurt me ter think Billy did that ter my Walter – even if he were larkin' around. I tret young Billy like me own son with him not having a mam of his own. Funny, he had no mam and my lads had no dad.' A look of realisation crossed her face and she pressed a contrite hand to her breast. 'Ee, I am sorry lass. Here's me goin' on about mams and dads and you've neither. What do yer think of me?'

'That's OK, Mrs Boothroyd,' said Amy. Her eyes bore deeply into those of Nipper's mother, almost mesmerising her. 'Billy's a good person. You have to believe he wouldn't tell a lie about how Nipper died just to save his own skin. He was locked up for two years for something he most definitely didn't do. Your son died happy. He died as he lived – just fooling around. It was nothing to do with Billy.'

Mrs Boothroyd was in tears. She took Amy in her arms. 'Well said, lass . . . well said indeed. He did die happy, did my Walter. He lived happy and he died happy and from now on I'll never believe no different. And thanks fer making me see what was plain all along.'

'I allus said it were nowt ter do wi' Billy Eccles,' said Napper, determinedly. 'I allus said that Hubert Heptonstall were a right liar.'

'Aye, yer did, lad,' conceded his mother, with a tearful smile at her son. 'Yer stuck up fer young Billy right enough, poor young beggar. My God, he's had it rough has the lad.'

'The trouble was,' said Amy. 'That Billy was caught out in a lie kinda trying to defend my honour. He thinks I broke a promise and I don't think he's really forgiven me. I want to make friends with him again, Mrs Boothroyd – and it would help if I took you with me. I guess he needs you to *tell* him you know it wasn't his fault that Nipper died.'

'How old are you?'

'Thirteen.'

'Yer've a lot about yer fer thirteen. Aye, lass. As a matter o' fact it'll do me good ter make things up wi' young Billy. Take away some o' the pain – some of his as well, I shouldn't wonder.'

Billy and Amy sat on the same rock by the same stream. A dwindling, late evening sun cast long shadows across the water. There was another swing, now called the Death Swing, and another dam, as there would be for years to come. The odd drowning doesn't stop kids having fun. No one was playing today.

'Should be great fun tomorrow,' Amy said.

'Thanks for inviting me. I've never seen the sea.'

'I've seen too much of it.'

Billy looked at her for a second before he understood. 'Yeah,' he said. 'I reckon you have. And thanks for bringin' Mrs Boothroyd round. It always bothered me that she believed I'd pushed Nipper in.'

'She didn't know what to think. Napper always believed you.'

'Aye, he's a good lad is Napper. Mrs Boothroyd called me son; did you hear her say that? She used ter do that sometimes before.'

116

'She told me she treated you like her own son.'

'She did an' all. I'm glad she's all right wi' me.' He threw a stone into the pool. 'It's not as good as our dam,' he observed. 'Kids today, eh? They can't do stuff like we used ter.' He was fourteen.

'By the way,' said Amy, who had waited for this moment at this place to tell him, 'I didn't break my promise.'

He frowned and looked at her. 'The coppers said yer told 'em that me an' you had . . . yer know.'

'Well, I didn't,' she said. 'I guess they were lying to try and make you into a liar.'

'Oh heck! They *did* make me into a liar, that's what got me locked up. It were my word against Heptonstall's.' He shook his head and sighed. 'The word of a liar like me against a trustworthy lad like Heptonstall.'

'I'm sorry.'

'I should have known yer wouldn't let me down.'

'You weren't to know the police would lie to you,' she said. 'In my opinion their lie was much worse than yours. Yours was a lie of honour to protect me.'

There was a long, contemplative silence, then Billy said, 'I won't forget that day I was here with you. It were the best day I can remember.'

'Me too,' said Amy.

A kingfisher dived into the pool and came up with a wriggling minnow. Amy went 'Ahhh' in sympathy with the fish. Billy put his arm around her and they watched the last of the sunlight dancing on the water, delighting in each other's company. Billy smiled at the memory of him and Nipper on the swing, both of them soaking wet; and of him and Amy in the stream that day.

'This'll always be my favourite place,' he said.

'And mine.'

Without warning he leaned across and kissed her flush on the lips, then drew away, apprehensively, to await her reaction. It was the first time he'd ever kissed a girl.

She didn't say anything at first. But to his relief she didn't act disgusted or annoyed.

'Hmmm . . . I think I'd like you to do that again,' she decided at length. 'I've never been kissed by a boy before.'

Billy obliged and this time, without the apprehension, it was better. It was a soft, warm kiss that neither would forget. A kiss by which all future kisses with other people would be judged.

Chapter Seven

Godfrey Farthing leaned back in his chair and stared suspiciously at the man sitting opposite. 'I didn't think you people worked on a Saturday. It must be something important.'

'It's . . . it's important to me,' John Sykes said hesitantly.

'I've paid you well, John. I hope you're not asking for more.'

Godfrey's office in Farthing's mill was designed to impress suppliers, customers and bankers, and to instill awe into whatever lowly employee was fortunate (or unfortunate) enough to cross the threshold. The walls were panelled in rich rosewood and decorated with two gloomy oil paintings – one of Samuel and one of Godfrey. The floor was expensively carpeted and on an outside wall was a window, heavily curtained in rich green brocade. On the inner wall, opposite, was a slatted blind that, with a flick, would give him a clear view of the main work floor of his mill. It had the feel of a room that hadn't known much laughter.

The desk befitted the man – heavy and wide. On it was

a black telephone, an inkstand and an open ledger in which Godfrey had been writing when his visitor was shown in.

John Sykes, now a full partner in Sykes, Sykes and Broom, solicitors, held out his soft hands in supplication. 'I'm not here to blackmail you, Godfrey, but I didn't realise how hard things would get, what with the war and all that.'

'I'm glad you're not here to blackmail me, because it wouldn't work.'

'No, I didn't think for one minute it would. It's just that I need to replace funds in our clients' account and money I was expecting hasn't materialised – so to speak.'

'Money has a habit of not materialising if you don't keep a grip on things. Am I to understand you've been stealing money from your firm's clients' account?' Godfrey sat back in his leather chair and tut-tutted.

'Stealing's much too strong a word, Godfrey. I simply diverted funds and I'm finding it difficult to divert them back. I wouldn't normally trouble you but–'

'How much?'

'Five hundred pounds.'

Godfrey nodded, slowly. It brought a smile of hope to John's face.

'Five hundred pounds, eh? I'd say that's about what you make in a good year.'

'Something like that.'

'And how many more times will you be coming back for money? If I give you this, and I'm not saying I will, it'll be two and a half thousand you've had off me since my father died. It can't go on, John. Times are hard for all of us.'

'This is the last time, Godfrey. That, I promise.'

'That's what you said last time – and the time before.'

John couldn't argue. He was intimidated by Godfrey, but the hold he had over the mill owner was so strong it overcame his fears.

'How is your granddaughter?' he enquired, innocently, deliberately striking at the mill owner's Achilles heel.

'How the devil would I know?' thundered Godfrey. 'And as far as I'm concerned she's not my granddaughter. That gold-digging bitch she calls her mother put it about all right, I've no doubt of that.'

'Unfortunately you have no proof,' pointed out John, 'and that's the problem. Legally she's your son's rightful heir.'

'No one has any proof,' retorted Godfrey, angrily. 'That last will of my father's ended up in the right place, the bloody fire-back. He obviously wasn't in his right mind – cutting me out at the last minute. What the hell was he thinking of?'

The solicitor thought he'd chance his arm. 'According to your father's last will,' he ventured, 'you'd been taking money from the company for several year–' Sykes stopped when Godfrey began to rise, threateningly, from his chair, then he added, 'I'm only repeating what was in the will.'

'You repeat it a bit too often for my liking,' snarled Godfrey. 'Whatever money I took was my right. I ran the bloody place. My lads had bugger all to do with it and the daft old goat goes and leaves the lot to them. The bloody lot to them and their bloody progeny.'

'And there's only *one* progeny,' John reminded him, unnecessarily. 'If the will ever came to light she would become the owner of – well, of everything.' The solicitor was becoming increasingly confident. Under the circumstance perhaps he should have asked for more. Was it too late?

'Aye, I'm well aware o' that,' growled Godfrey. 'But there's no chance o' this will coming to light, is there – because there isn't a will anymore.' He leaned forward and glared at John, with fierce suspicion. 'Is there?'

'Burned to a crisp, Godfrey,' John assured him. 'Both copies. And the only living witness, besides me, is a half idiot clerk who didn't know what he was signing, and in any case, just after the will was made, he moved back to Scotland where he came from. Never been heard of since.'

The solicitor, now confident of success, took a gold cigarette case from his pocket, opened it, and offered it to Godfrey, who waved it away.

'You know, Godfrey,' John went on, lighting up, extravagantly. 'In a callous sort of way, your sons both dying in the war has eased your situation. You didn't *insist* on them going off to fight the Hun, did you?'

Godfrey exploded and thumped his fist on the desk, but John remained outwardly calm. He had this man where he wanted him. Five hundred pounds was nowhere near enough.

'Are you saying I deliberately sent my sons to their deaths because of the bloody will?' Godfrey roared. 'Holy Jesus! What sort of a bloody monster do you think I am?'

'I don't think anything, Godfrey. I'm just pointing out that every cloud has a silver lining. Surely the same thought crossed your mind.'

Godfrey scowled and made no comment. He didn't trust this solicitor. Was this bloody man holding an ace up his sleeve – another copy of the will perhaps? Would he eventually bleed him dry? 'Confirm something for me, John,' he said. 'Tell me what the position would be if the will had come to light but both my sons and the girl were all dead.'

'Your father's will would have gone to probate and his fortune shared among the next of kin.'

'And I'm his only next of kin?'

'Exactly. Why do you ask?'

'No reason. Call back tomorrow. You shall have your money and let that be an end to this blackmail.'

The solicitor was thinking he'd take what was on offer now, and not be greedy.

One hour later Hubert Heptonstall stood smartly to attention in front of Godfrey's desk with all the awkwardness of an army recruit on his first day. Why he had been summoned he had no idea but he suspected he was in trouble. His fears subsided when Godfrey gave him a benign beam and lit up a cigar the size of a weaver's shuttle.

'Ah, Hubert . . . is that what your pals call you, Hubert? Or do they call you Bert. Proper man's name, Bert.'

'Bert's what all my friends call me, Mr Farthing,' said Hubert, who had no friends.

'Good man, Bert. Just been made up to jobbing lad, so I hear?'

'Yes sir.'

'How would you like to be an apprentice weaver, Bert?'

Hubert was startled. It was normally the mill manager who made such decisions, not the mill owner himself. Mr Farthing must think he was something special. Wait till he went home and told his mam and dad about this. As the seventh child they had always regarded him as the runt of the Heptonstall litter. 'Not all there,' was how he'd once heard his dad describe him to a neighbour after Hubert had been caught peeing over that neighbour's wall at the age of fourteen. It was said that the seventh child was marked for life, there being little enough to go round for the other six. He suffered from malnutrition, and a severe lack of affection.

'Five-year apprenticeship, lad. We don't offer them to everyone.'

'I know that, sir. Thank you sir.'

'Mind you, I've heard things about you, Bert,' said Godfrey, puffing a cloud of delicious smelling smoke Hubert's way. Hubert breathed in the luxurious fumes as his boss continued. 'I've heard people say you're not beyond a bit of skullduggery. I've heard you got a lad who crossed you sent away for something he didn't do. Word gets round, Bert.'

'Oh, that's not true, Mr Farthing, honest.'

Godfrey gave him a beam of disbelieving admiration. 'Good man, Bert. Always play your cards close to your chest. Could you play your cards close to your chest for me?'

Hubert was confused. 'What?' he said, dumbly.

'Would you like to earn a bit of extra money, Bert?'

'How much money?' enquired Hubert, greedily. When Godfrey told him he exclaimed, 'Cor blimey!'

'Cor blimey's right, Bert. Did you know what it means?'

'No, sir.'

'Well you do now. It means God blind me. Which is what will happen to you if you let me down, Bert. This is between you and me, Bert. Tell you what, take the rest of the day off, but don't tell anyone. I don't want the other workers accusing me of favouritism.'

As soon as Hubert had left, Godfrey called his mill

manager into his office. 'I want you to keep a closer eye on the workers,' he said sternly. 'Caught young Heptonstall stealing money from this very office. Had a mind to call the police. Sacked the little beggar on the spot because I don't want to make a fuss. If you make a fuss it affects the workers. If you affect the workers production falls. Say nothing about this to anyone but don't leave it up to me to catch the thieves in future.'

'Yes, Mr Farthing.'

'Do you know if the omnibus got away all right?'

'As far as I know, Mr Farthing. It should be in Scarborough right now.'

'Good, good. I think I might use it on works outings in future. Put the word around. Let them know I'm not the slave driver they think I am. Good work deserves reward. Remember about the thieves though.'

'I will, Mr Farthing.'

Chapter Eight

At first it was to be a charabanc trip, but as the numbers exceeded the 28-seat capacity of Wormald's charabanc it was decided to use Farthing's omnibus instead. Had Beth known this she might have baulked at the idea of travelling on a vehicle owned by him but O'Keefe had already paid a deposit for the three of them and it seemed daft not to go on the Cobbler's Arms annual trip; besides, it wasn't as if Farthing would be there in person.

Of the forty-two people on the bus only Amy, O'Keefe and a few ex-soldiers had seen the sea before – and Amy's memory of it was somewhat jaundiced. From the Spa Bridge the graceful sweep of Scarborough Bay with its jostling crowds and troupes of colourful Pierrots on the beach should have seemed a far cry from the unforgiving Atlantic that had swallowed up so many people that day, but bad memories have a sneaky way of creeping up on you. It was a blue, August morning with a fresh breeze embroidering the waves with sparkling white lace as they tumbled towards the shallow sand. The lighthouse at the end of the harbour wall had been recently rebuilt after being reduced to rubble early in the war by a

German naval attack on the town. The sight of it brought everything back; as did the fishing boats, the nimble yachts, the swooping, squawking seagulls, the smell of the sea, the gentle wind tugging at her hair and the friendly sound of O'Keefe's voice behind her. It was a fearfully happy moment, just like it had been on the *Lusitania*, minutes before the torpedo struck.

'D'ye feel it as well?' he said.

She turned, half expecting him to be standing there in his black and white waiter's uniform, carrying a tray of drinks for the impatient, doomed Americans. But only O'Keefe's smile remained the same. He was dressed in a tweed sports jacket and a straw boater atop his now snow-white hair.

'Yes,' Amy said to him. 'I sure do feel it.' Then she smiled at Beth, who couldn't understand what they were talking about but Amy chose not to explain; it would just prolong an unwanted memory. The soldiers returning from the Great War had dealt with their horrific experiences by trying not to talk or think about them. Authentic tales from the trenches were few and far between and more often than not told by men who hadn't been anywhere near front. 'Do you mind if Billy and I go off on our own for a while?' she asked.

'Meet you both back here at four o'clock sharp,' Beth said, pressing a coin into each of their hands. 'And don't give any of this to gypsies who seem down on their luck selling good luck charms.'

Beth had been tempted to pass on a warning given to her by her own mother on her eighteenth birthday. *'Never trust a man with testicles.'* But she thought Amy was too young for such adult advice, so O'Keefe had stepped into the breach with some whispered advice for Billy. 'Don't let any harm come to Amy or ye'll feel the length of me boot up yer arse!'

'What?' said Billy, backing away from him. 'What did you say that for? I wouldn't harm her. She's my friend. I wouldn't harm my friends. I wouldn't hurt anyone.'

There were sudden tears rolling down his face. O'Keefe took a step towards him, with his hands held out in contrition for his clumsiness, but Billy turned and ran away.

'What on earth did you say to the lad?' asked Beth.

O'Keefe ran over in his mind what he'd said to Billy and couldn't bring himself to repeat it. 'The wrong thing,' he admitted. 'I said if any harm came to Amy he'd – he'd have me to answer to. The lad took it the wrong way, that's all.'

Beth tutted at his lack of tact. 'He's been locked up for two years for harming one of his friends when we all know he didn't do it. I think he's entitled to be a bit touchy on the subject.'

'I'll go after him,' said Amy, who hadn't taken her eyes off Billy's retreating figure.

Beth pointed towards the Spa where a band was playing in the open air. 'We'll be down there, listening to the band.'

'Apologise fer me, Amy,' said O'Keefe, gloomily. 'I wasn't thinking.'

Amy took off after Billy who had by now disappeared into the crowd. She searched through the happy people watching the Punch and Judy and Pierrot shows. She checked the queues at the ice cream vendors and the many shellfish stalls to see if Billy might be spending his shilling there. She checked all around the harbour, as far as the lighthouse and even looked up at the castle to see if he might have climbed up there. Then she decided to go back to where they had parted company in the hope of finding him waiting there. Maybe Billy had regretted his impetuosity. He must have realised that O'Keefe wasn't the type to knowingly hurt him. He was just a man – and men said and did stupid things.

In the meantime Billy was making his way back to the main road, hoping to steal or beg a ride home.

And O'Keefe was proposing to Beth.

It was late evening when Ernest Eccles opened the door in response to O'Keefe's knock.

'Yes?'

'I thought I'd call round to check if young Billy got home safely.'

'No, he's not back yet. I thought he was with you.'

O'Keefe scratched his head awkwardly. 'He ran off on his own and didn't come back in time to catch the omnibus.'

'Oh dear. Well it sounds like something my son would do. He's at that age.'

'So,' said O'Keefe. 'Ye think he'll be all right, do ye?'

'All right?' Mr Eccles looked worried. 'I'm not sure. Scarborough's a long way. He's only thirteen and I only gave him threepence to go with.'

'He had another shilling on top of that.'

'That's very generous of you,' said Ernest sharply. 'But we don't need charity, you know. I expect he'll make his own way back. Billy's used to adversity. He didn't harm young Nipper, you know. Even Mrs Boothroyd believes Billy was telling the truth.'

O'Keefe was feeling worse by the minute for having said what he did to Billy. He had to unburden his guilt by confessing his sin. 'Look – it's maybe my fault he ran off like he did.'

'Your fault?'

'Billy and Amy were going off together for a couple of hours and er – well, young Amy and me, we've been through a lot together and I feel very protective of her. I told him not to let any harm come to her or he'd have me to answer to.' He winced at his own words as told the whole truth. 'Actually I said it a little more forcefully and the lad seemed to take exception to it.'

'I should damn well think he did,' said Mr Eccles. 'Sounds to me like you don't believe in my son's innocence as much as Mrs Boothroyd does.'

'But I do, I do,' protested O'Keefe. 'I'd have said the same to any young lad who went off with her.'

'But he's not any young lad, is he? He's a lad who's been badly done by and he's very aware of what people think of him. I've been treating him with kid gloves ever since he got home.'

'When he gets back will ye tell him I acted like an old fool and I'll apologise the next time I see him.'

Mr Eccles nodded with very little enthusiasm, then he closed the door on O'Keefe, who now felt two feet tall.

At eleven that evening Mr Eccles went round to the police station and reported his son missing to Sergeant Dicks, who had cause to remember Billy because word was going round that the lad had been badly done to by the police and courts. Dicks didn't like that one bit.

'Come back tomorrow, Mr Eccles. If he hasn't turned up by then I'll list him as missing.'

'Then what will you do?'

'We'll do what we can, which means keeping an eye out for him. If we put out a search party every time a young scallywag runs away from home we'd have no men left to police the streets. My guess is he'll be home by morning.'

At eleven o'clock that evening Amy had been in bed for an hour and was sound asleep. Beth was busy sewing while O'Keefe tried to rock away his worries about Billy. Both Amy and Beth had every faith that he'd turn up safe and sound. But they weren't the ones responsible if he didn't.

Beth looked across at him and allowed herself a contented smile. He had bought himself a noisy rocking chair from a house sale and a square of nearly new Axminster that just about covered the whole of the floor. It was a comfortable house and, with him and Amy in it, a proper home for the first time since Alfred. She didn't mind the squeak.

O'Keefe had sold what he had when he went off to America and all of his personal possessions had gone down with the *Lusitania*. His late wife's sister had sent him her copy of his wedding photograph, which stood on the mantelpiece alongside one of Alfred and his pretty bride, Beth. His two sons had written expressing their relief on hearing that he was alive and he had recently received a letter from his eldest boy, telling him he'd become a grand-father. News that had brought a fierce roar of delight from O'Keefe, and laughter from Amy and Beth as he danced an Irish jig to his own loud singing.

It had been a home of marital domesticity, without the marriage. But now all that could change. At first neither of them had wanted to rock any boats, especially with Amy so tragically bereaved. Their relationship had been strictly landlady and lodger. But recently he and Beth had been going out socially together; once to the Hippodrome Picture Palace to see *The Americano* with Douglas Fairbanks; twice to the Cobbler's Arms and once, two nights ago, to the Alhambra Theatre to see Vesta Tilley, the male impersonator. On their way back they had linked arms and sang one of Vesta's songs, 'Jolly Good Luck To The Girl Who Loves A Soldier', then Beth had broken down in tears as she realised she could well have been singing about her own daughter. O'Keefe had put a comforting arm around her and one thing led to another. Only a kiss, but it was on the lips and Beth felt a need for this kind man who had come into her life when she most needed someone. But she wanted more than just a kiss.

O'Keefe was aware of her eyes upon him in between her stitches. Eventually she put her work down. 'I'm sorry I couldn't give you an answer today,' she said. 'It came as a bit of a shock, that's all. I'll sleep on it tonight and give you my answer in the morning.'

'Any morning will do, me darlin' woman. I didn't make me proposal lightly. To be honest I'm more worried about the boy at the moment. D'ye think he'll be home by now? Will I go round to ask?'

She was put out that his proposal was secondary in his thoughts to young Billy, who would no doubt turn up, if he hadn't already. 'I don't think that would be a good idea,' she advised. 'Young Billy's a resourceful lad. You could drop him off in Timbuctu and he'd find his way home.'

'I do hope so. I offended the poor lad in a way I never should – oh, by the way,' he said, almost as an after-thought. 'I hope yer don't mind but I've seen a violin that might suit Amy.'

'O'Keefe, I can't actually afford one. Anyway she hasn't mentioned the violin in all the time she's been here.'

'It just caught me eye, that's all. And I remember talking to her on the ship about it. She seemed quite keen back then. Anyway, I been payin' for it these last three months and I pick it up tomorrow from Blakey's in town. All bought and paid for.'

'You're a good man, O'Keefe.'

'Then ye should snap me up while ye've got the chance.'

Beth laughed. 'I enjoyed the Alhambra the other night. Sorry I acted silly on the way home.'

He smiled. 'Ah, think nothin' of it. Unlike me, yer a person of great sensitivity. My Maggie was just the same. She could weep a lake o' tears over a distant memory. Half the time I didn't know what was going inside her head but she had the great heart and I loved her all the same.' His head went to one side as he surveyed Beth's face. 'I can see where young Amy and her mother got their good looks.'

She blushed for the first time in many years. 'Is this what they call the Blarney?' she asked.

He subjected her to his full attention. 'It's what they call the truth,' he said, earnestly. 'It's been a while since I enjoyed the company of a woman – and I enjoyed *your* company that night.' He left a deliberate pause before adding, 'Especially on the way home.'

It was there, in his voice. Beth wasn't so out of touch that she couldn't read a man. Or was it just wishful thinking? If it was she could well embarrass herself here. There was a long silence as she mulled over her thoughts. It was as though O'Keefe could read them.

'As a matter o' fact,' he went on, 'I wouldn't mind enjoying more of yer company.'

Beth smiled. He'd turned it into a game, which made it easier. 'Really?' she teased. 'How much more?'

He leaned forward in his chair and, with a twinkle in his eyes, he said, 'As much as ye'd like to offer and no more. Whatever company yer wish, I'm yer man.'

She felt her heart pounding. Oh God, he was offering himself to her. And she knew that tonight, for the first time since Alfred had died, she was going to make love with a man for whom she had great affection. Maybe even love.

'O'Keefe,' she said. 'Do you love me?'

'Ye mean like I loved my Maggie?'

She didn't answer this. He set the rocking chair in motion again as he gave her question some thought. His delay already told her the true answer.

'I have a great affection for ye, Beth.'

'And I for you, O'Keefe.'

'I feel a great contentment when I'm with ye. I enjoy our silences as much as our conversation. I like the cut of ye, and I think ye've the makings of a fine wife.'

It was as much as she could wish for – *more* probably. 'O'Keefe, I'd like to spend the night in your bed,' she said, amazed at her own boldness. 'It might help me make up my mind – that is if you're up to it,' she added, saucily.

'Would ye listen ter yeself? There might be snow on me roof but there's a good fire burning in the grate.'

Beth laughed and stood up, allowing him to envelop her in his strong arms. She wept soft tears into his shoulder as though unburdening herself of all the hardship she'd endured throughout her life. It was as if she wanted to rid herself of the pain before she enjoyed the pleasure.

'I think we should go up now, me darlin' woman,' he said. 'Before I'm destroyed with desire.'

134

Holding on to his hand she paused to turn out the gaslight before he led her up the stairs.

At one o'clock the next morning a dark figure poured two gallons of petrol into a funnel that he'd placed in John Sykes's letterbox. He then inserted a length of petrol-soaked rope. With a quick look around to make sure the coast was clear he struck a match, lit the end of rope and ran away to get on with his next job.

He was a hundred yards away when he heard the house go up in flames with a loud whooosh. He turned to admire his handiwork for a few seconds, still wondering why he'd been told to tie a rope between the doorhandle and the adjacent rainwater pipe. His next destination was two miles away. Beth's house in Cinder Yard.

Billy had found a signpost saying Leeds 65 miles and had set off walking. A colourful steam engine lumbered past pulling a wagon load of hay. Billy ran alongside and shouted up to the driver. 'Any chance of a ride, mister?'

'Jump on the wagon, lad. I'm goin' as far as Scagglethorpe.'

Billy had never heard of Scagglethorpe but he stayed on board for over 20 miles until it turned off the main road. The driver gave him a cheery wave that brought a smile to Billy's face as he waved back and shouted, 'Thanks mister.'

He passed an orchard, heavy with apples, and filled his pockets knowing he'd need sustenance if he had to walk the rest of the way. His dad wouldn't be so pleased; in fact Billy wasn't too pleased with himself, now that he'd had a couple of hours to see sense. O'Keefe was just looking after Amy's welfare. Billy had taken his threat too personally. When he got back he'd go round and apologise for being so daft. Still, it was a nice day and things weren't so bad. He had one and threepence in his pocket and he was pretty sure he was on the same road they'd travelled on that morning. All he had to do was keep an eye out for the returning omnibus. He began to whistle, in between taking bites out of an apple.

Passing vehicles were few and far between, but plentiful in their variety. Horse-drawn carriages and carts, steam engines, motor cars, charabancs, omnibuses, bicycles, motor bikes and in the distance a hunt in full cry galloping across the crest of Staxton Hill. All in all this was more of an adventure than Scarborough but he wished Amy was with him. The two of them would have had a fine time on this walk.

A bicycle leaning against a farm gate was too much of a temptation. He looked all around but couldn't see an owner so he convinced himself that it was lost and that he should take it to the nearest police station. At least that would be his story if he got caught. Billy had never had a bike of his own but he'd learned to ride one before he got locked up, during his days as a Saturday boy for Jessop's Butchers. This was a bigger bike and in need of a drop of oil, but it was faster than walking. There was also a cheese and onion sandwich in the saddle bag and a bottle of lemonade. Things were looking up.

The signposts had become confusing and he was a bit wary of asking anyone in case they recognised the bike. He knew by the sun that he was headed in vaguely the right direction, due west, but he thought he'd taken a wrong turning somewhere. By mid-afternoon he arrived at a bridge spanning a narrow river, with a field running right down to the water; an ideal place to take a rest and make further plans. Within half hour he was fast asleep under the cool shade of a willow tree. The sun had lost its height and warmth when he awoke and he knew he'd better make a determined effort to head for home if he was to be back before nightfall – which seemed unlikely now. Surely he and his bicycle were far enough away from the scene of his crime for him to ask for directions.

When he went to where he'd left the bike he gave a rueful grin. Some thief had stolen it. Maybe this was the way things were done in the country. You see a bike, you take it, then leave it somewhere handy for the next person to use. It seemed a reasonable way to carry on.

'Excuse me, mister. I'm looking fer the main road to Leeds and Bradford.'

He addressed his question to a bent old man in a battered bowler hat and a heavily repaired overcoat, standing by the roadside for no apparent reason.

'Don't know about roads, lad. Never had much use fer roads. All I do is gerron t' omnibus an' gerroff at t' other end. That's where I'm off now. Ter visit me mother in York.'

Billy was tempted ask how old his mother was. The old man looked to be ninety if he was a day. But he resisted the temptation and asked instead, 'Will a bus pick you up here?'

'I bloomin' hope so, lad. I've been standin' here an hour already. They have timetables yer know, just like trains. Only they never stick ter the buggers. D'yer smoke?'

'No,' said Billy, perplexed.

'I've just run out, yer see. Thought I might borrow one. Many a young lad o' your age smokes. It's a manly thing ter do.'

137

'I'll prob'ly be startin' very shortly,' Billy promised.

'You see yer do. Smokin' saw many a lad through t' war. It'll not be t' last war neither. You be prepared lad.'

'I will.'

Billy had tried smoking in reform school and it had made him sick so he was hoping he could get by without having to bother. It now seemed it might be a necessary evil if ever he was called upon to fight for his country. A motor horn sounded from beyond a nearby blind corner and within seconds an omnibus hove into sight. The old man placed himself in the middle of the road, trusting in the bus's brakes to stop in time. Billy held his breath and closed one eye as the vehicle stopped, virtually touching the old man's coat. The driver rose from his seat and waved his fist, angrily.

'Sid, you do that just one more time yer barmy owd bugger and I'll run yer over. This isn't a proper stop. Next stop's t' Horse and Trumpet in Claxton as well you know.'

'I can't walk ter bloody Claxton. I've gorra bone in me leg,' grinned the old man, gummily.

'Yer've gorra bone between yer ears.'

By this time the old man had boarded and was negotiating the fare with the conductor. Billy stood back, hesitantly. The driver looked at him.

'Are you wi' Suicide Sid?' he asked.

Billy shook his head and said, 'I don't suppose you go to Bradford, do you?'

'Yer suppose right, lad. We don't do foreign travel. York's as far as we go. Well, are yer gerrin' on or not?'

Billy stepped on the platform. The conductor assessed his age and concluded, 'I reckon that'll be threepence.'

At ten-fifteen Billy stepped off the bus in York and

headed for the train station. According to the obliging conductor a midnight mail train called at Leeds and Bradford on its way to Manchester.

'It'll cost yer t' thick end of a bob, lad.' The conductor warned. 'Highway robbery these trains.'

'I've only got a shilling,' said Billy. 'Do yer think I'll have enough left fer ha'porth o' chips?'

'I should check first.'

Billy checked and was relieved that the fare was only ninepence for a boy, leaving him enough left over for fish and chips which he ate sitting on the edge of the platform with his legs dangling dangerously over the line. He would remember it as one of the finest meals he'd had in his life.

It was quarter to two o'clock in the morning when Billy walked past the entrance to Cinder Yard and was knocked to the ground by someone running past him. He shouted after the man, making his feelings known before rubbing a sore elbow and reviewing his immediate future from his seat on the ground. Another two minutes and he'd be home. What sort of reception awaited him? Would his dad still be up? He'd already decided on telling the truth as opposed to an elaborate lie. The truth was as good as any lie he could make up. He wouldn't mention stealing the bike. No need for that. There was a light coming from Cinder Yard, much brighter than the usual dismal gas lamp. Out of curiosity Billy got to his feet and went over to the archway. There were flames coming from the ground floor of Beth's house.

'Fire!'

He was shouting at the top of his voice, running round the yard banging on and doors until a bedroom window scraped open and a stentorian voice gave a yell to match his.

'Fire!'

Within seconds people appeared outside their doors, clad in night apparel. The ground floor was an inferno. Amy appeared at the bedroom window, trying to open it.

Someone was shouting to fetch the fire engine but no one had a telephone and the fire station was nearly two miles away. They'd need to wake up the landlord of the Cobblers Arms and use his phone. By then it would be too late for Amy.

A man produced a ladder and leaned it against the wall just as Beth's living room window exploded with the heat, and hungry flames licked outwards and upwards, illuminating Amy's frightened face as she tugged at the window above. Within seconds the ladder was on fire. Amy had now opened the window and was screaming for help but it seemed there was no way of getting to her. Billy turned and galloped out of the yard. A crowd had gathered a safe distance from the heat, mutely looking up at Amy's terrified face and listening in agony to her awful screams, but offering no advice – they knew of none to give. Her death was a foregone conclusion.

One watching woman pointed up at the roof. 'Look,' she cried. 'There's a man up there. It's Sefton. Daft bugger's trying ter get hisself killed.'

'Sefton! Come away. There's nowt yer can do.'

Sefton was crawling, in his pyjamas, across the sloping slates towards the skylight that lit O'Keefe's attic. He kicked at the glass with his bare foot, shattering it with his third attempt. Trapped smoke poured out into the night air. Sefton reached inside, undid the catch and opened the broken window frame. He dropped down to

140

where O'Keefe and Beth lay unconscious from the smoke fumes that had risen, unhindered by doors, up to the attic and were now escaping through the open skylight, clearing the room sufficiently for Sefton to see the two figures lying in bed.

'Missis,' he shouted, shaking Beth. 'Missis, yer've got ter wake up.'

There was a banging coming from below, so Sefton banged back with his now bleeding foot, not knowing why.

Amy had looked back at the smoke pouring through the edges of the closed bedroom door. The flames had reached the landing, so there was no point trying to get up the attic stairs and out on to the roof. She had managed to open the window but her desperate screams for help seemed to be falling on deaf ears. Where was her grandmother? Was she okay? Had she got out? Her thoughts went, fleetingly, to O'Keefe who was a heavy sleeper. She took off her shoe, stood on a chair and banged with the heel on the ceiling.

'O'Keefe!' she yelled at the top of her voice. 'Wake up and get out on to the roof. The house is on fire.'

A loud banging came back from above. At least O'Keefe would be safe. The heat was becoming unbearable. Jumping out of the window through the searing flames licking out of the window below was looking to be her only option. Possible death weighed against certain death.

Amy gathered up her nightdress, leaned her head out of the window and immediately drew back from the blistering heat. There was only one thing for it. To stand back and run at the window. Her heart was pounding like a steam drill, tears of terror poured down her face and liquid of another variety ran down her legs. One way or another she'd be out of the burning house.

She stood there, clenching and unclenching her fists; summoning up the blind courage required to run and jump into what seemed certain death. Then suddenly the flames licking past the window vanished. There was something there. Some*body* there. Billy Eccles, urging her to get out. He was standing on the open, top deck of an omnibus that was tight up against the wall. The bottom of the bus was temporarily holding back the flames which had tranferred their fury to the lower deck.

'Come on,' Billy yelled. 'Before t' bloody bus goes up. Amy was out in seconds and ushered by Billy down the external spiral stairs to the street, where they fell into the arms of amazed onlookers. The omnibus was now ablaze from end to end, but it had served its purpose. Billy had taken it from the yard around the corner where it was kept, and driven it, with unusual expertise, to the rescue. As it happened it wasn't the first omnibus he'd pinched and taken for a joyride.

Someone pointed at the roof to where Sefton was heaving Beth's unconscious body out. Two men rushed into Sefton's house, up to his attic, and out on to the roof where they made their way across to where Beth's head was protruding from the skylight.

'I can't lift her,' Sefton was shouting. 'She's too heavy, mister.'

'OK, lad, we've got her.'

The men pulled Beth, unconscious, out on to the roof and across to Sefton's skylight. Her face was blackened from the smoke. Then another shout went up. 'There's someone else coming out.'

O'Keefe was only semi-conscious. With Sefton's help he heaved himself out on to the tiles. The Irishman lay there, coughing out great lungfuls of smoke as, a few yards away, Beth's rescuers lowered her into Sefton's house.

The men turned back for O'Keefe in response to shouts from below, but an explosion of fire burst through Beth's skylight and sent them crawling back. There was a scream from Amy as O'Keefe, burning now, began to roll down the roof.

'O'Keefe!' she screamed, but her shout was useless.

He rolled off the eaves, hit the front of the omnibus, and landed, with a sickening thud, on the stone cobbles. Men dragged him clear as the top floor collapsed and the fire became a roaring inferno. Someone shouted that Sefton was still in there but there was nothing anyone could have done. Then someone else remarked that he was 'a plucky bugger, choose what anyone says about him,' and the rest of the watching crowd murmured their agreement.

Amy knelt beside O'Keefe and stroked his smoke-blackened face.

'You're going to be OK, O'Keefe,' she told him.

His eyes flickered open and he tried a smile but gave up, as any movement obviously hurt like hell.

'I don't think I am,' he said, hoarsely. 'I think I'm about ready for the big dream.'

'You've got to be OK,' she commanded. 'I didn't spend all that time keeping you afloat just for you to leave me at the first sign of trouble.'

This time he smiled through the pain and said, 'I'm awfully sorry, madam.'

'I should . . . think you . . . you are.'

Amy's words were punctuated by sobs as tears ran down her grimy cheeks. Her hands shivered with emotion as she cupped his head and kissed him on his forehead. Beth was beside her now, with a man's overcoat covering her nightdress. O'Keefe's eyes went from Amy to her.

'Sorry,' he said, as though the whole thing was his fault. Perhaps in his confused state he thought it was.

'There's nothing to be sorry about,' Beth said. 'My answer is yes, O'Keefe. Yes, I will marry you.'

His lips were moving and Beth leaned down to listen. 'I think maybe I should have asked ye a bit sooner – yer a fine woman, Beth Crabtree. Mind you, I think I might have some explaining to do when I meet my Maggie.' His voice was audible only to Beth.

'I'm sure she'll understand,' Beth said, resigned to his fate now. The light was fading from his eyes and he had smiled his last smile.

'Goodbye, O'Keefe,' said Amy, sitting back on her haunches to allow her grandmother the last few seconds of O'Keefe's life.

Lit by a background of flames, Beth gently thumbed his eyelids shut and began to say the Lord's prayer. Amy joined in, as did everyone gathered around.

As Beth lay in her hospital bed her emotions surged from intense grief to guilt at having besmirched O'Keefe's beloved wife's memory by sleeping with her husband on his last night on Earth. She also knew she needed to explain her presence in O'Keefe's bedroom to her granddaughter.

'I expect you're wondering why I was in O'Keefe's room.'

'I don't suppose it's any of my business,' said Amy.

'He was as much your business as anyone's,' Beth said. 'He asked me to marry him when we were in Scarborough. I didn't mention it to you because of all the worry over Billy going missing.'

'Billy saved my life,' said Amy, who wasn't sure she wanted to hear all the details of her grandmother's love life. She didn't realise that people of Beth's age had such needs. 'Did you love O'Keefe?' she enquired.

'Now there's a question for a thirteen-year-old to be asking her grandma.'

'I thought that's why people got married. I know Mum and Dad loved each other. They argued like stink at times but you could tell they loved each other.'

'Yes, they did that,' remembered Beth. 'I can't honestly say it was like that with me and O'Keefe. He was a kind and comfortable man to be with . . . and he made me laugh.'

Amy nodded her agreement but she hoped there was more to love than that. 'I was hoping O'Keefe would propose to you. I'm glad he did.'

'It's just that at our age you feel as though you haven't as much time to wait for the formalities,' Beth went on, 'so, I went to bed with him. It was our first and only time.' She broke down in tears and hugged Amy to her. 'And now he's been taken from us and I feel so damn guilty. He'd been faithful to his wife's memory for all those years and I had to break that faith for him. What kind of woman am I?'

Amy had no answer for such a question. She just clung to her grandmother and wept with her. O'Keefe had been a trusted friend, grandfather and guardian angel all rolled into one. He had been the rock upon which she and her grandmother had built their lives and now they were on their own.

'The police have been in touch with his family in America,' she said, eventually. 'Apparently they can send messages by wireless. His sons are sending money for O'Keefe's remains to be taken to Cork so he can be buried next to his wife. One of them is making the trip, the other can't afford it.'

Beth gave a grey smile and wondered who he would have chosen to be buried next to, had he married her. It didn't matter now. 'We can't afford it either, my darling,' she said. 'I'll be out of here tomorrow. We'll say our goodbyes to him at this end.'

'He'd like that,' said Amy.

Chapter Nine

Late Summer 1917

Captain Rupert Franklyn DSO stood ramrod straight and held his salute as Sefton's body was lowered into the ground. Gertrude Earnshawe wept and Beth, unable to contain her disgust, shouted across the grave.

'Damn you, you hypocrite! You should have believed in him. You left your own son when he needed you most and here you are, crying crocodile tears into his grave because it turns out he's a hero after all.'

Gertrude hung her head and Beth followed by Amy, spun on her heels and walked away, leaving the mourners open mouthed, some of them suitably ashamed because they too had abandoned Sefton in his hour of need. Gertrude remained, with white hands knotted together, mumbling a prayer as the rest of the mourners moved away.

The officer hung back and held out a hand for her to shake. 'Mrs Earnshawe,' he said, with a slight nod of his head. 'I was proud to have known your son.'

'Beth Crabtree's right. I let him down, mister,' she said,

desolately, taking his hand. 'I let the poor little beggar down.'

'I understand from his letter he spoke well of you.'

'He spoke well of everyone. He even spoke well of the bloody Army. I just wish I could pay him back. Too late now. Thank you fer speakin' kindly of him.'

The captain nodded and hurried away. He caught up with Beth and Amy at the cemetery gates.

'Excuse me, ladies.'

They turned and met his smile with smiles of their own. He was a solid-looking man with even white teeth contrasting with a wide, dark moustache and he looked much older than his twenty-five years.

'I know it's none of my business but I trust you've found somewhere to live after having your house burn down.'

'Yes,' said Beth. 'For the time being we've moved into Sefton's old house. The landlord was only too pleased to let us take over the rent. It needs a lot of work but we're getting there, aren't we Amy? Don't know whether we'll stay. Too many ghosts in that house. All of them Sefton.'

Amy nodded her agreement, then had a thought. 'Are you the man who saved Sefton's life?'

Captain Franklyn regarded her, gravely. 'It was I who intervened when the firing squad was about to make a terrible mistake,' he said, walking beside them. 'Do I take it you disapprove of the way Private Earnshawe was treated by his mother?'

'She didn't treat him, lad, she disowned him,' Beth said. 'My granddaughter here.' She inclined her head towards Amy. 'She believed in him. She gave him back a bit of self-respect before he died.'

'His mother seems very remorseful,' remarked Franklyn,

glancing back at Mrs Earnshawe's huddled figure still at the graveside.

'So she should be,' said Beth, coldly. 'I'd never treat a son of mine like that no matter what he'd done.'

'I read about his heroism in the newspaper,' said the captain. 'Makes a complete nonsense of the way the Army treats its men.'

'How come you managed to save him from the firing squad?' asked Amy. 'The way Sefton told the story it all sounded so unreal. Like something in a dime novel.'

'Dime novel?'

'She used to lived in America,' Beth explained.

'Ah,' the captain smiled and said to Amy, 'I assumed you weren't local.'

'I didn't used to be local,' Amy said. 'But I am now – how *did* you save him?'

'Bent the rules somewhat,' said Captain Franklyn. 'As soon as I ascertained Private Earnshawe's true age I telegraphed HQ and pointed out that there would be an almighty hoo hah if they sent an underage boy before a firing squad. Heads would have rolled, believe me.'

'Sefton's head nearly rolled,' commented Beth, sourly. 'Poor beggar.'

'In point of fact,' said the captain. 'His head *would* have rolled had I played it by the book. You see, the order to reprieve him hadn't arrived when they marched young Earnshawe out to the block, so I had to assume that it was simply delayed and would arrive in due course.'

'What, you're saying you told a lie?' said Amy. 'To save Sefton's life?'

'I told them I'd received a message to say his reprieve was on its way,' the captain admitted. 'Had it not arrived, I'd have been in a spot of bother. Fortunately it did arrive

– three hours later. And now the poor blighter's bought it. God! What a mess. He'd taken a nasty knock on the head, y'know.' Franklyn tapped the left side of his head just above his ear. 'Lump the size of a duck egg. Affected his mind, I'm sure of it.'

'*Something* affected his mind,' said Beth. 'He was as right as rain before he went off to that damned stupid war.'

The captain nodded, sympathetically. 'The trouble was,' he said, 'he was seen running the wrong way without his rifle, crying like a baby. I suspect he had just recovered consciousness and was completely disorientated.'

'He'd seen his friend's head blown off,' said Amy. 'I imagine something like that will knock you off your stride no matter how old you are.'

'Sadly, we've all seen sights like that, young lady – that's the hell of it. In the heat of battle there's no time to hesitate. He was arrested on the spot lest anyone else got the same idea. I think the powers that be decided to set an example. I was at the court marshal. Poor blighter was in no fit state to offer a defence. When they sentenced him to death he apologised for his behaviour. I felt ashamed of my uniform that day. Shooting one of our own people just for not being up to the job.' He stopped and took out a packet of cigarettes. Amy and Beth paused as he lit up without offering one to Beth. Smoking in the street was unladylike and to do so would have been insulting.

'Y'know,' he said, walking on. 'With what he's had to endure since, maybe it would have been kinder had I not interfered.'

Amy exploded. 'Don't you dare say that! Sefton lived to save my grandmother's life and prove to the world that he wasn't a coward.'

'You're absolutely right and I apologise unreservedly,' said Franklyn, quickly and sincerely. Then he smiled at Amy's spirited defence of Sefton.

'If you want to do something really useful,' Beth said. 'You can get down to that police station and get Billy Eccles out of the lock-up. Young Billy was as big a hero as Sefton that night. He saved our Amy's life with his quick thinking and devilment – and the bobbies have locked him up because he pinched an omnibus to do it.'

'It was Godfrey Farthing's omnibus,' Amy explained. 'People say he's my grandfather, but he's not a proper grandfather. He made the police arrest Billy for theft. I don't think they really wanted to, but he's a magistrate.'

'We need a bit of influence to get the lad out,' added Beth addressing herself more to the impressive medal ribbons on his uniform than to him.

'Well,' smiled Franklyn. 'I'm not sure what influence I have, but my father's a member of the House of Lords. I'll tell him the story.'

Detective Inspector Gifford looked up at Sergeant Dicks. 'Another arson attack on the same night,' he mentioned, bleakly. 'Why the devil wasn't I told? Just because I don't wear a uniform doesn't mean you're not allowed to speak to me.'

'It, er, it wasn't on our patch, sir. It was over at Cottingley. I've just spoken to a sergeant on the blower, sir.'

'Blower, what's a blower?'

'It's what we call a telephone, sir. When I was in the Navy you had to blow dow–'

'I'm not interested in your naval exploits, Sergeant. Just tell me what you know.'

'The modus operandi was similar, sir.'

'Modus operwotsit? Speak English, man!'

'Yes, sir. The perpetrator used the same method in each attack. That is, he poured petrol through the letterbox and ignited it with a fuse made out of petrol-soaked rope.'

The inspector took out his pipe and began to load it with strong black shag. 'Hmmm. That's certainly how the Cinder Yard fire was started. And what time was this fire started?'

'One in the morning, sir. Less than an hour before the fire in Cinder Yard.'

The inspector was now enveloped in a cloud of acrid tobacco smoke that caused the sergeant to take a step back. 'And do you have anything else?' he enquired.

'No, sir – that is, yes, sir.'

'Which is it, yes or no?'

'It's probably nothing, sir. But the house in Cottingley belonged to a Mr Sykes who was Godfrey Farthing's solicitor – that's Godfrey Farthing the mill owner, sir.'

'And—?' The inspector's question came from within a foul smelling nebula that all but obscured him from the sergeant. Gifford waved away the smoke, as if it were put there by Dicks, and answered his own question. 'And the girl in the Cinder Yard fire is Farthing's grand-daughter. At least according to the *Bradford Daily Telegraph* she is. I wonder why they didn't report the other fire.'

'I believe they did, sir, the day before. The Cinder Yard fire missed the deadline for that day, sir.'

'How remiss of it.' Gifford puffed away, steadily, then looked up at Dicks who was standing there, uncertain of what to do. 'Well?' the inspector said. 'Don't you have a beat you should be pounding or something?'

'There is one other thing, sir. Godfrey Farthing pressed charges against William Eccles for stealing his omnibus and causing it to be destroyed by fire. We're holding the lad in custody.'

'Is this the same Billy Eccles who saved the Farthing girl's life?'

'Yes, sir – but the lad already has a criminal record. It wouldn't surprise me if he's our arsonist.'

'Perhaps you should have handed him over to us for questioning.'

'Well, we've been questioning him ourselves.'

'That's very helpful of you, Sergeant. Doing our job for us.'

His sarcasm passed over Dicks's head. 'Eccles was first on the scene,' said the sergeant, 'despite it being two in the mornin' – very suspicious, that. But when we ask him about the fire he simply gives us this cock and bull story about seeing someone running away just before the fire.'

'And have you got a description of this person?'

'Oh, we have more than a description, sir – and that's where young Eccles' story gets suspicious. He told us it was Hubert Heptonstall.'

'Hubert Heptonstall?'

'He's the young man who helped us with our enquiries the last time we locked young Eccles up, sir. So we have to take what the lad says with a large pinch of salt. A very large pinch indeed.'

'And have you asked this Hubert Heptonstall about his whereabouts on the night of the fire?'

'Er, no s–'

There was a knock on the door. A uniformed constable popped his head round and addressed himself to Sergeant

Dicks. 'A message has filtered down to us from the Chief Constable, Sergeant. It seems we're strongly advised to release the Eccles boy without charge.'

Inspector Gifford sat back in his chair and puffed on his pipe, luxuriously. 'Pity it took an instruction from the Chief Constable to drill a little common sense into you.' His voice was heavy with sarcasm. 'For God's sake, the lad's a hero! Tell you what, now that we have him in custody it'll do no harm to leave him where he is for the time being while we pick up this Heptonstall character. I want to see what he has to say for himself.'

'But we have no proof—' began the sergeant.

'Bugger that! Pick Heptonstall up and tell him you've got witnesses who saw him light the fires. Sound confident that you've got all the proof that you need. If he doesn't confess straight away we'll take another look at young Eccles.'

Billy was released within three hours with all charges dropped. As soon as Godfrey found out he went down to the police station to complain. Detective Inspector Gifford came to the desk and invited him into his office.

'We let young Eccles go because saving lives isn't a crime,' he said, sitting down at his desk and indicating for Godfrey to sit opposite. 'If I'm to be honest, Mr Farthing, I think you should be ashamed of yourself for pressing charges in the first place.'

'You are aware that I'm a magistrate.'

'I am. But far greater powers than you have been brought to bear in this matter.'

'Oh, what powers?'

'I'm not at liberty to say but you would be wise not to pursue the matter.' Inspector Gifford had other things to discuss and he wanted to make this pompous man as ill-at-ease as possible. Godfrey was annoyed at the policeman's tone.

'I had an expensive omnibus stolen and burnt out. If that's not a crime I don't know what is.'

'I'll tell you what a crime is, Mr Farthing,' said the inspector, coldly. 'Murder, that's a crime. The murder most foul of four innocent people. Mr and Mrs Sykes, their eighty-year-old mother – and Mr O'Keefe. Happily, with the help of young Billy Eccles, we have made an arrest.'

Farthing was startled for a second. He didn't know of Hubert's arrest. The game was afoot.

'Arrest?' he said, innocently. 'Murder? What does all this have to do with me?'

'Our prisoner says you put him up to it,' the inspector said, leaning forward and watching Godfrey's eyes to see what effect his words were having. Godfrey's eyes betrayed nothing. He slammed his fist on the table.

'This is preposterous! Who is this damned prisoner? Let me speak to him. John Sykes was not only my solicitor but a dear friend.'

The inspector was unimpressed by his protestations. 'It's odd,' he observed, 'that the two fires that night were both connected with you. One was your solicitor's house, the other was the house where your granddaughter lives.'

'I have no granddaughter.'

'All right,' said the inspector, who had been told about Godfrey disowning Amy. 'Your son's daughter – Bradford only had two house fires that night, each started within an hour of each other – one at your solicitor's house, one at your granddaughter's house. We have the person who admits to starting the fires and he says you paid him fifty pounds to do it. In fact he had that very fifty pounds on his person. Fifty pounds is a lot of money for anyone to carry about their person, let alone one of your own jobber lads, who I doubt earns much more than five shillings a week.'

'One of our jobber lads? What's his name?'

Gifford didn't answer, hoping that Godfrey might slip up and mention Hubert's name himself, thus incriminating himself.

'The lad's a liar!' stormed Godfrey. 'A fantasist, whoever he is. What's his name?'

'Come, come, Mr Farthing. Credit me with some intelligence. At least admit you must know the lad's name. Knowing your own employees' names is hardly going to land you in jail.'

It was a clumsy ploy and Godfrey didn't fall for it. 'I've got over three hundred employees,' he pointed out, 'and I know very few of their names. My job is to run a mill, not to know people's names.'

The inspector said nothing. He was sure Godfrey was behind the fires, but unless he slipped up it was going to be well nigh impossible to prove it. 'For what it's worth, Mr Farthing,' he said, 'I don't believe you. We've got the lad bang to rights. Four murders. He's singing like a canary. Scared to death in case they hang him – which in my opinion they will, despite his age. Why on earth would he make up a convoluted lie like this just to add perjury to his crimes and make himself look even worse in the eyes of the court?'

Godfrey narrowed his eyes and held up a finger, as though he'd just had an inspired thought. He knew what the inspector was trying to do and decided to play him at his own game. 'Perjury eh? As it happens I think I might be able to give you his name. I think I know a jobbing lad who's not averse to a bit of perjury to further his own ends. Told lies in court to get someone he had a grudge against locked up – common knowledge in the mill. The lad's got a big mouth apparently. In fact, now I come to think of it, the unfortunate boy who was locked up is the very same young man you've just let out – young Billy Eccles. You're right, of course. I shouldn't have pressed charges against him. What was I thinking of? It's just that my omnibus wasn't insured, you see – an oversight on my office manager's part, but it made me overreact.' He looked the inspector directly in the eye and said, unwaveringly: 'I'm talking about a jobbing lad called Hubert Heptonstall, Inspector. I personally sacked him on the day of the fires for the theft of a large sum of money that I never recovered. Are we, by any chance, talking about the same person?'

Frustration clouded the policeman's eyes. He knew Godfrey was lying. 'Can you prove this, Mr Farthing?'

'Prove it?' Godfrey sounded hurt. 'Of course I can prove it. Go to my mill and ask my manager.'

Chapter Ten

Mr Mathieson, the senior clerk at Sykes, Sykes and Broom gave Godfrey an emaciated smile as he sat down opposite and opened a thick file. A beam of dusty sunlight leaked through the unwashed office window and lit up the back of the clerk's wispy hair like a halo.

Godfrey was there to clear up a nagging doubt he had that John Sykes had left something in his father's file that shouldn't be there. He had asked if he could browse through the file himself but this nosey busybody insisted on helping him.

'Everything regarding your father's personal effects should be in here,' he sniffed. 'In fact there's an index of the file's contents.' He took out a sheet of paper and scrutinised it through the thick, scratched lenses of his spectacles. 'Two of the last three entries are regarding your father's wills.'

Godfrey's heart raced. If this idiot found something he shouldn't, what was the best thing to do? Snatch it from him and run – explain later after he had destroyed whatever it was? Better to snatch the whole file – leave nothing to chance. There wasn't much they could do, even if they wanted to. He put too much business their way for them to risk upsetting him. His hand was poised to grab the file as Mathieson read from the index.

'Will dated 4th February 1900 . . . just before my time all this . . . didn't start here until 1901 . . . Will dated 26th August 1900. Last entry, Samuel Farthing's Death Certificate. Hmmm . . . died September 20th 1901.' He peered at Godfrey and asked, tentatively, 'Why did he make a second will so soon after the first? Had he changed his mind about something?'

'A few minor bequests, if I remember rightly,' said Godfrey, casually.

He could have mentioned that the second will favoured Samuel's two grandsons, cutting Godfrey right out. He could have also mentioned that Mathieson's late boss had burned the only two copies of that will in return for money. What Godfrey hadn't realised was that there was a record of the second will's existence in the index. A record that should have been destroyed.

'There should still be a copy of his last will in here,' said Mathieson, riffling through the papers. 'Blessed if I can see it.'

Godfrey stiffened. According to John Sykes both copies had been burned. Godfrey himself had witnessed the burning. His hand hovered inches away from the file. If this idiot clerk pulled out the will Godfrey would have it off him in a flash – that and the file – and out of the door before the man knew what was happening.

'No,' said Mathieson, puzzled. Godfrey's poised hand relaxed. 'Two copies of the first will, no copy of the second.'

Godfrey breathed out a sigh relief. 'I believe I have two copies of the second will – somewhere,' he lied.

'Yes, that's what it says here. Two copies out to G.F.' He looked at Godfrey. 'I assume that's you, so one should be still on file – honestly, some people are so inefficient.'

'There were *three* copies?' said Godfrey, with ill-concealed alarm.

'Well, according to the index, there were. I don't know why. We usually only keep two.'

'But if there were three, there could be one lying around for anyone to see. I'm not happy about this, Mr Mathieson, not happy at all. This is downright incompetence!'

'Oh dear,' said Mathieson, wishing he'd kept his mouth shut about some people being so inefficient. 'I'm sure it was simply a clerical error.'

'You mean there aren't three wills after all?'

'Possibly, I mean – probably not. In fact I'd say most definitely not.'

Godfrey calmed down, realising that if his anger came to the notice of the partners it might raise unwanted curiosity about the will. Mathieson took off his spectacles, breathed on them and rubbed them vigorously with a handkerchief that was in need of a clean itself. 'Was there something specific you wanted to see?' he enquired, nervously, squinting at Godfrey through his unaided eyes.

Godfrey managed a casual shrug. 'Not really. I just wondered if there was any reason I couldn't take the file away for a while to have a good look at it. There might be something in it I find interesting. My father's estate was settled years ago. I'm sure the file's just gathering dust.'

Mathieson put his spectacles back on and blinked through them, disappointed that his lens cleaning hadn't improved his vision. 'I'll have to check with one of the partners but I see no reason why not. You'd have to sign for it. Was there anything else?'

'Your predecessor,' Godfrey mentioned, conversationally. 'Whatever happened to him?'

'Left and went up to Scotland, I believe. Edinburgh if I remember rightly. I understand he was from north of the border.'

'I heard he wasn't very bright.'

'Hmmm, well it's not what I've heard. I heard he went on to bigger and better things.'

'Remind me of his name.'

The clerk scratched his head. 'Oh, names, Mr Farthing. Now there's a thing. Now it was a familiar name if you get my meaning. It was a Scotch name, probably Mac something or other.' He scratched his thinning hair. 'Oh dear! I could ask Mr Sykes senior, I suppose.'

'Still call him Sykes senior eh?' mentioned Godfrey. 'Even after junior's dead.'

'Old habits, Mr Farthing . . . Burns,' he said, triumphantly. 'Robert Burns, as in the poet. I knew it was a Scotch name. How could I forget?'

It was with a feeling of unease that Godfrey instructed Josiah to drive him home. John Sykes had been lying about the clerk being a 'half idiot who didn't know what he was signing'. What else had he been lying about? Was there another copy of the will in existence? Probably not, but he couldn't afford the risk. The second will's sole surviving beneficiary had to go. He had already removed three of the threats, two by accident one by design. Although the tragic deaths of James and Henry had been deliberately engineered by him – if he cared to admit it to himself – he felt a certain sense of loss at their passing.

161

It was the price he had to pay for keeping what was right-fully his. It left him without an heir, but he had plans to remedy that. There was plenty of lead left in his pencil and a certain buxom young lady of his regular acquaint-ance had expressed her willingness to be sacrificed upon the altar of material gain. His money would guarantee her fidelity if she knew what was good for her. If not she'd be out in the streets before she knew it. She would be offered no affection, just bed and board until an heir came along – preferably a son, but it wasn't critical. The Farthing name meant little to him.

Chapter Eleven

Including his week in hand, O'Keefe had a two week's pay due to him. His erstwhile employers took it round to Beth who used it to tide her and Amy over until her next week's money came in. But she knew her wage wouldn't be enough to keep the two of them in any comfort.

'I'm sorry to have to ask this of you, Amy,' she said. 'But I think yer might have ter start work as a half-timer. Brammah's are taking on, at least they were last I heard. You'll have ter a get labour certificate from the education office, but your school attendance has been good so far, so I don't reckon you'll have any trouble. Your wage should just about pay the rent, my wage'll keep us in food and clothes. Mebbe even the odd treat – such as violin lessons.'

'But I haven't got a violin.'

Beth smiled and gave Amy a hug. 'As it happens there's one waiting for you in Blakey's in town. It's O'Keefe you have to thank. It took him three months to pay for it. I'm an old fool who didn't realise your violin playing was so precious to you.'

'It wasn't as precious to me as O'Keefe.'

'I know, love.'

So Amy began working as a half-time mill girl. Her first eight weeks were without pay, in return for being taught how to work a machine. She was given 6d a week pocket money with the prospect of earning 6s 4½d a week at the end of her training. She would start work at 6 a.m and go to school in the afternoon. The following week it would be vice versa, school in the morning and working from 1.30 until six in the evening. On Saturdays she worked from 6 a.m until one o'clock. It was a far cry from her comfortable life in America but she liked the people in the mill and she learned her trade a lot quicker then most. Life wasn't all that bad.

It would get worse.

Hubert Heptonstall was convicted of four murders and was destined to be the youngest person in England to be hanged since the turn of the century. He had pleaded guilty in the hope of being shown some clemency but such was the extent and deliberate nature of his crimes that this was a forlorn hope. He was hanged in Armley Prison, Leeds at 9 a.m on a rainy Friday in March 1918, the day before his eighteenth birthday. That same evening Inspector Gifford knocked on Beth's door. Rain was dripping from his Homburg hat as he stood on her step and introduced himself. It took her a few seconds to recognise him as the detective who had investigated the fire and O'Keefe's death.

'Won't you come in, Inspector. It's been a beggar of a day.'

'Worse for some than others,' said Gifford.

'What? Oh, I expect you mean young Heptonstall. I must say, I didn't feel good about him being hanged. What he did was wicked but–' She paused as she took his coat and hung it on a hook behind the door.

'But what, Mrs Crabtree?'

'There was just something about it that didn't fit. His family's all left Bradford; couldn't stand the shame I expect.'

'None of them ever went to visit him,' said the inspector. 'The lad was a gibbering idiot right at the end, so I'm told. Talking his head off. They had to gag him before they put the hood on. Everyone assumed he was talking gibberish, but I'm not so sure.'

Amy came into the room and smiled at the policeman. She wasn't like any mill girl he'd ever seen. She was more assured than most adult women of his acquaintance, and what's more she remembered who he was immediately.

'Inspector Gifford, how nice to see you. The kettle's nearly boiled, would you like a cup of tea?'

'I wouldn't mind at all,' he said. 'Nice and strong with a spoonful of sugar, if you have it. It doesn't matter if you haven't.'

'We have sugar, Inspector,' Beth assured him. 'We're not in the poor house yet.'

'I'm delighted to hear it. If you don't mind me saying so you seem to have come through your ordeals with a fortitude that's a credit to you both.'

'Thank you, Inspector,' said Beth. 'Won't you sit down and tell us why you've come.'

The inspector sat down in a nearly new leather armchair that had been given to Beth from the parish relief fund, along with other items of furniture. During the six months they'd lived there they had transformed it into a most pleasant dwelling with new wallpaper, curtains and a decent square of carpet. A warm fire burned in the Yorkshire range, above which was a mantelpiece carrying pictures of Amy's parents, O'Keefe, and Alfred Crabtree.

'I've come because of what I just said, Mrs Crabtree. I'm not at all sure that young Heptonstall *was* talking gibberish and, although I shouldn't be telling you this, feel honour bound to warn you both.'

'Warn us?' frowned Beth. She looked at Amy, who shrugged. 'Warn us about what?'

'Do you mind if I smoke my pipe?'

'Not at all.'

He worked at loading and lighting his pipe as he spoke. It seemed to help him with his thinking. 'Well,' he began. 'Were you aware of what young Heptonstall's other victims were?'

'Mr and Mrs Sykes,' remembered Amy, 'and Mr Sykes's mother.'

'And do you know who Mr Sykes was?'

'He was a solicitor.'

'Correct – but do you know whose solicitor he was?'

Beth shook her head as Amy went into the scullery to make the tea. Hubert's immediate plea of guilty had left the newspapers with little information about the background to the case. With British soldiers dying by the thousand every day a few local deaths wasn't exactly big news.

'He was Godfrey Farthing's solicitor.' Gifford lit his pipe and waited for the significance of his revelation to sink in. Amy picked up on it first and called out from the scullery, 'You mean my grandfather is the connection between the two houses that burned down?'

'Exactly, miss,' he called back. 'Not only that, but when I charged young Heptonstall with the crime he immediately blamed it all on Mr Farthing.'

'Didn't Hubert work for my grandfather?'

'I believe he did, but he had no connection with Mr Sykes.'

Amy found herself defending her grandfather and she didn't know why. He was an awful old man who had disowned her, but he was her father's father, that was why. 'Hubert had a habit of blaming other people for things he'd done,' she said. 'It was Hubert's lies that got Billy Eccles locked up.'

'That may be true. Unfortunately we've no evidence to support it.' Beth was now hanging on the inspector's every word. His pipe was now well lit and jammed into the right side of his mouth as he exhaled smoke from the left, leaving his hands free for gesticulation. 'But I'll tell you this,' he went on. 'I *believed* the lad. I make no excuse for him doing what he did, but there was neither rhyme nor reason to it – unless what he said was true. He told me Farthing had paid him fifty pounds to set fire to both houses. We found the fifty pounds on him.'

'Why didn't you arrest Farthing?' said Beth. There was anger mounting inside her now. In the scullery Amy had run out of arguments in her grandfather's defence and was pouring the tea into cups as she listened to the inspector.

'Because it was the lad's word against his, and Farthing had his story all ready. He reckons he'd sacked the lad that very day for stealing. His manager verified this. You know Farthing's a magistrate, don't you?'

'I *had* heard,' Beth said, scathingly.

'Thank you – the thing is,' said Gifford, taking a cup

167

of tea from Amy. 'I don't know why Farthing would want to do such a terrible thing, but if I'm right and he was behind it, it means the job possibly wasn't finished. It could be that he wanted one, or both of you, to end up as poor Mr Sykes ended up.'

'If it hadn't been for Billy and Sefton he'd have succeeded,' said Beth. 'My God! Do you really think Farthing was trying to kill us?'

'*Why* would he want to kill us?' said Amy, shocked at the very idea.

'I don't know,' said Inspector Gifford, scratching his head, 'any more than I know why he killed Sykes. I'm telling you this off the record because I think you have a right to know. But as far as the law is concerned the case is closed, and I would be really obliged if you didn't mention to anyone that I'd told you this. It could get me into deep trouble.'

'Well, I feel I should mention it to Mrs Earnshawe,' said Beth. 'She's evidently been in a bit of a state since her Sefton got killed. I've heard she's gone a bit funny in the head, to be honest. I feel a bit sorry for her.'

'You can tell who you like just as long as my name isn't involved.'

That evening Beth sat and listened to her granddaughter playing Chopin on her violin. Amy had said nothing about the inspector's visit. She silently refused to believe her grandfather had tried to kill her. Beth saw behind her silence and thought better of talking about it. Amy's eyes were fixed on the music on the stand but her thoughts were many miles away.

'I don't know much about that sort of music,' Beth said, 'but it sounds beautiful.'

'Thank you. Miss Small's a good tutor.'

'Go on, play me some of that gypsy music that Miss Small doesn't like.' Beth looked around the room and shielded her mouth with her hand as though the tutor could see her.

Amy hadn't played the violin for over two years but she had easily picked up where she left off and had been taking lessons for six months. Her tutor, Miss Dotty Small from Glasshouse Street considered Amy a real talent and bemoaned the fact that she had missed so many years of tuition.

But sometimes Amy found classical music to be a chore and turned her hand to gypsy violin music that she'd heard on a phonograph in Blakey's music shop. On Saturday afternoons she quite often went in there to browse and listen, then come home and play the music from the sheets she had bought. She replaced the Chopin with a gypsy violin concerto, and launched into a wild and vigorous tune that had Beth clapping her hands in delight.

'Hey, Amy, yer know that feller what carries a cross about, looking like Jesus?' Billy was standing on her doorstep, his face alive with enthusiasm, as it always was.

'I think so.'

'Well, he's up on Daisy Hill, givin' a show. There's loads o' people going. D'yer fancy it?'

'Why not? I'm going out with Billy, grandma,' Amy called out over her shoulder.

'Don't be late for your tea.'

'I won't.'

It was Saturday afternoon and any trip out with Billy was sure to be fun.

*

The bearded evangelist plied his trade beside a huge wooden cross that appeared to be resting on his shoulder but was in fact supported by a cleverly hinged plank of wood that neatly concealed itself within his biblical robe. A sad-faced, whiskery, old woman was reluctantly dressed in similar garb except that hers were more rags than robes. She was playing 'Jesu, Joy of Man's Desiring' on a slide trombone. Behind the pair was a sign proclaiming the man to be the Reverend Elias Mudd of the Church of the Divine Wind. He spoke above the music.

'I am the way, the truth and the life, sayeth the Lord. And what is the truth? The truth is that the Lord saved this brave woman's life and showed her the way. She came to me in torment just three days ago, stricken with the ague and not knowing what to do with her life. All she had in this world was her grandfather's trombone, that she knew not how to play. Which is when I felt the strength of the Lord upon me. Telling me to pass His strength on to the woman and lo, the ague is miraculously cured – do you hear her playing, my dear brethren? Do you hear the wonderful music pouring from this instrument. Is this the playing of a woman who had never played a note in her life until the day she met the Lord through me?'

The woman was blushing with shame and tried not to return anyone's gaze.

'I thank the Lord for the gift He gave to me. That same gift I passed on to this woman through my hands. I know not how it is done, my dear brethren, but it is not mine to question the Lord and his mysterious ways.'

Amy spotted a woman in the crowd calling out, 'Alleluia!' The evangelist, who was paying for two, waited for a man to do the same. 'Alleluia!' shouted the man,

170

on cue. Elias continued, as the trombone played on. A bent and tearful woman shuffled up to him and, leaning heavily on a stick, looked up at him. Both Amy and Billy recognised her as the alleluia woman.

'It's me back, yer reverence,' the woman said. 'Can yer do owt about me back? I haven't been able ter stand up straight fer twenty years.'

'That's right,' came a voice from the back – the alleluia man. Amy and Billy grinned. Surely the crowd wouldn't fall for this. But it seemed they did.

Elias placed a hand on the old woman's head and said what could have been a silent prayer. The trombonist looked away and played on. The crowd watched in fascination.

After a full minute the old woman took a step away from the evangelist, her back still bent. The crowd's initial disappointment turned into amazement as she tried to straighten up. Elias hushed them with a raised hand as they all silently willed the old woman onwards and upwards.

'You can do it, Florence!' shouted the alleluia man. 'Have faith. Alleluia.'

More alleluias followed, unpaid ones at that, as the woman slowly straightened up, inch by painful inch. Finally she stood erect just as the trombone woman moved on to 'Ode To Joy'.

The old woman's walking stick clattered on to the cobbled street as she turned to face the crowd who were now surging past her. Above their heads Elias's hand was held up high.

'Please, dear brethren,' he called out. 'I will do what I can. Some will be cured today, some tomorrow, others next week, some not at all. I am not a miracle worker. I just do what I can. There are people in this world who require more monetary help, and it is for those unfortunate people that I pass this hat among you.'

He picked up his top hat and gave it to the deliriously upright old woman who dropped her purse into it then carried it around the crowd. A man dropped a shilling into it then stepped up to Elias. He wasn't the alleluia man and Amy guessed he was the genuine article.

'Lumbago,' the man said. 'Can yer do owt about lumbago?'

'Can you pray, my son?' enquired the evangelist, piously resting a hand on the man's head.

'Aye, I reckon I just about can.'

They said a faltering Lord's Prayer as a queue formed. Others in the queue prayed as well. The trombone was now playing 'When I Survey The Wondrous Cross'. As the prayer came to an end Elias said, 'Amen,' and lifted his hand theatrically from the man's head. Amy and Billy were confident that the man would denounce Eli as a charlatan.

'Bugger me!' said the man. 'If it's not gone.'

The good news passed down the queue and there was a healthy tinkling as the hat filled up more rapidly.

'Don't just stand there,' said an impatient woman to the cured man. 'There's others with ailments as well. It's me knees, yer reverence,' she said to Elias. 'I'm a martyr ter me bloody knees.'

One by one the patients stood before him for their cure. Some went away happy, others disappointed but hopeful that they might have been given the delayed-action cure he'd mentioned. Maybe tomorrow, maybe next week – maybe never.

They could have stayed there all day and all night,

As Amy went to fill the kettle, Eli rubbed his chin between thumb and forefinger, as though adding up the years. 'Seven months,' he said. 'But I bring more contentment and well-being than most men of the cloth.'

'I imagine you do,' she replied, coming back into the room and sitting down. 'And what did you do before that?'

Eli sat down opposite. 'I was given to understand you are only thirteen years old,' he said. 'Why do I feel intimidated by you?'

'I just want to know what I'd be letting myself in for if I was ever foolish enough to go along with you, Mr Mudd. By the way, you didn't answer my question.'

'Did I not?'

'No, you did not.'

'I was mainly an actor. A very good actor if I may say so.'

'You may and I would believe you.'

'But I was a man who couldn't resist the temptation of the wager. A vice that kept me in permanent penury.'

'What sort of wager?'

'Oh, cards, race horses, cockfighting, the gaming tables. Had it not been for my ordination into the Church of the Divine Wind I would have been a lost soul. I won my parish in a card game from the former encumbent who really wasn't up to the job. The evangelical world needs a certain flair – this man was from Cleckheaton and whoever heard of an evangelist from Cleckheaton?'

Amy conceded that she had never heard of such a thing, but added, 'It seems an odd way to become a vicar. I always thought there was more to it than the turn of a card.'

'Oh – chacun à son goût.'

'Pardon?'

'It means each to his own thing. My thing was playing cards. Others prefer the more spiritual route. But sometimes a man of the world, such as me, can take a more balanced view of life than those who have led the cloistered existence.'

'And what's your balanced view of my life?' Amy asked. 'I'm thirteen years old and the only person in the world who gives a damn about me is in prison. If I don't pay the rent on this house my grandma won't have a home to come back to. I wonder if she thought of that?' She looked at Eli. 'Am I being hard on her, Mr Mudd?'

'I would prefer it if you called me Eli – and my balanced view of your grandmother is that she is unbalanced at the moment. Who was Mr O'Keefe?'

'He was a waiter on the *Lusitania*. He and I saved each other's lives. My parents both drowned and he came to live with us. On the day of the fire he had proposed to my grandma.'

'That's a mighty story, albeit somewhat sketchy. Perhaps you'll fill me in the details at a later date. I take it your grandmother believes this Farthing fellow was trying to kill the two of you as well?'

Amy shrugged. 'She's willing to believe anything bad about him.'

'Unlike you?'

She gave a shrug. 'Blood's thicker than water. He's my grandfather. My father was his son – Grandma is my mum's mother. I'm related to them both, but they're not related to each other.'

'Your grandfather – was he now? As fascinating as it is confusing. The plot thickens and my mind is in a whirl, dear girl. I must say, Farthing seems a very poor class of grandparent.'

Steam was drifting into the room from the boiling kettle. As Amy got up to make the tea Eli's eyes settled on her violin in the corner. 'Who's the musician?' he asked.

'Me, sort of. I've been taking lessons since I was three. O'Keefe bought me that. It's a real good one. Do you take sugar?'

'No sugar, no milk, thank you. Tell me, can you play hymns?'

'If I have the music I can play pretty much anything.'

Eli conjured up an image of Amy, orphaned survivor from the *Lusitania*, with honest dirt on her face, dressed in appealing rags and playing sweet music on the violin as he gave of his all to the assembled crowd. Far better than an aging trombone player. He had stumbled on a gold mine.

The following afternoon Amy was studiously writing when a police constable knocked on the classroom door and entered without waiting for an invitation. He was accompanied by a severe-looking woman. Her hair was piled up in a bun on the top of her head and she wore a black coat and button-up boots. Both she and the policeman glanced around the class, causing the pupils to look down lest they became the object of these searching eyes.

'Can I help you, constable?' asked the teacher, annoyed at this rude interruption.

'We're looking for Amy Farthing.'

'Why, what has she done?' The teacher sounded defensive. Amy was one of her favourite pupils and she couldn't think of any reason why she might be of interest to the police.

185

'She hasn't done anything. We need to have a word with her. It's to do with her grandmother.'

'Oh, dear,' said the teacher, concerned. 'Farthing, come to the front of the class.'

'Is Grandma OK?' called out Amy as she stepped forward, desperately worried. 'Have they done something to her?'

The constable gave an embarrassed cough. 'Well, she's all right in herself, it's just that—'

'It's just that she's been sent to prison as well you know,' cut in the severe-looking woman. 'Which means we need to find someone to look after you. You'll have to come with us.'

'I don't need anyone to look after me. I can look after myself.'

The teacher took Amy's hand and led her out of the classroom. 'Thank you for being so tactful,' she fumed at the woman. 'What are you going to do with her?'

'I'm not going with her,' said Amy, resolutely. 'I don't need anyone to look after me.'

'And just how will you pay the rent and feed and clothe yourself, girl?' said the woman.

'I have a half-time job.'

'Not any longer, you haven't. Your labour certificate has been rescinded. In any case a half-time job is insufficient to pay for your needs.'

'Just what are you going to do with her?' repeated the teacher.

The woman placed a custodial hand on Amy's shoulder and inserted herself between girl and teacher. 'We'll do the best we can. Unfortunately there's war on and the homes and orphanages are bursting at the seams with much more worthy cases than this one. There's a vacancy in a children's home in Huddersfield, which is where she'll be taken until her grandmother is released from prison and is deemed a fit and proper person to take care of the child.'

The policeman, who also took exception to the woman's tone, said to Amy, 'Are there any belongings you want to pick up from home, love?'

Amy couldn't think. She was reduced to tears now.

'We'll call round,' decided the policeman. 'There's bound to be a few bits and bobs.'

The severe woman, whose name Amy never learned, accompanied her in silence on the bus to Huddersfield where she was deposited in Kirkheaton Road Girls' Home. Amy had with her O'Keefe's seaman's bag and her violin. Both of which were taken from her as soon as she arrived. She was greeted by one of the largest women Amy had ever seen.

'There'll be no call for violin playing in here,' said the large woman. 'We don't want our girls thinking they're better than they ought to be, what with going round playing violins and the like.'

Some of the girls came to stare. They all wore the same. Boots, black stockings and dark-blue pinafore dresses.

'You'll call me Mother,' said the woman. 'Because to all intents and purposes that's what I am from now on. Now take off what you're dressed in and put these on.'

She handed Amy a bag of clothes. 'Do you have a name?'

'Amy Farthing.'

'Well, Amy Farthing, to me and the staff you'll be number twenty-seven. If the other girls want to call you

Amy that's up to them. We've got enough to think about. Are you deaf, girl? I said take off your clothes and get changed.'

Amy looked around at the sniggering girls. 'What, here?' she asked.

'What's the matter?' said Mother. 'Don't tell me you've got something we've never seen before.'

Amy stripped down to the new underwear that Beth had bought her only a week ago. She made to put on the pinafore dress.

'And the rest,' commanded Mother. The girls sniggered again. 'We have no favourites here. You all wear the same, then there's no jealousy.'

Blushing now, Amy got completely undressed and put on the coarse underwear, grimacing at its abrasiveness. Mother smiled, coldly. 'Not what you're used to, eh? Well, it's my way to get you girls used to discomfort, then it won't come as such a shock when you get sent out into the wide world. By the way, where d'you get that accent from?'

'America,' said Amy. 'That's where I was born. My parents died when the *Lusitania* went down. I was rescued.'

If she said it to elicit sympathy she was in for a disappointment. '*Lusitania*?' said Mother. 'Did your mam and dad work on board?'

'No, they were passengers.'

It was the wrong answer. 'Passengers?' remarked Mother. 'My word, girls, number twenty-seven's a toff. Passenger on the *Lusitania*. I don't know whether to bow or curtsy.'

Amy stood there in her ill-fitting clothes, feeling desperately miserable. The policeman had told her that her grandmother had been arrested for insulting a magistrate and that it wouldn't have been so bad had the magistrate not been Godfrey Farthing.

'He's my grandfather,' Amy had told him.

'I know, love,' the policeman said. 'But apparently it makes no odds. Your grandmother's been found guilty of contempt of court. It'll be three months afore she's out. Even then they might not think her a fit person to look after you.'

So Amy wasn't feeling well disposed towards her grandmother, and certainly had no sympathy for her being locked up in a prison. It couldn't be any worse than this place – and she was the one who had caused it all. 'What do I do now?' she asked Mother.

'I'll tell you what you do now. You look at the clothes you're wearing and be grateful to have them. Then you look closer and you will see that they are spotlessly clean, because in my book cleanliness is next to godliness. What is cleanliness, girls?'

'Next to godliness, Mother,' chanted the watching girls.

'Every Sunday there will be an inspection,' continued Mother. 'If I see so much as a speck of dirt I will reward you with a taste of this.' She produced a thin bamboo cane from under her voluminous skirt and swished the air with it. 'If I hear a dirty word from your mouth or see a dirty gesture or if I suspect you are thinking dirty thoughts, your reward will be the same.' She swished her cane again. 'Do I make myself clear number twenty-seven?'

'Yes, miss,' said Amy.

The cane flashed and struck her on her shoulder. 'I am to be called Mother!' thundered Mother, who didn't look a bit like anyone's mother to Amy.

189

'Sorry, Mother,' she said, rubbing her shoulder.

'I should think you are.' Mother took an oval badge, bearing the number twenty-seven, from her pocket and pinned it on the front of Amy's dress. For the first time Amy noticed that everyone wore one.

'You wear this at all times except when you are at school. Your bed is bed twenty-seven, your chair in the dining room is chair twenty-seven, when you line up for meals or assembly of any kind you are twenty-seventh in line. Do you understand that, number twenty-seven?'

'Yes, Mother,' said Amy, miserably.

'I have made arrangements for you to be taught at the local school. If I hear bad reports from the school you will be rewarded with this.' Another swish of the cane.

A strident bell sounded, quickly followed by a clattering of booted feet as girls seemed to appear from all over the building and lined up at a door marked DINING ROOM. Amy waited until the queue had assembled, picked out the twenty-sixth girl in the queue and then stood immediately behind her. Then a latecomer arrived and took up position two in front, so Amy moved forward a place.

'Hey! What ye think your doin' shovin' in front o' me?' The girl who was now behind her pulled Amy's hair, causing her to shout, 'Ow, that hurts!'

She had scarcely got her words out when she heard the swishing of the cane. This time it hit her on her arm. Mother had appeared in front of her as if by magic.

'I hope we haven't got a troublemaker here,' she snapped. 'Are you a troublemaker, number twenty-seven?'

'No, Mother.'

'I should hope not. Here we are, providing you with board and lodgings and all you want to do is make trouble.'

Amy said nothing. It seemed the best course of action with this unreasonable woman, who loomed over her like some gruesome monolith. The door to the dining room opened. Someone at the front shouted, 'By the left – march!'

It took Amy just a few seconds to realise what was happening. She skipped a couple of times to get into step and marched into the dining room, along with what seemed like a hundred girls of all ages from six to sixteen. In fact there were fifty-five but the home was supposed to house only thirty.

The girl who had pulled her hair sat immediately to her left. 'Thanks for getting me into trouble,' muttered Amy.

'Sorry, kid,' said the girl, who was a similar age to her. 'Thanks for not telling on me. They call me Daisy; what's your name?'

'Amy.'

By the end of the evening meal, which consisted of potatoes mashed up with swede and margarine, a slice of dried bread and a glass of milk, Amy had learned more than she wanted to know about this home and vowed to herself to run away at the first opportunity. She learned of the daily drill, the early rising, the cold baths, cruel discipline, inedible food, obsessive cleanliness, mopping, scrubbing, sweeping – and the way they were all treated as second-class citizens, despite the fact that most of the girls had fathers who had died fighting for their country.

'It's the third one I've been in,' said Daisy. 'They're all the same. Bloody awful places.'

'Doesn't anyone ever run away?'

'Loads of 'em. Most of 'em come back because they've nowhere ter go to. Have you got somewhere ter go?'

'No,' said Amy, after some thought. 'I haven't.'

'Pity,' said Daisy. 'I'd have come with yer. D'yer snore?'

'I don't think so.'

'Good. Me an' you'll be sharin' a bed. Top ter tail's the best way, unless yer fart. Yer don't fart do yer? The last lass in my bed farted like a foghorn. I didn't top ter tail with her. Me dad were killed wi' mustard gas. I reckon I'd have gone t' same road if she hadn't have left.'

'I thought I'd be getting a bed of my own.'

'Yer might, when yer've been here about six months. I've only been here three.'

'I won't be here six months.'

'That's what they all say.'

'Is there anything good about this place?'

'Not much. We have a few laughs now and again when t' bosses aren't listening. God help yer if they hear yer laughing. They'll think yer laughing at them – which we are most of t' time. If Fat Arse hears yer laughin' it's six of the best.'

'Fat Arse?'

'Mother – her real name's Mrs Fatorini. She married an Italian. We call her Fat Arse, but not to her face.'

That night Amy slept top to tail with Daisy, although she didn't sleep very much. A younger, smaller version of Mother came into the dormitory. It was customary for the girls to kneel beside their beds and pray to the Lord for the kindness they were having bestowed upon them. Amy, not realising this, was still folding her clothes as the others were praying. After the prayer the woman pointed a quivering cane at her.

'Which one are you?'

'Er, Amy Farthing, miss.'

'I don't want to know your name. What is your number?'

'Er, twenty-seven, miss.'

'You will attend punishment.'

'Punishment – why, miss?'

'I will not tell you why. You must find out why for yourself. Step out the girls down for punishment.'

Three other girls stepped out, each gave their number and the name of the person who had ordered them to be punished. Daisy was one of them. In turn they bent over a cupboard, pulled down their drawers and presented their bare backsides for punishment. They each received three vicious strokes of the cane.

'Now you, girl.'

Amy hesitated. Not so much that she was scared but because she thought it to be so wrong. Then, realising she had no option, she stepped up to the cupboard and received her punishment. The cane cut deep into her skin and it was all she could do not to cry out. But none of the other girls had, so Amy held it in.

'What did you do?' she asked Daisy when the woman had turned out the lights and left them with a threat of punishment ringing in their ears should they not be quiet.

'I put two spoons of sugar in me tea. We're only allowed one. It's rationed, see. I thought I might get away with it.'

'Does it hurt?' Amy enquired. 'Mine hurts like mad.'

'She really laid it on fer you,' said Daisy. 'She allus does fer new lasses.'

The other girls had begun sobbing after the woman left, but they were both much younger.

'I think it's cruel,' Amy said. 'Those other two are so young.'

'I've had worse,' said Daisy. 'It's worse when Fat Arse's husband does it. I allus think there's summat funny about a feller what hits lasses on their bare arse, don't you? I don't think she knows he does it, but he does.'

'He's not going to hit me on my bare ass. I'll tell on him.'

'Oh aye – an' how much bother d'yer think that'll get yer in?'

Amy had no idea. The only idea she had was to get out of this place as soon as possible. If she could get to Billy she knew he'd help.

It seemed as though she had only just dropped off to sleep when her slumber was disturbed by a loud bell. Daisy was out of bed in an instant.

'What time is it?' Amy asked.

'It'll be six o'clock. We're first in t' bath today. Lucky us, eh? Come on.'

Most of the girls in the dormitory were forming a queue at the door. Amy followed Daisy straight past the queue and into a room containing six deep, cast-iron baths. A woman in a white overall was filling the last bath with water from a hose pipe. All the others were filled. There was an ominous lack of steam in the room.

The girls all took off their nightdresses, hung them on a numbered hook and lowered themselves gingerly into a bath. Two to each one. The water looked extremely uninviting.

Daisy and Amy waited until the woman had filled the last bath. Daisy stepped in and sat down with her arms crossed, as if for warmth. Amy followed. The water was icy. She stood there hesitantly for a second then shouted out as the woman aimed the jet of water directly at her.

'Builds character,' she chortled as Amy sat down. Then

she went round each bath and dropped in two lumps of carbolic soap. 'Right girls, you got five minutes ter wash all last night's sins off yer filthy skin.'

That five minutes seemed like five hours to Amy. She and the other girls got out, dried themselves on flimsy, abrasive towels and hurried back to the dormitory to get dressed. For the next hour she and six other girls scrubbed floors before going back to the washroom to wash their hands and faces, then they lined up in number order to march into breakfast.

The staff sat at a long table, elevated above the others. Mother and her husband sat in the middle. He was older than she, jowly, bald and mean faced. On either side of them sat three women, one of whom had caned Amy the night before. None of the women looked as though they could summon up a smile. Amy sat down next to Daisy.

'How can you stand it here?' she asked. 'It's like being in the worst prison. It wouldn't surprise me if they gave us gruel, like in Oliver Twist.'

A voice from a serving hatch shouted, 'Table two.'

'That's us,' said Daisy. 'Get in line or yer'll get yer arse reddened again ternight.'

Amy got in line and shuffled forward with the others. A woman in an off-white apron ladled stodgy porridge into her dish, then she held out her cup for tea to be poured into it from an urn. Beside the urn was a large bowl of sugar and a small spoon. Amy decided not to risk it. While she was here she'd drink her tea without sugar.

The porridge was just about edible and the tea tasted strong but OK. The worst thing about the breakfast was the smell of eggs and bacon coming from the staff table.

After fifteen minutes a bell sounded and the girls arose to let the second sitting in. A car door slammed outside and some of the girls looked out of the window.

'What is it, girl?' called out Mother.

'It's a vicar, miss – and a nun and a feller in uniform. They're coming in.'

'Then run along and tell them to wait in my office.'

'Yes, Mother.'

Amy's heart lightened as she heard the unmistakeable sound of Eli's voice booming along the corridor. He stopped at the dining-room door and gallantly allowed the nun to enter first. Then he stepped in and surveyed the room as though he owned it.

'Splendid!' he boomed.

He was wearing a shirt of ecclesiastical purple, glistening white dog collar, dark morning coat, black trousers and highly polished shoes. He removed a homburg hat to reveal well groomed hair and beard. Amy was impressed. He had gone to enormous trouble. All this, and the expensive motor car parked in full view of the window plus the small entourage identified him as a churchman to be reckoned with, not some bumbling country vicar.

Mother got to her feet. 'I asked the girl to, er – to ask you to wait in my office.'

'And so she did, madam, so she did. But I'm in a deuce of a hurry so I took the liberty of pursuing my business post-haste as it were. By the way, how rude of me not to introduce myself. Reverend Elias Mudd at your service, madam.'

He neither shook her hand nor asked her to introduce herself. It was as if her identity was of no interest to him.

196

'Er – what is your business, might I ask?' enquired Mother, uncertainly. She lowered her gaze under the force of his glare.

There was complete silence. Suddenly the person in command of this room was no longer Mother, but this vicar. It made a welcome change.

'My niece is my business, madam. I understand she has been seized from her home in Bradford and brought here. Her grandmother was recently placed in custody for being in contempt of a most contemptible court. I am here to check on her welfare.'

'Your niece? I didn't realise any of the girls here were related to—'

'Related to anyone, I imagine, poor girls,' said Eli. 'Innocent victims of a cruel war. I trust they are being well cared for here.'

'We do our best,' said Mother, casting a warning eye around the room to curtail any contradiction.

The nun walked slowly between the tables and the man in uniform – a chauffeur's uniform – stood by the door, as if guarding it.

'Do the children look well cared for, Sister Agnes?' Eli called out. 'Can we go back to the diocese and report that all is well with the girls here?'

Amy got to her feet. 'All is not well, Uncle Elias.'

'Amy,' called out Eli. His face broke into a wide beam. 'How are you, my dear?'

'I'm not well at all, Uncle.'

'And how is that?'

'I've been here just one day and I've been cruelly beaten, dressed in ghastly clothing, made to take a freezing bath and scrub floors. And the food here isn't fit for pigs, unless you happen to be sitting at that table.' She pointed,

197

accusingly, at the staff table. 'They had eggs and bacon and we've had a plateful of slop.'

'Dear me!' exclaimed Eli. 'This cannot be. Tell me this isn't so, madam. Surely these poor children have suffered enough without you adding to their woes.'

One of the younger girls had burst into tears and was being comforted by the nun. Amy recognised her as one of the girls who had been beaten the night before. Mother was speechless. She sat down and muttered something to her husband. He shook his head and she turned away from him in disgust.

'He gets the girls to bare their bottoms then he beats them with a cane!' Amy pointed, accusingly, at the Mother's husband.

Mother sprang to her feet and cried, 'That's a damned lie!'

'It isn't a lie,' shouted Amy. 'He's her husband. He shouldn't be allowed to do that.'

A timid voice said, 'He did it to me once, Mother.'

'And me,' said Daisy.

'And me.'

Half the girls in the room were claiming to have been similarly treated. Mother's face went white. She sat down again. The rest of the staff looked distinctly uncomfortable. Eli's face was like stone and it seemed to Amy that he wasn't acting.

'I will be removing my niece here and now,' he thundered. 'And you, madam, if you have grain of decency, will attend to the decadence of this—' he looked at Mother's husband with an expression of deep disgust '—this loathsome creature.'

Mother jabbed her husband in the ribs with her considerable elbow. 'Get out,' she hissed. 'I knew you were up to something with the girls.'

He got up and left. Amy was by Eli's side now. 'I need my things,' she said, her eyes fixed accusingly on Mother. 'She took my violin from me.'

'Another sacrilege,' said Eli, angrily. 'Denying a talented girl the means to express herself. Madam, I shall have to report you to the appropriate authorities. It wouldn't surprise me if you end up incarcerated yourself, along with your husband.'

'Oh, surely, Reverend, there'll be no need for that,' whined Mother. 'We're desperately overcrowded here – overcrowded and understaffed. I have to impose strict discipline or the girls would run riot.'

The girls looked on, open mouthed. She seemed powerless and human and scared – and they liked it.

'Discipline's one thing, madam,' thundered Eli. 'But unwarranted cruelty and perversion – now there's another thing altogether.'

'Well, now you've pointed it out to us I think we can be a bit more lenient with the girls, can't we, ladies?' pleaded Mother. She turned to her staff for support and was rewarded by a row of vigorously nodding heads. They all knew of her husband's bare-bottom smacking, but none had dared mention it to her. Some suspected he had done worse.

'I would be failing in my duty if I didn't report my findings to the authorities,' Eli said. Amy tugged at his sleeve, urging him not to push his luck. One of the staff got to her feet. She was younger than the others and was taking grave offence at him.

'I'll thank you not to tar us all with the same brush as him,' she snapped, jabbing her thumb in the direction of the departed husband. 'It isn't easy. We have far too many girls to take care of. We do things our way. I admit we should have reported him for what he had been doing but–'

'There's no "buts" about it,' interrupted Eli. 'Will someone get my niece's belongings, I don't wish her to stay here a moment longer than she has to.'

'If you're sending her to a church home,' persisted the young teacher, 'I think she'll find the discipline even stricter than here.'

'That's nothing to be proud of,' growled Eli. 'She will stay in the presbytery until her grandmother is released.' He glared at Mother, then gradually allowed his anger to subside. 'Madam,' he said, shaking his head, 'unless you give me your word that the inhuman treatment of these young ladies will cease forthwith I will do my utmost to see you brought before the courts. And I can assure you that I am a man of considerable influence.'

'Oh, you have my word of honour, Reverend,' said Mother, unable to conceal her relief.

'Good. I will leave you to deal with your unspeakable husband in your own way.'

'Oh, he will be dealt with, Reverend, you can be assured of that,' she told him, with deep sincerity.

'In that case, as I am in the business of forgiveness I will not take any action personally other than to alert the authorities to keep a sharp ear open for any complaints.' He turned to the girls. 'Did you hear that, girls? The authorities will be on the lookout for any complaints about this establishment. So, if you make a complaint it will be taken very seriously. Tell your teacher at school or anyone you can think of.'

'They're a shower o' proper evil bastards if you ask me,' said the nun as they drove out of the gate. She took off her wimple and lit a cigarette.

'Well said, Florence,' remarked Eli. Then to Amy, 'Oh, by the way, this is Florence and our chauffeur is her husband, Norman Attercliffe. They help me out from time to time.'

'I think I might have seen you before, shouting alleluia,' grinned Amy.

'They're the ones,' chortled Eli. 'Best Alleluia Chorus in the business. How would you like to join us, Amy? Our trombone player has gone to join a travelling circus.'

'As the bearded lady,' sniggered Norman.

'Don't be unchristian, Norman,' chastised Eli.

'Won't someone find out what you've done and send me back?' asked Amy.

'There's hundreds o' kids gone on the run from these homes,' said Norman. 'No one ever bothers goin' after 'em. It's not as though they're criminals or nowt. I ought ter know, I went on the run meself when I was twelve. Got a job on the chimneys. Ran away from that as well. Climbed up from the fireplace, out on to the roof, down the drainpipe and away.' He laughed at the memory. 'I reckon that miserable boss of mine thinks I'm still up there.'

'I hardly think anyone at that foul home is going to make any noises,' Eli declared, confidently. 'No, I think they'll be keeping their heads down hoping there will be no repercussions. By the time your absence comes to the notice of the authorities your grandmother will have been home for many months, if not years. Well done, by the way at picking up on my act with no prior warning. Such talent tells me you're a natural and should join the show without further ado.'

'What about school?'

'I'm afraid we dare not risk your returning to school,

that might be tempting providence. But, if I'm not mistaken will you not be fourteen very soon and of school leaving age?'

'I'll be fourteen in July.' She counted the months on her fingers. 'About three months.'

'You'll learn more with me in those three months than you will at school in three years.'

'That's for sure,' said Norman. 'By the way, who's job is it ter take this car back?' He adjusted his mirror and looked at Amy. 'The Reverend Elias borrowed it on a day's approval yesterday. I reckon it'll be my job ter take it back and explain why the Reverend doesn't wish to buy it.'

'Tell them it's a bit too racy for a clergyman of my nervous demeanour,' advised Eli. 'That should do the trick.'

Amy looked out at the passing countryside and wondered what she was letting herself in for.

Chapter Thirteen

March/April 1918

Beth was sharing a cell with a prostitute and a pickpocket. Both were serving much longer sentences than she, and in Beth's eyes they deserved all they got, but she didn't tell them that. The story of her performance in court had reached Ashinghurst Women's Prison and it did her reputation with the prisoners no harm at all. The prison staff looked upon her as a potential troublemaker who would need taming before she got above herself.

She was placed on C Wing which was staffed by a mixture of male and female officers. Bog Nose was the sobriquet of the senior warder on the wing. He wore the expression of a man with a permanent bad smell under his nose. In fact what he had under his nose was a stained moustache and foul breath. Beth's cellmates, in exchange for certain favours, such as cushy jobs in the kitchen, rewarded him with the only favours it was in their power to bestow.

In Beth's opinion he couldn't have got a woman any other way so it came as a surprise to her, therefore, when she found out he was married – it occurred to her that this might be used against him should the necessity arise.

Even if she had felt so inclined she was never given the opportunity to offer her body in return for a plum job in the prison offices. There had been a time many years ago when she had been asked to be nice to a man in return for favours. Her refusal that time had blighted her whole life, but she wouldn't do any different if she could have her time over again.

Bog Nose came to see her in the mailbag room and made it quite plain why her services weren't required. 'Thirty years ago, mebbe,' he sniggered. 'But not now. I'm a bit fussy where I put it. I don't shag dried-up old bags like you.'

Beth shot him a look of disgust. 'Go away from me. You stink like a pig.'

He sidled up close to her and spoke into her ear; his breath was rancid and made her cover her nose. 'Just for that,' he sniggered, 'I'll put you in the same cell as Fat Hilda. She prefers women to men. She'll make your three months seem like three years – if you survive, that is.'

Fat Hilda was a twenty-stone prostitute, by far the most vile woman in the prison. Beth inwardly shuddered, but continued sewing. The man was a pig and life wouldn't be worth living in this place if she didn't get the better of him. It was time to test his vulnerability.

'I wonder what your wife would say if she knew what you got up to at work,' she said calmly, biting off the end of a thread and throwing the finished bag on a pile.

'My wife – what's my wife got to do with anything. You leave my wife out of it and mind your own business, or else I'll mind it for you.'

Beth played her trump card early; it was the only card

she'd got, so it had better work. 'If you put me in with Fat Hilda I'll change my mind and apologise to the court for my contempt, which means I'll be out inside a week. The minute I walk through that gate I'll tell the world that I was forced into apologising by a low, fornicating bully who's not fit to be a prison officer.'

Bog Nose curled his lip. 'Oh yeah – d'you think anybody'd believe an old slag like you?'

Beth detected the weakness in his voice. She glanced up and allowed the deep contempt in her eyes to wash over him, causing uncertainty, then fear. Oh yes, this was something he most definitely didn't want brought to anyone's attention – especially his wife's. Satisfied that she now had the upper hand, she folded her arms belligerently. The other inmates in the room had gone quiet and edged nearer to catch the conversation.

'Why shouldn't people believe the truth?' Beth said. 'The only reason I've been locked up is for telling the truth and refusing to back down. As a matter of fact I'm absolutely sure people would believe me – especially if they read it in the papers. Anyway, you know what they say, no smoke without fire. What I said to Farthing got in all the papers. I don't expect that did his reputation any good. I know at least one reporter who'll be waiting to interview me the minute I get out. Who's side do you think the other women in here will be on if questions are asked about you?'

'Your side, love,' shouted an anonymous voice, raising cackles from others.

The prison officer just stood there, not knowing how to handle this hostile inmate whom he wished he'd never crossed. She wasn't like any other woman in here. Crabtree was a loose cannon who could do him a lot of harm.

'If anything bad happens to me in here,' Beth went on, jabbing a threatening finger at him, 'I'll make sure you pay for it a hundred times over. It'll cost you your wife and your job – and maybe your liberty.'

'You tell him, missis,' called out another voice.

'You wouldn't dare,' sneered the officer.

'Of course I dare, you ridiculous man.'

Later that evening her cell was unlocked, her name called out and an order given for her to pack her belongings and step out on to the landing.

'Sounds like Bog Nose,' said the prostitute. 'Well, it's either the shithouse or the sunshine fer you, dear. I just 'ope yer get what yer deserve.'

There had been friction between the three cellmates since news of Beth's confrontation had got out. If he'd been frightened off them it could spoil their cushy life. Beth took a deep breath and walked out of the cell. Her big mouth had got her into a lot of trouble recently. She knew she wasn't going to get away with it this time. No way would an officer back down so publicly. What she didn't know was that the prison governor had also heard about the confrontation and had decided to nip matters in the bud.

Bog Nose stood there with a silly grin on his face which, under other circumstances, Beth would have loved to have wiped off.

He laughed, without a trace of humour. 'Hey, you *do* know I was kidding about putting you in with Fat Hilda, don't you?'

'*I* wasn't kidding.'

His voice was lower now, confidential and out of the side of his mouth. 'I know that – but going to the papers about me. I'm just a workin' lad doin' me job.'

Because she didn't want to overplay her hand, Beth too kept her voice down. 'Working lad? You make me sick! There's men a lot younger than you fighting and dying for their country in France while you're over here with your bullying ways, fornicating with thieves and prostitutes. You're no better than the worst of the women in this place.'

'All right,' he hissed. 'What is it you want? You can have anything within reason.'

Anything within reason? It was obvious to Beth that he wasn't acting on his own authority. Orders had come down from above. Might as well make the most of it.

'I want a cell of my own, permission to have at least one book a week sent to me, a nice office job – and I want to be able to serve out my time with no aggravation from anyone.'

Bog Nose ran her list through his head to check that she wasn't asking for anything beyond his scope of authority. He nodded. 'OK – and do I have your word that you won't go to the newspapers?'

'My word? Ah, so my word *does* mean something?'

'I'm told you're a woman of misguided integrity,' he muttered.

Beth allowed herself a faint smile of triumph. 'Then you have my word on it – providing you keep your side of the bargain. I've got much bigger fish to fry than a stink-mouthed fornicator.'

She was moved to a single cell on another wing and found the solitude more disturbing than she had anticipated. Just her, four brick walls, a few spiders, a bed, a cupboard and a bucket. The floor was bare flagstones and the only light came through the barred windows from the prison yard, which was lit by a gas lamp. Eli had sent her a cryptic letter telling her that he was successfully honouring her recent request but that a visit from the subject of this request might be difficult to arrange. So Amy was all right, but why couldn't she come and visit? Beth didn't like the sound of that. Maybe she should apologise, throw herself at the mercy of the court in order to get released early. Then she changed her mind when she thought of Godfrey Farthing and his evil ways – especially that foulest of crimes he'd committed on All Hallows Eve thirty-six years ago. The events of that night were deeply etched into her memory.

Chapter Fourteen

April 1918

'All you sinners come gather round me, and through me let the Lord lay His gentle hand on you and cure you of your worldly ills. But let me warn you, brothers and sisters. Be true to the Lord for if you are not true to the Lord then be sure as hell the Lord will not be true to you.'

Eli's booming, theatrical voice rose and fell in the convincing but counterfeit manner of all true evangelists. He was standing beside his cross which was now fixed in its own slot on his evangelical platform. He was on Woodhouse Moor in Leeds the day before Woodhouse Feast started and he had attracted quite a crowd. The show people were putting the finishing touches to their fairground rides and attractions, and passers-by were getting off the trams and buses to see what the fuss was about. Amy was up there with him, dirty faced and appealingly scruffy, playing the violin. Billy Eccles hopped around the crowd's perimeter on crutches bought for him by Eli.

'What's goin' on, mister?' Billy addressed himself to the back row of the onlookers.

'It's a sort of a preacher,' said a man. 'He's got some gob on him, I'll say that fer him.'

Billy tried to hop up and down to get a better view. 'What's that big wooden thing?'

'It's a cross,' said a woman. 'Just like the one Jesus died on, only I reckon this is a bigger bugger.'

People around her went 'Ooooh!' at such blasphemy and the woman hunched her shoulders and placed a penitent hand to her mouth. 'I've heard about this feller,' she said. 'I heard he can cure lumbago by just puttin' his hand on yer 'ead.'

'Only if yer true ter the Lord,' said another woman, piously. 'If yer not true ter the Lord it dunt work. I wonder if he can fettle my hip? It's been givin' me some right gip this week has my hip.'

'I bet there's a collection,' said a man in a mutton-chop moustache and beard. 'Where there's God yer can bet there's a collection.'

'Course there's a collection,' said the woman with the hip. 'The Good Lord's disciples don't live on bloody fresh air, yer know.'

'I bet he couldn't cure me,' muttered Billy, summoning up a tear. He did this by plucking at his eyelashes, but once the tears started he could keep them coming. It was a useful talent he'd learned as a small child.

'Would yer say yer true ter the Lord?' asked the woman with the hip.

'I go ter Sunday school every week,' lied Billy. 'So I reckon I am.'

The woman jabbed her hand in the air and shouted at Eli in a stentorian voice. 'Here, see what yer can do fer this young cripple lad.'

'If he cures yon lad I'll show my arse on t' Town

Hall steps fer a week,' muttered the mutton-chop man.

'Well let's hope he dunt cure him, then,' said a woman standing next to him, presumably his wife. 'I'd sooner look at yer face than yer arse, an' that's sayin' summat! If he cures the lad I'm sending you up. Happen he can stop yer farting!'

There was coarse laughter and the crowd automatically parted to allow Billy through. The mutton-chop man placed his hand on Billy's shoulder and said sincerely, 'Don't expect miracles, lad. I reckon this feller's all me eye an' Tommy Martin.'

Billy nodded, tearfully, and hobbled through to the front where Eli awaited him. The crowd went quiet as Billy, with Eli's help, mounted the platform.

In the distance, on the far side of Woodhouse Lane, a Salvation Army played 'Nearer My God To Thee'. Amy effortlessly took up the tune, like the first violinist in an orchestra, with a sound sweet enough to extract a few ooohs and aaahs and 'isn't that lovely'? from the audience.

'Tell me your name, son,' said Eli. His voice carried to the back of the crowd and was accentuated by Amy's playing.

'Thomas,' said Billy.

'Thomas – after the apostle, Doubting Thomas,' said Eli. 'Do you doubt the Lord, Thomas, as did your namesake?'

'Oh no, mister.'

'How long have you been a cripple, Thomas?'

'All me life, mister.'

Eli gave Billy a munificent smile and placed his hand on the boy's head. Some members of the Salvation Army Band could see what was happening and they stopped playing, as did all the other musicians, one by one, until Amy was playing alone.

Eli closed his eyes and looked heavenwards, then suddenly he took his hand off Billy as if he were on fire. Where Eli had been touching it the boy's hair stood on end.

'Did you feel it, my son?'

Billy nodded. There was an amazed murmur from the crowd. Billy remained as he was, supported on his crutches, as if he daren't put Eli's miracle to the test.

'Try and stand up on yer own,' called out the woman with the bad hip.

Billy looked at her and shook his head.

'Go on, lad,' shouted someone else. Others joined in.

'It'll do no harm.'

'Go on, lad, it's worth a try.'

'Yer've nowt ter lose.'

'Leave him be,' commanded Eli holding up his arm. 'The Lord works in mysterious ways. Maybe it isn't the boy's time.'

'Aye, an' mebbe yer a bloody fake!' shouted the mutton-chop man who was relieved at not having to stand on the Town Hall steps revealing himself to the world. Billy allowed one of his crutches to fall away. Eli's arm was still dramatically aloft, bringing the crowd into silence. The other crutch fell to the floor and Billy stood there, swaying, to gasps of astonishment from the crowd. He took a step forward, then another, then collapsed dramatically, as taught by Eli, who held up a staying hand as the crowd swayed forward to help the boy.

'Don't doubt the Lord now, son,' called out Eli.

'Have faith, lad,' shouted the woman with the hip, others shouting similar encouragement.

212

Billy frowned and pushed himself to his knees, then to his feet.

'Don't do too much too soon,' cautioned Eli, loud enough for the crowd to hear. 'Just a few steps, lad. A few steps today and a few more tomorrow.'

Billy walked unsteadily towards a chair which was prepared for him at the far side of the platform, and sat down heavily, with sweat pouring from his face. This would have been less convincing had the crowd known it was caused by nervous adrenaline rather than physical effort.

'Alleluia!' shouted Florence Attercliffe, whose job had been done for her up until now by the woman with the bad hip.

'The Lord be praised!' shouted Norman Attercliffe from the other side of the crowd, which had now swelled to 200 or more. The woman with the bad hip was now standing by the front of the platform, along with half a dozen others in need of healing.

'Dear brethren, let me introduce you to the miracle girl who showed me I had such a gift,' called out Eli.

There was a murmur of curiosity from the crowd as Amy stepped to the front of the stage and began to play 'Abide With Me' – the old tried and tested crowd pleaser. Eli held up a recently acquired back copy of the *Bradford Telegraph* which showed Amy's picture under the headline, 'Miracle Girl Survives Lusitania Sinking', and as she played he told the crowd her part in the *Lusitania* story. He'd had a printer reproduce a hundred copies of the front page, ten of which he allowed the people to pass amongst themselves.

'Miracle indeed, dear brethren,' he called out, with engaging humility. 'Not only did she survive the sinking but she learned to play the violin within days of meeting me. If ever a girl was blessed by the Lord it is young Amy, who will be passing among you with a collection box. Do not give if you cannot afford it,' he implored. 'We require scant payment to get by on.'

The more he implored them not to give, the more they gave. Florence Attercliffe set the ball rolling by tossing a whole florin into the collection box, shaming those who could only afford sixpence, but not as much as those with only copper coins to spare – which was most of them.

Underneath the box was a velvet bag, into which some or all of the coins could be periodically tipped by releasing a catch in the side of the box, allowing its base to flip down – thereby ensuring it would never be so full so as to have people think they needn't contribute any more.

The woman with the hip was now on the platform. Eli had asked her name and she'd told him it was Lizzie Frampton and that she came from Hunslet and her hip was giving her some gip and she thought it was the damp weather they'd been having.

'Lizzie, short for Elizabeth?'

'With an ess, not a zed,' she said, with some pride at being different.

'Aha, Elisabeth – mother of John The Baptist, wife of Zebedee.' If nothing else Eli did his homework. A good working knowledge of the Bible always impresses, he would say.

'Well, they call my husband Fred and our lad's norra Baptist and he's called Norman. We're Roman Catholics when we go.'

'Your Fred's a Roman Alcoholic,' someone shouted, to accompanying laughter.

214

Eli placed his hand on her head and the crowd went quiet. He had a piece of sandpaper stuck to his palm which, under gentle pressure, she couldn't feel. The money stopped dropping into Amy's box as all eyes were on the woman. The girl edged towards the perimeter of the crowd, not wanting any obstacles between her and freedom if she needed to make a quick getaway. Eli applied downward pressure for a split second and twisted his hand before drawing it quickly off the woman's scalp. The sudden friction had her hair standing on end, much to the crowd's amazement.

'Did you feel it?' he asked her.

The woman flattened her hair with her hand. 'By the 'eck!' she said. 'I bloody did an' all!'

Then she put her hand on her hip. 'Well, there's still a twinge but I have ter say, it dunt feel as bad as it did.'

'Have faith in the Lord,' said Eli. 'And it shall be healed.'

'I will have faith, mister,' she said, taking his unsand-papered hand in both of hers.

Amy closed her eyes and shook her head, impercept-ibly, asking herself how on earth he got away with it. When she opened them he was smiling down at her with a look that said: Faith can move mountains – and some-times fix a dodgy hip.

Florence went up next to have agility restored to her chronically arthritic knees. She was followed by a variety of people, none of whom wanted to admit that they were the ones who had so little faith in the Lord that He didn't see fit to cure them – although a large percentage of them actually felt much better. Norman went up after half an hour, his back bent and his face creased with the pain of his crippling lumbago. He had no hair to stand on end,

215

but he left the stage upright and painless, waving to the loud applause from the crowd.

As the curees came and went the bag beneath the collection box began to bulge to the point that Amy was worried it might tear off under the weight. She took it up on to the platform and emptied it into Eli's suitcase, then waited a respectable few minutes before starting her collection once again.

Eli's credibility was boosted when one of the Salvation Army cornet players had sufficient faith to go up to have his warts removed. Amy wondered how Eli intended handling this. Unseen aches and pains were one thing, but warts were there to be seen and therefore a real challenge.

'This is not an ailment, my son,' said Eli, with mild reproach in his voice. 'It is but a blemish that offends your pride, and what is pride if not one of the Seven Deadly Sins?'

The blushing musician hurried from the platform accompanied by disapproving looks, especially from the Salvation Army captain who didn't believe in Eli but couldn't figure out how he did it.

After two hours solid healing Eli asked his congregation to kneel down and say Psalm 23 along with him. As they chanted 'The Lord Is My Shepherd' Amy emptied her third full collection box (and bag) into Eli's case. She couldn't begin to calculate how much money they had collected but this time she didn't feel quite so guilty. Many of the people now had smiles on their faces, especially those who seemed to have cured themselves through their own blind faith. At worst they had all been entertained. The Salvation Army Band was now playing at the edge of Eli's congregation which he was about to freely hand over to them. As the psalm ended he called out, 'My dear brethren, thank you for your generosity. But do not forget the Lord's orchestra which is now playing for you. Be as generous to them as you were to us.'

This was highly unlikely, but it would boost the takings of the band more than on a normal day and generate for Eli some reluctant goodwill from an unlikely source. The captain threw him a curt nod of thanks and wondered if the Good Lord would approve of the Sally Army copying Eli's beguiling dishonesty to swell the coffers.

After paying Florence and Norman five shillings each the day's takings were a massive three pounds four and three-pence. Billy was delighted with the ten shillings that Eli gave him and even happier when he got to take the reins and guide the caravan home; driving things was Billy's forté. After they had dropped him off at his house, Eli looked across at Amy and asked, 'Am I still a fraud?'

Amy thought for a moment as she remembered an incident from earlier in the day. 'There was a fortune teller at the feast called Madame Du Barry,' she said.

'Madge Barraclough, I met her in court once,' said Eli. 'She was fined twenty-five shillings for selling the elixir of life in the street without a hawker's licence.'

'It said on her booth that she could tell your future from the stars,' said Amy. 'I think she'd set up a day early because of the crowd you attracted. When we left there was a queue waiting to see her.'

Eli nodded. 'She calls herself an astrologer. It's a good, scientific-sounding name – like astronomer, which is a proper science. You give them your hard-earned shilling and they'll make up a thing they call your horoscope which is where all the stars were at the time you were born.'

'Presumably they get this information by consulting an astronomer,' guessed Amy.'

'Presumably,' said Eli. 'But I doubt you'll ever catch an astronomer consulting an astrologer.'

'So, it's all trickery?'

'Who's to say? It gives people something to believe in, which makes them a bit happier. Give the poor man something to believe in and you make him a little richer.'

'Who said that?' Amy enquired.

'I did, just then. I've got another for you: Give money to the poor and you make them richer still. Here's a pound for your work today.'

He was a rogue, but a generous boss. By the time Beth was released her granddaughter had saved eleven pounds fifteen shillings and sevenpence – and there was a well-paid job going as the Virgin Mary if Beth wanted it.

Chapter Fifteen

Beth turned the corner towards the gates of Brammah's mill and was met by a few uncomfortable stares from her workmates. This puzzled her. It was her first morning back after serving the full three months of her sentence. Remission would only have been possible had she offered an apology to the court. There had been a time when Beth had weakened to the point where she had been on the verge of knocking on the governor's door to offer such an apology. Then she thought about the satisfaction Godfrey would derive from this and she remembered the look on his face when she had thrown her accusations at him in court, and the newspaper account the following day which had quoted her absolutely verbatim – as anything else could have got the newspaper in trouble for libel. She knew that if nothing else, mud sticks, and it would stick much longer if she refused to be brow-beaten by the courts. Her resolve strengthened and she was rewarded by a follow-up article written by the same reporter, who was waiting to interview her at the prison gates on the day of her release.

'I'm surprised you had to serve the whole three months,' he said.

'I could have been out much sooner had I gone back to court to say I was sorry for what I said to Farthing,' Beth had told him. 'But that would have been a lie – perjury, in fact – and perjury is even more serious than contempt.'

Once again her statement had been printed, verbatim, in the *Bradford Telegraph*. Godfrey had been asked to make a statement but he had rudely refused, prompting the reporter to phrase this refusal in such a way that it harmed Godfrey's reputation a lot more than it harmed Beth. All in all it had been three months well spent.

'Morning Beryl.' Beryl Osgoby had worked with her for twenty years and was at the other side of the street. Beryl dropped her eyes for a second, then hurried over to Beth.

'Mornin' love. How was it?'

'Hard, but worth it. Anyway, it's all behind me now. Old man Brammah wrote to me while I was inside and told he'd be keeping my job open for me. I must say I'll be glad to get back into the swing of things. Catch up on all the gossip.'

'Have yer not heard?'

'Heard what?'

By way of an answer Beryl nodded towards a figure standing by the gate, smoking a fat cigar.

'Farthing, you murdering bastard!' shouted Beth, instantly incensed at the very sight of him. 'Why don't you crawl back under your stone?'

Godfrey managed a broad sneer without bothering to remove the cigar from his mouth. It waggled up and down as he spoke to her. Other workers passed them by as she stopped to confront him; Beryl paused awkwardly in her stride.

'I hope you don't think you've got a job here,' Godfrey said, as if surprised to see her.

'It's nothing to do with you whether I have or I haven't.'

He gave a loud laugh. 'Nothing to do with me? Haven't you heard, woman? I own this mill now.'

The wind was well and truly taken from Beth's sails. 'That's what I were trying ter tell yer,' whispered Beryl, before going on her way. 'Owd man Brammah sold out to him last week.'

Beth stared at Godfrey and said derisively, 'Just to spite me, eh? By God, you must be scared of me. Why's that, Farthing? Frightened one day that I'll have you strung up for the murderer you are?'

The eyes of passing workers went from one to the other as they hurried through the gates without pausing. There'd be plenty to gossip about over the looms that day.

'Any more talk like that and I'll sue you for slander,' hissed Godfrey.

'Sue me?' Beth gave a manic laugh. 'Do your worst, you poisonous bastard. You're a damn murderer! You've killed six people to my knowledge – that's on top of all the other foul things you've done!'

She shouted this at the top of her voice, causing Godfrey to spin on his heels and storm through the gates, wishing he hadn't come out for this confrontation. Threatening to sue her had been a bit stupid. You don't sue people who have no money.

It soon became apparent that Godfrey had done more than deprive her of her job at Brammah's. Every mill owner in the district was a member of, or in some way associated with, the Bradford and District Heavy Woollen Lodge, of which he was this year's president. If Beth wanted a job in a mill she'd have to move well out of

221

town. Eli, of course, had the solution to all her problems, but she was dead set against it.

'I can't parade round dressed in blue and white, looking all holier than thou.'

'Do no harm to try it, Grandma. It's actually quite good fun. And there are loads people who swear that Eli has cured them.'

'Is this true?' Beth asked Eli.

Eli shrugged. 'If I ever got arrested again they'd have a job proving I'm a fake. I've got the names and addresses of many people who, I'm sure, will stand up in court and vouch for me.'

'What about all the people you haven't cured?'

'I always make it quite clear that I can't cure everyone.'

'When people hear that he's already cured someone, it strengthens their belief in him,' said Amy, repeating what Eli had told her. 'If they're absolutely sure he can do it, whatever inner powers they've got start working overtime on their ailments.'

'So, it's done by people believing it can be done?'

'Grandma, belief is ninety per cent of the battle.'

'I could make *you* a healer, if you like,' said Eli to Beth. 'Then we could work in shifts. You've got a very believable face.'

Beth sat down in the armchair, her head buzzing. She had only been home for ten minutes after a day going from mill to mill looking for work, only to be turned down as soon as she told them her name. Godfrey had spread his poison well.

'Eli,' she said. 'You're a nice fellow, but this is all trickery and bamboozlement.'

'So are half the pills and potions doctors give you,' he countered. 'But it doesn't stop you swallowing them. Beth, we live in a world of trickery and bamboozlement, but we give them entertainment as well, and all for a few pennies.'

So it was with great reluctance that Beth agreed to play the part of Mary in Eli's Church Of the Divine Wind gathering. But after a while even she conceded that he brought a certain happiness and hope to a small corner of the world in exchange for a few coppers per person. Some of the healed would remain so; at the very least those who exchanged their hypochondria for faith in Eli's God-given healing powers.

The summer of 1918 went by with them travelling all over Yorkshire. The news from the war was good, the money was good, the rent easily paid and all would have been well with Amy's world had her grandmother not gone on incessantly about Godfrey Farthing being a murderer. Amy believed him to be a mean and curmudgeonly old man, but nothing more, definitely not a murderer, not her dad's father.

It was two days after Armistice Day, 13 November 1918. Three quarters of a million British soldiers had died; the total war dead numbered 12 million. As far as Amy could tell the whole affair had been totally pointless. There were no winners, only losers. So it was high time, she decided – without telling her grandma – that things got sorted out with Grandpa Farthing. She would make it clear to him that she wasn't interested in his silly old mills or his money, she just wanted to know why he'd never liked her and her grandma – and her mother for that matter. What had happened in the past that made him hate them all so much? She was his granddaughter and she had a right to know.

It was a cold morning, with a frosty nip in the air that clouded the breath of the people passing by her in the street as she strode towards Farthing's mill. The younger kids were all out playing kick-the-can, marbles, conkers and skipping. At fourteen Amy had pretty much outgrown all this but she couldn't resist the temptation of jumping along a set of faded hopscotch squares chalked on to the flagged footpath.

Way in front of her a knife and scissor sharpener pushed his one-wheeled cart along the road. When he stopped and turned it over the wheel became a pulley, worked from a pedal. He gave a cry of 'Knivesanda-sizzersasharpennnedaa!' and within a minute he had a small queue of chattering customers, whose chatter stopped when a funeral approached and everyone in the street who wore a hat – which was everyone except Amy – removed it as a mark of respect for the departed stranger. Just one of far too many of late. Amy stopped walking and bowed her head. The hearse was pulled by two black-plumed horses, followed by a procession of dark-clothed mourners and a Salvation Army band. The coffin looked quite small which prompted one of the watching women to comment:

'It looks like a kiddie, poor mite. It'll be that Spanish flu. I've heard it's killing more than that damn Kaiser ever did; our Beattie's girl's none so good; she's gone as skinny as a rake, poor little beggar. There's no meat on her at the best o' times.'

Union Jacks and bunting from the armistice celebrations fluttered disrespectfully above the gloomy cortege. A one-legged man on crutches with his surplus trouser leg folded up with pins stopped and saluted the coffin – and Amy made a good guess at where he'd lost his leg.

It was a strange world, where celebration and mourning marched side by side.

The funeral disappeared around the corner and the daily life of the street resumed as though it had stopped for no more than a heartbeat: a butcher's boy on his squeaky delivery bike; a woman pushing a squeakier perambulator – or pram as they were coming to be known; a whistling window cleaner; and a young woman riding past on a motor cycle. This latter brought a smile to Amy's face. How the war had brought women out of the dark ages. At this rate they'd be voting and smoking in the street by the time she was twenty-one. At least they would if Amy had anything to do with it.

She saw Mrs Harrison from Pennypot Terrace sneak into one of the many pawnshops with something bulky under her coat, probably the wireless set she was always boasting about. Amy's grandma had done that before today. Pawn it Monday redeem it Friday if you're lucky. If you couldn't redeem it the pawnbroker would eventually get lucky. It was the way of things.

Amy knew that the iron gates at the entrance to the mill would be closed until midday so she timed her visit to coincide with the dinner-time hooter going at 12 o'clock. A stooped man in a worn bowler hat and grimy waistcoat came out of a wooden hut and swung the gates open. Amy sauntered through and asked him, with an air of superiority born in New York but still thriving in Bradford, 'Could you direct me to my grandfather's office, please.'

'And who might you be, young lady?'

'Amy Farthing,' she said it with just enough superior irritation for the man not to give her an argument. He pointed towards the mill.

'Through yon big door, up the steps, first door on yer right. Best knock, he might be busy.'

'Not too busy to see me, I hope,' smiled Amy. The man returned her smile and said, 'I expect not.'

She went through the huge, mill door and took a deep breath before mounting the stone staircase that led to her grandfather's office, passing a flurry of people coming down. The first door on the right had one word on it: PRIVATE. Amy turned the handle and peeped around the door. Inside was the empty office of Godfrey's secretary who had just left for lunch. She stepped inside and looked at a door at the far end, knowing that behind this door would be the old curmudgeon whom she was going to put right about a few things. She took another deep breath and set her shoulders straight as she opened this next door and walked inside.

Godfrey was standing with his back to her, not having heard her come in. He was looking through a glass screen down on to the mill floor where work had just stopped for dinner. The two of them stood there for a while, with Godfrey unaware of the presence of his granddaughter. It was she who broke the silence.

'Why do you hate me so much?'

'What?' Godfrey spun around and didn't instantly recognise her. At fourteen she could have been one of his workers. He had only seen her once, for a brief time three years ago in Liverpool, and she had changed since then.

'Don't you remember me?' It was the accent that gave her away. He gave a curt nod.

'Aye, I remember you. What I don't know is what you're doing in my office.'

'I'm here because you're my grandfather and I want

226

to know why you hate me.' She had left her grandma out of the equation because she felt Godfrey might have a reason to hate her that she hadn't told Amy. Keeping things between the two of them left him with no surprise excuses.

Godfrey went to his desk and sat down without offering her an invitation to do the same. She sat down anyway, on the chair opposite, and folded her arms to await his answer.

'Well?' she said. There was a charming belligerence about her that would have brought a smile to most adult faces. But not to Godfrey's.

'You're a cheeky young beggar,' he barked. 'Has no one ever taught you any manners?'

Amy blushed and wished she'd been more polite. 'I'm sorry if I've been rude,' she said.

'I should think you are. Now, what have you come for? I'm a busy man and you haven't got an appointment.'

Amy's contrition evaporated. He was being much ruder than she had been. 'Do I need an appointment to see my own grandfather?' she said, boldly. 'To ask him why he hates me when he doesn't even know me.'

Godfrey took out a cigar and lit it slowly, as Amy looked on, wondering how he would react to her assertiveness.

'Hate you?' He turned the words over in his mind as he puffed a cloud of smoke in between him and her. 'I expect your grandmother's put you up to this.'

'No she hasn't. If she knew I was here she'd go mad.'

Godfrey gave a short laugh. 'Aye,' he said. 'I expect she would. I expect she'd not be best pleased at all, knowing I've got you in my clutches. She thinks I'm a murderer, y'see.'

'I know,' Amy said.

'And do you think I'm a murderer?'

'I know you're my paternal grandfather. And no murderer could be the father of such a good man as my dad.'

Godfrey nodded and puffed away as he framed his thoughts. 'So, you know I'm your paternal grandfather, do you? You're a bright girl judging by the way you think and speak – a very bright girl indeed. Under any other circumstances I might be proud to be your grandfather.'

'But you're not proud of me?'

Godfrey shook his head. 'I take no pride in being your grandfather, that's for sure.' He looked at her, steadily. There was no love in his eyes. They didn't look as if they were capable of loving anyone – except perhaps their owner.

'Why not?' she asked him. 'What have I done wrong?'

He gave a mirthless laugh that displayed two uneven rows of brown teeth. 'The wrong was done before you were born, girl. The wrong was done by that hag you call your grandmother. But it doesn't stop you being a part of it.'

Amy's heart sank. She knew there was some hidden secret – some justifiable reason her grandmother had kept from her. A reason for her grandfather to hate the two of them.

'Please tell me what she did.' Amy scarcely dare ask the question.

'What she did?' He gave another of his empty laughs. 'It's what she didn't do – that's the problem. What she didn't do.'

'What didn't she do?'

Godfrey shook his head and shuddered. Then he looked

at Amy through eyes narrowed with distaste. 'I'll tell you this, girl, and I'll tell you only once because it sticks in me gullet to have to tell you it at all.'

Amy gulped in fearful anticipation.

'Many years ago,' he began, 'your grandmother worked here. She was only a young lass at the time and not a bad looker at that. I was only young meself and – well, to put it bluntly your grandma and me had a bit of a fling.'

'You and grandma–?' Amy's eyes widened trying to grasp the implications of all this.

Godfrey scratched his ear, then rubbed his mouth. 'That's right, me and your grandmother. It happens. Boss's son takes a fancy to a flighty piece in the mill and before you know it she's tempting him to take advantage of her in the hope he might father her child and have the decency to marry her.' He leaned forward on his desk. 'I'm ashamed to say that in your grandmother's case I fell for her charms. Next thing I know she's telling me she's pregnant and will I be doing the decent thing by her?'

'You made my grandma pregnant?' Amy gasped. It was only recently that she'd learned, from Effie Slack, how babies were made. 'But who was the baby?'

'Your mother.'

'My mother? You mean you're my mother's father?'

He nodded, grimly. 'I should have said something, I know. But I had a fiancée of my own by the time I found out and I didn't want to lose her. So, I told your grandma straight. It was her own fault for leading me on the way she did and she wouldn't be getting me to the altar, nor any money neither. That's why she snapped up the first man to come along – Alf Crabtree.'

Amy had gone quite pale. The enormity of all this was sinking in, but there was no pity in Godfrey's eyes.

'Happen you're too young to be taking all this in,' he said, 'but I reckon you've a right to know why I can barely stand the sight of you. You're an unnatural child, girl. Your parents were brother and sister – that's why you've got such a strange look about you. They didn't know – right up to the end they didn't know because the one person who could have told them chose not to, to spite me.'

Amy had nothing to contribute to this conversation. It was all way, way beyond her scope of understanding. He was saying she was an unnatural child. What did that mean? Godfrey sat back in his chair, silently satisfied with the effect his words were having on her.

'I know it's not your fault,' he went on, benignly, 'but it's types like you that fill up the prisons, and I should know, I've sent enough of them there in me time. Cousins interbreeding's bad enough, but brothers and sisters – what can I say . . . ?' He shook his head in despair. 'All the badness comes out in adulthood, you see. A lot of them commit suicide when they see it coming on – not that I'd ever advocate anything as drastic as that, but in some ways it's the best way out.'

Amy found her voice, but it was a quiet one. 'It can't be true – it can't be.'

'I wish to God it wasn't,' said Godfrey, sadly. 'But I suggest you ask your grandmother. She may lie about the actual circumstances of your mother's conception but not even she can lie about who your mother's father was. Not even she is that evil.'

'Why didn't *you* tell my parents that they couldn't marry?'

'Why? I'll tell you why. It's because I made the mistake of leaving it to your grandmother to tell them. I didn't go to the wedding because I didn't think there'd be one – I thought she'd stop it before it went too far, but I didn't realise how spiteful she was, how much of a grudge she harboured against me for not agreeing to marry her. There can be no other reason for her letting that marriage go ahead than for her to spite me. After the wedding there was nothing I could say or do to put it right.'

Amy stood up and walked out of the office like a zombie, without waiting to hear any more. She didn't like this old man and his fat cigars and bad teeth and she no longer regarded him as her proper grandfather. By the same token Beth wasn't a proper grandmother either – and her parents hadn't been her proper parents. He was right, she was an unnatural child. A freak.

'Goodbye, girl,' Godfrey called out, but Amy didn't hear him. This wasn't at all what she had expected. This was the very worst thing that could happen. How could she go back home after this. How could she even look at her grandma? What she had done was an act of pure evil.

Godfrey could scarcely conceal his delight at the child's wretchedness. All in all he was easily winning his feud with Beth Crabtree, but he knew a time would quickly come when he would have to rid the world of these dangerous and irritating women for good.

Chapter Sixteen

'Is Euphemia back yet, Mrs Slack?'

Amy was aware that some mothers didn't like their children's names shortened into something common. Instead of going home to face her grandma she had wandered around the streets and parks all afternoon until she knew that Effie would be in from her job at Brammah's.

'She's not, love. She's going straight to her Auntie Hilda's from work.'

'OK, tell her I called round.'

'I will, love. She'll be back about eight if yer want ter call back then.'

'I might do that, thanks.'

Auntie Hilda's. Amy's face dropped. Effie had a big family. A big, proper family with brothers and sisters, aunties and uncles and two grandmas still alive. Both of them *proper* grandmas. Maybe it wasn't Effie she wanted to see. Effie with her big happy family. She'd try Billy Eccles. He only had his dad, who was a pain in the ass most of the time, according to Billy. Billy came to the door and beamed when he saw Amy.

'Are yer lookin' fer another cripple boy?' he grinned.

Billy was only part time with the show, being one of the few kids in the district who had got into grammar school. In fact he was the only kid who had got in late, via approved school. His well-publicised heroism had helped. That plus his natural aptitude and probable innocence.

'No,' Amy said, unable to keep the sadness from her eyes.

'What's up?'

'I can't tell you. I just wondered if you wanted to come out for a while. I don't want to go home – ever.'

Billy needed no second asking. He slipped into his jacket and threw a friendly arm across her shoulder. It seemed to him that she needed a pal right now. She reached up with her hand and took his fingers as they lay across her shoulder. Both of them knew that whatever was between them was more than just friendship, but as far as Amy was concerned, being more than just friends with a boy could lead to all sorts of trouble, for generations to come. Maybe Billy's dad and her mother–? No, that was just too stupid for words. Laughable really. But they had lived in the same area as children, and they were of a similar age.

Amy looked intently at Billy, trying to spot some resemblance. Then she mentally slapped herself for being so silly. But she couldn't get it out of her head. There could be all sorts of kids, all over the world, who didn't know they were brother and sister. And they, according to her awful grandfather, were the ones who filled up the jails.

'If yer don't want ter say what's up it's all right with me,' Billy said, as they walked through the darkening streets. 'I get stuff I don't want ter talk about. But if yer do want ter talk about it, that's all right as well.'

'I'm going to run away and never come home,' she decided, suddenly.

'I'll come with yer,' he said, almost before she had got her words out. It was as though he'd been waiting for her to say it.

'You can't. You have to finish school.'

'Why? *You* never finished and you're loads cleverer than me.'

'That's different. I'm a girl. There's no place in this world for an educated girl.'

'Where are yer thinking of going?'

'New York,' she said it as though she'd been planning it for weeks. In fact she had only just thought of it. 'I'm going to stow away. It only takes five days.'

Billy whistled, excitedly. 'New York? I'm definitely comin' with yer. When do we go?'

'Tonight.'

'It's a bit cold ter be goin' at night,' pointed out Billy, practically.

Amy gave this some thought. 'We can catch a train,' she decided. 'I know there's an early morning train that goes from here to Manchester because Eli checked. He wants to take the show to Lancashire.' She gave her first smile for many hours. 'He figures there's a lot of pains in the ass in Lancashire all waiting for the cure.'

Billy gave a loud laugh. 'Hey! My dad comes from Wigan, so happen he's right.'

'And it's not far from Manchester to Liverpool,' said Amy, still thinking.

'All we've got ter do then is get ter New York,' said Billy. 'How far's that?'

'What? Oh, about five days on a ship.' She was planning their journey as she spoke. 'We'll need food and

234

warm clothing and as much money as we can raise. I figure we can sneak on the ship OK. We can mingle with the well-wishers who go on board with the passengers. You're supposed to have some sort of a pass but there's such a crush of people it's easy to get on without one. About half an hour before it sails there'll be an announcement asking all non-passengers to leave the ship – by that time we'll be hidden away in one of the lifeboats.'

Billy eyes were dancing with excitement. Stowing away on board a ship to New York was the adventure of his dreams. Not only that but he was doing it with the girl of his dreams. But he wouldn't mention that to her – he didn't want to put her off.

'I've got two pounds ten and six left from me Eli money,' he said. 'I've been giving half ter me dad ter stop him moaning.'

'Is that what you call it, your Eli money?'

Billy laughed. 'Good as owt,' he said. 'What do you call it?'

She shrugged. 'Just savings, I guess. I've got nearly four pounds in cash. There's more in a bank but I can't get at that. My gran– Mrs Crabtree organised it for me.'

'Mrs Crabtree eh? Blimey, things must be bad at your house.'

Amy couldn't bring herself to discuss it and Billy decided to leave further questions until later; it would be something to talk about when they were on board the ship.

They strolled around for a while making further plans, then went their separate ways with Billy having arranged to tap on her window at 5 a.m for them to catch the train that left at six.

*

'Oh dear God, Amy love! Where've you been? You had us worried sick.' Beth flung her arm around Amy who stood there and didn't respond. Her grandmother stood back, still holding Amy by her arms.

'There's something wrong, isn't there. I can tell by the look on your face.' She turned to Eli who had been sitting with her as she waited and worried. 'There's something wrong with her, Eli.' And in a flash she remembered her frozen reactions when Godfrey had raped her all those years ago.

'Has somebody done something to you, love. Because if they have I understand and you can talk to me about it. Eli, happen you'd better leave us for a few minutes. I'll give you a knock if I need you.'

Eli got up to go and Amy said, 'No, Eli. I don't want you to go. No one's done anything to me. I'm OK.'

He sat down uncertainly.

'I don't feel too good, that's all.'

'It'll be your age,' diagnosed Beth, thankful that it wasn't what she had suspected. 'Your body goes through all sorts of changes at your age – and your mind for that matter. Is that what you've been doing love, having a good think?'

'Kinda,' said Amy, non-committally.

'You'll be hungry as well. Me and Eli have not eaten, what with worrying about you – I'll make us a nice bit o' tea.'

Amy realised that she was hungry, not having eaten since breakfast. She would need a good meal inside her to start her off on her journey. Beth smiled at her – a real grandma's smile. Only Amy knew it was a fake smile. If Beth had been a decent person Amy wouldn't even have been born. She shouldn't be here, standing

236

in this room, planning to run away with Billy Eccles.

'Thank you,' she said, with no gratitude in her voice. 'I am hungry. I'll go up to my bedroom and come down when it's ready.'

'OK, love. I'll have it ready in no time if Eli'll peel some spuds.'

Amy went upstairs and left Beth and Eli looking at each other.

'I don't know what to think, I'm sure,' said Beth. 'She's sickening for something, I know that.'

'Mebbe it's a young man,' suggested Eli. 'She's growing up fast is young Amy, practically a young woman.'

'A lad? Do you know, I hadn't thought of that. It'll be a lad all right.' She smiled at him. 'Young love, eh? I don't think I can advise her on young love.'

'You must have been in love once.'

Beth gave a long sigh and went into the scullery, with Eli in close attendance. 'Not that I can remember. Alfred and me – well, it was just something that happened. He loved me though, bless him.'

'And no one since?'

'A few disasters, then I gave up looking.'

'What about O'Keefe, didn't he ask you to marry him?'

'He did, God love him. Oh he was a good man was O'Keefe – but he never tore at me heart strings. No one's ever done that.' She turned to look at him. 'What about you?'

'My wife left me years ago. I don't blame her. I'd have left me if I'd been her. Our union was childless which I thought was a blessing at the time.'

'Oh, how long ago was that?'

'Over twenty years ago now. She was a very forceful

woman. Had ambitious plans for me that I found didn't suit my tranquil demeanor. After several years she left me, with an uncalled-for black eye, a mountain of debt and an incontinent cat. I have to say the debt was mostly mine but the cat was stroke of pure malevolence.'

'What about the black eye?'

'I called her an evil old lizard, which wasn't strictly true as she was barely thirty years old at the time. How many potatoes do you want peeling?'

'What? – oh – half a dozen big ones. I'll make sausage and mash. Amy likes that. And – have you never thought about marriage since? I reckon you could be fair presentable-looking under all that face fungus.'

'I thought about it,' he mused, peeling a potato with the expertise of a man who had spent hours learning his trade doing jankers during the Boer War. 'But she would have to be someone very special.'

'Aye, me and all,' agreed Beth, lighting the gas ring.

'The trouble is,' said Eli, 'tempus does tend to fugit a bit faster when you get to our age. You'll be surprised to learn that I'll be fifty in two weeks.'

'Fancy.' Beth tried to sound surprised. She thought he might have the decency to be at least as old as she was – not five years younger.'I'm dreading fifty.'

'I imagine you are,' he said, gallantly. 'But you have young skin. I've met thirty-year-old women who look older than you.'

'I bet you say that to all the girls.'

'Beth, I stopped sweet-talking women the day I met my wife.'

But you're sweet-talking me, she thought, as she pricked the sausages. There was something about his nearness that pleased her. It was an odd feeling that she'd never

238

known before. God he was a rogue! 'Eli,' she said. 'You sweet-talk everyone you come across. You're a professional sweet talker.'

He laughed and tapped his knife against his chest. 'There's sweet-talking that comes from the wallet and sweet-talking that comes from the heart. I'm strictly a wallet man.'

Beth thought that was a shame but she didn't say so.

Chapter Seventeen

At five o'clock the next morning Amy was inching her way down the scullery roof to where Billy was waiting in the back alley. She threw O'Keefe's seaman's bag down to him, in which she'd stuffed most of her belongings; Billy carried his things in a canvas shopping bag that had seen better days.

'Did you leave a note?' she asked him.

'No, did you?'

'Yeah, there was something I had to get off my chest.'

'I'll write ter me dad when we get there,' Billy decided. 'Tell him it's nowt ter do with him. He'll not know I've gone till tonight when he gets home from work.'

It was cold and dark with no sign of dawn as yet. Flickering gas lamps did their best to light up the streets but they couldn't offer cheer and warmth. No one was abroad apart from a knocker-up and his young assistant. He was tapping on bedroom windows with a long pole and calling out the name of the person to be awakened. Those who didn't want to be awakened at this hour had hopefully learned to ignore the shout. At the other side of the street his assistant (probably his grandson) was doing the same job with a pea shooter, combining fun with work. They'd get threepence per house per week. As they did forty houses it was good money for an hour's work six days a week. Billy went over to the the younger knocker-up, gave him a coin and said, 'Thanks'.

'Is that how you managed to wake up?' Amy asked.

'Penny well spent,' grinned Billy. He tapped the side of his head. 'When yer running away you always have ter think on. I've checked the train time as well. It leaves at 5.50., gets into Manchester at 6.55. Four stops on the way. Half fare's a shilling return so it'll probably cost us about seven pence one way. With a bit of luck we should get a train to Liverpool pretty sharpish. I reckon we could be there by dinner time. We might have to hang around for a few days before we can find the right ship but we've got loads o' dosh. Enough ter stay somewhere really posh.'

'Tell you what,' said Amy, her dampened spirits now lightened by the company of such a stalwart and resourceful friend. 'Let's go to Manchester first class. Start as we mean to go on.'

'Suits me,' said Billy. 'Suits me right down to the ground.'

As things turned out it would have been far better had they stuck to third class.

They sat side by side facing the engine, hoping that no one else would join them. The compartment was plushly furnished with walnut panelling and armrests on each seat. The porter who, uninvited, helped them with their inferior baggage said, 'Will anyone else be joining you?' implying that presumably such young people would surely be in the care of an adult.

'My mum and dad are meeting us at the other end,' smiled Amy, dismissively, using her New York accent to its full effect and giving the man a sixpenny tip. It had a suitable affect. The man touched his cap and left them to it.

'I hope we have the compartment to ourselves,' said Billy, regretting their choice of travelling first class. 'I don't fancy sharing with some upper-class toff.'

Amy, who had spent five days on the *Lusitania* travelling with the real upper crust, was amused. 'Hey, we're as good as anyone,' she assured him. 'When we come back from America we'll be millionaires, so you'd better start getting used to it.'

Billy looked at her and felt a powerful urge to give her a kiss but knew it might spoil things between them. Suddenly she asked, 'Billy, do you think I have a strange look about me?'

'Well, I suppose we both look a bit strange, doing what we're doing.'

'No, I don't mean that. It's nothing to do with what we're doing – I mean in general. Do I have a strange look about me?' She turned and presented her face to him for examination. 'Tell me what you see.'

'I don't know what you want me to say. I think you've got a nice face.'

'Nice – just nice, that's all? Oh, come on Billy. I know I'm no raving beauty.' She paused, realising he'd need more to go on if he were to give her a proper opinion. 'Someone told me I had a strange look about me and there was a possibility I'd turn bad as I got older.'

'Well that someone wants their head testing,' said Billy. 'If yer must know one or two of the lads have started talking about you. "She's a bit of all right is that Amy

Farthing", that's what I've heard 'em say. And if yer must know, I agree with 'em.'

'So, you don't think I've got a strange look about me.'

'Yer've got a look about you all right, but there's nowt strange about it. Beautiful, that's the word I'd use.' He blushed as he said it.

Amy gave him a peck on his cheek and said, 'Thanks, Billy.'

A man walked down the corridor past their compartment, glanced in at them, then slid open the door.

'Are these seats taken?' he asked.

Amy and Billy looked at him, sizing him up, each prepared to lie, but he seemed OK.

'No,' said Amy eventually.

'Good, I'll park meself here then. It's all right, I don't smoke or anything and I had a bath this morning.'

Amy and Billy smiled. Although he was a very big man, well over 6 feet, he seemed a genial sort, probably nearing fifty now, and going to fat. His accent was pretentious working class. He sat down heavily on the seat opposite them, carrying a large attaché case on his lap.

'Samples and stationary,' he explained. 'It's for me work. If I put it up on the rack I'd forget it. Memory like a sieve.' He looked at them and gave a blink that seemed to act as a switch that worked his smile. 'Fancy a couple of kids such as you travelling first class? I reckon I'm in the company of millionaires.' Without waiting for a reaction from them he went on, 'The firm pays for me, y'see. When the firm pays I always travel first class. It might be the only chance you get – Wallace Peet, at your service.' He held out a fat hand for them to shake in turn.

Amy opened her mouth to introduce herself but Billy beat her to it.

243

'Jack Brewer,' he said. 'And this is my cousin from America, Jill Brewer.'

'Jack and Jill, eh? Easy to remember. America eh? Long way from home.' He looked out of the window with narrowed eyes. The glass caught the soulless glint in them, but the youngsters didn't.

After a while he got up to go to the dining car and Billy said to Amy, 'He talks a lot but he seems OK.'

'I guess he's a travelling salesman,' said Amy.

The train slowed as it climbed into the clouds that were draped over the Pennines, obscuring the lights from nearby houses and roads. Dawn was still over an hour away and Amy huddled inside her coat, glad she wasn't out there. As they began the descent into Lancashire, Wallace came back. He stopped outside the compartment door and gave a loud belch that had Billy grinning from ear to ear.

'Better out than in,' said the man apologetically as he came back inside. 'It's eating on the move that does it. Plays havoc with the digestive system. Always on the move, Wallace Peet. You ask anyone in ladies underwear.' He laughed at his much used double-entendre. 'That's what I sell – ladies underwear. If anyone asks me what I travel in I say ladies underwear; always gets a laugh that.'

Billy and Amy accorded him a suitable laugh. He was lively enough company and Billy figured they'd only have him for another twenty minutes or so.

'Have you two eaten?' Wallace asked them suddenly.

'We're not hungry,' said Amy. 'We'll get something in Manchester station.'

'We swap trains there ter go ter Liverpool,' Billy explained.

'We're meeting our folks there,' added Amy.

'Then we're going to America,' said Billy. 'That's where she's from.'

Wallace gave him a long, benign stare that had Billy shifting uncomfortably in his seat. 'You're running away aren't you?' He glanced up at the luggage rack above their heads. 'I've seen transatlantic luggage in my time and there's nothing transatlantic about that. Scarcely transpennine, if you ask me.'

'Well we're not asking you and whatever we're doing it's none of your business,' remarked Amy, defiantly.

Wallace held up his hands. 'Never said it was. I ran away meself when I was your age. Cruel stepfather. Never looked back. Best thing I ever did – and do you know what I've always said to meself ever since? Wallace, I said, if you ever see a kid running away, help him – or her. What is it you're planning?' He narrowed his eyes again, but this time he disguised the soulless glint with one of benevolence. 'A stowaway job?'

Billy gave an involuntary nod. Wallace clapped his hands in self-congratulation. 'I knew it. I was sittin' through there, eating me eggs and sausage and I said to meself, them two's a pair o' potential stowaways if ever I saw them. Stowed away meself. Thought I was going to Dublin, ended up in Valparaiso. Gave meself up after two days. They put me to work in the galley. Fourteen years old. Trouble was I got seasick. I was at sea for six months before they brought me back and there wasn't a day went by that I wasn't sick. Never got me sea legs. Seamen are born to it I reckon – never took to it meself. Pity really, as I like to get around.'

No, he didn't look like a seaman, Amy thought. His complexion was quite pallid, his hair was thinning, he had a waxed moustache and obvious false teeth. He wore his dark-blue trousers high above his bulbous paunch, held in place by both belt and braces and she caught a whiff of body odour, despite his claim to have had a bath that morning. All in all, he was a big man who was all right in small doses. The train began to slow and she saw a sign saying Stalybridge. Wallace took out a pocket watch.

'Not too bad,' he said. 'We'll be in Manchester at seven o'clock. My good lady will be waiting for me in the motoring car.'

'A motor car,' said Billy, impressed. 'What kind?'

'I believe it's called a Wolseley, although you would have to ask my good lady. She's the motoring enthusiast. Drives like the wind.'

'Blimey! Fancy letting a woman drive a motor car.'

Amy frowned. 'Why shouldn't women drive cars? They're just as capable as men.'

Billy opened his mouth to reply but Wallace intervened. 'I'll tell you what. Why don't you both have a go at driving, then we'll see who's best.'

'We haven't got time,' said Amy, firmly.

'I think you may have,' said Wallace. 'You see, the first Liverpool train doesn't leave until ten, which will leave you nearly three hours. I only live a short drive from the station. Why don't you you come home with me for a bite to eat? I'll have you back in good time for the train – and I might have some invaluable advice for you in your forthcomin' venture. Only don't mention this to Mrs Peet.'

'Great,' said Billy, before Amy could stop him. 'Can I be first to drive?'

'Well, I think we'd better let my wife get us to the quieter roads first.'

*

Mrs Peet was a severe-looking woman, more than a match for her husband, despite his size. She herself was a large woman and took up more than the seat space allotted to the driver. It surprised Amy that she didn't ask who they were. She just gave them a nod and opened the back door for them.

'Yer husband said I could have a drive,' said Billy, following Amy in. 'Didn't yer, mister?'

'I did, lad, I did,' conceded Wallace, who was cranking up the engine with the starting handle. 'But Mrs Peet's in charge of all things motoring. What d'yer say, Mrs Peet? Shall we let the lad drive now, or shall we leave it until we drive them back?'

'Leave it,' she said, to Billy's disappointment.

'On the way back, lad,' said Wallace, getting into the front passenger seat.

Amy felt distinctly uncomfortable. Events had been taken from her control and she didn't like that. Not under the circumstances. 'I've changed my mind,' she said. 'I think we should be on our way.'

'Changed your mind?' said Wallace. 'Nay, lass. This is no time to change your mind. Depriving yourself of a good meal and good advice, not to mention young Billy of a chance to drive this contraption. No lass, I'll not hear of it. Drive on Mrs Peet.'

The noise of the car engine meant there was little conversation for the next fifteen minutes. Amy told herself that she was being silly, worrying about nothing. All Billy was worrying about was whether or not he'd get to drive the car on the way back.

They were out in the suburbs now, the motorised traffic had thinned out and there were more horses than engines. Winter dawn had finally made an appearance but the sky remained grey and cold. Mrs Peet turned the vehicle into a grass track that led through a copse of trees then opened out to reveal an old brick-built house almost large enough, were it of grander design, to be a mansion.

'Blimey!' exclaimed Billy. 'It's bigger than our school.'

'We only occupy part of it,' said Wallace. 'Now that there are only two of us.'

His wife threw him a glance of admonition – which Amy caught – but she thought it was simply the woman's general character to be morose.

Mrs Peet led the way to the door as Amy and Billy followed on behind, examining their surroundings. There was a garden of sorts that had seen better days. The winter cold had stopped the tangled growth of weeds and the whole place had an eerie look about it. She whispered to Billy, 'The quicker we get out of this place the better.'

'We'll be OK,' he assured her, without much conviction.

The inside of the house matched the outside – cold and unloved. Just like Mrs Peet, Amy thought. It was a house without warmth, neither physical nor emotional. Wallace reached up and pulled a cord that fired up the gas mantle, adding illumination to the dark hallway. It was wide, high and sombre. On the wall was a silent clock and a large photograph of a stern-looking family, who didn't have a smile between them. Their feet clicked on linoleum flooring that had seen better days. In front of her a balustraded staircase led up to forbidding gloom. Amy had an urge to turn and run out but she'd have to alert Billy to do the same and he was walking on ahead of her. Mrs Peet had fallen behind to close the door. Amy felt a hand on her back, then on her wrist, twisting her

248

arm up her back until she shouted with pain. At the bottom of the stairs the same was happening to Billy, who was kicking out at Wallace and getting a heavy blow to the side of his head for his trouble. Amy tried to kick back at Mrs Peet's shins but the woman was ready for her and forced her arm further up her back until it was at breaking point and Amy was shrieking in agony.

'No one can hear you, girl,' she was saying, through Amy's howls of agony. Billy was screaming as well. 'Let me go yer big bastard!'

Wallace had him by his hair and was dragging him effortlessly up the stairs. Mrs Peet pushed Amy up behind them.

'What are you doing to us?' she screamed.

'You'll find out in good time, girl,' snarled the woman. 'Just behave yourself and get in that room.' She pushed Amy with such violence that she slid across the floor and banged her head on the wall. Dazed she got to her knees, sobbing with fear now. Billy was being taken to another room – she could hear his yells of protest and the thumping sound of Wallace subduing him.

'Strip,' said Mrs Wallace.

'What?'

The woman took a step towards her and slapped her hard across the face. 'If I have to ask you again you'll get another of these and so on until you do as you're told. Now strip.'

Crying quietly now, so as not to earn herself any more punishment, Amy stripped down to her undergarments. She could hear Billy's cries coming from a nearby room.

'Stop him,' she sobbed. 'Stop him hurting Billy.'

'Shut up and stand up straight,' commanded Mrs Peet.

Amy straightened slowly, as she had been trying to

hunch her shoulders and turn away from Mrs Peet's searching gaze.

'What's the matter, girl. Ashamed of what you've got? Arms behind your back, legs apart.'

The noise in the other room had quietened to a heavy sobbing. Amy did as she was ordered and Mrs Peet cast a critical eye up and down the length of her body. 'You're a bit scrawny but you'll have to do. Right, get your clothes back on before my dirty husband sees you. You're too good for the likes of him.'

'What do you mean?'

'What do I mean? I mean what I say, girl. I'm not here to explain myself to a little tart like you.'

She was barely dressed when Wallace came into the room. No longer the bluff, amiable travelling salesman, but a snarling, salacious animal, with blood spattered on his shirt – Billy's blood. Amy screamed. 'What have you done to Billy?'

'Done to him? I've quietened the noisy little bugger down, that what I've done to him.'

He was looking at her through lascivious eyes and she was glad Mrs Peet had ordered her to get dressed again. The woman had a stick in her hand and she whacked Amy hard across the buttocks, drawing a loud laugh from Wallace.

'What are her titties like, Mrs Peet? I reckon they're beginning to sprout.'

She threatened him with the stick. 'Don't you use your dirty language in this house. You save that for your dirty friends!'

Wallace roared with laughter. 'I've saved *you* for me dirty friends before now,' he howled, 'but only when we've been hard up. They'll not be wanting you now – not now we've got this beauty.'

His wife poked her stick in Amy's face and asked, harshly, 'Are you a virgin, girl? Have you ever been with dirty men? What about him you're with? Has he been dirty with you? By God I'll flay the skin off his dirty body if he has!'

'No,' sobbed Amy.

'What does that mean? No you're not a virgin or no you haven't been with dirty men?'

Amy collapsed to her knees, almost unconscious with misery, unable to respond to the woman's offensive questioning. Wallace started forward, reaching for Amy.

'Leave her,' snapped Mrs Peet. 'I think she's a virgin – and virgins such as her command a high price. I don't want you soiling the goods. There'll be plenty of time for that once we've broken her in.'

'You're right as usual, Mrs Peet,' he conceded. 'We'll be able to make a fair living out of this one for a long time to come. She's American – did you spot that?'

'I did, but there'll be no need for her to talk, not in her line of work,' said his wife. 'And I want her better treated then the last one. If she ends like her I'll bury you in the same grave. There's years of business in this one.'

Amy could hear the sound the woman's words made, but mercifully not the words themselves. Her mind was too numbed with shock.

'If you must satisfy yourself, do it with the lad.' Mrs Peet spoke to her husband as though she was chastising him for some minor, irritating habit. 'But leave it till tonight when some of the stuffing's gone out of him. I don't want you making a racket. I want to read me library book tonight.'

'Tonight it is, Mrs Peet. And tomorrow I'll be about my lawful business.'

'Have you done much business this week?' she asked, conversationally, as if the traumatised girl at her feet didn't exist.

'Oh, I've had a fair week,' he said. 'Ladies underwear's the thing for a man to be in nowadays.'

His wife laughed as if she'd never heard it before. It was his only joke, and if she didn't laugh at that she wouldn't laugh at anything. Amy heard the door close and a key turn in the lock. Was this just the beginning of her worst nightmare? These people seemed sublimely confident of their power over her. Why was that? Surely they couldn't keep her here against her will; such things didn't happen. At least she'd never heard of such things happening.

Amy sat up with her back against the wall and looked around her. The room was furnished with a double bed and a bucket. She took a blanket from the bed and wrapped it around her for warmth as she went to the only window and drew the curtains back. It was barred, with no possible means of escape. She sat on the bed and tried to consider her options. There weren't any. Then she began to recall snatches of the words Mrs Peet had been speaking when Amy's mind had been too numbed with shock for her to understand.

'Virgins such as her command a high price' . . . 'We'll be able to make a fair living out of this one.'

She was only fourteen but old enough to have a fair idea what this woman meant.

Amy lay on the bed beneath the blanket because there was nothing else to do and she needed to keep warm. Hours went by and all she heard were the normal sounds of a normal household. Footsteps; the low, modulated sound of people who might be talking about everyday things; the wind whistling outside where Amy so longed to be. She thought about Beth and had she been right to judge her simply on the word of Godfrey Farthing, the wealthy, sour-faced grandfather who had paid her off with a farthing the first time he saw her; the man who yesterday had practically advised her to commit suicide. Whereas her grandma had no money but had taken her in gladly. She had loved her and fed her and put a roof over her head. So why on earth had she run away without giving her grandma the chance to answer Godfrey's allegations?

What sort of world was it that spawned such awful people? If she got out of here she would go back to Beth and believe her. Believe every word she said. *If she got out of here.*

She lay there all day with such thoughts coming in and out of her mind. Ghastly images of violation, death and burial with no one knowing what had happened to her. Nightmare. The thin blanket couldn't keep out the cold which was exacerbated by the creeping dread of what was to happen to her. She shivered and sweated at the same time. Never in her life had she been so scared. Even in the sea as the *Lusitania* went down. Out there her survival had been in her own hands. People were trying to rescue her. Good people. In this house she had no friends except Billy who was in the same fix as she. Possibly worse. What if they had killed Billy because he was of no use to them and they didn't want to risk him telling anyone? In her naivety she couldn't think of any way a boy could be of interest to dirty men. She shouted at the top of her voice.

'Billy!'

Nothing.

'BILLY!'

Nothing.

She feared the worst and began to cry, her tears mingled with the cold sweat of her fear. She cried for hours until there were no tears to cry with. The daylight outside had gone when she heard a hideous, high-pitched screaming coming from not very far away. It was a scream of agony and it went on and on. A death scream. Her blood ran cold when she saw the handle of her door turning.

Beth looked at Eli as the sky darkened outside. 'Maybe I should have shown the police her note – they might have taken it a bit more seriously. I just can't imagine what's going through her mind.'

For the hundredth time that day she read the letter Amy had left her:

Dear Mrs Crabtree,
Today I learned the truth from my grandfather about my awful parentage. He also told me that you could have prevented my parents from marrying but didn't because you hate him so much. I feel as though I am an abnormal person, and that I belong to no one and I blame you for it.
This is why I am running away.
Amy.

'Oh, Eli. Why didn't she just ask me before jumping the gun like that? I could have set her mind at rest. What must she think of me?'

'She ran away without giving the matter any thought,' said Eli. 'Kids do that. Given time – in fact in no time at all, knowing Amy – she'll sit and think about it and realise she should at least have asked you for your side

254

of the story. I must admit, when you told me I was taken aback, so what effect d'you think it had on her?'

There was a knock on the door. Beth sprang to her feet and had it open in a flash. It was Ernest Eccles.

'Have you seen her?' she asked him. 'Is she with your Billy?'

He was shaking his head, although her questions had been as good as an answer to him. 'I take it your Amy's missing.'

'Since this morning.'

'Our Billy's missing as well. I thought he might have called somewhere on his way home from school. By the sound of things he never went to school. He's a bit unpredictable is our Billy. But as time dragged on I began to get worried. Ah, well, I suppose they must be together.'

'We've told the police,' said Beth. She had mixed feelings about Amy being with Billy. But at least he'd look after her.

'I don't think the police would worry too much about my Billy going missing for a couple of hours,' said Ernest. 'No doubt he'll be back when he's good and ready. I don't know why he's done it. It's not as though I'm harsh on the lad.'

'Lads do daft things,' said Eli. Then to Beth he added, 'I'd best get back to my caravan. If there's anything else you need, give me a knock.'

He said it as much to preserve Beth's reputation as anything else. Having O'Keefe living under her roof had set tongues wagging and he didn't want to add to her problems.

'I blame that Heptonstall lad,' said Ernest Eccles. 'He's ruined my Billy's life with his damned lies. If only people were a bit more truthful it'd save a lot of trouble.'

255

For a second Beth thought he knew about the truth she'd been keeping from Amy, but how could he? Still, he was right. If only. Life was full of if onlies.

Billy was shivering on the floor, unable to get to the bed. His face was bruised and his body ached. He was gagged and bound hand and foot to stop him screaming and fighting. But his bonds only served to heighten the hatred he felt for Wallace Peet. It was a deep hatred, brought on not only by what had been done to him, but what they might be doing to Amy. His beloved Amy. He remembered the time he'd kissed her on the lips and wondered if he'd ever get the chance to do it again. He promised himself, first chance he got he'd do it.

All day he lay there, with no food or drink. There was a bucket in the corner which he couldn't reach so he simply peed on the floor and rolled away from it. He had heard her call out his name but he couldn't respond. Her cry was so pitiful and he couldn't help her. What were they doing to her?

Outside the barred window the early dusk closed in. Billy's heart raced when the door opened and Wallace came in carrying a paraffin lamp. It cast scary shadows all around the bleak room. He tried to sit up, but Wallace kicked him back down again.

'Stay there, until I say different.'

Billy nodded. This foul man had far too much physical superiority over him for him to do otherwise.

He stood there, naked and grotesque in the flickering light. *With a knife in his hand.* He waved it under Billy's nose, then he cut the ropes binding the boy's hands and feet, but leaving the gag in place.

'I'll use this again if I have to. It's – it's to encourage

you to do the right thing without too much argument. Every time you don't do as you're told I'll open up a neat little hole in you. Best to do as I say, eh?'

Billy said nothing but kept his eyes on Wallace as the gross man grabbed his arm, pulled him to his feet and threw him on to the bed. Then he climbed in beside him.

'Now lad. I want you to take my dick in your hand and do to me what you most likely do to yourself every night.'

Billy pulled the gag from his mouth. 'No,' he said.

'Didn't you hear what I said, lad?'

Billy was weeping with revulsion. 'I'm not doin' that. Yer can't make me do that.'

'I can and I will!' Wallace jabbed the knife at Billy, who drew away. The blade missed him by a fraction. Wallace tried again. Billy leapt from the bed and grabbed the bucket, which he swung around his shoulders and caught Wallace on his head with a resounding clang. The knife dropped to the floor. Billy picked it up; Wallace, cursing loudly, came for him. Billy thrust out the knife and felt it sink into the man's stomach. He flung himself backwards, away from the fountain of blood that was spurting from Wallace's belly.

Billy dropped the knife and made for the door. He stood on Wallace's discarded jacket and looked down. A wallet was sticking out of the inside pocket. Billy picked it up and stuck it in his own pocket, then he pulled the door open. Someone was running up the stairs. He ran along the corridor to where he'd seen them take Amy. The key was in the lock. He turned it and went inside. The room was dark but he could just make her face out, peeping fearfully from under the bedclothes.

'Billy – are you okay?'

'Amy, come on. I've just stabbed the fat bastard!'

She was out of bed in an instant, running to him. A minute ago there had been no hope and now there was. He took her hand and led her out of the room. The screaming from Wallace was now hideous. There was another sound as well – someone shouting at him, telling him to shut up, probably his wife. Mrs Peet came to the door and saw them running towards the stairs. Billy pulled Amy to a halt and let the woman come to them, then, as she drew level with the stairs, he flung himself at her legs and brought her to the ground. As Mrs Peet struggled to her feet he kicked out at her and knocked her off-balance, sending her tumbling and cursing down the stairs. Her fall was halted at a half-landing where she banged her head against the wall and lay there, dazed. Her moans were drowned by her husband, who was screaming that he was dying.

Billy and Amy ran down the stairs, past the groaning Mrs Peet, out of the house and into the bushes where the cold was forgotten.

'Aw, bloody hell!' said Billy. 'Bloody, bloody hell! I think I've killed him Amy – I think I've killed him!'

'Billy. It doesn't matter.'

'Doesn't it? Are yer sure? I stabbed him in his belly.'

'No,' said Amy, 'it doesn't matter a fig. Just let's get away from here.' She checked her pockets. 'Oh heck! My money's gone.'

Billy took Wallace's wallet from his pocket and examined it. 'I nicked this off him. There's enough in here for us.'

'You shouldn't steal,' remonstrated Amy. 'It makes you as bad as them.'

'Blood hell, Amy! After what they did to us? Are you kidding?'

She shuddered. 'It's what they were *going* to do that bothers me.'

'There was definitely worse to come,' said Billy. 'A lot worse.'

'I'm sure there was,' she said, 'and they stole our money.' Her conscience was satisfied and she watched with approval as Billy tucked Wallace's wallet back into his pocket.

'What do we do now?' she asked. 'I've no idea where we are.'

The screaming in the house had died away. They feared the worst. 'I reckon I can start his car,' Billy said. 'We could drive to Liverpool if I could find the way.'

'Billy, I don't want to go to Liverpool. I want to go home.'

He looked disappointed for a second, then said, 'That's OK by me.'

'You don't mind?'

'Why should I mind? It was your idea in the first place. I only came with you to look after you.'

'Which you did. Will you tell your dad about what happened?'

'I don't know. Mebbe I shouldn't tell anyone.' He was looking at the house as he spoke. 'I can't understand why she hasn't come out. Do you think she has a telephone? Mebbe she's rung the police.'

'I can't see a telephone wire going to the house,' said Amy, looking around. It was a clear night, lit by a good moon. 'There'd need to be a pole or something to carry the wire.'

She didn't know whether Billy had killed Wallace, and there was something inside her that didn't want to know. The last twelve hours had been the most horrific of her turbulent life. But Billy needed to share his burden with someone, she knew that much. If Wallace was dead she was as much to blame as Billy. She'd make that clear to him.

'I'm going ter nick the car,' he said, decisively.

'Don't you need a key or something?'

'Mebbe,' he said. 'Mebbe not. He might have left the key in.'

'I'll help.'

Darting from shadow to shadow they went back to the car which was parked only yards away from the house.

'There's a key in it,' Billy whispered. He gave her instructions to switch on the ignition and put her foot on the accelerator as he turned the starting handle. A face appeared at the landing window, then disappeared as Billy inserted the handle. He gave it a couple of turns with no response from the engine. He called out to Amy in a low voice.

'Is it switched on?'

'Yes – oh, sorry, no – it is now.'

The house door opened and a dark figure emerged just as the engine fired into life. Amy saw it first; she pressed her foot on the accelerator as she called out.

'Jump in, Billy.'

Mrs Peet hurled herself at the car, landing on the running board and trying to stab Amy with the knife Billy had discarded. Amy dodged to one side of the flailing weapon, narrowly avoiding being stabbed in the shoulder. Then she pushed one hand into the woman's face and with her free hand released the handbrake and sent the car jerking down the grassy driveway straight into a bush which knocked Mrs Peet off, leaving her incandescent with rage, stabbing wildly at the leaves.

Billy had managed to jump on to the other running board and was clinging on for dear life as the car careered through the bushes. Mrs Peet's hysterical howling died away in the distance and eventually Amy found herself back on the grassy track; the engine was howling and the car seemed to have a mind of its own. The quicker she handed over control to Billy the better.

'I don't know how to stop it!' she shouted.

'Take yer foot off the pedal,' yelled Billy, above the scream of the engine.

'Oh,' called back Amy. 'Never thought of that.'

The car was going up a slight incline and slowed down enough for Billy to swap places with her. 'Don't you dare say anything about women not being good drivers,' she said.

'What gear are you in?' he asked.

'Gear, what's a gear? All I did was jiggle this handle about and take the brake off.'

'Yer must have got it into first gear,' grinned Billy. 'Good job, or the mad woman would have got us.'

He got to the main road and turned back in the direction they came. A sign saying 'Manchester 8 miles' told them they were headed in the right direction. By this time Billy's excitement had turned to something more sombre.

'I stabbed him,' he said, without taking his eyes off the road. 'I stabbed him in his belly with his own knife. Amy, I think I might have killed him.' He began to cry and Amy didn't know how to soothe him. 'Amy, I might have killed someone.'

'Why did he have the knife?' she asked, gently.

'To make me – to make me do something to him – yer know. He came in the room, and said he'd make holes in me with the knife if I didn't do as I was told.'

'His wife used much the same method with me,' said Amy. 'Only, all I had to do was strip down to my underwear.'

'I'm glad that's all that happened to you,' he said, sincerely. 'I was really worried – really mad. Anyway, I said I wouldn't do it and we fought and he let go of the knife so I grabbed it and I stabbed him good and proper. If I hadn't, God knows what would have happened to us.'

'I'd have been raped by a lot of dirty men then killed, that's what would have happened to me,' Amy told him. 'I think they intended making money out of it, selling me to their customers.' She placed her hand on the steering wheel over his. 'Billy you saved me from all that. I don't care if he's dead. He deserves to be dead. I hope she's dead as well.'

Her outburst seemed to have a remedial effect on him, his tears dried and he turned to smile at her, starting to think more clearly. 'Are our bags still in the back?' he asked.

She leaned over the seat to take a look. 'Yes – that means we've left nothing to connect us with what happened.'

'So, we just do a bunk and say nothing?' said Billy.

'Don't see why not. We can leave the car in Manchester and get the train home. No one will be any the wiser.' Then she remembered something else Mrs Peet had said.

'Billy, there was a girl before me. Something happened to her. They buried her. Billy, we've got to tell the police. These people are monsters.'

Billy corrected her. '*Were* monsters – Amy, I can't go to the police. I've already been locked up once for killing Nipper.'

'But that was a mistake. You didn't do it.'

'According to the law, I did.'

'Billy, if that man doesn't die, he'll still be a monster. He'll do it to someone else.'

'Amy, tell me what to do and I'll do it.'

There was such trust in his voice that she knew she couldn't put him in harm's way. The law had already let him down once. Then she remembered a certain newspaper that Eli read every day. 'I think I know a way,' she said.

Chapter Eighteen

The post-room boy led them to the desk of Vernon Haslett, the crime correspondent of the *Manchester Guardian*, who had just got up to leave.

'They wouldn't take no for an answer, Vern,' said the boy, who looked about the same age as Billy. 'I told them you were a busy man and you didn't like wasting valuable drinking time. But they said they'd got a real exclusive for you. A scoop.'

'I'll scoop you, one of these days, you cheeky young blighter,' grumbled Haslett, who looked in need of a drink. He took a watch from his waistcoat pocket, looked with some distaste at Amy and Billy, then sat back down and said, 'Unless you have proof who Jack the Ripper is I'm not interested – unless you've come to tell me I've been given a raise or my wife has left me or some other good news.'

'Well, it's nothing like that,' said Billy, bemused.

'We've got a real good story for you,' Amy said. 'But we don't want anyone to know we're involved. We want your word on that, don't we?' She looked at Billy.

'We do,' he said. 'You don't have to pay us any money or owt.'

The bruises on Amy's face, courtesy of Mrs Peet, were now quite livid. Billy looked as if he'd been run over by a large bus. Haslett lit a cigarette and sucked on it deeply, as if to give him the energy to deal with this unexpected addition to his day's work.

'You look as if you've been in the wars,' he remarked.

'We were beaten up,' said Amy. 'Do we have your word?'

'What? Oh, yes.' He held out his hand to them. 'You have my word.'

The two of them solemnly shook hands with him and Amy looked around the large, almost empty news room to see if anyone else might overhear their conversation. No one was in their vicinity.

Billy put Wallace's wallet on the desk. 'This bloke and his wife did it – his name and address are inside.' Haslett picked it up, looked inside and counted ten pounds.

'There was sixteen,' said Amy. 'But they stole six off us so we took it back. That's all right, isn't it?'

'Sounds fair,' said Haslett, who didn't know what she was talking about, but their story had possibilities so he took out a notebook and began jotting down shorthand. Mainly a vivid description of them both. For reasons he couldn't explain they were the most interesting-looking kids he'd seen in a while.

'We were running away, you see,' Amy said.

'From what?'

'From home.'

'I see. Any particular reason?'

'Yes,' said Amy. 'But that's private. Do you want to hear our story or not?'

Haslett grinned at her belligerence. He put his feet up on his desk and sat back in his chair. 'I'm hanging on to your every word. So, you were running away from home, what happened then?'

'He kidnapped us.' Amy looked across at Billy to confirm that kidnapped was an appropriate word. He gave his version:

'Well, he tricked us into going to his house with him, then him and his wife locked us up.'

'We were in separate rooms,' added Amy.

'They kept us there all day,' Billy went on. 'It were freezin' and I thought we were gonna die. All there was in this room was a bed and a bucket.'

'Same in my room.'

'Then Wallace came into my room with a knife and tried to make me – do stuff to him –'

'Whoa! Hold it right there,' said Haslett, swinging his feet off the desk. 'I think you should be telling this to the police, not me. I'll take you along and write the story but—'

'No buts,' said Amy firmly. 'There are very good reasons why we don't want to become involved.'

'I'm afraid you *are* involved,' Haslett pointed out. 'Without you there isn't a crime.'

'Ah, but we think there is,' argued Amy. 'I heard them talking about another girl who they've buried.'

'For all we know there might be loads of 'em,' said Billy, 'buried in their garden. All the coppers have ter do is go and dig that garden up and arrest them for murder when they find the bodies.'

Haslett shook his head sadly. 'I'm sorry, kids, it doesn't work like that. The police can't go around digging people's gardens up for no reason.'

266

'Well, supposing the last kid he tried it on stabbed him in his big fat belly,' blurted Billy, 'and there was blood all over the place and he screamed like a pig – and he might be dead for all I know.' He ended up in tears as his story tumbled out. Amy put her arm around him.

'He saved our lives,' she said. 'He saved me from having awful things done to me by dirty men. I heard them talking about it.' She was crying now, as if talking to someone about the horrific events of that day had unlocked the floodgates. The reporter handed her a handkerchief then went back to scribbling notes. 'Do you know how to use a telephone?' he asked.

'I guess we could figure it out,' said Amy. Neither had ever used one.

'OK. I'll go with the information you've given me. If it's not enough I'll put a notice at the bottom of page two in Friday's edition asking you to telephone me at this office. It'll still be confidential.'

'OK,' Amy said, getting up to leave. 'Thanks mister.'

'Do you want to tell me your names?' asked Haslett. 'Confidentially?'

'Jack and Jill Brewer,' replied Billy. 'We're cousins. By the way, I stole Wallace's motor car. It's parked outside. You can have it if you want.'

'He's a good driver,' said Amy. 'Better than me.'

'It were me what took it,' said Billy, 'not her. She had nothing ter do with it. It were me that stabbed him as well. I want ter make that clear, just in case.'

'Just in case what?' asked Haslett.

'Just in case the police get it wrong,' said Billy. 'It'll not be the first time if they do.'

Haslett watched them leave and knew in his bones that

this could be the best story he'd ever had. He picked up the telephone and rang the police.

Within an hour an ambulance was rushing Wallace to Wythenshawe Hospital and a police van was taking his wife to Gatley Road Police Station. In her younger days she had been a nurse and knew enough to stop her husband bleeding to death. As things turned out she wished she'd let him die there and then.

In his confused and weakened state, knowing he was near to death, Wallace told the police it was all his wife's doing and that he'd only gone along with things to keep the peace. He wasn't sure if there were two or three bodies buried in the garden. His wife did all the gardening. He had a job to do. He travelled in ladies underwear. Making a joke on his death bed would put him in a more favourable light, or so he thought. The police didn't see the funny side. They were more interested in a list of names they found locked in a bureau drawer – names of some very influential Manchester and Cheshire citizens. A repentant Wallace, with his dying breath, was very forthcoming about them all.

After the police had gone the doctor told him he was over the worst and wouldn't die after all.

Amy and Billy stood on platform 5 of London Road Station. Billy was in no rush to board the train for Leeds and Bradford; the last minute would do. He had the weight of possibly being a killer bearing down upon him, and was becoming increasingly distrustful of the reporter.

'He could have had us followed,' he said. 'That's what reporters do.'

'Don't be daft, Billy.'

'I'm not being daft. I've just told him I might have killed someone. He's bound to have told the cops. I'm not getting on that train 'til the last minute. You can be trapped on a train. Amy, if I smell a copper on me tail I'm on the run. They're not gonna lock me up again. You're OK, you haven't done nowt.'

'Neither have you, Billy, except save my life – twice now. Anyway, whatever happens we're both in it together.'

'No we're not,' he said adamantly. 'You haven't done nowt. If anyone's gonna cop fer this it's me. There's no point both of us gettin' locked up.'

'Billy you're being silly.'

'Happen I am. But if I think they're coming for me I'm on me toes.'

They were sitting on an iron bench opposite their train, listening to the noises of the station. A distant whistle sounded to herald the approach of an incoming train as an echoing loudspeaker announced its imminent arrival on platform 2; porters shouted, steam hissed from boilers, a hot chestnut vendor shouted his wares, a child cried and a parent scolded; all the fun of the fair. Two men climbed into first class, wearing seasonally unfashionable boaters, presumably to distinguish them from their flat-capped, third-class counterparts. It crossed Billy's mind that they might be detectives looking for him but he said nothing, although he was ready to run. Steam from the stationary locomotive drifted past the seated pair as the odd third-class passenger climbed on board and porters kept glancing down at them suspiciously, so Billy thought. He muttered his fears to Amy.

'They're just wondering what we're doing here, that's all,' she explained. 'This is the last train tonight; we should be either getting on it or getting off it, not sitting here like Pithy on a Rock.' It was a saying she'd got from Beth, although she didn't know what it meant.

The discordant trill of a police whistle came from the exit end of the platform. Billy was on his feet in an instant.

'Oy, you – stop!'

Heavy running boots followed the shouted command. To Amy's amazement Billy kissed her on the lips and shouted, 'I love you, Amy Farthing.'

Over his shoulder she saw a policeman heading at speed directly towards them. Within seconds Billy was over the edge of the vacant platform behind them, on to the track and disappearing behind a stationary carriage. She daren't shout after him lest she alert the policeman.

She eyed the approaching constable with displeasure. Who did he think he was, scaring off a hero like that? He would get a piece of her mind. The policeman didn't even pause in his stride when he reached her, but continued running before eventually opening a carriage door and jumping inside. Seconds later he emerged dragging a young man by the scruff of his neck.

'I never picked nobody's pockets,' protested the struggling youth.

'I saw yer wi' me own eyes, lad. We'll deal with you down at the station.'

A porter shouted out, 'All aboard that's goin' aboard!' Amy let out a sigh of exasperation and walked across to the other side of the platform to see if she could spot where Billy might be hiding.

'Billy,' she shouted as loud as she could. 'The train's going in a minute.'

But there was no sign of him. She wondered if perhaps

270

he had made his way back and had got on board secretly. Yes, she convinced herself. That was it. This was the last train tonight and he wouldn't want to miss it. A porter was walking down the length of the train, slamming the doors. She slung her bag over her shoulder, stepped inside a third-class carriage and began walking up and down the corridors, looking in each compartment for him.

She did this all the way to Bradford, searching the whole train, even standing at the door to the baggage car and calling out his name. But he was nowhere to be found.

Beth was still awake, listening for sounds outside that just might be Amy. Eli was doing the same 20 yards away in his caravan. He heard her first and drew the curtain back on his tiny window. Within seconds he was outside, wearing slippers and a voluminous greatcoat over his nightshirt, striding along in her wake. She was carrying O'Keefe's bag over her shoulder like a homecoming sailor.

'Amy!' he called out. 'Are you all right?'

She turned and smiled at him. It was the right thing to say to her. He hadn't said, *where on earth have you been?* or any such words of chastisement. He was just concerned about her. 'I'm OK, thanks, Eli.' Her breath steamed into the wintry night air. 'Just cold, that's all.'

'Thank heavens. We were so worried about you.' He looked at the light in Beth's house. 'I think your grandmother's still awake.'

'Then I suppose I'd better go in and face the music.'

'You'll find there's no music to face.'

'I don't think you understand, Eli.'

Beth was at the door with a look of wretched relief on

271

her face. Her arms were open wide. 'Oh, Amy love. I'm so sorry I didn't tell you.'

Amy fell into her arms and suddenly felt closer to this woman than she ever had. This wasn't the Mrs Crabtree she'd so coldly referred to in her stupid note. This was real love coming from a real grandma.

'Sorry you didn't tell me what?'

'Oh, come inside love, and shut the door, you look starved to death. You as well, Eli, if you're decent under that coat.'

'Modest night attire,' said Eli, 'as befits a man of the cloth.'

The three of them went into the front room where Eli set about resurrecting the dim fire in the grate. Beth and Amy watched in silence as he he placed a few strategic lumps of coal on the dying embers then stretched a newspaper, the *Manchester Guardian,* across the fireplace to draw the flames up the chimney. After a few seconds the fire began to burn brightly behind the newspaper and Eli expertly drew it away to prevent it bursting into flames.

'I read your note,' said Beth, still with an arm around Amy, 'And I understand why you ran away. The old devil was bound to poison you with it sometime and I was wrong not to tell you.'

'So, it was true? They were brother and sis–'

'No, of course they weren't.'

Eli was building up the fire as he listened to the conversation. He felt as though he had no right to be part of something so personal, but he also felt a closeness to Beth and Amy that he'd never felt for anyone in his life.

'Not brother and sister?'

Beth smiled at the relief on her granddaughter's face. 'No, love. It's a bit complicated but they were never brother and sister. Maybe I never told you because I never told them, and at the time I thought that was for the best.'

Amy dropped her bag on the floor and sat down. 'I'll put the kettle on,' said Eli. 'I think a brew's in order.'

Beth sat on the arm of Amy's chair and tinkered with her granddaughter's hair. 'When I was seventeen,' she said, 'Godfrey Farthing – well, he raped me in the mill and made me pregnant. So, as you obviously know, Alfred wasn't your mother's father, Farthing was.'

'That's what he told me – apart from the bit about – how it happened.'

'Well, I can't prove it, you'll just have to take my word for it.'

Amy placed her hand over Beth's. 'I do take your word, grandma. I'd take your word against his any day of the week.'

Beth allowed the pleasure of Amy's faith in her to sink in before she continued. She now had a faint smile on her face. 'So you see why I didn't tell your mother.'

'I guess. Anyway, how come mum and dad weren't brother and sister?'

'Your other grandmother's name was Lydia.'

'I know that, dad told me. She died when he was very young.'

'She committed suicide. She couldn't stand Farthing's cruelty. What your dad didn't know was that Godfrey wasn't his father.'

'You mean she had a lover? Grandma that's so romantic. Who was he?'

'She never said. If his name got out it'd have got him into a lot of trouble. She said he was a good man, though.'

'Did she love him?' Amy asked.

Beth looked at her granddaughter and didn't want to disillusion her. 'Yes,' she lied. 'But some loves are not to be.'

'Oh, Grandma this is just so romantic,' breathed Amy, 'and so sad. 'I assume Grandfather Farthing doesn't know this?'

'Of course not. God knows how he would have treated your father had he known. This is why I had to keep quiet about the whole thing – until now.'

The kettle began steaming in the scullery. 'I'll go and make the tea,' said Eli. 'It's all getting too complicated for me.'

'Actually, he knows most of it,' said Beth to Amy. Her eyes followed Eli as she spoke and Amy noticed great affection there – affection she'd never noticed when she'd looked at O'Keefe. 'I told him today.'

'So,' said Amy, trying to sum things up. 'I've got a grandfather that I've never met. Do you think he knows about me?'

'I'm not sure. He knew Lydia had his child. To be honest, I don't even know if he's still alive.'

'Gee, this is so romantic,' said Amy, 'Are you following all this, Eli?'

'I got lost way back. I know if it carries on like this you might end up as my long lost Auntie Amy. How did Henry and Amelia meet?' he enquired. 'I don't mean to be rude but they seemed to have come from very different stratas of society.'

'My Amelia was a very bright girl,' explained Beth. 'Clever enough to win a scholarship to St Hilda's at Oxford.'

'You must have sacrificed a lot to put her in that position,' Eli remarked.

'It was more than worth it. Anyway, that's where she

met Henry. Just friends at first, nothing more. They continued their friendship after university. Amelia became a teacher and Henry went to work as an architect.

'Are you still following this, Eli?' asked Amy.

'Oh, you'll have to make out a family tree for me to study. Are you my long lost Aunt Amy yet?'

'I think we're getting there.'

Beth flashed them both a look of irritation. This was a story she'd wanted to unburden herself of for many years and it needed to be taken seriously. But Amy had had enough serious thoughts for one day. This was light relief compared to what she' just endured. She'd learned all she needed to know – that she wasn't an abnormal child. The rest of the story was simply interesting, albeit confusing, trimmings. Her grandmother's next revelation made her sit up, though.

'Then Amelia told me she was pregnant and would be marrying Henry Farthing – right out of the blue like that. "Mum," she said, "Henry and I are having a baby and we're getting married a week on Saturday." What could I say but, congratulations?'

'Then I had Godfrey banging on my door, demanding that I put a stop to this unnatural marriage between two people with the same father. I told him to put a stop to it himself if he felt so strongly about it. Maybe I should have told him the truth there and then, but his manner was so obnoxious I chose to let him stew in his own juice. If he plucked up the courage to tell them why they shouldn't get married I'd have told them why it was all right to do so. Needless to say, Godfrey hadn't the backbone to come clean. Rather than face any scandal he allowed his son to marry a woman he thought to be his daughter. I must admit, it always does my heart good to see him suffer.'

'How did you feel about them having to get married?' Amy asked.

'How did I feel? Well, it was as plain as the nose on your face that they were in love. To tell the truth I couldn't have been happier for them. I'm sure Lydia would have approved. Godfrey was absolutely foul to her. Her two boys were the only joyful things in her life.' Beth went to a drawer and, after some searching, took out a letter – the one Lydia had written to her just before her death, telling of how Godfrey had admitted killing Alfred and that he wasn't the father of her first child.

'Lydia asked me to destroy this,' Beth remembered, reading it herself. 'I'm glad now that I didn't. If you look at the date on it you'll see the child she refers to can only be your father.' She showed it to Amy who burst into tears when she read it.

'Oh, Grandma. Why is the world so full of bad people?'

It wasn't just the letter, or Beth's revelations. It was the whole day. The terrible events she couldn't reveal to Beth or to anyone. But at least she wasn't an abnormal child. That made up for a lot – but not for all of it. Nothing would ever compensate for those twelve awful hours. How she wished she could tell Beth and Eli. But a promise was a promise.

'I don't know, child,' said Beth. 'What I do know is that for every bad person there's a hundred good ones. It's just that we tend to notice the bad ones a lot more. Oh, by the way,' she added. 'Billy's dad was round earlier. I assume he got back all right?'

'Billy?' Amy was tempted to say he hadn't been with her. But that was too big a lie. 'We got split up,' she said, truthfully. 'In Newcastle Station. I think he might have got on the wrong train.'

'Ee, daft lad,' said Beth. 'I expect it'll wait 'til morning before we tell his dad. Happen Billy will be back by then.'

'I guess so,' said Amy.

'Newcastle eh?' said Eli. 'Whatever made you go to Newcastle?'

'We just got on the first train that came.'

'I see.'

Amy detected disbelief in his voice but thankfully he didn't pursue the matter.

'Whatever have you done to your face,' exclaimed Beth. 'I thought it was dirt at first, but it's all bruised. Has someone hit you?'

Amy felt she was getting deeper into a mire of deception and she didn't like it.

'We had trouble with a couple of people,' she admitted. 'But it would have been a whole lot worse if Billy hadn't been with me. He's a real hero is Billy.' His last words to her had been running through her thoughts ever since he'd made his unnecessary getaway. *I love you, Amy Farthing.*

Her grandmother and Eli looked at her in anticipation. 'Well?' said Beth, at last. 'Don't keep us in suspense, what happened?'

Oh dear, Amy thought. Then she had an inspiration. 'You'll have to ask Billy,' she said. 'With his police record he thinks he might get into trouble and he made me promise not to tell anyone what he did. But honest, Grandma, he's a real hero. I wouldn't be here if it wasn't for Billy.'

Beth took her in her arms. 'Oh, Amy love. Whatever would I have done if you'd not come back?'

*

Billy didn't come home the next day. Mr Eccles wasn't pleased with Amy's reluctance to tell him exactly how Billy had been a hero, but respected the promise she had made to him.

'He'll be back in his own good time, Mr Eccles, I'm sure of that. He thought I'd broken a promise to him once before and he ended up in a reformatory.'

'What about these people he defended you from? Maybe they've got him?'

'No, Mr Eccles, that wouldn't be possible.'

The day after that she saw Eli reading the *Manchester Guardian*, more intently than usual. Beth was out shopping. He looked up at Amy. 'There's a front page story in here about two mystery kids who turned up in the *Guardian* offices two nights ago with information about a man and his wife who were kidnapping young girls. The police dug up three bodies from the garden.'

'How is he–?' said Amy, without thinking.

'How's who?'

Amy just shrugged and continued sewing the ragged garment she'd be wearing for the next evangelist outing.

'There's a description of these youngsters,' said Eli, innocently. 'Both around fourteen or fifteen, she had bruises on her face but nowhere near as bad as the bruises on the boy's face. According to this the girl had intelligent, blue eyes, dark curly hair and was wearing a navy blue coat, just like yours, fancy that. Hmm – if he'd said the girl was pretty I'd have sworn it could be you.'

'I imagine lots of girls fit that description.'

'The young lad,' continued Eli, 'had fair hair that needed a comb, and a cheeky face. Now who does that remind me of?' He rubbed his chin, contemplatively. 'It can't have been you, because you were in Newcastle. Oh, by the way, your grandma asked me to give your coat a brush down this morning. It was looking a bit muddy.'

'Thanks.'

'Something fell out of the pocket; it's on the sideboard. It's something that probably needs throwing away but I thought I'd let you see it first. I don't like throwing other people's things away.'

Amy got up and went to the sideboard. On it was a Manchester/Leeds train ticket, third class. *He knew.* She stood there for a while, wondering what to say. If Eli had found out on his own, then she wasn't betraying Billy – or was she? She turned round and asked, 'Does it say how the man is?'

'He'll live to be tried for murder, apparently. I take it these children were you and Billy.'

'What?'

'Come on Amy, I wasn't born yesterday.'

'OK. Sorry I lied to you.'

'It was your duty to lie.'

'Anyway,' she said, 'I'm glad you found out.' Her relief was obvious. 'Billy thought he'd killed him. He was really upset about it.'

'Does this make any difference to the promise you made to Billy?' enquired Eli. 'According to this the police want to speak to the two youngsters and it says they are not in trouble – especially the boy, who the police say seems to have been quite a hero.'

'He was,' said Amy, sitting down again. 'Oh, Eli, it was the most awful thing that ever happened to me.'

'My dear girl, I can't imagine how dreadful you must have felt. The story you told the reporter is all down here. I don't wonder the police want to speak to you. Apparently several men have been arrested as well; men who might have been implicated in the murders.'

'Dirty men,' said Amy softly. She shuddered as she remembered.

'I suspect the police might want to pin a medal on Billy. I know your grandma will when she finds out.'

'I just wish I knew what had happened to him,' said Amy. 'He was so convinced he'd get into trouble.'

'I imagine he'll be back once he reads about all this.'

'I hope so,' Amy said. 'I do hope so.'

Right at that moment Billy was passing The Old Head of Kinsale in a merchant ship heading for Central America. He couldn't see the scene of the *Lusitania*'s sinking because he was in the galley peeling potatoes. He wouldn't read a British newspaper for years but he had sent two letters, one to his dad and one to Amy, saying he was going off to seek fame and fortune. They both wept when they read them.

Seven months later he had visited many ports in Central and South America and had now rounded the Horn. He was in a bar in Valparaiso, drinking a glass of Chilean plonk, unaware that at that precise moment Wallace and his wife were being simultaneously hanged – Wallace in Strangeways, his wife in Holloway. On the advice of one of his shipmates who was in the same boat as him – in more ways than one – Billy hadn't written home again. It would have revealed his whereabouts. And that was too risky.

Chapter Nineteen

June 1919

Godfrey Farthing read in the *Bradford Telegraph* about how the 'Manchester Monsters' were hanged and of how two local youngsters had bravely brought them to book, one of whom was Amy Farthing, the granddaughter of millionaire mill owner, Godfrey Farthing. It told of how Amy was living in reduced circumstances since her miracle survival of the *Lusitania* sinking, but the newspaper left it to the readers to wonder just why a millionaire should abandon his brave and beautiful granddaughter. When asked, Beth had simply said, 'You'll have to ask Farthing that.'

'Blast and damn that woman!'

It meant that reporters would be banging on his door before the day was out. The readers would expect a re-action from him in tomorrow's edition. Before he knew it the whole thing could be in a national newspaper. He cursed Beth, he cursed Amy, he cursed the hanged Peets for not doing their job properly – and then he cursed that solicitor's clerk in Scotland who had witnessed his father's will and whose very existence was hanging over Godfrey like the sword of Damocles. Supposing he read the story and wondered why Amy hadn't inherited the money?

Godfrey had a new wife whom he expected to provide him with a child, preferably a boy. He was sixty-one now and couldn't realistically expect to father more than one. But even if it was a girl at least it would be a natural child and a fitting person to inherit his wealth – unlike the mongrel whose picture smiled out at him from the front page. He screwed up the paper and threw it on the floor.

Josiah came into the room, picked up the paper, smoothed it out and was reading it with a smile just as Godfrey was planning his next move. The man in Edinburgh had to be quickly dealt with, the one with the familiar name – Robert Burns. First him, then those two meddling females. All Godfrey had to find was another Hubert Heptonstall to do his dirty work for him.

Weather permitting, Robert Burns was in the habit of taking a lunchtime stroll out of his firm's offices in Frederick Street, crossing Princes Street, and eating the sandwiches packed for him by his wife in the castle gardens. Now forty years old he was a junior partner in the firm and his prospects were good. He had a great love for the law despite all its discrepancies, but his main asset was his memory for things in the past. Before anyone in the firm headed for the filing cabinet to look up an old case or a name they would first ask Robert, to see if he could save them time.

It was this memory that had provided him with something to puzzle over while eating his lunch. An article in yesterday's *Evening News* about the hanging of the so-called Manchester Monsters had had him pondering all morning as to why Samuel Farthing's great-granddaughter was living in reduced circumstances and hadn't inherited all his money. He remembered the look of amusement on old Samuel's face the day he altered his will. It was that look which persuaded Robert to read through the will to see what was in it that was so funny and had been amazed to find the will altered to cut out his son completely. Shortly afterwards John Sykes had reminded him of the will's confidentiality and had warned him not to breath a word of it to anyone, not even to anyone within the firm.

That morning Robert had telephoned his old firm, Sykes Sykes and Broom to learn that both grandsons were dead and Amy Farthing was the only surviving great-grand-child. According to the will she should now be a wealthy young lady.

That afternoon he would pursue the matter further. Samuel Farthing's solicitors said that both copies of the will had left their files so they weren't able to throw any light on the matter and it was only as Robert was leaving his office that he remembered there could well have been a third copy of the will in his old office file back at Sykes's. They made a third copy under certain circum-stances, such as if they thought the will might be disputed. It was probably down in their storage right now but it shouldn't be too difficult for them to dig out. If nothing else the matter merited another telephone call to Sykes, Sykes and Broom whose responsibility this was.

As he waited for the traffic to clear he looked across Princes Street and up at the castle. It was a nice place to eat his sandwiches and think. And the more he thought about it the more he suspected that Godfrey Farthing had been up to no good. Then he remembered that other business where John Sykes had died in his burning house. Tragedy that. But hadn't young Amy Farthing been involved in the second burning that night? If his memory served, and it usually did, the same man was convicted of both crimes. Was there a connection? Yes, there was much to think about as he ate his lunch.

In the gardens a pipe and drum band began to tune up. The discordant howl carried across the street and brought a smile to his lips. His own attempts at the bagpipes had sounded much like this, only these pipers would hopefully get into tune before long. The noise was enough to drown the sound of the car approaching him at speed. Someone shouted a warning but they were too late.

The following evening Eli was in Beth's house, perusing the *Bradford Daily Telegraph*. He was in the habit of reading out interesting snippets, which he often embellished to make them sound more dramatic or funny or just plain silly. Eli reading the newspaper was an entertainment for all of them.

'Oh dear, poor chap,' he exclaimed.

'What's happened?' Beth asked, putting down her sewing. Amy paused in her violin practice.

'Solicitor chap, used to work for a Bradford firm. Got knocked down by a motor car on Princes Street in Edinburgh. Know the place well. Last time I was there motor cars were few and far between. More likely to get trampled by a horse than run down by a motor car. They're becoming a menace, you know.'

'Is he all right?' asked Amy.

'Well no, he's not all right. Poor chap's dead. Worst thing is the driver of the blasted vehicle simply drove off and left him in the road. The police are calling it a suspicious death.'

'Oh dear,' said Beth. 'Was he married?'

'Wife and fourteen-year-old daughter. Used to work for a firm in Bradford called Sykes, Sykes and Broom. Left in 1900, long time ago. Still, hence the local interest, I suppose.'

Beth and Amy glanced at one another. Eli looked at them over the top of the paper, narrowing his eyes.

'What?' he asked.

'Probably nothing,' said Beth. 'It's just that when Hubert Heptonstall burned our house down he burned down Mr Sykes' house about an hour before, killing him and his mother.'

'Of course,' exclaimed Eli. 'I remember you telling me. My word! Is this just a coincidence or is it a conspiracy? Perhaps we should tell the police.'

'If this poor man had some connection with Godfrey Farthing it might raise a few eyebrows,' remarked Beth. She looked at Amy who held up her hands.

'It's OK, I agree. It's a long shot, but maybe he is behind it all.'

'I'd like to say it's only a question of time before he's brought to justice,' sighed Inspector Gifford. 'But all the evidence against him is what we call circumstantial.'

'Circumstantial?' repeated Beth.

The policeman scratched his head, then rubbed his neck and added, 'There's a lot of it, but it's all very flimsy. We don't have a motive, you see. He has connections with a lot of murdered people, but the question is why. All he has to say is that it's just a series of coincidences. Our only witness against him was hanged.'

'Do you think my grandfather did it?' asked Amy.

Gifford stared at her, as if wondering if he could trust her not to go round blabbing to all and sundry about his suspicions. 'If I were a betting man,' he said, 'I'd bet my pension on it. But I'll thank you for keeping my suspicions to yourselves. If word of this conversation gets back to him he could make trouble for me. That's the trouble, you see. He's got power he's not really fit for.'

'That's the trouble with the whole world,' commented Beth, philosophically. 'Men with power they're not fit for.'

Chapter Twenty

A group of men stood outside Rawson Market, chatting, watching the world go by and talking about anything but the war; those who had been there rarely talked about the war. Most of them had left body parts on the battlefields of France and had been rewarded with a lifetime's unemployment. Some sold matches, others, the ones with voices, just stood and sang on street corners.

'Makes you feel proud,' said Beth to Amy, cynically.

'Makes me feel guilty,' Amy said. 'We seem to make money out of people's misfortune. I'd hate to think we made money out of those men.'

'We give people hope,' argued Eli. 'We sell them hope and very often relief from a pain that's mostly up here.' He tapped the side of his head.

'Hey, vicar,' called out a legless man, who had obviously recognised Eli from one of the meetings. He was propped up on crutches and sounded as though he'd had a drink or two. 'I wonder if yer could do summat ter help me get me leg over.'

Eli normally had an answer to everything, but not this time. The man's friends laughed raucously and the man himself gave Eli a big wink that said he meant no harm. Eli returned the man's wink with a broad smile and the trio went on their way with Beth and Amy each linked into one of Eli's arms.

It was a mild autumn afternoon. Amy had dealt with the trauma of Manchester in the same way as the men did with the trauma of the war – she put it out of her mind until it existed only in her nightmares and then, after Wallace and his wife had been hanged, not at all. That day had been a day of violent and mixed emotions that she desperately wanted to share with Billy because only he would understand. The memory of Billy remained with her. He was a memory that wouldn't go away because she wouldn't allow it.

'Amy, I need advice,' said Eli. 'Advice on an affair of the heart.'

'I'm only sixteen,' Amy said. 'What do I know?'

'Everything,' said Eli. 'I've yet to come across a sixteen-year-old that doesn't know everything.'

Beth frowned. She didn't like the sound of Eli seeking advice on an affair of the heart.

'Normally,' said Eli. 'I'd have hitched up my caravan and been a hundred miles away by now, curing the heathen Lancastrians or maybe enabling the benighted Geordies to see the light, and line my pocket. But, tragically, I'm emotionally tied for the first time in my life.'

'Emotionally tied?' said Amy. 'That's not tragic, that's romantic. Well, so long as you're not leaving us.'

The two of them unconsciously gripped his arm more tightly, much to his delight. 'Wouldn't dream of leaving you,' he said. 'We're an excellent team, bringing hope and joy to the unsuspecting masses. I just need to find new premises.'

'So,' said Amy. 'What's this affair of the heart you're on about? Do you have a lady friend?'

Beth had deliberately kept him at arm's length, fearing that any romantic involvement might turn sour and ruin a perfectly good living for them all. Eli nodded in answer to Amy's question and Beth's heart sank. Her feelings for him were deeper than for any man she'd ever known if she cared to admit it. He was a rogue and a charlatan but he had something that she desperately wanted. If only she knew what it was.

'I have indeed. I've had this lady friend for some time and I have very benign feelings towards her, very benign indeed.'

'Benign,' said Amy, unimpressed at his depth of feeling. 'Is that all?'

There was little traffic about that Monday afternoon. A horse pulling a delivery wagon paused to evacuate its bowels, causing them to stop halfway across Kirkgate. Before they had reached the other side of the road a man with a patch over one eye and a hideously mutilated face ran out and shovelled up the steaming manure. As soon as he had a bucketful he would be on his way to Thornton Road allotments, offering it for sale to supplement his army pension.

'Deeply benign,' said Eli as they reached the kerb and proceeded down the footpath. 'My feelings for this lady are most deeply benign – and what is more I believe she has feelings for me which are, so far, unexpressed. She also has premises of a most comfortable nature.'

Beth was feeling quite miserable now. Eli spent a lot of his time away from her, and he'd had ample opportunity to strike up a deeply benign relationship with this other woman and her comfortable premises. However, it puzzled her that he hadn't mentioned it. Over the time she'd known him they had become almost soulmates, exchanging thoughts and stories and ambitions and jokes. Never in her life had she been so taken with a man.

'How benign are these feelings?' enquired Amy. 'Are they benign enough for you to propose marriage to this lady friend?'

Shut up, Amy, Beth was thinking. *Don't put such thoughts into his head. Apart from anything else, if he goes off with this lady friend we'll lose him and then where will we be?*

'You mean get down on bended knee and say the four magic words?' said Eli.

'Why not?' replied Amy, encouragingly. 'If anyone can talk her into it you can.'

They were in a crowded street, passing a jeweller's shop. Eli stopped to look at a tray of rings, glittering in the window, under an electric light.

'I thought if I bought her a betrothal ring it might demonstrate my feelings towards her more than mere words can,' Eli remarked. 'And this is where I need the advice. What sort of a ring would impress a lady of great quality.'

'A solitaire diamond,' said Amy without hesitation. 'The bigger the better.'

Beth twisted the narrow wedding ring that Alfred had bought her all those years ago. It was the only ring he could afford but it meant more to her than the world's biggest diamond. It was the wedding ring of a good man. 'Rings don't impress ladies of great quality,' she said, gruffly, remembering the massive diamond ring that Godfrey had bought Lydia.

'Do they not?' said Eli.

'No, they don't. A ring has to mean something. My

290

Alfred bought me this ring with his whole week's wages. It didn't amount to much but I wouldn't swap it for all the rings in this shop.'

'Hmm,' said Eli. 'I have a ring that belonged to my mother. It's not exactly one of the crown jewels but it's my greatest treasure. Perhaps I should give her that?'

'If she's got anything about her she'll prefer that to any of the rings in here,' muttered Beth, who hated this lady friend.

'I hope you don't live to regret those words,' said Eli. He took a ring from his pocket. It was an opal between two small diamonds, not hugely expensive, but pretty enough. 'It's all I have to remember my dear mother by,' he said, gazing at it with some fondness. He took the glove off Beth's left hand and went down on bended knee. Amy caught her breath as Eli said, 'Elizabeth, will you marry me?'

It seemed as though everyone in the street had stopped to hear her answer. 'Why you dozy beggar,' whispered Beth. 'Get up. Everyone's looking at us! What would your lady friend say if she could see you acting the goat like this?'

Eli spread his arms. 'I will get up when you have given me your answer.'

'What?'

'I think you *are* that lady friend,' said Amy, happily. 'Grandma, he's proposing.'

'Is he? Are you?'

'Well, I'm doing my level best,' said Eli, shifting his position so that his bended knee was no longer resting on a crack in the flags. 'My features are humble but my heart is bursting with love for you . . . ouch!' His knee found another, sharper crack.

'I should tell him yes, love, afore he knackers his knees,' advised a watching woman, holding a nose-picking child by its hand.

Beth glared at her. 'I'll make up my own mind, thank you very much.'

'I'm just saying, that's all. Yer can't afford ter be choosy at your age.'

'You're no spring chicken yourself!' retorted Beth.

'Ee, there's no helping some folk. Arnold will you stop jumpin' up and down?'

'Granny, I want ter go for a wee,' said Arnold, urgently.

The woman looked at Beth. 'Will yer be long deciding? The lad's wetting hisself.'

Beth looked back down at Eli, whose ardour looked to be on the wane.

'Say something, Grandma,' urged Amy.

'Say yes,' said Eli. 'Please say yes.'

His plea was echoed by some of the crowd, much to Beth's embarrassment. 'Aw, go on then,' she said. 'If only to shut you up.'

'Is that a yes?' asked Eli, uncertain.

'Course it's a flamin' yes,' said Arnold's granny. Others in the crowd confirmed this.

'Yes,' said Beth, eliminating all doubt. She gave an embarrassed smile at the round of applause she got. Arnold escaped from his grandmother and ran down a back alley, unbuttoning his trousers as he ran. Eli got back to his feet and put the ring on Beth's finger. 'I love you, Elizabeth Crabtree,' he said. 'And I'd like to make you Mrs Mudd.'

'Oh heck!' said Beth. 'I never thought of that.'

Arnold's grandmother smirked, some people in the crowd groaned their sympathy, but it was too late for Beth. She'd said yes.

Chapter Twenty-One

March 1920

On some days Amy still felt Billy's kiss lingering on her lips, even though it was two years ago and she had only been fourteen when he had planted it there; the memory of him was far stronger than the reality of all the boys she had been out with. It worried her that he might never return home, her heart would be stranded and her childhood love for him left unrequited. Perhaps he had found someone else, or had forgotten about her or was dead. She had confided in Eli, who seemed to understand such things. In many ways her grandmother's heart had been hardened by the events of her life, although marrying Eli had knocked some of the sharp edges off her. They were walking in Roundhay Park where Eli was planning an evangelical spectacular.

'I thought you and grandma had a beautiful wedding.'

'The word I'd use is economical,' said Eli, after some consideration. 'Economical but romantic.'

'And cold,' Amy added.

'Deep amid the winter's snow,' said Eli, with a grin.

'Trudging from chapel to inn, all wearing gumboots and singing lustily. Just my small family, and friends who really matter.'

'It's a shame you have no other family,' said Amy, ever curious. 'What happened to them?'

'Oh, dead or nor worth bothering with.'

Amy kicked some dead leaves, still lingering in the grass from the recently departed winter. 'Eli, do you think I'll ever become happily married like you and grandma? If I do, I hope I won't have to wait quite as long.'

Eli chuckled. 'You're flowering into a real beauty, Amy – a real heart melting beauty. You're so young, at the beginning of your life with the world at your feet. It's not a time to be thinking of marriage. Marriage is for boring old adults such as me. You should be thinking of romance.'

'What's the difference?'

He shook his head and gave her a sad smile. 'The difference is that romance is fun, marriage is hard work. Somewhere out there is a man who is worthy of you and who can make you happy every day. He might be a pedlar or a prince, you won't care.' He winked at her. 'But, take it from me, it's better that you don't meet him just yet.'

Billy returned to her thoughts. He had been no more than a boy when she last saw him. Was she fooling herself. Was she in love with a memory? She sat down on a wooden bench by the lake. Eli joined her. A hopeful duck approached them, hoping for titbits, then swam away with a disappointed quack.

'Sorry,' called out Amy. She turned to Eli and asked, 'Are you happy with Grandma?'

He took out his clay pipe and packed it with tobacco as he considered his reply. 'I'm as happy as a man can be,' he said. 'She has her own point of view on many things. The trick is to change her opinion without her knowing it.' He struck a match and sucked the flame into the bowl.

'I imagine you're good at changing her opinions,' Amy said, catching a whiff of the smoke. She always liked the smell of a pipe outdoors. Inside the house was a different matter altogether.

'I do have a certain talent in that direction,' Eli said, puffing away, contentedly, with arms folded and legs crossed. 'It's the secret to all happy marriages. Usually it's the woman who does all the trickery, because men are so gullible.'

'I never looked upon grandma as gullible.'

'*Susceptible* is more the word I'd choose for Beth. She's a woman who doesn't quite know where her talents and preferences lie. All she needs is a nudge in the right direction.'

'Without her knowing it?'

'If she knew, she wouldn't budge an inch.'

'She seems to have budged many inches since marrying you.'

'The length of a cricket pitch,' smiled Eli.

'Do you think she'll ever make peace with Grandfather Farthing?'

'Not if I could nudge her the length of the Great North Road. And I have no reason to nudge her in his direction. I'm afraid I share her dislike of the man. The death of that solicitor in Scotland worried her. There's something venomous about that man that I simply don't understand.'

'The police didn't make a connection with the man in Scotland's death,' Amy remembered. 'They said he was killed by an unfit motorist rather than it being a deliberate act.'

'I would rather trust your grandmother's instincts than the police.'

Amy tossed a stone into the water, earning herself a look of rebuke from a nearby fisherman. As she watched the widening circles she thought about Billy again. 'Eli,' she said. 'I keep thinking about Billy. Do you think it's because I'm in love with him?'

Eli put an arm around her and gave her a squeeze. 'If you have to ask, I'm afraid the answer's probably no. True love's a rare bird. When it comes along it smacks you in the eye and leaves you shuddering from top to toe.'

'You make it sound very painful.'

'Painful? It can be agonising, especially when you're young. That's why it's better to leave it until you're older.' His pipe went out, as it often did, and he paused to light it.

'So, I'll definitely know when I'm in love?'

'You'll be in absolutely no doubt,' he assured her, between puffs.

'And are you in no doubt about being in love with grandma?' she enquired, ingenuously.

Eli smiled. 'No doubt all,' he said, '– not even a shadow.'

'I wish Billy would come home,' Amy said, 'then I'd know for sure.'

Eli's thoughts had strayed on to his imminent task. He was surveying the scene and mentally planning the positioning of his stage. 'This is a magnificent venue,' he said. 'I do hope there aren't any last minute hitches.'

*

'Beth, I should have had that tooth out.'

Eli lay beside his wife in bed with a hand cupped under his jaw. 'Do we know a dentist who could pull it today?'

'Doubt it, love, not on a Sunday. Will you be all right to do the show?'

'Please, Beth, it's a gathering, not a show – and a fine healer I'd be if can't cure my own toothache. I'll try and ease it with a drop of juniper juice.'

Beth got out of bed, opened a drawer in the dressing table and took out a bottle of aspirin. 'Never mind gin, take a couple of these every now and again. Alcohol doesn't agree with you, it makes you giddy, as if you're not giddy enough to start with.'

There was a good crowd in Roundhay Park that afternoon. It was mid-March and there was a Spring Fair, the first event of the year. A brass band was playing in the bandstand overlooking Waterloo Lake. It had attracted a good audience, and it was near here that Eli decided to set up his stage. His bad tooth throbbed away but he was keeping the pain at bay with a mixture of gin and aspirin – although Beth didn't know about the gin. She thought the stuff in his flask was water for his dry throat.

The weather was cool but sunny and the people in the park were glad of an additional attraction, especially one as entertaining as the silver-tongued Eli. It was a time of year when there was still damp in the air and winter aches and pains were still at their peak, not yet soothed by summer warmth. The faithful were persuaded to make their way to the stage and be cured by Eli's healing hands. All was going well and Beth's collection box was becoming nicely filled with not just copper but with a few threepenny bits and the odd silver tanner. During the day Eli had drunk almost a full bottle of Gordon's – a drink which made him uncharacteristically maudlin. He was looking at his beloved Beth moving through the crowd, and dear Amy playing *Nearer My God To Thee* more sweetly than he'd ever heard it before. Then, for no reason he could think of, Godfrey Farthing sprang to his thoughts. All the evil things this foul man had done to his beloved family and yet he was still free to walk the streets. It just wasn't right. He picked up his tin megaphone so that he could reach the people at the back.

'My dear brethren,' he called out. 'Today is Sunday, the Sabbath Day, the Lord's Day. And it is only fitting that I should tell you a modern day parable.'

Amy stopped playing and Beth stopped collecting. In the audience, Norman and Mrs Attercliffe, both ready to present their ailments for his miracle cure, were stopped in their tracks.

'My story,' boomed Eli, 'is of an evil man who fortunately does not live among you, but in your neighbouring town of Bradford. This man tried to kill my dear and charming wife who is among you now, and the delightful Amy who plays the violin so beautifully.' There was a murmur in the crowd, which had taken to Amy. Eli took another sip of his gin. He swilled it around his mouth, baring his teeth and drawing in a throat-ventilating breath before swallowing it. The pain was there in the background but the gin – and now his new mission – were helping to ease that pain.

'This evil man,' he went on, 'ordered the burning down of their home, and the home of another family, killing a total of five good people. Five good people died an excruciating painful death, my dear brethren. He ordered their deaths simply because he is an evil man. And, my dear brethren, this profoundly evil man has escaped justice.'

There were shouts of, 'How,' and 'Why?' from the audience.

'You may well ask how,' said Eli. 'How can such a man escape British justice of which we are so proud? He escaped, my dear brethren because he is a rich man. He is a man of power. He is part of the establishment. He is a magistrate and man of great influence.' Warming to his theme, Eli took another large swig and pointed to the heavens. 'But none of us can escape the justice of the Lord, my dear brethren. On judgement day his money and power and influence will count for nothing, and he will be sent to burn in the deepest bowels of hell.'

'Alleluia!' shouted Norman Attercliffe.

'Who is this man?' came a shout. Other people joined in.

'Who is he?' shouted Eli. 'I will tell you who he is. I will tell you who he is so that his name will be burned into your minds for ever. He is a mill owner in Bradford. But he is also a murderer, a rapist and an abuser of women.'

'Tell us the bastard's name,' screamed a woman who had just been cured of arthritis.

'Godfrey Farthing, that's his name,' bellowed Eli through his megaphone. 'Godfrey bloody Farthing!'

Beth was nodding her approval of Eli's denunciation of the man she hated most in the world. Amy was wondering if such a public censure might get Eli into trouble. Eli had forgotten his toothache and was now launching into old testament stories and parables. Within minutes his words became jumbled, his speech became slurred and he collapsed into his chair, where he snored away soundly. In the bandstand a brass band struck up and the crowd, having been well entertained for a few pennies in a collection box, now transferred its attention to the free music.

Beth caught the eye of a young man she'd seen before. He smiled at her and scribbled away at the copy he'd be taking back to the *Bradford Telegraph* that very afternoon.

Amy took the reins of the caravan as they drove back to Bradford. Eli slept all of the way, only waking up as they rattled over the cobbles of Cinder yard. He yawned and stretched his arms.

'Where are we?'

'Back home,' said Beth.

'Really? I must have nodded off for a moment.' He was silent for a while, trying to collect his thoughts. Beth looked down on him.

'I found your flask of juniper juice,' she said. 'You were drunk.'

'I was easing the pain,' said Eli. He pressed his hand to his forehead. 'It seems to have transferred itself to my head.'

'Eli, do you remember anything about this afternoon?' Amy asked.

'What – you mean the gathering? Yes, of course I do. How did it go? I didn't nod off before the end, did I?'

'Not before you told everyone about Godfrey Farthing,' Beth said, with no condemnation in her voice.

'Oh dear. Did I say too much, do you think?'

Beth grinned. 'Well,' she said, 'you'll be able to read about it yourself in the *Telegraph*. A reporter was there.'

'Did I say anything that might be construed as slander?'

Beth shook her head. 'You told the truth,' she said. 'Since when was telling the truth slander?'

Eli looked at Amy for a more balanced opinion. 'What do you think?'

'Well, you *were* very forthright,' she said. 'And when you went on to tell your bible stories you got a bit mixed up.'

'Mixed up?'

Beth nodded her agreement. 'I'm not worried about Farthing finding out, but if they print everything and Doctor Rosenberg reads it he might kick us off his panel.'

'Doctor Rosenberg? Oh dear, I didn't offend the good doctor did I?'

'You might have,' said Beth. 'I think Samson slew the Philistines with the jawbone of an ass – not the arsebone of a jew.'

The telephone rang downstairs. Godfrey woke up and looked at the clock, then roundly cursed the late hour. Josiah should have woken him two hours ago, it was half past eight. Why the hell hadn't he been with his morning tea? Dammit! It was Josiah's day off. His wife was supposed to wake him – the one who was snoring beside him. Couldn't she do anything right? He knew one thing. If she didn't produce a child soon he'd kick her out on her arse and to hell with the Farthing dynasty. He'd sell up and go to Paris and spend all his money on whores and high living. That thought put a smile on his face as he heaved himself from his bed.

The telephone bell echoed up the stairs as he waddled down in his dressing gown, shouting, 'I'm coming, I'm bloody coming!' He was out of breath when he picked it up and snarled, 'Yes?'

'Geoffrey Broom here, Mr Farthing. Sykes, Sykes and Broom.'

'I know who you are, Broom. What the hell do you want?'

'I wondered if you saw the *Bradford Telegraph* yesterday evening.'

'Don't even get the bloody *Telegraph*.'

'Well, there's a particularly scurrilous piece about you. Apparently this Eli Mudd character denounced you as a rapist and a mass murderer at one of his evangelical meetings. It seems, among other things, he's accusing you of ordering the burning of John Sykes' house.'

The veins in Godfrey's neck were bulging and throbbing. His knuckles were white as he gripped the telephone. 'It's all damned lies!' he screamed. 'How the hell can they print such damn lies? John Sykes was my friend. Why the hell would I want him dead? It's that bloody mad woman he's married to who's put him up to this. She'll sink to anything to try and get to me.'

'He also says you tried to kill Amy Farthing, who I believe is your granddaughter.'

'I want you to sue that bloody rag and put it out of business!'

'I doubt we can sue the newspaper. It's worded in such a way where they can say they're only quoting another man's words, which is allowable in law. We can sue Mudd. He must have a few quid from all this faith healing nonsense. We could take all that off him and leave him bankrupt into the bargain. That should quieten him down.'

'Do that.'

'Very good. I think ten thousand's a nice round figure. We'll also send notice to the newspaper telling them of your intent. They'll probably be asking you for your side of the story, which might not do any harm.'

'I've no intention of speaking to any bloody papers. Ten thousand eh? Do you think we've got a chance?'

'I doubt if he's got anything like that amount of money, but we'll strip him of everything he has.'

'You're sure of this?'

'Have you been found guilty of murder or rape in a criminal court?' asked Broom.

'Of course I damned well haven't.'

'Have you ever been accused by the police of either of those crimes?'

'Never.'

'Then, Mr Farthing I think we have a cast-iron action against him. We'll relieve him of every penny he has and every penny he's ever likely to earn.'

'Eli Mudd?'

'Yes.'

'Duly served.'

The man on the doorstep pushed a sheaf of papers into Eli's hand and walked away before Eli could respond. Beth came up behind him.

'What did he want?'

'He gave me these.' Eli looked at the top sheet that had the words *Writ of Slander* written on it.

'Oh dear. I do believe I'm being sued.'

'Farthing?' She spat the name out as if she couldn't bear to have it on her lips.

Eli nodded as he perused the documents. 'Ten thousand pounds, no less. Where does he get the idea that I've got ten thousand pounds? I'd struggle to raise a hundred.'

'He doesn't want the money,' Beth said. 'He just wants to destroy us.'

'Well, I did give him good reason to get annoyed,' Eli conceded. 'Perhaps I should have been a little more circumspect.'

'Circumspect my eye!' snorted Beth. 'You told the truth about an evil man.' She took the papers from him. The legal jargon made little sense to her. 'How much damage can he do to us?'

'Quite a lot if we don't fight it.'

'How can we fight him through the courts. We don't have his sort of money.'

'Then we fight him on our own terms,' said Eli, 'and we use the only weapon at our disposal.'

'Which is?'

'My jawbone. It'll be like Samson fighting the Philistines.'

'I think we should forget Samson and the Philistines,' said Beth. 'Let's settle for David and Goliath.'

Josiah opened the door. His face lit up, imperceptibly, when he saw Beth. 'Is he in?' she asked.

Josiah didn't move. 'Mr and Mrs Farthing are taking port in the drawing room, madam.'

'It's Josiah, isn't it?' Beth said, kindly

'It is, madam.'

'You know who I am, I take it,' she said. 'I believe we met before, under unfortunate circumstances.'

'I do remember you, madam. Mrs Crabtree isn't it?'

'It used to be but I got married again. My name is Mudd now.'

'My congratulations, madam.'

'And this is my husband, Eli.'

304

'Pleased to meet you, sir.' He stepped to one side. 'Might I take your coats?'

'No thank you, Josiah' said Eli. 'We might be leaving in a hurry.'

'Very good, Mr Mudd.'

Josiah led them to the drawing room, tapped lightly on the door, opened it without waiting for permission, ushered them in and announced, 'Mr and Mrs Mudd.' He then hovered beside the door, awaiting developments with interest.

The new Mrs Farthing stood up, Godfrey remained sitting in his chair with a glass of port in one hand and a cigar in the other. His wife slowly sat down again, taking the lead from her husband.

'What the hell are you doing here?' growled Godfrey, getting to his feet. His wife once again followed suit. 'I can only assume you've come to apologise. Put your ten thousand on the table and clear off.'

'I've come to tell you why you'd be a fool to pursue this ridiculous litigation,' said Eli, loftily.

Godfrey glowered from beneath sullen brows. '*You* might think it's ridiculous.'

'I do indeed think it's ridiculous. A man in your precarious legal position having temerity to sue me, a man of the cloth.'

'Man of the cloth my arse,' sneered Godfrey. 'The only man of the cloth in this room's me. Without such as me there'd be no bloody cloth. Who the hell do you think you are, coming into my house, laying down the law after what you've done?'

Beth sensed that things had got off to a bad start. 'I'll tell you who *I* am,' she snapped. 'I'm the girl you raped and made pregnant when I was seventeen. I'm the mother of your daughter who drowned on the Lusitania. And I was a friend of your poor dead wife who killed herself because of your brutality.' She turned to Godfrey's wife, who was listening with interest, but showed no sign of springing to her husband's defence. 'Does he beat you, love? Does he beat you like he used to beat my friend Lydia?'

Mrs Farthing found her voice. 'He once tried,' she admitted. 'But he learned his lesson. Doesn't do it any more.'

Godfrey glowered at her.

'He murdered my first husband, did he ever mention that?' Beth said

'No – he never mentioned it.'

'Get out of this house before I have you thrown out,' roared Godfrey.

Beth ignored him. 'Well, he mentioned it to his first wife,' she said. 'In fact I have a letter that she wrote to me. It tells how he mistreated her and how he boasted of killing Alfred Crabtree.'

'Don't believe her, there's no such letter!' snarled Godfrey. 'She never knew Lydia.'

Beth took the letter from her pocket and showed it to Mrs Farthing. 'I had a facsimile made for you to keep. I'll be giving the real one to the police now that things have come to a head.'

As Mrs Farthing read the letter Eli decided it was time he took up the cudgels. 'You see, Mr Farthing, in a court of civil law all these things will be pertinent to the case. Including the last words of a certain Hubert Heptonstall who was hanged for setting fires on your instruction.' Mrs Farthing looked up from her reading as Eli went on: 'He was a young man about to die, with no reason to add to his sins by telling a last lie. He said you paid him fifty pounds to set the fires that killed five people.'

'It's all lies,' said Godfrey, uncertainly.

'This letter doesn't sound like lies,' said his wife, handing the letter to Godfrey.

'They'll have bloody written it themselves.'

'Really?' said Beth. 'If you read it you'll also see why I didn't object to Amelia marrying Henry. You see Henry wasn't your son. Lydia had taken another man to her bed to produce him. There wasn't a drop of your blood in his veins.'

'You what?'

Godfrey scanned the letter then screwed it up and threw it, contemptuously, to the floor. 'This is all bloody rubbish,' he sneered. 'The truth is that Lydia was a raving lunatic at times and if it's not a forgery all it proves is that she was a whore as well. Maybe you saw the good side of her but I had her all the time. And I treated her well.'

His attitude had Beth fuming. 'You're a rapist and a murderer, Farthing!' she screamed. 'A man who beats women. A man who sends his sons to war when he daren't go himself. You've never treated anybody well in all your life.'

Godfrey, seeing Beth was rattled, maintained his composure. 'Tell you what,' he suggested. 'Let's hear the truth from someone who remembers my first wife and all her strange ways. A reliable man who will be prepared to say these things in court.' He walked towards Josiah and stood facing him, with his back to Eli and Beth.

'Josiah, I want you to tell these people how well I treated the first Mrs Farthing. You were here during that time. I want you to tell them how I treated her with great respect and kindness. And tell them about her mental problems. How she wasn't right in her head.' There was no threat in his voice but there was one clearly visible on his face, which only Josiah could see.

'Mental problems, sir?'

'Yes mental problems. It's a long time ago but surely you remember it.'

Josiah rubbed his chin. 'I remember Mrs Farthing very well, sir. She was a fine lady, sir – but I'm blessed if I remember her having mental problems.'

'I said tell them, dammit!'

'Yes tell us, Josiah,' said Beth scornfully, 'before he sacks you.'

'You want me to tell them that you treated the first Mrs Farthing with respect and kindness – and that she had mental problems. Is that what you want me to tell them sir?'

'Are you paid well enough to tell such terrible lies, Josiah?' asked Eli.

'No, sir, I'm not,' said Josiah, gruffly.

'Not what?' screamed Godfrey.

'I'm not paid well enough to tell such terrible lies, sir.'

With that Josiah left the room with a sense of pride in himself that he hadn't felt for years. He'd stood up for Lydia's memory. But at what cost?

Eli now spoke with a calm confidence that Godfrey found unnerving. 'You're in a lot of trouble Farthing. Your own manservant can't bring himself to defend you. Is this the sort of damning evidence you wish to face in a court of civil law? Because if you lose – and lose you will – the criminal authorities will take an interest. And when they take an interest, the next step for you is the gallows, which is more than you deserve!'

Godfrey went white with a mixture of rage and fear. Mrs Farthing hurried from the room. 'Where the hell are you going, woman?'

'As far away from you as I can!' she retorted. 'There's too much of this stuff for it all to be lies.'

'I think we'll take our leave as well,' said Eli to Godfrey, who stood there open-mouthed at the events of the past few minutes. 'Hope we haven't troubled you too much. It's all right, we'll see ourselves out.'

Josiah had made himself scarce. From the window of his basement room he had watched Beth and Eli leave, then he sat and read his book until ten o'clock when he went to bed. With a bit of luck Godfrey would, by now, have drunk himself into one of his stupors and forgotten all about what had happened.

As he lay there in the dark he contemplated his life – his past and his future, what there was of it. He was now seventy-three years old and he knew he hadn't much work left in him. His hip had been troubling him for some time. Climbing the stairs to take Godfrey and Mrs Farthing their morning tea was becoming a major effort. There had been some mornings when he had only just managed it. He was more than ready for retirement.

Samuel Farthing, the boss he'd worked for from being a young man, had been dead well over twenty years. He had no retirement agreement with Godfrey and he knew he hadn't much work left in him. For the thousandth time he remembered Mr Samuel's dying words:

'I've left you well catered for, Josiah. My grandchildren should be pleased as well . . . mind you, Godfrey's got a bit of a shock coming to him.'

The thought of being well catered for had sustained Josiah throughout Samuel's funeral. He would take what was coming to him and leave; there was no way he could ever work for Godfrey.

In the event neither he nor the two grandsons had merited so much as a mention and Josiah's personal circumstances had forced him to stay on for a further twenty-two years of most disagreeable employment. Apart from his personal financial loss the will was a puzzle that had always troubled Josiah. Samuel wasn't a man to make false promises. But a will was a legal document, signed, sealed and witnessed by a lawyer, so there couldn't have been any mistake – or could there? Not for the first time he went to sleep with this mystery on his mind.

The next day was a Sunday and it was nine o'clock when he climbed the stairs and rested on the landing chair for a while before knocking on Godfrey's bedroom door.

'Come.'

The voice seemed no more harsh than normal. Josiah took a hopeful breath and entered. The bedroom stank of alcoholic breath and cigar fumes. There was reason for optimism. Godfrey was standing by the bed, peeing noisily into the chamber pot, bleary eyed from drink. His wife wasn't there.

'Has Mrs Farthing risen early?' Josiah enquired, politely.

'Mrs Farthing walked out on me last night, thanks to your bloody treachery!'

Josiah's heart sank. He had remembered.

'What surprises me is that you didn't follow her!' Godfrey, having empted his bladder, walked over to where Josiah was standing with the tray in his hands. 'It was your fault, you damned old fool! I expect loyalty from my employees. I expected you to back me up when I asked you about my first wife.'

'I, er, I was confused, sir,' said Josiah lamely.

Godfrey punched him in the face with all the force he could muster. Josiah dropped the tray, staggered and fell flat on his back. The pain in his hip was even more agonising then the pain in his nose.

'If you wonder what that was,' Godfrey snarled. 'It's my way of giving you a week's notice. I want your bags packed and you out of this house seven days from today.'

Josiah struggled to his feet and held on to the back of a chair for support, breathing heavily, blood dripping down his face. 'But I've nowhere to go,' he said.

'What the hell has that got to do with me? You should have made provision for yourself. Did you not think of that in all the years my father and I have been good enough to employ you?'

'No, Mr Godfrey. I thought you migh–'

'Thought? I've never known you think in all the years I've known you. Seven days, and think yourself lucky I'm not kicking you out on your scrawny arse right now.' Godfrey picked up the newspaper and shook a few drops of tea from it. 'Now clean this mess and bring me a fresh cup of tea or I'll do just that!'

Josiah had never felt so wretched in all his long years. He turned his face away so that Godfrey wouldn't have the satisfaction of seeing his tears of despair. Would that Mr Samuel were around to right this terrible wrong.

In damp-eyed desperation he descended the stairs with the tray and the empty cup, knowing he wouldn't have the strength to get back up again. The wicked bastard would have to make his own tea now and to hell with him.

*

That afternoon Josiah was snoozing on his bed when Godfrey burst in to his room. Mrs Farthing had not returned and he had been drinking all day. There was no one in the house to make him his meals and he was hungry and drunk – and needed someone upon which to vent his anger. Josiah.

'What the hell are you still doing here?' roared Godfrey. 'If you don't work here you don't live here. Pack your bag and get out!'

'But, Mr Godfrey. You said I had a week–'

'A week's notice means you work a week. If you don't work you leave; I'm not a bloody charity. Now are you going or do I have to throw you out?'

Josiah summoned up whatever strength and dignity he could muster. He swung his legs off the bed and winced in pain. 'I'm sorry, I can't move very fast,' he said, quietly and defiantly. 'Would you please leave and let me get my things together. I wouldn't dream of trying to live off your charity. I was labouring under the assumption that you were some sort of human being.'

The veins in Godfrey's thick neck pumped with anger. He needed a witty response to Josiah's insult, but wit was in short supply.

'One hour,' he snarled. 'Out in one hour or I'll personally throw you out.'

'I'm due a month's wages,' Josiah said.

'And I've been due a month's work,' retorted Godfrey. 'The way you've been performing of late, you're lucky I've kept you in bed and board.'

Josiah limped to the door and held it open for his employer to leave. His face, which was set in an expression of disdain, collapsed into one of distress the second Godfrey was out of the room. He shook his head, despairingly, and sat on his bed.

'Oh my,' he muttered. 'Whatever am I to do?'

He opened his bedside drawer and took out a purse, which he emptied on to the bed. His worldly wealth consisted of ten shillings and seven pence three farthings. He had three guineas to come from his last month's wages but he held out little hope of ever getting that. He'd been on three guineas a month all found since old Samuel died. Nowadays it barely kept him in clothes and tobacco. If he had no money coming in did it mean he qualified for old-age pension? How much was it? Five bob a week at the most. Five bob a week for the over seventies with no other money coming in.

Josiah packed his pipe with strong black shag and, as he filled his room with acrid fumes, he ran through his limited options. He had no family to speak of, apart from his dead brother's boy who lived in Leeds. His world had been centred around the Farthing family for most of his working life and he had no real friends who might put him up. Ten shillings might buy him a week's board at half-decent lodgings, or a month's board at a dosshouse. After which he'd have to throw himself upon the mercy of the parish.

He looked in through the door of the drawing room as he passed with his packed suitcase. Godfrey was slumped in a high-backed chair, dead to the world in a drunken, drooling slumber. The old manservant took the time for a last look around what had been his home for over fifty years and, with a deep sigh, he limped out of the door.

Godfrey's brand new Daimler was parked beside the house and Josiah always carried a key in his waistcoat pocket. The pain in his hip was excruciating – even after a few strides – so there was no way he could walk any distance. He threw his suitcase on the back seat, inserted the starting handle and turned it with a jerk that seemed to set his back on fire, then he stood up with great relief as the engine burst into life.

Josiah opened the driver's door and addressed his last words to the house and it's sole occupant.

'Godfrey Farthing. I hope you burn in the deepest fires of hell!'

Then he got in the car and drove away. It was early Sunday evening on a grey spring day that threatened rain. The thought of taking Godfrey's car brought a smile to his face – a wintry smile but a smile nevertheless.

But as he approached the centre of Bradford guilt overcame him. Thoughts were buzzing about inside his head like bees in a bottle. He had never stolen anything in his life, not even wine from Godfrey's cellar, and here he was, stealing a valuable car. It didn't do to cross Godfrey Farthing. He sent people who crossed him to prison – such as Beth Crabtree. How Godfrey had laughed at that. Laughed fit to burst. Josiah had secretly admired the woman for standing up to him. Good for her. Had he done all the stuff she accused him of? At the time he had thought she was going over the top but he wasn't so sure now. Godfrey had a real streak of evil in him. Maybe he should have stood up to Godfrey and to hell with the consequences. But he couldn't go to prison like she had – not at his age. Prison would kill him. Michael, that's what his nephew was a called – Michael Simms. Good sort, young Michael, bound to put him up. Regular in the army last time he heard, which was a long time ago. He'd probably be out by now. Hopefully he still lived in his father's old house in Headingley, not far from the Yorkshire cricket ground. Josiah had been there to visit his brother once or twice – years ago and he couldn't remember the number. No matter. He'd drive to the station, leave the car there, catch a train to Leeds and make his way to Headingley. Surely he'd remember the house, if not, he had a tongue in his head. A boy ran out into the road, Josiah swerved and drove into a lamp post.

'Are you all right, mister?'

A small crowd gathered, more to examine the damaged car than to help Josiah, who had cut his head.

'It's a Daimler. Posh motors, Daimlers.'

'By the heck. He must have some brass must this feller.'

'He dunt look as if he's got much brass. Dunt look as if he's gorra tanner ter scratch his arse.'

'Yer can't tell. There's millionaires in Bradford wanderin' round wi' their trousers arse hangin' out.'

'Here, mister, are yer all right. I'll give yer an 'and.'

Josiah allowed several young men to help him out of the damaged vehicle.

'Shall I fetch a bobby, mister?'

'No, no. It's all right. I'll be fine.'

Josiah took his suitcase from the back seat and pushed his way through the crowd, who paid little attention to him. The damaged car was all they were interested in. Ten minutes later he was sitting on a low wall waiting for the pain in his hip to ease and wondering how far it was to the station. He put his hand in his pocket to take out his pipe and as he did so he realised something was missing. His purse. He'd been robbed.

He raised a desperate hand to attract the attention of a passing policeman then realised that he himself was a thief of a much more reprehensible kind than the one who had robbed him of a few shillings.

'Are you all right, sir,' asked the policeman.

'Yes, thank you. Just stretching my arms, that's all. I get stiff in my joints, you see.'

'You should try my job, sir. This is the job for stiffening of the joints. Out in all weathers. Having to chase fleet-footed miscreants in these great clod-hopping boots.'

'Oh, I couldn't do that, constable.'

'No sir, I don't expect you could. I bid you good day, sir.'

'Good day, constable.'

Josiah sighed and set off walking down the road. Perhaps he could steal a ride on the train, then somehow make his way to his nephew's house when he got to Leeds.

But Josiah didn't even get to the station. Very soon his hip gave way again and sent him tumbling, heavily, to the ground from where he couldn't get up. Something had taken away his power of speech and all he could summon up was a low, rasping moan. His body felt completely numb all down one side. Passers-by walked around him assuming he was just another drunk littering the streets. One man even poked him with a walking stick, urging him to have some dignity and get up. Whatever dignity Josiah had left drained away from him in the form of tears as he laid his head on the cold flagstones and closed his eyes as rain began to fall. It was a poor way to end his days, but it seemed he had no option.

As he drifted in and out of consciousness it seemed to him that dying was a slow business and he wished God would get on with it instead of leaving him here, littering up the pavement. He pondered on what they'd do with him after he'd gone. How long would it be before they realised he was dead? Probably not before morning. His vision was blurred but as far as he could tell it was dark now. Dark and wet. He couldn't feel much but he didn't suppose men on the verge of death would be able to feel much – which was a blessing. Dying out here like this was very uncomfortable, not to say embarrassing, but it wasn't painful. He'd swap painful for uncomfortable and embarrassing any day of the week. Please God let Godfrey Farthing die a painful death and let it be soon. So, why had Samuel let this happen to him? He'd promised on his deathbed that he'd be taken care of, so what had happened? If Josiah was in a position to make a promise right now it wouldn't be a false one. There'd be no point making a false promise to anyone at this, the fag end of life – the bit just before you got snuffed out. Now was a time for truth. If only he had someone to tell the truth to. But what was the truth? He allowed his imminent demise to condense his thoughts into what could only be the absolute blinding truth. Just before death was a very good time to think as it turned out. Yes, a jolly good time to think, come to think of it. Everything was there, and he could see it, plain as day. Plain as the nose on your face. Why hadn't he seen it when he was alive and kicking? The truth was that Samuel *had* been telling the truth. That's what the truth was. Plain as a pikestaff. The truth was that Godfrey must have done something to make that will – the one which apparently cut him off without a penny – disappear. Made sure no one saw it. The will that was read out was the will *before* Samuel changed it. It had to be. Godfrey could make things like that happen all too easily. It was all so clear to him now. At the fag end of his life with no one to tell all this to. What a pity. Trouble was he didn't know who he could tell it to anyway, even if he hadn't been due to die very shortly. The boys, the true beneficiaries of the will, were both dead, so he could only tell them in the afterlife, which shouldn't be long now. What about young Amy, the one Godfrey seemed to disown for some reason? She would be the sole beneficiary. No wonder Farthing had disowned her. Sole beneficiary, now that really would be something. If he had any duty in this life it was to tell Amy the whole truth. He should have told her, or at least told that woman. What was she called again? Beth Crabtree. No, Mrs Mudd. My word, she'd have kicked up a storm had she found out. Probably got to the truth as well. Determined woman like that. Pity he was going to die. He had so much truth to tell. Someone was cursing and pulling at his feet and his head banged against something hard. Knocking him into merciful oblivion.

At five-thirty the next morning Josiah was the subject of a discussion between a policeman and the knocker-up who found him.

'I dint know where ter send my lad – fer thee or fer t' undertaker.'

'Well, I suppose yer did right in sending fer me first,' said the policeman, writing a note in his book. 'How d'yer spell cadaver? It's one o' them words that never looks right when yer write it down.'

'I've never had much call fer writin' it down meself. Why don't yer just put body?'

'It's procedures yer see, sir,' said the constable, studying his spelling and shrugging. 'We all have procedures ter follow. Would yer mind waitin' here with him while I ring the station?'

'I could leave t' lad if yer like. There'll be folk late

fer work already. It's bad enough me losin' trade to a bloody alarm clock without losin' it to a stiff.'

'He's not a stiff until he's been officially declared a stiff,' said the policeman. He glanced at the knocker-up's young assistant who was standing several yards away, looking decidedly unenthusiastic at the idea of guarding Josiah's body. 'He looks a bit too young fer such a task.'

'Why, what yer expectin' to happen? The bugger's hardly gonna gerrup an' run away, is he?'

'Body snatchers, sir,' said the policeman, dramatically.

'Oh, I see.'

'Even in this day and age there's people who'll pay good money for a fresh cadaver.'

'Oh, go on then. Horace – yer'll have ter finish t' round on yer own. Can yer manage that?'

'Will I be entitled ter more brass?' enquired Horace.

'Yer'll be entitled to a bloody thick ear.'

'I'll be as quick as I can, sir,' said the policeman. 'I need a doctor to declare him dead before I can have him moved to the mortuary.'

Chapter Twenty-Two

Beth was in the scullery winding washing through a mangle when the postman delivered the letters, both of which, in a roundabout way, were to change their lives. Eli opened the first and read it through squinting eyes.

'It's about time you got yourself some glasses,' commented Beth. Amy was in the living room practising her violin, which she did every spare moment.

'My eyes are fine. They just wake up about an hour after the rest of me, that's all. Ah – this is from Messrs Sykes, Sykes and Broom. Farthing's offering to withdraw his action providing I promise not to make any further malicious and unfounded statements about him. What a kind man.'

'*Will* we be making any further malicious statements?' asked Beth.

'Not today.' He opened the second envelope. 'Chap here wants us to give a show for nothing. I wish people wouldn't call it a show.'

'We're *always* supposed to work for nothing,' Beth reminded him. 'The collection's supposed to be just enough to cover our expenses.' She was finding that living on the edge of a law that had served her so badly provided her with a sort of recompense that eased the bitterness.

'The fact is that our expenses keep us living well,' said Eli, stroking his beard, 'and will hopefully pay for Amy's music college fees.'

'If she gets that scholarship it might not be so bad.'

Amy's music teacher had entered Amy for a scholarship to Manchester College of Music. Eli and Beth paused to listen to Amy's playing. 'I think the scholarship's a forgone conclusion,' said Eli. 'Then we'll have to get a new musician.' He looked at the letter again. 'Maybe it wouldn't do any harm to have it known that we do good work as well. If we could get it in the newspapers, it might stop the law in their tracks if they ever come looking for us again.'

'I thought the law had left you alone now you've got this reputation as a genuine healer.'

'It would do no harm to have a reputable organisation batting for us – if ever it were needed.'

'Reputable organisation? What reputable organisation?'

Eli waved the letter at her. 'The Knights of the Saint Jude Home for the Homeless. They want us to be part of their Christmas celebrations. By the sound of it there'd be no point having a collection. I doubt if they've got a pot to piss in.'

'Eli!'

'Sorry – I was speaking biblically. I believe it's in the Old Testament – *And Jacob had no coat to wear or pot to piss in.*'

'You make it up as you go along.'

'Do I? I think not. Anyway, I think we should do it.

Yes, I'll let them know – then I'll ring the *Yorkshire Post* and the *Argus*.'

The senior Knight of Saint Jude was a retired railways clerk called Cedric. The home was an old school and where the desks had been there were now beds, mostly taken up by ex-servicemen, a lot of them disabled. Cedric himself only had one arm, having left the other in Mafeking some twenty-two years earlier.

'Bloody Mafeking,' he grumbled to Eli. 'Bloody Baden Powell got all the bloody glory and I lost a bloody arm. Mind you, there's them as lost a lot more than that. Still out there, most o' me pals.'

'Ah – *If I should die*,' quoted Eli, '*think only this of me: That there's some corner of a foreign field that is forever England . . .*'

'Is that the sort of stuff yer do?'

'What? Oh, no. That's the sort of stuff Rupert Brooke wrote. He died in the last lot. I was in the Boer War too. Not Mafeking. I was at Ladysmith, though. Rose to the dizzy heights of corporal.'

'And now yer've taken up religion?'

'It appears I have a gift,' said Eli.

'It'll have ter be a gift,' said Cedric. 'I'm afraid my lads have nowt ter give.'

'Are they all men?'

'All us residents are. We have women poppin' in fer meals during the day. We can't put both sexes up. We've neither the room nor the brass.'

'Well, we shall ask for nothing. Except that you extend your hospitality to the odd newspaper reporter.'

'Bread and soup is what we offer,' said Cedric. 'We've not the means ter spoil anyone.'

'Their publicity would do your organisation no harm at all,' pointed out Eli. 'It might boost your charitable subscriptions.'

'Well, they need a boost right enough,' agreed Cedric. 'Right, I'll put some pies on for 'em. Soup and pies for them and your lot.'

'You're a most gracious host. Me and my lot will be here to set up at six-thirty in the evening a week on Friday. The gathering will begin an hour later. We can't restore lost limbs but I may be able to heal aches and pains and broken spirits.'

'In that case yer've got yer work cut out.'

Eli persuaded Norman Attercliffe to hobble in on a crutch and become a resident a few days before the show. He protested until Eli offered him ten shillings a day. Florence, Norman's wife was to call in as a day visitor a few times before the day of the show. Eli always found it handy to have a couple of miraculous cures to set the ball rolling. Once the audience had it in their minds that he was the genuine article their powers of self-healing increased by leaps and bounds. This was the theory upon which Eli based his livelihood.

Beth, who usually took the collection dressed in Virgin Mary blue and white, was redundant that evening. She spent her time helping the Knights of Saint Jude settle people into their seats, which were set out in rows in the dining hall where Amy was playing carols on her violin. Some people were singing along, mainly discordantly, some were chatting, others were staring vacantly into space.

An old man in a wheelchair was being pushed down to the front. His face was twisted and he looked in such

323

a bad way that she felt incredibly guilty this man might be placing his hope in Eli. Maybe she should have a word with the man straight away; tell him not to get his hopes up; that there were many ailments that Eli could not cure.

She went over and squatted down in front of him. There was something familiar about his face. The man's twisted mouth attempted a smile.

She hesitated, trying to place him. 'I'm Mrs Mudd,' she said, 'Eli's wife.'

He gave a twisted grin. Beth pretended to chastise him. 'Don't you dare laugh at my name, you cheeky man.'

He slowly brought his hand up to his mouth by way of self-recrimination.

'I was only joking,' Beth said. 'Anyway, do I know you from somewhere?'

He made several attempts to get his words out. Cedric came up. 'He had a seizure or summat,' he explained. 'Given up for dead, one bit over. He'd been on a slab down at t' mortuary for half an hour before somebody saw him twitchin'. Any road, he got took to hospital an' when he perked up a bit they asked us if we could look after him. Believe it or not he's improved no end since he's been here. Can't speak. We only know his name because it were written inside his coat. At least we assume it's his name. Could be somebody else's coat for all we know. He's our star man is owd Josiah. Maybe Eli'll be able to help him along a bit.'

'Well, he's not very good with seizures,' said Beth, who had too much on her mind to recognise the name. 'But he'll do what he can, I'm sure.'

By half past seven there were about a hundred people in the room – a dozen or so woman and the rest men.

Eli's wooden cross was positioned on a makeshift stage

at one end of the room. On either side sat Amy and Eli. She was no longer the scruffy urchin figure she'd been when she first started working with Eli, but an unusually pretty young woman in a chastely buttoned-up black velvet tunic which did little to hide the shapely figure beneath. Eli wore his trademark top hat and a long frock coat.

He got to his feet, removed his hat, positioned it under the crook of his arm, adopted his Jesus expression and looked up at the ceiling. Some of the audience followed his gaze to see what was up there, but quickly looked back down again when his booming voice took command of the room.

'My dear brethren,' he began. 'We of the Church of the Divine Wind come here in all humility, knowing many of you have fought for your country.'

'Aye, an' a fat lot o' good it bloody did us!' shouted a man with a patch over one eye. He got little support from the audience who thought that swearing at a reverend was a bit much.

'I take it you were a soldier, sir.'

'I was,' said the man, 'and proud of it. King's Own Yorkshire Light Infantry. Picked up an arse full o' shrapnel in France. Couldn't sit down proper for two years.'

'And a fat lot of good it did you indeed,' said Eli. 'For you are here and they who sent you into battle are in their ivory towers with their limbs intact and their bellies full.' There was strong murmur of agreement and Eli knew he had them on his side.

'I am not here to put back missing limbs or to restore eyesight,' he went on. 'I am not here to bring back lost comrades or to make scars disappear. I am here to show you that there is a strength within you that can heal the invisible scars that torment your broken bodies. The aches and the pains and the melancholia.'

He noticed with some satisfaction that a couple of men at the back were scribbling down his every word. The reporters had turned up.

'We normally ask for a collection for us to keep body and soul together,' he went on 'but the good news is that the kind people at our other gatherings have contributed sufficient for us to come here and not add to your burden by sending round a collecting box.'

'Knowin' some o' these buggers there'd be more taken out than goes in,' called out one wag. This raised a good laugh, to which Eli and Amy joined in.

'That was the other reason for us not taking a collection,' Eli admitted with a broad beam that had his gold tooth glinting in the light from the single bulb hanging above him. He looked, benignly, at the man with the shrapnel. 'I trust, sir, that you haven't come here to have your shrapnel publicly removed. I suspect that the removal of shrapnel from such an area may be beyond me.' The man grinned and shook his head as the audience howled with laughter. They were warmed up now, the ball was rolling. Amy began to play 'Hark The Herald Angels Sing'. Eli raised his arms and asked, 'My dear brethren, do you have faith in the Lord?'

A few people muttered, 'Yes.'

'That's what I thought. You probably see no reason to have faith. But the Lord only put you here on Earth and left you to it. He didn't send you into battle. He didn't tell the politicians to treat you badly. He's simply waiting at the other side for you – how you go on down here is up to you. But if you have faith in Him you will feel the faith in your bones, you will feel it in your mind, you will feel it in your heart. Do you have faith in the Lord?'

'Yes.'

It wasn't loud but it was fairly unanimous. Eli put a hand to his ear.

'I can't hear you.'

'YES!!'

'Now I hear you. Now the good Lord hears you. Is there anyone in this room brave enough to put their faith to the test?'

There was a silence as they all looked round at each other. Most had come as spectators, not as participants. Norman Attercliffe got slowly to his feet. Beth went across to help him. He was clutching at his hip as he had been since he'd hobbled into the home four days previously, earning himself two pounds ten, including today's money. Florence, sitting at the back, had called in three times as a day visitor. She was on half a crown a day plus ten shillings for today. Beth helped Norman on to the stage, Amy played 'Silent Night' and the audience were hushed in silent expectation.

'It's me hip,' mumbled Norman, leaning heavily on a stick. Bad hips were his speciality. 'I've had it years.'

'What is your name, my son?'

'Norman Attercliffe.'

'Can you stand up straight, Norman?'

'Not fer ten years.'

Eli placed a hand on Norman's head, mumbled something to himself, then asked 'Can you feel it, Norman?'

Norman frowned, the audience were open mouthed. Norman said, 'Well I can feel summat.'

'That's good, Norman. Now I want you to have faith. I want you to *know* that there's a power beyond you or

I, that is working here today. That's all I'm here for, to introduce you to that power. Can you feel the power, Norman?'

Eli took his hand off Norman's head with an imperceptible twist that had the sparse hairs on Norman's pate lifting up. Those in the audience who could see it gave a gasp. Eli stood back and hid his sand-papered palm behind his back. 'Straighten your back, Norman,' he commanded.

'Nay the heck, mister,' protested Norman. 'I can no more straighten me back than fly to the moon.'

'All I ask is that you try.'

Norman winced and pushed down on his stick. The audience winced along with him as if his pain were theirs. Slowly he pushed himself upwards. The audience willed him along, their frowns turning to smiles of triumph as he stood erect and looked at Eli in amazement.

'By heck, Reverend,' he said. 'I feel right champion.'

Those in the audience who had two arms clapped as Norman walked back to his seat, not too sprightly as to give the game away, but much improved.

'Your faith is great, Norman,' called out Eli. 'But remember, it wasn't I who healed you, it was you and your faith. Does anyone else have faith?'

Amy switched to 'O Come All Ye Faithful' and most of the audience were singing now. Three women came up from the back, including Florence. Eli, miraculously, cured two of them as the crowd sang joyously on. The uncured woman went back to her seat with her head hanging low. She obviously didn't have the faith. 'It may come tomorrow,' called out Eli, 'or next week. Is there anyone else?'

Josiah's arm went up, slowly. Cedric wheeled him to the front and Beth glared at him as if to say, 'I've already told you Eli can't do anything for him.' Eli stepped down from the stage.

'This is Josiah. He's not said a word since he came to us well over a month ago,' Cedric told him. 'He's had a seizure.'

Eli saw something in Josiah's eyes that told him he might have a bit of luck with this man. The ones with this look – that spoke of self-determination – usually worked out well for him, and for them. All they needed was the confidence to get them going. On top of which he'd seen Josiah, or someone very much like him, before.

'Do you have faith, Josiah?' Eli asked him.

Josiah looked at him, then at Beth. His mouth contorted as he tried to form a word. He gave up trying and just nodded his head.

'Put yer hand on 'is 'ead, Reverend,' shouted a woman from the back.

Eli looked at Josiah's sparse scalp and put his non-sandpapered hand on it. Josiah tried harder. 'Just relax my son and have faith,' said Eli, soothingly. His voice was hypnotic and many people in the audience found themselves relaxing to the point of nodding off. Josiah nodded his understanding, then summoned up all his willpower. Three words exploded from him. 'Godfrey bloody Farthing!' His voice was distorted but the words were plain to hear.

'What?' said Eli who wasn't sure why Josiah's chosen words should be Godfrey bloody Farthing, who seemed to have his finger in just too many pies.

'By the heck!' shouted Cedric. 'If that dunt put the bloody tin hat on it. Owd Josiah's never said a word all the time he's been with us. Two minutes wi' you an' he's shoutin' louder 'n my missis.'

'That's it!' cried Beth. 'That's who he is. He's Godfrey Farthing's man. I remember him now – but he's changed so much. Good grief! What happened to you, Josiah?'

Josiah took a deep breath and blurted, 'Sacked!' It seemed to come out more through his nose than his mouth.

'Alleluia, it's a miracle,' yelled Norman.

The reporters scribbled away, much to Eli's satisfaction. 'Godfrey Farthing sacked you?' Beth exclaimed, loud enough for them to hear. 'But you've worked for the Farthings for as long as I can remember – over fifty years if I'm not mistaken. And he's thrown you out on to the streets.'

There were grumblings of anger from the audience. Beth turned to address them. 'It's not just old soldiers who get thrown on the scrap heap by the men in their ivory towers, it's decent, hardworking men like Josiah, who was manservant to Godfrey Farthing of Farthing's mill – and Samuel Farthing before that.'

Josiah put his hand on Beth's arm and summoned up his next speech. The audience went quiet. 'There's something,' he said, 'yer should know.'

'Something I should know?' said Beth. 'What's that?'

Josiah tapped the side of his nose and shook his head, indicating it was between him and her. Eli saw that he wasn't going to top this miracle and decided to call it a day.

'Ladies and gentlemen. I think I have demonstrated to you the power of self-belief. You see, you don't really need me. All you need is faith in the Lord and faith in yourself. We wish you a happy and peaceful Christmas.'

'Alleluia,' shouted Florence from the back, who had been cured of lumbago for the eightieth time. The audience, who were now due soup, meat pies and Christmas pudding cheered and clapped and Josiah smiled because he felt that something good was happening to him for the first time in a long time.

The following morning Josiah was sitting on the best chair in Beth's living room. It had never occurred to Beth, Amy or Eli that the old man had anything of value to tell them. He had been sacked for standing up to Godfrey on the night Eli had confronted him, which made him Beth's responsibility. He would live there for as long as was needed. He was as much a victim of Godfrey as she was.

Josiah was very bad on his feet but his speech was returning, hastened by Eli's shock tactics of the previous evening. The decision to take Josiah in had been taken by Beth with Amy's agreement. Eli just went along because he knew it was the wisest course of action, although he made sure the two reporters knew about the altruism of the Church of the Divine Wind.

He also pointed out to Beth that Josiah wouldn't be able to take himself to and from the lavatory out in the yard and Beth pointed out that until that time arrived they'd just have to rely on Eli. Unless of course Eli could work yet another of his miracles and get Josiah up and walking before nature called.

'Last night,' Beth reminded Josiah, 'you said you had something to tell me.'

'Something she should know,' added Amy.

Josiah, who had said little since last night, summoned up some more words. He framed them in his mind before he sent them out through his half-numbed mouth.

'I don't think . . . his will's right,' he said.

'Who's will? Samuel's will?' prompted Beth.

He nodded.

331

'I see,' said Beth.

Amy stepped forward and asked, 'Why isn't it right?'

'He . . . cut Goff . . . Godfrey out. Told me.'

'He cut Godfrey out of his will?'

'I think so – he told me on his . . . death bed.'

'Ah, you only think so,' said Beth. 'Well, I'm afraid, Josiah, that only thinking so's no good. Never mind, you can stay here until you're up and running.'

Josiah shook his head at her disbelief. Once again his words were distorted. 'Told me he'd left . . . most of it to his grandchildren. Some for me . . . and a nasty shock for Godfrey.'

'So, how come no one saw this will?' asked Amy.

'Mr Godfrey can make things . . . happen.'

'You're telling me.'

'Well, I have to say,' said Beth, 'I know old Samuel had no great liking for Godfrey, and it came as a surprise to me that he left Henry and James nothing. If what you say's true then Amy here's the next in line.'

'Check with the soliciss–,' said Josiah. It was too big a word for him to cope with.

'You mean solicitors?' translated Eli. 'You think Amy should check with the solicitors?'

Josiah nodded.

'I don't suppose it'll do any harm,' admitted Beth.

'Didn't you say his solicitor was killed in a house fire the same night your old house was burned down,' Eli asked.

'He was, but I'm not sure I can see the connection,' replied Beth.

'If the solicitor knew the truth about the will, Godfrey would want him out of the way,' deduced Amy. 'And me as well.'

'That's right,' exclaimed Beth, banging a fist down on the table. 'It makes sense. He was trying to cover his tracks and eliminate the true heir all in one night. My God, what a monster!'

'Then there was the other chap in Scotland who was killed by a car,' remembered Eli. 'The one who used to work for Farthing's solicitors. Suppose both of them had something to do with the will?'

'That's right. That would be the connection,' said Beth. 'Inspector Gifford could never make a connection.'

'So, what have we got?' summed up Eli. 'We have the word of a good man here that Samuel Farthing told him on his death bed that he'd changed his will to favour his grandsons. But the changed will was never found. Which means somehow Godfrey managed to hide it, possibly with the help of a crooked solicitor or solicitors, both of whom have since died violent deaths. Is that what we're saying?'

'Not sure how the man in Scotland could have been involved in it,' said Beth. 'If I remember rightly, according to Inspector Gifford, he moved to Scotland years ago, probably before Samuel died. He wouldn't have been around when the will was read out. I think that was just an unhappy coincidence.'

'There's a few too many unhappy coincidences surrounding that awful man,' said Amy. 'I think we should go to see Inspector Gifford. At least we know he's on our side.'

'And tell him what?' asked Eli. 'That a sacked employee of Godfrey's, who obviously has a grudge against his old boss, has come up with an unsubstantiated story about a bogus will.' He looked down at Josiah. 'Sorry, Josiah, we all believe you. But without the will there's nothing that can be done.'

'I'm going to see them solicitors,' decided Beth, she

already had her coat on.

'I'll come with you,' said Eli. 'Just in case you say something you shouldn't.'

'You'll have to stay here and look after Josiah,' Beth pointed out.

'In that case, I'm coming,' said Amy.

As the two women went out of the house Eli looked at Josiah and shrugged helplessly. Josiah pulled an apologetic face and shrugged back. But, will or no will, he was happy to be with these people.

Chapter Twenty-Three

Ordinary Seaman William Eccles stepped off the gang-plank of the tramp steamer *Oriole* and vowed that he was done with the sea for good. He was sixteen now, although his papers, which had been dubiously acquired, said he was eighteen. Despite many surreptitious enquiries, he still wasn't sure if he was wanted for murder.

He was in Barry Docks in South Wales, about a hundred or so miles south of Liverpool from where his journeys had begun, a year and a half and many sea miles ago. If there was music to be faced he was ready for it now.

It wasn't just his piercing whistle that attracted the stare of many a passing girl. The roll of the sea had given him the jaunty walk of most sailors, especially those used to smaller ships. Billy was almost six feet tall and his skinny frame had filled out with eighteen months of hard work and general growing up. His fair hair was bleached blond from the Caribbean sun and his face was cheerful and suntanned. On top of which he had money in his pocket. He turned up the collar of his reefer to shield him from the March wind and slung his seaman's bag over his shoulder.

In those eighteen months he had sent just three letters home, the last one to hopefully arrive on his dad's birthday. He gave no address. His fear of being caught was constantly reinforced by a certain shipmate who was on the run from a genuine crime of violence.

He'd been tempted to write to Amy but thought it would be better if she forgot about him. The whole reason for his running away was to distance himself from her – for her benefit. Trouble was he'd found it hard to forget about her. Despite the tales of sailors having a girl in every port, Billy found a seaman's life to be a romantically unencumbered one, which had suited him. It would be nice to see Amy though. He'd never met a girl like her.

Beth and Amy sat opposite Geoffrey Broom who was twiddling his fingers, trying to decide where his loyalties lay.

'Let me get this straight,' he said. 'One minute I'm representing Mr Farthing in a slander action against your husband and now you're expecting me to investigate his integrity – and by the sound of it, one of our deceased partners.'

'Did you ask Farthing why he wanted to drop the action against my husband?' asked Beth.

'He dropped it,' said Broom, 'because suing people who have no money is a pointless and expensive exercise. I was happy to proceed because it's how I earn my living, but Mr Farthing saw sense.'

'In that case why did he bother to sue Eli in the first place?' The scorn in Beth's voice had Broom blushing. 'It doesn't take a genius to work out that he hasn't got much money.' She thrust her face towards him so that he wouldn't miss any of her words. 'Farthing dropped the action against my husband because he was scared of opening a can of worms that could lead to the gallows. He had my house burned down and killed two people, and he also had John Sykes' house burned down, killing another three.'

'There's also the former employee of yours who was killed in Scotland,' added Amy, 'in very suspicious circumstances.'

'Ah, Robert Burns,' said Broom. 'Good man, Robert – I remember him well. Tragedy that.'

'Murder more like,' said Beth. 'Especially if he had anything to do with Samuel Farthing's will.'

'Look Mrs, er, Mudd. I'm obviously aware of your antipathy towards Mr Farthing but I'm not sure I'm the right person to deal with this.'

'Mr Broom,' said Amy. 'My grandma and I have come to you before going to the police. If it turns out that your deceased partner was crooked, then surely it's better that you're seen to be co-operating with them.'

'Inspector Gifford is as certain as he can be that Godfrey Farthing was behind the fire that killed Mr Sykes and my friend Mr O'Keefe,' said Beth.

Broom had remembered something of significance during this conversation. He got up and went to his office door.

'Mr Mathieson,' he called out. 'Do you have a moment?'

Mathieson, the clerk, came into the office and stood beside where Amy and Beth were seated.

'Mr Mathieson,' said Broom. 'I want you to cast your mind back to last summer and the tragic death of our former employee, Robert Burns, up in Edinburgh.'

'Oh dear,' said Mathieson. 'You know what my memory's like, Mr Broom. Still, I'll do my best.'

'It sticks in my mind that he made a telephone call to this office on the day of his death, right out of the blue. I seem to remember someone saying how they'd been talking to him on the telephone not an hour before he was killed. Such coincidences stick in one's mind. I thought it might have stuck in yours.'

'It did indeed stick in my mind, sir,' said Mathieson, delighted he could be of help. 'It was I to whom he spoke.'

'And what did he speak to you about?'

'Let me see, it was to do with a will . . .'

Amy and Beth looked at each other, then at Broom who was beginning to look uncomfortable. 'Which will?' he enquired, already knowing the answer.

'I, er, I believe it was Mr Samuel Farthing's will, sir.' He looked from Broom to the two women, wondering if he should be discussing such matters in front of them.

'Tell me what you remember of the conversation,' said Broom, knowing he didn't want to hear this, but he had no alternative.

'Well,' remembered Mathieson. 'To the best of my recollection he said he was the person who witnessed Mr Farthing's last will and he was asking if the grandsons had survived. I believe he'd read something in a newspaper that puzzled him. He didn't tell me what. He didn't say as much but he did seem surprised that Mr Farthing was the beneficiary.'

'Did he now?' said Broom. 'Thank you, Mr Mathieson. Oh, Mr Mathieson, could you get Samuel Farthing's file out of records and bring it to me?'

'Certainly, sir.' Mathieson turned to go then stopped in

the doorway and rubbed his chin, trying to remember something else. He snapped his fingers and said, 'Oh dear!'

'Oh dear what?'

'Now you have got my memory working overtime, sir. I remember Mr Godfrey Farthing coming in some years ago and asking about the will. He asked if he could take the file to peruse it. I believe I checked with you or Mr Rodney, sir. Trouble is, I've no knowledge if the file was ever returned.'

'Well, I wouldn't bet on it,' said Beth.

'There was one thing I remember, sir. On the file index it said the file contained three copies of the will, but in fact it contained none. Mr Godfrey Farthing said he had two copies himself. He did seem concerned as to the whereabouts of the third will. In fact, if memory serves he got quite angry that the will might be lying around for anyone to see. I remember because it's not often voices are raised in here. I calmed him down by saying it was almost certainly a clerical error.'

'And was it a clerical error?'

'I've no idea, sir. It seemed an expedient thing to say at the time. To calm the man down, so to speak.'

'Quite so, Mr Mathieson.'

Geoffrey Broom walked into Rodney Sykes's office with a face as grey as putty. He sat down opposite the deceased John Sykes's elder brother and sighed, heavily.

'I think we might have a problem on our hands.'

'What sort of problem?'

'It's possible your brother was killed on Godfrey Farthing's intructions.'

Rodney sat back in his chair and said, 'Go on.'

Ever since Amy and Beth had left to tell Inspector Gifford all they knew, Broom had been sitting in his office trying to work out what might have happened. The most obvious scenario stared him in the face.

'It may have a connection with the money we found missing from John's clients' account. It could be that John was blackmailing Godfrey Farthing so that he could return the money.'

Rodney sighed. He'd always suspected a skeleton or two might fall out of his brother's cupboard after they'd found he'd been embezzling the firm. If this were true it could do them a lot of damage.

'What did he have on Farthing?'

'You're not going to like this,' said Broom. 'I think John made Samuel Farthing's last will disappear. There are those who believe Godfrey was cut out of his father's will.'

'Such as?'

'Such as Robert Burns, the chap who was killed in Scotland a few years ago – he witnessed the will. Plus Godfrey's old manservant. The whole thing's beginning to stink, Rodney.'

'It only stinks if the will rears its ugly head,' pointed out Rodney calmly. 'Is there a copy of the will in existence?'

'I don't know. Godfrey took two copies and presumably destroyed them.'

'That's it then,' said Rodney. 'There isn't a problem.'

'But the file index says there's a third copy.'

'Ah,' said Rodney, getting to his feet. 'In that case we'd best send the staff home early and turn this place upside down and find it.'

'Then what?'

'Don't be stupid, Geoffrey. If a will turns up we burn it. A scandal like this could ruin us!'

'Not if we co-operated,' protested Broom. 'If we're seen to be co-operating, we'll get through it. I'm not going to be a party to a cover-up.'

'In that case I'll look for the bloody thing on my own!'

Inspector Gifford drummed his fingers on his desk as he read the letter from Lydia to Beth.

'I'm afraid this is like everything else we've got on Farthing,' he said. 'All supposition, no substance. Besides, it's forty years old.'

'If I thought it might have done some good I'd have shown it to someone when Lydia died,' Beth said. 'But under the circumstance it would have done more harm than good.'

'Quite so,' agreed Gifford, his brain still ticking over. 'If there's a will in that office I'd like to get to it first. A solicitor won't want this sort of scandal.'

'What do you mean?' asked Beth.

'I mean that will's better in my hands than in theirs,' Gifford said.

'Mr Broom seemed a decent sort of man,' said Amy. 'I don't think he'd do anything wrong.'

'I'm sure he wouldn't, but I don't like to leave temptation in anyone's way.' He got up from his desk and took his coat from the hook behind the door. 'Ladies, I think you and I will pay Messrs Sykes, Sykes and Broom a visit.'

Mr Mathieson was just leaving as Amy, Beth and the inspector arrived. Gifford looked at his watch, half past three. 'Going early?' he said.

Mathieson looked at Amy and Beth and wondered what was going on. 'Er, yes,' he said.

'Do they often let you go early?' asked Gifford. 'My name's Inspector Gifford, Heaton Royd Police.'

Mathieson was at a loss what to say. 'Er, no.'

'Well, don't close the door, sir. Save us the trouble of knocking.'

Rodney was just coming through to the reception area to lock the door behind his departed staff. 'I'm sorry, we're closed for the day.'

'My name's Inspector Gifford, sir, Heaton Royd police – and you are?'

'Rodney Sykes. How can I help you?'

Gifford glanced at a filing cabinet with several drawers open. 'It appears you've already begun to help us, sir.'

'What?'

'Well, I assume you're searching for the missing will.'

'Am I?'

'I do hope so, sir. I do hope I'm right in thinking you're going to be of invaluable assistance to us.'

'We'll do our best,' said Rodney, through gritted teeth.

'I'm sure you will, sir.'

Broom appeared and offered a hand to Gifford, who shook it. 'Geoffrey Broom,' he said. 'I assume you're Inspector Gifford.'

'I am.'

'We were expecting you, weren't we, Rodney?' Rodney gave a thin smile. 'We're just about to start looking for the will, Inspector,' Broom went on. 'We let the staff go because it's a very delicate situation. Not the sort of thing we want everyone to know about.'

'Quite so, sir. Miss Farthing here tells me you've been very helpful.'

'I'm not sure how much help we *can* be,' said Broom. 'If there is a missing will in here, then wherever it is, it's been gathering dust for twenty years.'

'Unless of course someone's given it the odd dusting down in the meantime,' commented Gifford. 'Did the late Mr Sykes have an office of his own?'

'Yes, he did,' said Broom. 'We didn't replace him when he er, left us. So his old office is used for general storage.'

'What Geoffrey means,' said Rodney, 'but is much too polite to say, is that my dear, late brother was an idle sod and didn't merit a replacement.'

'I understand he took money from his clients' accounts,' Gifford said.

'So we found out after his death,' Rodney told him. 'His old office is upstairs. I doubt very much if the will's in there. People have been going in and out of there for six years, so it would have turned up at some stage. The only thing of my brother's that's left in there is his precious desk and it's not in there. We searched it thoroughly when we realised he'd been embezzling money. Pity he didn't spend as much time sitting at it as he spent *on* it. The damn thing cost him a fortune. If he *has* hidden it my second guess would be under the floorboards.'

'What would your first guess be, sir?'

'Somewhere in his house,' said Rodney. 'The one that was burned down.'

'It would suit you not to find it at all, wouldn't it, sir,' said Gifford.

'Down to the ground, Inspector,' admitted Rodney. 'My brother created problems for me all through his life. I'd rather him not close this firm down after his death.'

'I'm sure it won't come to that, sir. Would you mind if we all had a look round?'

'I most certainly would, Inspector. This place is full of confidential files.'

'It won't be in a file,' Amy pointed out. 'Or in anything where someone's likely to look. If I was hiding it I'd put it somewhere secret. A personal place only I knew about.'

'Is his desk still in his old office?' Gifford asked. 'I always find desks tend to be very personal.'

'Er, yes,' said Broom. 'I'd have had it for myself but it's too big to move easily. It's hidden under a mountain of books and stuff. As Rodney said, we checked it thoroughly.'

'Well I don't suppose another check will go amiss,' said Gifford. 'Could you show me the way please?'

Up in John Sykes's old office the inspector swept the top of the desk clean with a couple of sweeps of his arm that scattered the books all over the floor. The drawers were all unlocked and more or less empty. Amy, who had her hopes up, sighed. Beth examined the floor for loose floorboards but it was covered in seamless linoleum; she sighed as well. There were cupboards and piles of files and papers all over the room but Gifford was only interested in the desk. He ran his fingers under the top right-hand drawer. 'Hello,' he said, 'what's this?'

There was a click and he pulled out another drawer, no more than an inch deep, beautifully hidden between the top drawer and the surface of the desk. He pulled it right out. Although it was very shallow it ran the full length of the desk and had room enough to hide a large amount of papers. All that was in there was the last will and testament of Samuel Farthing dated 26 August 1900. He took it out and handed it to Broom.

'Would this be what we're looking for, sir?'

Geoffrey Broom examined it carefully, then he looked

344

at Gifford and said, 'I think we'd better go down to my office.'

Within an hour Amy and Beth were on their way home in the police car with Gifford. Amy was the sole surviving heir to Samuel Farthing's fortune. There had been a bequest to Josiah of one thousand pounds and one of the mill cottages. Sykes, Sykes and Broom had sent a messenger to Godfrey with a letter telling him that they were no longer his solicitors in view of them now acting for his granddaughter who was the main beneficiary of Samuel Farthing's will. And in that respect they had written to Godfrey's bank with a formal request that all his accounts be frozen until the matter be sorted out.

'What will happen to Godfrey now?' asked Beth.

'I'm not sure,' said Gifford. 'Off hand I still can't think of a crime we can prove him to have committed. He could play dumb and say he's never seen this latest will and I'm not sure what we can do about it.'

'But we all know he's as guilty as hell,' said Beth.

'Yes we do,' agreed Gifford. 'And we've stripped him of all his wealth. It's just a question of time before we nail him.'

'When will Amy come into her money?'

'No idea. I'm sure Farthing will want to contest the will. Hopefully he won't have any money to pay lawyers with. Young Amy here doesn't have to do anything except sit and wait. I'm very happy with the outcome so far.'

'So am I,' said Beth.

Amy was thinking of Billy and wondering if she'd ever see him again. It never occurred to any of them that if Amy had a tragic and mysterious accident all the money would revert back to Godfrey. However, it wouldn't be long before this occurred to him, and he had enough cash stashed away to fight his corner.

Godfrey's new manservant opened the door to the messenger boy, who had come on a bicycle. 'Yes?' he said, loftily.

'I've brought a message for Mr Godfrey Farthing. Is he in?'

The manservant held out his hand. 'I'll give it to him.'

'I've been told to put it in his hand and no one else's,' insisted the messenger, who was only fourteen.

'I'll give you the back of my hand for your insolence.'

'It's from his solicitor,' persisted the boy. 'If I don't give it to him I'm in bother.'

'Well, in that case you'll have to wait because Mr Farthing's not in.'

At that moment Godfrey's Daimler came purring up the drive, with him at the wheel. The messenger turned to look. 'Is that him?' he asked.

'No, that's the flaming dustbin man. Who the hell do you think it is?'

The messenger boy grinned and took a couple of steps towards where Godfrey had stopped his car. 'I've brought a message fer yer, Mr Farthing, from yer solicitors.'

'What the devil's so urgent it has to be sent by messenger?' grumbled Godfrey to himself as he snatched the envelope from the boy. He was still muttering to himself as he opened the letter and read it, while the boy and the manservant looked on. As his eyes scanned the page his brow gradually creased into a deep frown and he began to mouth the words in silent disbelief. The colour, quite visibly, drained from his face and his hands began to shake so much that the letter dropped to his lap.

'Are you all right, sir?' called out the manservant.

Godfrey made no reply.

'Will there be a message to take back?' asked the messenger boy.

Still no answer. Godfrey began to take in huge chunks of air, choking as he did so. His pale face now went red as the vein in his neck pumped blood upwards. His eyes bulged and he made a low, moaning noise.

'I think he's having a funny turn,' commented the messenger boy, knowledgeably. 'Me granddad had one o' them just afore he popped his clogs. Happen we ought ter do summat.'

The manservant opened the car door and between them they pulled Godfrey out and placed him on the ground where he lay gasping for breath and moaning.

'Shall I fetch a doctor?' said the boy. 'There's one just down t' road.'

'Yes, do that. Tell him to come straight away. Tell him Mr Farthing's having a fit or something.'

The boy mounted his bike and pedalled off as Godfrey stared up at the bleak, January sky and wondered how the hell he could get out of this. Even as he lay there, fighting for air, he knew the answer. Get rid of that conniving bitch who calls herself his granddaughter. Get rid of her once and for all – and get rid of her quickly. With no conniving bitch to inherit what was rightfully his, the will was meaningless. It would all revert to him. He was rambling to himself now, with the manservant trying to make out what he was saying.

'I'll get it,' called out Beth, from the scullery. 'Although heaven knows who's knocking at this time of night.'

It was a hesitant knock, a knock without authority or

347

urgency, so it wasn't Inspector Gifford, nor was it the knock of a neighbour. Beth opened the door and it took her a few seconds to identify this strapping, suntanned, young man.

'Billy?' she said.

'Hello Mrs Crabtree.'

'Billy Eccles as I live and breathe. I'm not Mrs . . . Oh never mind. Come in, it's freezing out there.'

'Thank you. I don't suppose Amy's here, is she?'

Amy appeared behind her grandma. 'Hello, Billy,' she said. 'Long time, no see. You've changed.'

'Hello Amy. So have you, er, you look very nice.'

'Thank you, so do you. So, you came back.'

'Yes. I, er, I thought it about time.'

'I'm glad you came back.' She wanted to hug him to her but felt inhibited by her grandma's presence. Instead she offered her cheek for him to kiss. Beth had no inhibitions – she took Billy in her arms and almost squeezed the breath out of him.

'By heck I've wanted to do that for a long time, Billy Eccles.'

Eli came clattering down the stairs. 'Did I hear the name Billy Eccles?' he called out.

'That you did,' said Beth. 'Here in the flesh, large as life and twice as handsome.'

'Well, it's a name that's welcome in this house any time of the day or night. Isn't that so, Mrs Mudd?'

'Yes it is,' said Beth, taking Billy by the hand and leading him into the living room.

'Mrs Mudd?' said Billy. 'You mean you two are married?'

'Four blissful months,' said Eli. 'Isn't that so, Elizabeth?'

'If you say so, Eli.'

'You've been away a long time,' Amy said, with a hint of reproach in her voice. 'I would have written but you didn't send your dad an address.'

'I didn't want anyone to know where I was. It was better that way.'

The four of them sat down, with three of them looking at Billy, waiting for him to tell his story. He looked from one to the other then his eyes settled on Amy. His lovely Amy.

'It's good to see you, Amy, really good. I thought about you a lot.'

'Perhaps we should leave them to it for a while,' suggested Eli, tactfully.

'No, no,' said Billy. 'I'm pleased to see all of you.' He paused for a long time before asking, 'Has, er, has everything been all right since I've been gone?'

'Billy,' said Amy. 'Have you heard *any* news from home since you went away?'

'None at all. Oh, I read a few old newspapers, but they don't deliver the *Argus* to the South Seas.'

'I suppose your dad was pleased to see you,' Beth said.

'I haven't been home yet.'

'What? Billy he's been worried si–'

Amy interrupted her grandmother. 'So, you won't know about the Peets, then,' she said.

'I had no way of knowing. I tried to find out, but short of coming home and askin–'

'They were hanged for murder, Billy.'

'Hanged? So I didn't kill him?'

'No, everybody thinks you're a hero. The police, the papers, especially me.'

'And me,' said Beth. 'Saving my granddaughter's life like that.'

349

'So, I'm not in any trouble?' said Billy with huge relief. 'I thought I might get done for murder. It wouldn't be the first time I got done for something I didn't do. That's why I ran away from that copper in Manchester.'

'He wasn't after you, he was after a pickpocket.'

'A pickpocket? Blimey, I wish I'd known.'

'Oh Billy, come here,' said Amy, losing all her inhibitions. She took him in her arms and kissed him in front of her grandma and Eli, who both looked on approvingly.

'Poor little rich girl eh?' remarked Effie. 'It'll be tuppence ter talk ter yer now, I expect.'

'Don't, Effie,' scolded Amy. 'It's all come as a bit of shock. And I'm not a rich girl yet. The courts have to sort things out.'

They were linking arms as they walked to the pictures to see *Daughter of the Night*, starring Bela Lugosi. It had been described on the billboards as 'Sinister', which suited Amy and Effie.

'What's happening at the mills?' Effie asked.

Amy shrugged. 'Shut down. I think the courts will be sending someone in to manage things until the will's sorted out, which could take ages. The good thing is that my grandfather can't go near them until it is.'

'He's gonna be very mad.'

'Serve him right,' said Amy. 'What he did was downright wicked. If it all comes to me he won't get a penny of it. Did you know he kicked Josiah out and left him to die on the streets?'

'I heard – I heard summat else as well.'

'What?'

'I heard Billy Eccles is back.'

350

'Yes, he came back last night.'

Effie jabbed Amy with her elbow. 'And you didn't tell me! I shouldn't have had to ask you about something like that, you should have told me.'

'It's only Billy.'

'Only Billy? You haven't stopped going on about him ever since he ran off. How he saved yer life, how he told you he loved you–'

'Hey! You're not to mention that to anyone.'

'Keep yer hair on! I've said nothing to no one. Mind you, it'll not be long before everyone knows – now that he's back. Are yer going to marry him?'

'Effie! Will you stop it? All that's happened is that Billy's back. He came round last night, we said hello, nothing more.'

'Nothing?'

'Well, we kissed – like old friends do.'

'*We're* old friends, we never kiss,' Effie pointed out.

'I'm very fond of Billy. He's always been there when I've needed him, but when he really needed me, I let him down.'

'Not on purpose.'

'Doesn't make any difference. I owe Billy my life twice over. I think the absolute world of him.'

'Absolute world – is that all?'

'Isn't it enough?'

'Maybe – but it doesn't sound to me as if you love him,' observed Effie. 'Did he make your heart sing when he came through the door after all them years?'

'I've never been so pleased to see anyone in my life.'

'So, he made your heart sing then? It says in the *Woman's Weekly* that your heart sings when the right feller comes along.'

Amy, who couldn't honestly remember her heart singing when Billy came back, looked at the ground and scuffed her shoes against the pavement as she walked. She remembered Eli's definition of true love: *It smacks you in the eye and leaves you smouldering from head to toe.* None of this had happened. All this time thinking she was madly in love with someone and all the time she was just in love with a memory. She knew that now. She'd realised it when she hugged Billy the previous night. He was her most precious friend in all the world. But that was all.

'If it's true love you're talking about, I'm not sure I know what love is, Effie.'

Had either of them turned round they'd have noticed a large man walking just behind them, within earshot of their conversation. Godfrey wore a heavy overcoat, a flat cap pulled right down over his eyes, a muffler covering the bottom half of his face and he walked with his head down.

'When are yer going out with Billy again?' Effie asked

'If you must know, Miss Nosey Pants, I'm going out with him on Friday night. We're going to the Eccleshill Picture Palace on Friday to see *Oliver Twist*.'

'I hope that's a film and not a naughty trouser trick he's learned on his travels,' giggled Effie.

'Effie Slack, you rude thing!' Amy pushed at her friend in mock disgust.

Godfrey had heard enough. He turned around and walked away. Friday night couldn't come soon enough. He would put an end to all this nonsense.

Chapter Twenty-Four

Godfrey unscrewed the top of the brandy flask. He'd been there half an hour and had nearly drunk the lot. He could think of no better way of killing her. It had worked up in Scotland so it should work here. Although in Scotland he'd paid someone to do his dirty work – two hundred pounds. He'd insisted it look like an accident; money well spent as it turned out. Didn't need any help for this job – in fact, given all the grief the conniving little bitch had given him it would be a pleasure. It would be simple enough. The streets were dark, and it would all be over so quickly no one would think to see what sort of a car it was or who was driving it. Anyway, to most people all cars looked alike. He looked at his pocket watch. 7.45. According to the cinema adverts in the *Telegraph* the second house started at eight fifteen. He was banking on her meeting her boyfriend there, rather than him pick her up, which could be awkward.

The night was cold with drizzle in the air. It was glinting on the cobbles, reflected by the flickering light of a gas lamp. He turned up the collar of his coat, pulled his motoring cap down over his eyes and rubbed his gloved hands together his breath steaming out into the cold night air. Although the car was a convertible, only the rear passenger saloon had a hood; the driver's cab was open to the elements.

The engine ticked over quietly and he could now hear a voice echoing from under the archway. Any second he expected her to appear, where the hell was she? His adrenaline was surging and his heart was pounding in anticipation. Then she emerged, silhouetted by the street lamp. He eased off the handbrake and sent the car rolling quietly forward, engine just ticking over, lights turned off, and picking up speed down the steeply sloping street. As she stepped off the kerb Godfrey slipped the car into gear, put his foot hard down and aimed the heavy vehicle directly at her, leaving Amy with no chance to get out of his way.

Last second squeamishness had Godfrey closing his eyes just before the moment of impact. There was a loud bang, followed by two thuds as something bounced off the hood at the back of the convertible car, then onto the road. Godfrey didn't stop to see what damage he'd done – it sounded pretty final. He switched the lights on and drove around a corner out of sight of any prying eyes and headed north, in the opposite direction to his house and mills, just in case anyone mentioned seeing the racing car to the police.

Godfrey circled the city and approached Farthing's Mill from the south-east; he had told his new manservant he'd be spending the evening there, catching up on some work. In the distance, from the direction of Cinder Yard, he heard a clanging ambulance. It brought a grin to his face. They'd be better off sending a hearse.

Using keys he shouldn't have he unlocked the yard gate and drove in, leaving it open for his exit. The mill had been closed since the new will had reared its ugly head. His mind was racing with elation and excitement. As soon as he was officially informed of the conniving bitch's death he'd be round at his solicitors insisting they reinstate him. After which he'd find another solicitor and sue Sykes, Sykes and bloody Broom for negligence. While he was at it he'd press on with his slander writ against Mudd. That family needed destroying completely.

He parked up and brought out a storm lantern from one of the sheds to examine the damage to the car. It was a sturdily built vehicle and there was little, if any, damage to be seen. Just a few shreds of fibre which he removed from the radiator. He then went round the back and found blood on the canvas hood. Ten minutes scrubbing with cold water still left an incriminating stain. Godfrey cursed. It took him another fifteen minutes to detach the hood completely and take it into the boiler room where he threw the whole lot into the furnace and stoked it into life. Then, satisfied with his night's work, he went up to his office where he had a bottle of brandy in his drawer.

'Young men collected their young ladies at their house in my day,' commented Eli, looking up from his evening paper.

'That was back in the olden days, Eli,' said Amy. 'It doesn't make sense Billy walking past the bus stop to call here then both of us walking back. It's called equality. We've got the vote now, you know.'

'I've got the vote,' said Beth. 'You've got to wait until you're thirty.'

'It'll change,' said Amy confidently. 'By the time I'm twenty one we'll all have the vote.'

'I don't doubt that,' said Eli, 'if you've got anything to do with it.'

'Right then, I'm off,' said Amy. 'I'll get Billy to bring me home to the door. We should be back around eleven.'

'And no later,' said Beth. She watched through the window and shook her head, despairingly. 'I don't know. She's gone out without her gloves, and I did remind her.'

'Would you like me to go after her, Mrs Mudd?' asked Josiah, putting on his coat. With the aid of a stick he had been exercising his legs inside the house and fancied taking them outside for a real test.

'Well, if you feel up to it,' said Beth. 'I'd go myself but I've got nothing on me feet. They're on the sideboard where she left them. Just give her a shout, she'll wait for you.'

By the time Josiah hobbled from the house with the gloves Amy was under the archway. 'Miss Farthing,' he shouted, walking after her.

She stopped and looked back. 'What?'

'You forgot your gloves.'

'Oh, so I did, thanks Josiah. Wait there, I'll come and get them.'

'No, no – I need the exercise.' She waited under the arch for him to hobble over and give her the gloves. 'Here you are, miss. Have a nice evening.'

'I will, thanks Josiah.'

The old man stood under the archway and watched her cross the road. He smiled. It had been a good day when she and her grandmother had chanced upon him. And now Amy's good fortune was linked with his. A cottage and a thousand pounds. He knew old Samuel wouldn't let him down. That knowledge pleased him almost as much as his inheritance; on top of which Godfrey Farthing was getting his just desserts at last. He turned to go back, and was startled by the roar of a car engine. He spun round just in time to see the Daimler hurtling at Amy.

Whatever strength and speed was left in Josiah's body came together in a massive surge of energy that had him dashing across the road and flinging himself at Amy's back. He gave her an almighty push that sent her flying out of harm's way whilst he took the full force of the impact. He flew over the bonnet and landed first on the roof and then on the road behind the speeding vehicle.

Amy was on her knees, winded. Her coat was torn and her face grazed. She went rigid with horror at the sight of Josiah's twisted body lying motionless in the road. She crawled across to him and listened for breathing. 'He's alive,' she shouted to anyone who might be listening.

Two young men ran over to see if they could help. 'What's happened, love?'

'A car hit him. Please, I need help,' gasped Amy. 'I need to get him to the hospital.'

'There'll be telephone in t' Cobblers,' someone said. 'I'll phone from there.'

A coat was placed over Josiah to keep him warm. Within minutes Beth and Eli appeared. Eli put an arm around Amy as Beth knelt beside Josiah.

'He won't die, will he, grandma?'

Beth noticed the blood bubbling from Josiah's mouth as he struggled to breath. 'I'm sure the doctors will do what they can, love,' she said, inadequately.

Josiah didn't look well at all. Under the light of the street lamps all the colour had drained from his face and his eyes were flickering. A police constable arrived at the scene, kneeling down beside the old man. He looked up at Beth. 'Does he belong to you, madam?'

'In a manner of speaking.'

Josiah was trying to say something. 'Don't try and talk,' said the policeman. 'Just try and stay calm until the ambulance comes. We'll have you as right as rain in no time, sir.'

Josiah shook his head. He didn't feel as though he'd ever be as right as rain again. This all felt very different from last time. A bit more final. As if last time had been a dress rehearsal. Perhaps God's way of allowing him time to sort things out before he left for good. That thought brought a thin smile to his face. This was a better way to go. He'd done what he had to do. The cottage and the money would have been nice but it had come twenty years too late. He hadn't the energy left to enjoy it, Godfrey had seen to that. He remembered the smile on old Samuel's face as he prepared himself to die. A smile brought on by what he had done to Godfrey.

'He's smiling, missis,' said the policeman. 'He can't be feeling too bad, then.'

Beth wasn't so sure. 'You've saved Amy's life, Josiah,' she said. 'We'll never forget you for that.'

The thought of being well remembered by these good people pleased him. Yes, this was a good way to go. But before he went, there was something else he had to do. What was that? Oh dear – me and my memory. Then his eyes lit up for one last time as he remembered. He summoned all his remaining strength because he wanted this to be heard as plainly as possible.

'It was Godfrey Farthing driving that car,' he said, in a voice only audible to Beth and the policeman. Amy was being comforted by Eli.

'Godfrey?' repeated Beth. 'What? Godfrey was driving the car that knocked you down?'

'Are you sure, sir?' said the policeman.

'Yes,' said Josiah. 'I'm . . . I'm . . . very sure.'

'Are you talking about Mr Godfrey Farthing the magistrate, sir, because if you are this is very serious.'

'Godfrey Farthing . . . the magistrate,' confirmed Josiah.

'He used to work for him,' said Beth. 'He's a very bad man is Farthing.'

Josiah smiled up at Amy, who sat down on the road and put an arm around him. Her nearness at this moment in his time made up his mind for him.

'Amy, there's something you should know.'

'Don't try to talk, Josiah,' Amy said. 'You must save your strength.'

Josiah managed a smile. 'Strength?' He gave a feeble laugh. 'I think I've just used the last of my strength up.'

'You saved my life.'

'It's a life worth saving. My lovely Lydia will be so proud of me.'

'Your lovely Lydia?' said Beth, incredulously. 'You mean – you and Lydia?'

'Me and Lydia,' he confirmed. Then he looked at Amy and spoke in little more than a whisper. 'I'm your grandfather, you know.'

'My grandfather?'

'Yes, I'm terribly sorry. Never did anything for you up until now. I hope I've now made up for things.'

The revelation left Amy speechless. She looked from him to Beth and back again. Her tears were falling on to his face. 'My grandfather?'

'I should have guessed,' said Beth, looking down at him with great affection. 'She said you were a decent man.'

Josiah smiled at her. 'Decent man? I loved her with

359

all my heart. And I always kept an eye on Henry. Watched him grow into a fine young man. Couldn't tell him, you see. It would have done too much damage.' His eyes moved back to Amy. 'Amy, it was lovely to have known y–' There was a rattle coming from deep within his throat. The amount of blood trickling from his mouth increased as, with a supreme effort, he forced out his last words to his granddaughter. 'I love you, Amy Farthing.'

'I love you too, grandfather – and now that I've found you, I want to keep you.'

But the light had gone from Josiah's eyes. A small crowd had gathered, including Billy, who had run from the bus-stop when he heard that someone had been knocked down outside Cinder Yard. At first he felt immense relief when he saw it wasn't Amy, and then sadness when he saw it was old Josiah whom he'd met at Amy's house. An ambulance and a doctor arrived. Josiah was examined, pronounced dead, and taken away. Amy was being comforted by Billy and Eli. Beth was pacing up and down; her fists opening and closing; her face contorting with mounting rage.

'Eli,' she said, 'there's something I've got to do.'

'What sort of something?'

'Something I should have done years ago.'

'I'll come with you.'

'No, it's better you stay here and look after Amy.'

'Of course I will, but wher–?'

He didn't get to finish his question. Beth was gone.

Half an hour later. Inspector Gifford turned up at the house. Amy was sitting on the settee with Eli. Billy was brewing a pot of tea. 'I just heard,' the policeman said. 'I'd like to express my condolences.'

Amy's face was still damp with tears. 'He was my grandfather,' she told him. 'I didn't know.'

'So I understand from the constable. It must be an awful shock.'

'The old boy saved her life,' said Eli. 'Damn car just drove off.'

'I hope you catch the driver, Inspector,' called out Billy, 'and do the bugger for manslaughter.'

'It won't be manslaughter, Billy,' said Gifford, 'it'll be murder. I assume you know who was driving the car?'

All three of them shook their heads. Gifford gave a puzzled frown. 'According to my constable the deceased gentleman recognised him.'

'It must have been before he told me he was my grandfather,' Amy said. 'He was saying something to grandma and the policeman but I didn't catch it.'

'Nor did I,' said Eli.

'And Mrs Mudd didn't tell you?'

'No.'

'Where is she now?' enquired Gifford, expecting the worst.

'She went off,' Eli said. 'Told me she had something to do.'

Gifford squeezed his eyes shut and shook his head. 'Josiah identified the driver as Godfrey Farthing. By the sound of things his intended victim was young Amy here. I just hope Beth hasn't gone off to do anything silly.'

'Oh dear. I wouldn't count on it,' sighed Eli.

'Neither would I,' said Amy, getting to her feet. 'We need to find her.'

'I have a constable waiting in the car,' said Gifford. 'I came here to get Mrs Mudd's confirmation of Josiah's statement before we went off to arrest Farthing. It might

361

be to our mutual benefit if you people came along with me. She strikes me as a woman who won't listen to reason, but she might listen to those she loves.'

'We can but try,' sighed Eli.

Chapter Twenty-Five

'He's at the mill,' said Godfrey's new manservant, who'd come to the door in answer to Beth's thunderous knocking.

'They're not his mills any more. You're lying!' She had him by the scruff of the neck and was pushing him backwards into the hall. 'Farthing!' she yelled into the echoing depths of the house. 'Get out here you murdering bastard!'

'Madam, I don't know who you are, but I must ask you to leave,' insisted the manservant.

'Farthing!'

'Mr Farthing is out and I don't know what time he's coming back. Now will you please leave before I call the police.'

'You won't have to call the police. They'll be here to arrest him soon enough. All right, where is he then?'

'As I said. He told me he was going down to the mill to sort some papers out. I believe he still has a set of keys.'

'What mill? There are two mills.'

'Farthing's Mill.'

'If you're lying I'll be back here to shove your lies down your throat.'

'I'm not lying. Now will you please leave.'

Godfrey had been dozing in his chair, a three-quarter full bottle of brandy on his desk. His own snoring woke him up and he thought he heard a noise from somewhere in the mill, on the next floor up – probably a bird but it'd do no harm to have a look. He climbed up to the next floor where the loading-gantry door had been left open to the elements and any passing thieves.

'Damn and blast! I'll have someone's hide for this when I get my mills back.'

He went across to the same gantry where he'd sent Alfred hurtling to his death over forty years ago. Although he'd now killed someone else he felt no remorse – that's what life was all about, kill or be killed. He'd been responsible for the premature ending of the odd life, but no more than many other people in his position. Politicians, army generals, surgeons experimenting on the poor, police. No – lined up against that lot he was quite a saint.

Was she dead? That was the question. From the force of the bang whoever he hit was sure dead. If he'd done for her – and he probably had – it was the end of everything, and a new beginning for him. His assets freed, his money restored, his worries over. Godfrey smiled as he looked out into the night and breathed in the smoky air of Bradford. An almost full moon came out from behind clouds being hurried along by the cold night wind. It shone its milky light on the dark chimneys of a score of mills, pointing into the night sky, sending up grey smoke that would come down as soot and further pollute the town. Pollution, the price of industry. Everything had its price, whether it be money, pollution or death. The price had to be paid. And that conniving bitch had paid the price tonight.

There was a faint noise behind him. He had only half turned when a shovel came arcing towards his legs. The pain had him shrieking in agony. Sparrows nesting in the eaves flew away with a loud flurry of wings. Godfrey fell to the floor, rolled over on his back and clutched at his left shin which had been smashed with the shovel.

'You stupid bloody woman!' he howled. 'You broke my leg.'

'I meant to,' she said, coldly. 'I didn't want you running away.'

'Running away? Running away from what?'

'From your Nemesis.'

'Nemesis? What's a bloody Nemesis when it's at home? Owww! Christ this hurts. You'll have to get me an ambulance.'

'You won't be needing an ambulance.'

As she approached he kicked at her with his good leg. She brought the shovel down on that knee with a bone-smashing crack. His second scream was even louder than the first.

She bent down and picked up the chain that was attached to the ginny wheel. Then she looped it around his neck and linked it with the hook. Each movement had him howling in agony.

'What the hell are you doing to me, woman?' he wept. 'Are you mad. I have money, I can pay you money.'

That remark earned him an eyeful of contemptuous spit. 'Money, what use do I have for money?' She grabbed his arm and dragged him to the edge of the gantry. He tried to roll away but she threatened him with the shovel again. 'You're a killer, Farthing, and you've killed just one too many. I can't live with that any longer. I'm going to kill you.'

She pushed him with her foot, right to the edge. Sweat was dripping down his fat face, mingling with the tears of terror.

'They'll hang you for this!'

'I won't be around for them to hang. Are you ready to die, Farthing?'

'Please don't kill me!'

One final push and he dropped from sight. Halfway down he came to a neck-snapping halt. He gave a throttled groan and kicked his legs a few times, enough to set him swinging like a pendulum before all the life went out of him. She leaned over and looked down on him, satisfied that his death hadn't been instantaneous. He'd lived long enough to know he was about to die.

Gifford, Amy and Eli had followed Beth's trail down to the mill after being directed there by an extremely irritated manservant. The inspector saw the hanging body as they turned the corner. 'Oh, Christ, what's happening here?' he said to the constable, who was driving.

'Please, let Elizabeth be all right,' beseeched Eli.

Amy jumped from the car before it stopped and was running towards the hanging man shouting, 'Grandma!'

Eli, Billy and the two policemen followed at speed, all of them shouting.

'Look up there, sir,' shouted the constable. 'There's someone up there, sir.'

'Where?'

'Standing in that gantry, sir. It's a woman sir.'

'Oh dear God, no,' said Eli. 'Oh, Elizabeth what have you done?'

'Mrs Mudd,' shouted Gifford. 'Is that you? What's happened here?'

In his heart he knew who it was and despite Farthing's crimes he also knew this was a hanging offence. People just couldn't take the law into their own hands. Not in this inhuman manner.

'Mrs Mudd, I want you to come down.'

She stood there, motionless.

'Grandma,' screamed Amy. 'Could you come down please?' She screamed louder when she saw her grandma topple forward, like a felled tree, and fall, head first, past Godfrey's body, on to the stone-cobbled yard; just like her grandad had all those years ago – only there wasn't a horse to break her fall. She landed with a sickening, bone-splintering crunch. The men ran across to her. Amy clasped her hands over her face and sank to her knees.

'Oh Grandma. Why did you do this to me?'

'I haven't done anything to you,' said a voice from behind. 'I've just got here.'

Beth was standing there, looking up at Godfrey, who was still swinging gently. Amy flung herself at her. Eli was beside her a second later. The constable was shining his torch on the body. Gifford called out.

'You don't know how pleased we all are to see you, Mrs Mudd.'

'Thought that was me, did you?' Beth said, walking cautiously towards the mystery body. 'Whoever it is did us all a big favour.'

'I think it's Sefton's mam,' said Billy, identifying the corpse by the light of the constable's torch.

367

Beth took a closer look, then stepped back. 'It's Gertrude Earnshawe all right. Her lad lost his life saving mine. She always treated him badly when he was supposed to be a coward.'

'I remember,' said Gifford. He looked from the shattered body of Gertrude Earnshawe up to the swinging body of Godfrey. 'And she took her guilt out on Farthing.' For a few, silent, seconds Amy and Beth looked up at the lifeless remains of the man who'd had such a devastating affect on their lives. It was the body of a man who would be mourned by no one but remembered by many.

It's over, Amy,' Beth said. 'He can't hurt us anymore.'

Amy looked away and took Billy's hand. Beth linked arms with Eli and they walked with Gifford and the constable towards the mill gates.

'I told Mrs. Earnshawe he was behind the fire,' said Beth. 'So I suppose it's my fault in a way. I knew she'd gone a bit loopy.'

'You told her the truth, love,' said Eli. 'She was entitled to know the truth, loopy or not, isn't that so, Inspector?'

Gifford gave a non-committal shrug and said, 'The woman must have had a lot of anger inside her to do this.'

'It's what Farthing was good at,' said Beth, '– making people angry. By God he made me angry tonight. Trying to murder my granddaughter.'

'What did you intend doing to him?' Gifford asked, curiously.

'To be honest I don't know. I've never in my life felt such a rage. It's as though it had been building up over the years and suddenly came to a head. All I know is that the anger left me the minute I saw him hanging there.'

'Sounds to me like you and Mrs Earnshawe had some-thing in common. She did you a massive favour. This could have ended very badly for you.'

'Poor, poor woman,' said Beth. 'She had all that guilt to cope with as well.'

'What do we do now, sir?' enquired the constable.

'Ideally,' said Gifford, rubbing his chin, 'I'd like to go to the Cobblers Arms for a stiff drink.'

'I think I could do with one of those,' said Eli. 'Large juniper juice – settle the nerves and all that.'

'Trouble is,' said Gifford, 'I've got two murders and a suicide to deal with.' He rubbed his chin, thoughtfully. 'Luckily for me, there's no one left alive to question, so it then becomes a job for our uniformed colleagues. Find a telephone, constable. Get them down here.'

'Yes sir.'

'Well,' said Beth, 'it's sounds a bit inappropriate under the circumstances, but I think we've got cause to cele-brate. Amy gets her inheritance and I feel as if a weight's been lifted off my shoulders; a weight I've been carrying around for fifty years.' There was shout from behind them.

'Excuse me,' called out Billy. He sounded annoyed. 'Amy's not so good.'

The adults turned back to where Amy was sitting on a low wall with her head in her hands. Billy was sitting with his arm around her.

'She lost her granddad the minute she found him,' he explained. 'And she thought she'd lost her grandma as well. Shakes you up a bit, stuff like that. She's only a kid.'

'Not like us eh, Billy?' said Beth, somewhat chastened at not seeing this herself.

'I just know how she feels, that's all, Mrs Mudd – you know, inside.'

'She'll never have a friend as good as you, Billy Eccles.'

'I know, Mrs Mudd – and I know that's all I'll ever be to her. I'm not daft.'

'You're a wise and kind lad, Billy.'

'And a brave one,' added Eli.

The shock of that evening had taken its toll of Amy. She put her arm around Billy and got to her feet. He didn't make her heart sing or make her shudder from head to toe.

But he was the one she needed right now.

Epilogue

Josiah's was the last of the three funerals that Amy organised and attended. It was either that or have Godfrey and Gertrude Earnshawe buried in pauper's graves – no one else seemed to be forthcoming with the necessary funds.

Like the other two, Josiah had a good turnout, mainly due to the extensive newspaper coverage of the three related deaths and the attempted murder of Amy. After the burial a shabbily dressed middle-aged man went over to the grave and looked down at the coffin. He was screwing a cap in his hand and saying what seemed to be a prayer. Amy spotted him as she looked back, over her shoulder.

'Do we know who that is, Grandma?' she asked.

'No idea, love.'

After a minute the man looked up to catch Amy and Beth staring at him. He gave an embarrassed nod and hurried away. Amy called after him. 'We're having a funeral tea. You're welcome to come.'

The man stopped in his tracks, considered the offer, then walked over to her. He had a pronounced limp.

'Were you a friend of Josiah?' Beth enquired.

The man looked embarrassed. 'Josiah Simms was my uncle.' He made it sound like an admission of guilt.

'Really?' said Amy.

'Look I know – with me being his only family – I should have coughed up for the funeral but the truth is I hardly knew him and my financial circumstances are what you might call reduced.'

'So, you didn't keep in touch, then?' said Amy.

'No, I spent most of my time overseas. I was in the army.' He held out his hand. 'My name's Michael Simms. Uncle Josiah was my dad's older brother. Dad died before the war, so did my mam.'

'You certainly don't look in the best of circumstances,' observed Beth, rather rudely Amy thought.

'I make do,' said Michael, 'as best I can. Got booted out of me dad's house when I were pensioned off from the army wi' this.' He tapped his leg. 'They were bills that hadn't been paid – bills I never knew about. Army pensions don't pay bills.' He gave a wry grin. 'Sounds like I'm making excuses, doesn't it?'

'You don't have to make excuses,' said Amy. 'This is my grandma, Mrs Mudd, and I'm Amy Farthing. Your uncle was actually my grandfather – so his funeral was my responsibility.'

'Grandfather? But he never married.'

'Doesn't stop him being my grandfather, in an illegitimate sort of way.'

'Well, the old dog. I'd never have believed it.' He looked at Beth.

'Er, don't look at me,' she said, quickly. 'It was Amy's other grandma.'

'So,' said Amy, 'you and I are related. Who would you say Josiah's next of kin is – you or me?'

He thought for a second. 'You I suppose – you being a direct descendent.'

'That'd be hard to prove in a court of law,' Amy said. 'Legally it's still you. Which makes you his heir.'

'I doubt it'll make much difference. It was in the papers that he'd been living in a shelter for the homeless. I think poverty must run in the family.'

'After the funeral tea,' Amy said, 'I'll take you down to our solicitors. Before he died Josiah had just inherited a cottage and a thousand pounds. We were wondering what would happen to it if no legal relative turned up.'

'I bet you're glad you came,' said Beth.

Amy tossed a stone into the stream. She and Billy were in Granny Beck Woods.

'Grandfather Farthing was a lot wealthier than anyone realized,' she said. 'He might have been awful as a person but he was evidently very good at business. It's all mine now. I feel really queer about it.'

'My dad says big businessmen are all bastards,' commented Billy. 'He says you have ter be a bastard ter succeed in business.'

'Well Grandma and Eli will be keeping an eye on the mills from now on and I don't think they'd thank you for calling them bastards – they're bringing two managers in to do the stuff Grandfather Farthing used to. Eli says running a business is all about delegation.'

'Is he giving up being an evangelist?'

'He hasn't said yet.'

Billy laughed. 'By the heck, we had some laughs working with him. What about you – what are you going to do?'

373

'I'm going to Manchester College of Music to study the violin.'

Billy nodded, approvingly. 'Yer'll do well. Best violin player I've ever known.'

'You don't know any other violin players.'

'Wouldn't make any difference.'

Amy smiled at the way he never failed to give her his full support and help in everything she did. She owed him so much and yet he never asked for anything in return. Just whatever friendship she could offer.

'Billy – Eli suggested to me that you could have a good career in the mills. You could go to college and take a course in textiles. Maybe take over the whole lot one day.'

Billy thought about it for a while, then began to laugh. 'Billy Eccles, mill boss? Can yer see it, Amy. Fat cigar and big belly – bossin' everyone around. I don't think so, somehow.'

Amy laughed as well. No, she couldn't see it. 'It was just an idea,' she said. 'What do you want to do?'

'I'm goin' back ter sea.'

'To sea? I thought you didn't like the sea?'

'Well, I've been thinkin' about it ever since I got back and I miss it. I want ter make me own way in life.' He turned to her. 'When I was at sea last time I were scared of what were waiting fer me back home. Every time we came into a port I looked around to see if the local police were waiting for me. Sometimes, at night, I dreamed I were bein' hanged.'

Amy put her arm around him. 'That must have been awful.'

Billy put his arm around her; it felt comfortable and right. 'I didn't dream about that every night, some nights I dreamed about you.'

'About me?'

'About you and me and this place. That was the best day I've ever had, when you and me – yer know.'

'I know. Hey – I'm not going to do it again if that's what you're thinking, Billy Eccles.'

He gave a cheeky grin. 'There's no law against thinkin', Amy Farthing. Any road, it wouldn't be the same, I don't suppose.'

He took a packet of cigarettes from his pocket and offered her one. It was a habit he'd acquired at sea.

'I don't smoke,' she said.

'Take one. We've all got ter start sometime.'

Amy took one and ended up coughing out a cloud of smoke.

'Takes time,' he said, sagely. 'But it's worth it in the end.'

'Billy,' Amy said, 'I'm going to give you some money, whether you like it or not. You can use it to make yourself an officer – now that's a job I *can* see you doing. Captain William Eccles. There's probably enough money to buy you a ship of your own.'

Billy half closed his eyes and pictured it. 'All the girls love a sailor,' he said, 'especially a captain. How about you? Could you ever love a ship's captain?'

'Sounds like something I could very easily do,' she said.

'In that case,' Billy decided. 'I think I'll take you up on yer offer.'

Other titles by Ken McCoy, also available from Piatkus . . .

Jacky Boy
Ken McCoy

On the day of his dad's funeral, ten-year-old Jacky Gaskell
meets Frank McGovern for the first time. For when Frank
is hanged for a murder he did not commit, Jacky's mother
Maureen feels she must tell Jacky the truth: Frank was his
real father. On the day of the execution Maureen loses the
only man she ever truly loved and must now raise her three
children, Brian, Ellie and Jacky, alone.

Once the scandal gets out, there is little sympathy from
the neighbours, and Jacky has a hard time at the local
school from children and teachers alike. And there is
little comfort to be had at home as Brian suddenly turns
against his younger brother, constantly provoking arguments and fights. Although he only met Frank briefly,
Jacky is convinced he was innocent and feels duty bound
to clear his name. Enlisting the help of his sister Ellie,
the pair embark on a series of plans and stunts to bring
the real killer to justice. However, when their actions
backfire, they not only attract the attention of the police,
but the more sinister attentions of the real murderer, who
will stop at nothing to silence the Gaskells.

978-0-7499-5659-2